HALLS
OF
IVY

Roland Nuñez

This book is dedicated to every college student, former college student, or prospective college student out there working hard to develop a sense of purpose, identity, and integrity.

CONTENTS

Acknowledgments   vii

Prologue   1

1.   Cheyenne Winters   3

2.   Interview- Benjamin Blake   11

3.   Orientation   21

4.   Cheyenne Winters   35

5.   Interview- Lisa Perez   47

6.   Transitions   55

7.   Cheyenne Winters   63

8.   Interview- Miyu Kaneko   69

9.   Recreation   77

10.   Cheyenne Winters   85

11.   Interview- Mitch Adams   93

12.   Midterms   101

13.   Cheyenne Winters   109

14.   Interview- Sarah Holmes   115

15.   Foul Play   123

16.   Cheyenne Winters   131

17.   Interview- Rachel Davis   139

18.	Winter's Eve	147
19.	Cheyenne Winters	155
20.	Interview- Lisa Perez	161
21.	Hushed Holiday	167
22.	Cheyenne Winters	175
23.	Interview- Benjamin Blake	183
24.	Spirits	191
25.	Cheyenne Winters	199
26.	Interview- Miyu Kaneko	209
27.	Maverick Madness	215
28.	Cheyenne Winters	225
29.	Interview- Sarah Holmes	231
30.	Retribution	237
31.	Cheyenne Winters	247
32.	Interview- Rachel Davis	253
33.	Farewells	259
34.	Interview- Mitch Adams	267
	Epilogue	271

ACKNOWLEDGMENTS

The creation of this book is attributed in large part to my wonderful wife, Jasmine, who put up with me from the original idea through the making and publishing of this novel. Her patience and support is greatly appreciated. I am also thankful of my wonderful family. My mom, who has continuously encouraged me throughout college, giving me an experience wonderful enough that I would write a whole book about it, as well as Illiana and Michael, my two younger siblings who support everything I do. And thanks to my dad for believing I could do everything I set out to achieve. Some other individuals I would like to thank are Dr. Foubert, as well as the many theorists and researchers of student development, for teaching me what I know about the field of student affairs. My close friends Olimpia, Jonathan, Jenny, Rachel, Tony, Valerie, and the rest of my friends are also very dear to my heart for teaching me how an amazing friendship can brighten up your life. I also want to point a nod to writer Max Brooks, whose writing style and format for his books gave me the idea on how to structure the interview portions of this book.

And finally, a huge thanks to both my undergraduate and graduate universities, as well as everyone in them whom I've interacted with, for providing me such a wonderful college experience and influencing my decision to move into a career in student affairs. A lot of the great moments and great characters in my book were inspired by experiences in these schools. I have full loyalty to my alma maters and would recommend both universities to anyone for a delightful college experience.

PROLOGUE

"I would like to call forth Ms. Winters. Please state your full name and occupation."

After hearing his bass voice booming throughout the packed room, I walked forward, nervously clutching my folders full of notes.

"My name is Cheyenne Winters. I am a Student Affairs professional. My primary job is to aid in college student development."

The gentleman's tone softened as he continued speaking. "Ms. Winters, you do understand the harsh implications that this testimony will have on your career."

"Yes sir."

"Very well then. You may proceed."

"Thank you. I'm holding here samples of the documents and notes I've accumulated in my time at Sun Valley University. I first came here to conduct research for my dissertation. It was planned to be a four month ethnography consisting of campus observations and student interviews. Much to my surprise, this study brought results that neither I nor anyone else could have anticipated. My interaction with these students surfaced some... issues, which led to the crisis."

"Ms. Winters, I'm going to have to ask you to be more specific."

The piercing stare of the room made me feel anxious, but I held my ground. I pulled out the files from my folder.

"I've provided each member of the committee copies of these files. I've included biographies of the students I've met with, as well as select interviews that are relevant to the case. Lastly, I've worked countless hours with students, faculty, and staff to compile a chronological document outlining the events that led to this crisis. I did my best to leave it as unedited and unhampered as possible, so they may contain strong language or themes. I felt it was the only way to fully portray the lives of these students and their reasoning for exhibiting such unusual unethical behavior."

"Are these documents supposed to serve as your story?" the gentleman said as he placed his glasses on to review the files on the table.

"Not at all. They are merely supplements to represent the voices of those that made this possible. To fully understand the crisis of Sun Valley University, you need to hear the perspectives of all of those involved. This isn't my story, sir. This is our story."

CHAPTER 1: CHEYENNE WINTERS
JANUARY

Police sirens echoed throughout the campus, forcing me to pull over at least three times to let them pass. Despite the delay they caused on the road, I was still on schedule. I finally pulled into the lone road that led into the university. Although it wasn't too long past six, darkness had already swept in. At one point, the single road split into a huge circle, with a patch of trees isolated in the middle. It was hard to tell in the dark, but it seemed to be a small park adorning the entrance to the campus. I turned left onto the circular road, then made another left and followed the sound of the sirens.

Driving down the campus's side road showed me the true enormity of the university. Despite everything I've learned, all the people I've interviewed, I could never have imagined a liberal arts college of this size. It rivaled that of the state universities. I felt both intrigued and intimidated.

I pulled into a parking lot, empty except for a few cars scattered around here and there. I looked around for the administration building, but it was nowhere in sight. Just a few empty parking lots, some residence halls, and a closed deli. The majority of students were still gone for winter break. I looked back at the residence halls down the street with the emergency vehicles parked by them. There was an ambulance and three police cars parked by Miller Hall, right across from the campus safety office. There was a man standing outside talking to a police officer. Figuring he could help me, I walked towards him.

Looking like he may have just gotten out of work, the man was tall and skinny, wearing a peach-colored polo that meshed well with his dark brown skin tone. The police officer seemed disgruntled during their conversation, hands in pockets as if Floridian winter was too cold for him. A part of me wanted to know what was going on. I've examined campus emergencies for two years in my case studies, but haven't actually been near a real one. The officer saw me approaching and directed his attention towards me.

3

"May I help you?" he asked with a slightly condescending tone. I could tell he didn't want me to be there. I could smell his garlic breath from all the way over here.

"Hi… umm… hello," I responded as I nervously fiddled with my silver-tinted glasses. "I'm Cheyenne Winters. I have an appointment in the administration building. Could any of you direct me to where it is?"

The officer looked over at his watch. "Listen, miss, in case you haven't noticed, we're in the middle of a possible crime scene. There's a university directory down the road. I suggest you take a look at it and clear the area. We don't have time for this."

He turned around and looked back at the other gentleman, as if gesturing for some backup. Upon closer inspection, I noticed that this police officer wasn't a police officer at all. He was just one of the campus safety officers that patrolled the university.

The other gentleman looked back at the officer, shook his head, then looked at me. "Listen, Randy. We're done here. I told you what you needed to know. Nothing has changed. Now, please excuse me while I help the lady with her directions."

The man walked towards me, much to the officer's dismay.

"Hello Ms. Winters. My name is Travis Coleman, Associate Director of Housing and Residence Life," he said with a sympathetic smile as he reached out to shake my hand. "Don't mind Randy here. He's just in a bad mood because the Sun Valley police officers left him on guard duty out here to direct the non-existent traffic. If you'll just follow me, I'll show you where Admin Hall is."

Travis led the way. Back in Miller Hall, I saw two men wheeling out a body into the ambulance. I really had an urge to find out more. Travis could tell that I was curious.

"Yeah, that's a body back there," he told me before I asked. "Freshman male. His roommate found him dead in his room. Signs point towards a suicide."

"A suicide?" I asked in disbelief, partly surprised with how relaxed he was acting through all of this. I would've been panicking all over the place. "Haven't there already been two suicides on this campus this year? In the past three months even?"

"Yeah," Travis responded. "Which is exactly why everyone around here is getting worried. Three suicides in one year is unprecedented at this university. People are quickly starting to believe that these aren't isolated incidents. Yet at the same time, it's almost becoming a normal occurrence. That's the scariest part."

"What happened to the other two?" I asked him.

"We're not sure, to be honest. We managed to figure out how they killed themselves, but we never found out why. We're under the impression that this is a cause of depression among our students. Depression is the most common reason for suicide among students in universities. So, of course, that's what the others in my department have concluded."

"Do you think it was depression?" I asked him.

"I don't know," he responded. "It's really a lot to think about, lots of variables involved. But anyways, take a look over there."

Travis pointed to a building down the road.

"That's Admin Hall. Just go right on through the first entrance you see and it'll lead you to the reception desk. They can help you out from there. Now I need to go back to Miller Hall and check on the other students. It was nice meeting you, Ms. Winters."

"Likewise, and thanks," I responded as we both parted ways. Questions raced through my head about the whole ordeal. If there were so many suicides, why was everyone so calm and relaxed? Why wasn't this in the news? This should've been the police department's number one priority! Had I been running this university, things would've been completely different.

I headed on over to Admin Hall and went inside to find the Dean of Students, Shandra Giles.

I spotted her standing by the reception desk engaged in conversation with a few people. Her dark brown hair was neatly tied in a bun as she stood there with near-perfect posture. Her tall stature and firm disposition exuded a great deal of authority. She seemed to be in her mid-forties. I had only met her once before, during a brief encounter at the ACPA (American College Personnel Association) conference.

"Hi, Dr. Giles?" I cautiously chimed in. "I don't mean to interrupt. My name is Cheyenne Winters, and I had a meeting with you scheduled."

She turned over and looked at me. "Ahh, yes, Cheyenne, I was expecting you today, wasn't I? Cheyenne, I'd like to introduce you to our university provost, Dr. Scott, and Detective Lynn Sawyer, from the Sun Valley Police Department."

I looked over to the other two individuals accompanying Dr. Giles. Dr. Scott was an older man in his mid-fifties. His raised hairline from his hair loss made his shiny forehead the center of my attention. He was a skinny man dressed in a pair of dress pants and a polo shirt, similar to Travis Coleman. It was an odd choice of wardrobe, considering his position was much higher than that of Dr. Giles', yet she looked like his superior. Lynn Sawyer was much shorter in comparison to Dr. Giles and Dr. Scott, but her fierce stare more than made up for it. She didn't seem to put much effort into her appearance. Her hair was frizzled and her outfit needed some ironing. It was hard to look at her without staring into her intimidating grey eyes as they glared at me like a territorial predator.

"This is Cheyenne Winters," Dr. Giles continued. "Graduate from East Central Florida University and now working on her PhD in... what was it dear? Psychology?"

"Student Affairs," I corrected her. "I met you at a student affairs conference, remember?"

"Ahh, yes, ACPA," Dr. Giles said. "You wanted to talk to me about some study you wanted to do on our students, correct? Question them about something?"

I opened my mouth to respond, but Detective Sawyer jumped into the conversation.

"Hold on a second, Shandra," Detective Sawyer said in a slightly aggravated tone. "What do you mean she's here to question some students? We have some really pressing issues at hand. I'm planning on interrogating students in the next coming days as they arrive from their winter break. I would prefer if I was the only one doing the questioning around here."

"I really don't believe I'll be a bother," I nervously told her. "It's for my dissertation. I'm doing an ethnographic study on college students. I'll be learning about how they think, how they behave, and what their college experience is like from the students themselves."

"Listen, Ms. Winters, I understand you have your work to do. But I have my work to do as well, and frankly, this investigation takes precedence over your little school project. I have enough of you officials to deal with already. Shandra, I'm going to have to ask that you tell Ms. Winters here to postpone her study."

"Absolutely not," Dr. Giles responded for me. "Cheyenne is involved in a very important area. Her study of these students is invaluable to the student affairs work that we as university staff do here."

"Excuse me, but what exactly is student affairs?" Detective Sawyer asked in irritation.

"We're the field that makes your life easier, detective," Dr. Giles responded coyly. I could almost see the hint of a grin on her face. "While university professors help students grow academically, we're the ones that are left to help them develop everywhere else. We help them with their social, emotional, and out-of-class problems that they face. It is our job to help them grow into mature, responsible adults, and keep them out of your hands and out of trouble."

Detective Sawyer smirked. "Well, based on this streak of suicides, it seems your student affairs department has been slacking on the job. Problem with the management, maybe?"

I could tell there was some tension between Dr. Giles and Detective Sawyer that was present before I even entered the building. If I ran this university, problems like this wouldn't exist. I had so many ideas I wanted to implement once I graduated and actually had the power to change anything at these colleges.

The provost, Dr. Scott, finally spoke up.

"Ladies, ladies, please," he said. "Detective Sawyer, I'd like to discuss with you the specifics of your investigation. There are a number of things we need to address before you begin interrogating my students. Let's let Dr. Giles and Ms. Winters have their meeting."

Dr. Scott led Detective Sawyer up to his office. She gave Dr. Giles and me a stern look for a brief second before heading off with him. I looked over back at Dr. Giles.

"Thank you so much, Dr. Giles," I told her, relieved. "I wasn't sure what I would've done if-"

"Listen, Cheyenne," Dr. Giles interrupted. "I stood up for you because Lynn Sawyer has been a pain in my ass since the first suicide took place here. She's wanted to turn this place upside down with her investigation and I haven't let her. Now with this third one, she really has it in for me and has been giving me grief about it ever since. The truth is, your timing doesn't sit well with me. With all of this going on, and all the pressures I'm getting from the admins above, your study is more of a hindrance than a help. Babysitting you is something I don't need to be worrying about right now."

I watched her in silence, turning red with embarrassment.

"However, since I've already agreed to it, you can do your study here. I've arranged with Professor Garcia for you to meet with his class on the Monday after winter break is over. You can introduce yourself to the class and tell them the purpose of your study. I will allow you to meet with them, and only them, for your interviews, observations, and field notes. Do not get in the way of our faculty, our staff, Detective Sawyer, or me. Especially me. Otherwise, you're finished here. You got that?"

"Yes Dr. Giles," I responded sheepishly. "Though I promise I won't be a bother to anyone. My study isn't just for my benefit. It's for the benefit of the students. Maybe if I can find out what's making the students unhappy I can help improve the college retention rate. Maybe even, who knows? Discourage future suicides, maybe?"

"Oh, Cheyenne, you're so young," Dr. Giles said. "Sun Valley University's retention rate is a little over fifty percent. Do you know what that means? That only about half of the freshman class that entered this year will reach graduation. It's been like that for a while now. No matter what we do, how hard we try, it is unrealistic to assume that it will change. Students have problems, and only the students themselves can choose whether or not they want to deal with them. We can only help those that want the help.

"A little word of advice, from professional to professional. Don't get too attached to these students. And don't expect to change the world with one study. That path will lead to disappointment. Just do the best you can with what you have, and set realistic expectations."

"Thank you," I told her as I turned to leave. So much for having her as my mentor.

"And one more thing," she added. "We have a strict rule of confidentiality at this university. Any information gathered here that you intend to publish or share with the public has to be approved by me first. Failure to do this will result in some serious legal ramifications. Do I make myself clear, Ms. Winters?"

"Yes, ma'am."

BIO: BENJAMIN BLAKE
CLERMONT, FL

My name is Ben Blake. I'm nineteen and I'm studying Marine Biology. I've always loved studying animals. Aquatic animals are a particular favorite of mine, though animals in general are fascinating. It probably has a lot to do with my childhood. I grew up in a sheltered environment. My mom was very protective of me. She was a housewife, choosing to work at home instead of pursuing a career to take care of me. We weren't dirt poor, but we weren't made of money either. I spent a lot of time either indoors or right outside our apartment, collecting bugs to study under my microscope. It was very exciting when I got my first pet fish. It was a bug-eyed goldfish. I loved it and started adding more to the aquarium. I had fish, snails, algae eaters, and aquatic plants. I eventually got turtles, until they started eating my fish and I had to separate them.

I don't have any siblings. It's just my parents and me. My father was the only one who brought income to the house and we had many expenses. His accident made everything that much worse for us. It's been 6 years since he died. My mother has never been the same since then. While she continued to show me her love and support, there was a sense of joy in her smile that just wasn't there anymore. It was pretty hard for us after that. My mom had to live on welfare for a few years, we moved from apartment to apartment when we couldn't afford to pay rent, and she had to make the difficult decision to go back to work. My mother and I are close. She's both my mentor and my best friend. The hardest thing for me to do was move to college. Once I left, I feared she had no one else left. Nevertheless, she wishes the best for me and believes that I will make it big. I'm grateful for the amazing mother she has been to me. Now that I'm on my own, I'm not sure what to do.

I've had a few acquaintances growing up, but never any real friends. Just people to hang out with every now and then. Since they went to out-of-state colleges, I don't really keep in contact with them anymore. Some of my hobbies involve reading, writing poetry, spending time online, and of course, studying nature. I'm hoping that college will be a great place to branch out and do more. At orientation they kept telling us to get involved, listing all these different clubs and organizations to join. Sounds like a good idea. We'll see.

ROLAND NUÑEZ

CHAPTER 2: INTERVIEW #BB01
BENJAMIN BLAKE

[Benjamin enters my office a few minutes ahead of schedule. I hand him a permission form for him to sign that allows me to proceed with the interview. I turn on the voice recorder.]

Good morning Benjamin. Do you go by Benjamin? Or just Ben?

Good morning, Ms. Winters. My friends call me Ben, but Benjamin is fine too. Whatever you prefer.

Okay. And for the record, feel free to call me Cheyenne. This isn't a formal interview or anything, just a casual conversation so we can get to know each other better. And if at any point you feel uncomfortable or I'm doing or saying something that makes you feel uncomfortable, please let me know, okay?

Sure, no problem.

Great! Now Benjamin, like I said when I visited your class, I'm here to do a study on college life. I'd like to get the perspectives of college students from the students themselves. Learn about what you think, feel, and do. You are free to talk about whatever you would like that you feel represents you as a college student and as an individual. Now, I've read your biography here that your professor asked you all to write. Could you tell me more about it?

Yeah, sure. In the beginning of the year Dr. Garcia asked the whole class to write a one page biography, around the ball park of three to four hundred words, which answers the following statement: "Tell me about yourself".

That's it. He gave us no other prompt, no other direction, no other guidelines as to what to write about. It was the strangest thing. He said that we could write about anything, and even use whatever language we preferred. I know a couple of us were wary, thinking this was some sort of test or a trick. But he assured us that this was just a writing exercise to help loosen up our minds and do some self-reflection. He said he wasn't going to grade it. He just wanted to learn a little bit about us. Something he wouldn't have guessed upon first looking at us.

He's actually a pretty cool professor. He didn't judge us based on what we wrote. In fact, he used whatever details he learned about us to strike conversation. Like me, for instance. Occasionally, he would ask me how my turtles were doing. It felt great knowing that someone cared about something that was important to me. I would usually give him an update on how Shelly and Blinky were doing based on my phone calls with my mom.

I guess the activity helped with our writing, as well. Dr. Garcia made it a point to allow us the freedom to write in whatever manner we wanted. While he occasionally collected our work, he didn't put a grade on them until the final draft. This took some of the pressure off of writing. It's impressive, too, though, cause he isn't even a writing teacher! He actually teaches many of the physical science courses on the college of Applied Sciences. It's just that he, like many other professors, have to sign up for at least one freshman orientation class every year to teach. With all the new students coming in and funding the way it is, they have to make the professors work double duty. At least, that's what he tells us.

He's upfront about it, at least. He tells us that he was assigned this classroom, but that this in no way affects the quality of the class. He says he would provide just as much effort and quality of instruction as he does for his other upper level courses. So yeah, I wrote my biography for him, and have enjoyed his class so far. At first I was kind of annoyed that this course lasted the whole year. Every other course lasted only one semester, but this one lasted much longer. How much can they possibly teach you about being a maverick?

A maverick?

It's what they call freshmen at this university. I don't really get it, but the university has a unique ranking system for class standing. Apparently, some students years ago didn't like the freshman through senior ranks since they didn't want to be identical to their high school counterparts. They wanted to be distinct, so they popularized their own ranking system. First years are mavericks, unbranded and unaffiliated with any particular field. They're still testing out the waters. Second years are called pathfinders. Third years are called trailblazers, and fourth years and above are called vanguards. I don't fully understand the logic behind it, but it's university tradition. Spend a couple of months here, and it grows on you. You find yourself saying it without even realizing it. It's not official, as the university officials don't acknowledge it, but it's what's considered normal here. I've even heard some professors slip it out every once in a while.

Interesting. It seems you've gotten quite accustomed to the lifestyle of Sun Valley University. Would you mind telling me about your experience when you first arrived here? Back when you were a new freshman, or maverick, as you call it. I'd like to start from the beginning.

Mhmm. Well, I'm originally from Florida, so the transition from home to here wasn't that rough. Same hot weather, about the same proximity to the beaches, and generally the same number of people. The big difference here was age. Florida, and more specifically where I'm from, Clermont, isn't really known for its youthful population. It is more famous for being a place for retirees to settle and relax. And there's some truth to that. Around my neighborhood there are senior citizens everywhere. The retirement homes are packed, the handicap parking spots are always full, and there's always a long wait at the clinic. It's why I've always hated going to the clinic. Needles? Fine. Physical check-ups. Fine. But put me in a waiting room for a couple of hours before I'm seen? Now that's torture!

Anyways, it was just my mom and me driving down to Sun Valley. We didn't have money for a trailer, so all I took with me was whatever we could fit in my mom's dinky Sentra. The drive was only a few hours. Much closer than Miami, that's for sure. It was pretty amazing, though. Just a few minutes into Sun Valley, Florida and we see signs pointing to the campus. The initial entrance isn't very big. Just a sign pointing to a road surrounded by trees.

We pulled into the road, and after about half a mile, we finally saw the real entrance to the campus. It was beautiful! I mean, I haven't seen any other campuses to compare it with, but what I saw was really something wonderful. The first thing we saw was Clifton Memorial Park. It was a park created in memory of Sun Valley University's founder and first President, Andrew B. Clifton. The road split into two roads which formed a circle, with the park nested in the middle. Driving around the circle would let you see the park from every angle. It wasn't big, but it was nice. It had a small little pond in the middle, trees around the sides, and a couple of benches for people to relax on. You'd always see students lying on the grass reading or napping.

As we drove around and past the park, we had a clear view of the university's four major college buildings: the college of Applied Sciences, the college of Allied Arts, the college of Education, and the college of Business. Their placements formed a neat square near the center of the campus, which gave that area the nickname College Square. However, these buildings paled in comparison compared to the Union Tower. Planted right in the center of College Square was the Student Union. Many students call it the tower, since its massive size can be seen well before you even enter the campus. The entire building contains beautifully tinted glass windows from top to bottom, giving it the appearance of a glass tower. However, as you get closer to the building, you'll notice it's much more than that. The tower appears to be a tall cylindrical building, or a circle if seen from above. However, upon closer inspection, you notice that it is in fact two half cylinders, or two half circles if seen from above, connected by two walkways where the gaps are supposed to be.

As my mom parked the car in the visitors' parking lot and we headed to the union, I could see her glances of approval as she carefully examined the place she was going to drop off her son for the next four years.

"Wow, Ben, are you sure you won't get lost here?" Mom joked as she tried to make sense of the campus map we brought along.

"Don't worry about me, Mom. I'll manage. Worst case scenario I'll call 911, kay?" I told her with a smile.

She raised an eyebrow as if trying to make sure I was indeed joking.

Fortunately, the size of the Student Union made it easy to find. When we arrived, I was surprised at just how tall this tower was. Florida isn't exactly known for its buildings.

"So what room do we go to in this building?" Mom asked me.

"My orientation packet said to meet at the Union Epicenter. I'm not sure what that means."

As we entered the union through one of its glass doors, I walked up to the lady at the information desk and asked for directions.

"Oh, the Epicenter?" she responded courteously. "It's located right down the hall. Make a left by that plant over there and out the double doors."

We followed her directions and opened the door. I couldn't believe what I was seeing. Right at the center of the union was actually an outdoor area with a small field! There were some tables and chairs draped with white tablecloth and a buffet table full of appetizers for the taking. Further down there were a bunch more chairs facing a stage. The reflectivity of the circular building around it lit up the place very beautifully. I could tell my mother was definitely impressed now.

"This school doesn't hold back on its presentation," she said to me. "But presentation alone isn't enough. Let's see if there's substance behind their smokes and mirrors."

There were already students at the Epicenter, some of them at the buffet table grabbing a bite to eat, others at the round tables eating, and some were already finished and waiting by the stage chairs. Had I known that food would be provided, I wouldn't have eaten those sandwiches on the way here.

After about fifteen more minutes, a lady walked up to the stage and told us to please finish our appetizers and take our seats by the stage. As people began to migrate towards the seats, a girl sat right by me wearing some strange-looking clothing. It appeared to be a loose-fitting dress with fall colors, designs meshing brown, tan, green, and darker greens together. She looked over at me and caught me staring.

"I made it myself, you know," she said with a smile. "It's one of my earlier attempts, but I still think it exhibits the right Zen I was aiming for, don't you think?"

This girl had a very natural look to her. She had long, straight, platinum blonde hair, with flowers on her head. She looked like she had fallen into a flower garden. She continued to smile at me, waiting for a response. I started to stutter as I tried to find something to say, and then my mom decided to chime in.

"Oh, look, Ben! Isn't she sweet?" she said enthusiastically. "What's your name, sweetie?"

"Oh, greetings! My name is Grace. Grace Collins. It's very nice to meet you."

Grace shook my mom's hand, then she reached out for mine.

"Hi, I'm Ben," I finally managed to say as I shook her hand. I noticed that she was sitting alone. "Who did you come with?"

"Not a soul," she said. "It's more of an adventure when you tackle it on your own! Grab it by the horns and say 'okay adventure, I'm the boss of you, you hear? I own you!' Yeah, it's great."

I looked at her in confusion. When my mom warned me that college was full of strange people, I didn't realize just how literally she meant it.

I opened my mouth to say something else, but she interrupted me.

"Ooh! Ooh! Shhh!" Grace said. "It's starting!"

We turned our attention to the front, and the lady was once again back on stage, this time ready to begin.

"Good morning students and families. My name is Nancy Wei, Academic Advisor for Student Services. On behalf of the rest of the administration, I would like to formally welcome you all to Sun Valley University!"

The students and families began to applaud. Some students began to scream and whistle, others just seemed bored. I looked over at Grace who listened intently with a smile on her face.

"As some of you may or may not know, this year we decided to split up orientation into several groups due to the growing number of students on our campus. This pre-orientation meeting is for students with last names of A

15

through E. If your last name isn't A through E, then please meet with our orientation leaders by the entrance who can direct you to your scheduled pre-orientation time. The reason we ask that you come back later is because at the conclusion of this meeting we will be handing out identification cards, dorm room keys, and math and reading test placements for those students with these last names. We'll have your items ready later today."

As she said this, a couple of students got up and left the stage. I wondered how many students were in the freshman class in total.

"As I speak, please take a look at the orientation schedules that are being passed out by my student assistants. The items on the list are pretty self-explanatory, with the name of the event shown, as well as the time, building, and room number of where it will take place. If you are not familiar with any of the areas, please consult with any of the orientation leaders that will be roaming the campus for the next few days. I also want to make note tomorrow's big orientation event. We will all be meeting at 9am in Renfield Entertainment Center, abbreviated as REC in your campus map, for the freshman convocation ceremony. Our university president Dr. Lambrick will be there to give you all the official Sun Valley University welcome. It is a very big event with lots of music and of course, families are more than welcome to attend."

The students all listened as Nancy Wei outlined the specifics of orientation over the next few days. My mom, however, leaned over to me and gestured for us to go.

We got up and walked over to the registration counter.

"I'm terribly sorry to be an inconvenience," Mom told the student working the registration counter. "I can't be here long and have to get back home for work. Is it possible to get my son's room keys so we can move his stuff inside?"

"Yeah, sure ma'am. No problem," the student responded cheerfully. That's definitely one thing I'll never forget about this school. The students in the orientation team are some of the most cheerful, energetic people I've ever seen. They can be a bit overbearing at times, but there's no doubt they're helpful.

We spent the next few minutes filling out all sorts of forms: vaccination forms to make sure I was up-to-date on shots, emergency contact forms, ID card forms, then took a poor-looking picture that was made into my ID card. They finally gave me the room keys to my dorm.

"So where did they end up putting you?" my mom asked me.

"Miller Hall," I responded.

Sun Valley University, being a residential campus, has several dorms specifically for freshmen. Some are better than others. Miller hall... well... it was one of the others. Still, I was glad to finally have my room keys and we walked back towards the car. My mom had a saddened expression on her face as we walked.

"It's okay mom, I'll be fine, I promise," I tried to reassure her.

"I know, Ben. It's just… I feel so bad just leaving you like this. You're my only son. I should be here for you through the entire orientation like all the other parents are doing for their children. I know this is hard for the both of us. I just wish there was more I could do."

Her voice began to tremble as she finished the last few words. I reached out and grabbed her hand.

"Mom, look, don't give yourself such a hard time about it. I completely understand. You have to work. I'm just grateful they let you take off this morning long enough so you can at the very least come drop me off. I care about you mom, and it's going to be really hard for me to enjoy my time here knowing that you're working so hard at home just to pay the bills."

"Don't say that Ben!" she said in a sudden louder tone. Her anger caught me by surprise. "Ben, these will be the greatest years of your life! Your father and I never went to college, and to this day I consider this our biggest mistake. It is my pride and joy to know that you have this wonderful opportunity. Don't you dare take that away from us! Don't you dare!!" She paused for a moment to calm herself down. "I want you to make the most of your time here, you promise? Don't spend your days worrying about me. Please, make friends, do well in your classes, and have a great time, okay?"

"Okay," I responded.

We were quiet for most of the next hour as we moved my stuff out of the car and hauled it all the way to my room in Miller Hall. I was disappointed that my roommate got there first. My dorm room already seemed small without all his stuff scattered around everywhere. And by the looks of it, it seemed he had already claimed the top bunk as his own. That was a bit irritating.

"You want to grab some lunch?" she asked me when we finished moving.

"Sure."

Our lunch was silent. Even more silent than the move in. My mom seemed to be in deep thought the entire time, and I didn't want to upset her by asking her what she was thinking about. I knew what she was thinking. It was the same thing I was thinking. It was almost time to say goodbye.

I was dreading this moment for days. It was silly, I know, considering I only lived a few hours away. But it was the meaning behind this big step. After this moment, I would no longer live at home. From here on out, at least in part, I was no longer her little boy. It wasn't so much for me that I ached and worried, it was for her. She was getting old. She put up with so much, sacrificed so much to get me where I am today. And here I was, leaving her alone as I moved on with my life.

Near the end of the lunch, all she said to me was that I have my father's eyes.

When we left the restaurant, I began to ponder my schedule for the rest of the day to keep my mind busy. There were many events going on, some for students, some for parents, some for both. I needed to figure out which ones I needed to attend, and then what to do with my free time. Then I started wondering about my roommate. Who was he? Would we get along?

My thoughts were interrupted when I saw that my mom pulled over at a bus station.

"Mom, what are we doing here?" I asked her. "I need to get back to the campus."

"I know," she said. "Here."

She pulled out the keys from the ignition and handed them over to me.

"Mom, what are you doing? This is your car!"

"Ben, listen. We don't have much. We've never had. It is your intelligence that managed to get you enough scholarships to come to this school. Other than food and shelter, I haven't been able to provide much to you. Please, take the car. It's all I have. I want it to serve you well."

"You can't do this! You need it for work. I can't take the car!"

"Please, Ben, do this for me. I'll manage my own affairs, don't worry. It's my gift to you. Let it be a piece of home you can take around with you. I want you to know that I love you and I would do anything for you." Her eyes began getting watery.

I looked at her, trying to hold back my own tears. I could tell that giving me this car meant a lot to her.

She handed me over the keys and stepped out of the car. As she headed to the bus station, I got out of the passenger's seat and ran over and hugged her.

"I'll miss you…" I told her. At this point, I just let the tears flow down. I didn't care.

"I'll miss you too, sweetie," she told me as she embraced me. The moment lasted all but a few seconds, but it felt like hours. I could feel her pain through the embrace. "I have to go now, sweetie. The Greyhound leaves in a few minutes."

I finally let her go and walked back to the car. What a dinky car. But it was my car. Sitting in the driver's seat and turning on the engine was a bittersweet moment for me. I was very grateful with my life, despite our difficulties. I looked out the window to catch the last glimpse of my mother as she entered the bus station.

BIO: ZACHARY MYERS
TALLAHASSEE, FL

I grew up with football. It's been my passion since I was a kid. My dad played for FSU, and it was his dream that I follow in his footsteps. Living in Tallahassee, he took me to all the games, really got me into the school spirit. He would constantly tell me that I was his best achievement. And what can I say? I love the sport. I learned to walk as a toddler just so I could learn to tackle.

See, there wasn't much to do in my town. I come from a family of farmers. My dad was the first to break the mold and get a college education. Unfortunately, things really didn't work out for him. Now, I'm not naïve. I know he's trying to live all his failed achievements through me. But I really don't mind. I enjoy the sport and I want to make my dad proud. Well, to an extent. As I'm sure it's obvious by now, I didn't go to FSU like he wanted.

I got accepted, but I had no way of paying for it. My family's income is at that point where we make too much money to be given financial aid, but not enough for them to help me with my college education. And as a white male, forget about scholarships. Just about all the college scholarships around here are saved for minorities or women. Not that there's anything wrong with that, but it makes it that much harder for guys in my situation to get into college.

Fortunately for me, I played runningback in high school, and SVU liked what they saw. They offered me a full scholarship to be runningback for the Sun Valley Sliders. It was hard breaking the news of my decision to my dad, but I knew it was the best option for me. He'll understand eventually, at least I hope he does. Still, I look forward to playing with my team. We've already started conditioning and the rest of the guys seem pretty cool.

CHAPTER 3: ORIENTATION
AUGUST

Kimberly Shaw scrambled through the orientation booths with the box full of dorm keys. The summer heat was already in full swing as temperatures rose well into the hundreds. Sweat poured down the short sleeves of her polo, further fueling her stress. The residence hall registration line was already full of people coming from the lunch rush before Kimberly realized she had forgotten all the keys in the housing office.

"So sorry I'm late, everyone!" Kimberly said as she sprinted towards the table with the large key shelves. She suddenly lost her footing and almost fell onto the ground spilling all the keys.

"Look out!" her fellow RA Robert yelled as she caught her footing just in time. "For Christ's sakes, Kimberly! Do you know how long it took us to organize those keys by room number last night? Do you realize what could have happened if those keys fell out of their slots on the shelf? Think before you sprint, Kim! This line ain't going anywhere."

"I'm sorry," Kimberly said as she placed the key box on the table.

"Alright, registration can now continue," Robert told the irritated families waiting in line.

Kimberly felt awful. While she and the other RAs were sitting comfortably in the shade under by the tents, constantly supplied with water and Gatorade every half hour, these families were being sent all through campus for meetings, registration forms, parking passes, and other events going on in this unbearable heat. Sweaty, greasy, angry faces stared her right in the eyes, as if they were blaming her for the scathing heat brought upon them. She turned her focus towards the messy piles of registration forms and documents sprawled on the wooden table.

The next family up was a male student with his parents right behind him. His mother seemed preoccupied on the phone, and his father cranky. The student was tall, about six feet, had short, light brown hair, well-built, and sported a button down shirt with a pair of cargo shorts and flip flops.

"Name please?" Robert asked.

"Zachary Myers," the student responded.

Robert looked through a list of names until he found Zachary's name on the second page.

"Kim, could you grab the keys for Miller Hall, room 326?"

Kimberly reached out for the keys and waited for Zachary to sign the key-acceptance form before she gave them to him. She gave him a welcoming smile.

"Hi Zachary. My name is Kimberly Shaw. It seems you've been placed in my hall this year. I'll be your RA!"

Zachary smiled back. "It's very nice to meet you Kimberly. I guess I'll be seeing you around, then?"

"Yes, of course!" Kimberly responded. "We'll be having a hall meeting tonight."

Zachary nodded his head, then motioned for his parents to go. They followed their campus map to Miller Hall.

"Is this really the kind of school you want to be in, Zachary?" his father grumbled. "Long lines in this blazing heat? What kind of a crap service is that?"

"It's not a big deal, Dad," Zachary responded calmly. "Registration goes by last name. My last name unfortunately scheduled us to register during the lunch rush, which also happened to be the hottest part of the day. It's not their fault."

"This never would have happened at Florida State," he said. "They've always prepared for rushes like this so this kind of shit wouldn't happen."

"Owen, watch your language!" Zachary's mother said automatically without diverting any attention away from her phone conversation.

Zachary rolled his eyes and continued lugging his bags along to Miller Hall.

One elevator ride and two wrong turns later, they finally made it to room 326. Much to his surprise, his roommate was already in there. He was a very muscular guy, looked like he lifted weights.

"Hi, my name is Zachary," Zachary introduced himself.

"So you're my roommate, huh?" the student said as he inspected Zachary. "Sup? The name's Dylan."

Zachary and Dylan shook hands. Dylan reached out to shake Zachary's father's hand, but he refused to uncross his arms, choosing instead to inspect the room.

"Okay, then," Dylan said. "Hey, Zachary, if it's okay with you, I unbunked the beds. I've never been a fan of bunk beds. You cool with that?"

"Yeah, sure. No problem," Zachary responded.

"This room's a bit small, isn't it?" Zachary's father said snidely. "Hmmph. Well, gotta take what you can get in a school like this. I'm going with your mother to pull the car around so we can move the rest of your stuff. I'll call you when we're ready." He headed out with Zachary's mother, who was still on the phone.

"Pleasant fella, isn't he?" Dylan joked.

"Try living with him," responded Zachary. "Though you get used to it. He's just irritated now since I decided to play football for the Sliders instead of his Alma Mater."

Dylan's eyes lit up. "Dude, you play football?"

"Yeah, why?"

"Well, I'm a football guy myself. You're looking at my high school's best quarterback right here. What did you play?"

"Runningback."

"Cool. Guess we'll be having lots of practice together."

Zachary put his bags on his bed, then began to look around. It seemed the room hadn't been renovated in quite a while. The walls were chipped and small holes were scattered around the ceiling. He walked over to the shelf and saw all of Dylan's trophies. He saw some for wrestling, swimming, and of course football. He saw the name "Dylan Wright" etched on the trophies.

"Your last name's Wright?" Zachary asked. "I thought registration for you didn't start until later this afternoon. How did you get into your room so soon?"

"My brother goes to this school. He's a senior now. He has a few contacts, pulled a few strings, and got me my room keys since yesterday. I've been chilling here ever since."

Zachary felt his phone vibrate as he was unpacking, and saw that his mother texted him to go outside. As he walked out the door of his room, he heard loud noises outside. It sounded like someone was running down the hall.

"Dylan! Dylan, what the hell, man?" Luca Palmer shouted outside. Dylan went out into the hall to join Zachary.

"What do you want, Luca?" he asked with a smirk on his face.

"You ass! I know it was you! I found shaving cream all over my room! You know this isn't over. I'll get you back!" Luca told him.

"Hey! You started it, bud. Trying to sneak some crickets into my room last night! Don't dish it out if you can't take it."

"Oh, really Dylan?" Luca answered. "Is that a threat?" He walked right up to Dylan and glared into his eyes.

"Listen, British boy. I'd suggest you get outta my face before I crush your scrawny little European body and dump it in the trash room."

"Oh, you'd like that, wouldn't you? Come on. Go ahead bugger! Give it a try!"

Luca began taunting Dylan by shoving him backwards.

Zachary could tell this was getting out of hand.

"Guys, let's just chill. School hasn't even started. Let's not do something we'll regret."

"Oh, he's gonna regret this," Dylan told Zachary. Dylan shoved Luca back even harder.

"That all you got, macho man?" Luca taunted.

Suddenly, Dylan sprang forward, grabbed Luca by the shoulders, then shoved him against a wall. He grabbed him by the neck and began strangling him.

"Stop! Stop! You're... choking... me!!" Luca shouted in despair.

"Stop it Dylan!" Zachary shouted.

"Stay out of this, Zachary! Don't get involved!" Dylan responded.

Zachary ran towards Dylan to try to loosen the grip, but Dylan shoved him out of the way and continued to strangle Luca. Zachary was getting angry.

"Don't make me have to fight you Dylan!" he said in a huff as he headed back towards him.

Suddenly, much to his surprise, Dylan started laughing. He released his grip, and Luca started laughing too.

"Did you see his face?" Dylan said through his laughter.

"Yeah," Luca responded. "He looked like he was about to crap his pants when the fight broke out!"

Zachary looked confused. Dylan walked over to him and patted him on the back.

"Welcome to Miller Hall, Zachary. Word of advice, don't take things too seriously here."

"Oh, shut up," Zachary responded with a smile. "I gotta go, anyways. My parents are waiting downstairs with the rest of my stuff." Zachary headed towards the stairs.

"Think he'll fit in with our group?" Dylan asked.

"Yeah, he seems cool," Luca added. "But I'm still getting you back for that shaving cream, jerk."

"Oh, I'll be waiting. But hey, did you see the girls that just moved in at the end of the hall?"

"Who? The Hispanics? I haven't seen them since they put their stuff in their rooms."

"No, not them. The ones in the rooms nearby. Room 345. Did you see the blonde one? She was fine!"

"Dylan, didn't you come here with that one girl you're with... what's her name? Rachel?"

"Hey, I'm just looking, not touching. Don't spoil this for me, kay man? Besides, you're fair game. I'm sure you'll knock 'em dead with that British accent of yours. Just stick with me and I'll find you some tail."

"Oh, please. Like I need any help chatting up a totty. Watch and learn."

Luca went over to room 345 and knocked on the door. Some shuffling was heard inside, and a girl with thick, wavy blonde hair opened the door. She wore a pair of faded jeans and a button-up shirt.

"Hey there, doll. The name's Luca. Looking at the door tag on your door leads me to believe that you're either Amy or Grace. Let me take a shot in the dark and say that you're Grace."

"Nope, Amy," she responded while still at the door. "Now, if you'll excuse me, Luca. I have lots of unpacking to do. I'll see you at the hall meeting tonight." She then went back inside and closed the door.

"Nice one," Dylan applauded.

"Oh, shut up," Luca snarked.

*****

It had been a long day. All the work running errands and making registration go as smoothly as possible had Kimberly exhausted. But her work wasn't done. Before she could go to bed, she had to have her first hall meeting with her residents. And despite how tired she was, she knew she had to put on a smile and make them all feel welcome, even if they could care less about the hall meeting.

Kimberly remembered her first year at Sun Valley University's residence halls as a freshman. Students really didn't care for their RA at the time or any "hall meetings" he had planned. Kimberly was determined to learn from his mistakes. She put up signs on their doors early in the day, and advertised snacks to be provided during the meeting.

She got up from her bed, wincing in pain as her feet ached from wearing uncomfortable shoes all day. It was dark outside. Despite how tired she was, she couldn't sleep a wink in the half hour nap she had planned. Instead, she got up and out of her room, went to the room next door and knocked. Amy came to the door.

"Hey Amy, how are you doing?" Kimberly asked in her friendliest tone.

"Doing great. Just about done unpacking everything. You never realize how much stuff you have until you have to move it three thousand miles to a school on the other side of the country."

"That's right, you're from California, correct?"

"Yeah, Lancaster. Very different from Florida. Getting here was a pain. Two layover flights and a delay that took me much longer to get here than it should have. I still wonder if I would have been better off driving. At least my roommate had an easier time."

"Speaking of Grace, where is she? I haven't met her yet."

"Oh, she's been in and out a few times. She's an… interesting girl. Very cheery all the time and, I don't know. She seems to live in her own little world."

"Interesting, I can't wait to meet her. Anyways, Amy, I have some snacks that I need to set up out here for the hall meeting that starts in a few minutes. Would you like to help me set them up? I've got a lot of stuff here."

"Sure!"

Amy left her room and helped Kimberly set up a table in the hallway, as well as chips, drinks, and cookies that Kimberly bought for the staff meeting. Other students started to come out of their rooms as nine o'clock approached, wondering what the meeting was about, but mostly just to grab some snacks. Ben and his roommate were the first to come out, followed by a few others from the other side of the hall. Luca came in with Dylan and his friend Sam with some sodas from the local dining place on campus, laughing and joking around.

Amy opened the bag of chips and poured them in bowls, then handed out plates to the students in line for the snacks.

Kimberly began counting heads to see if everyone was accounted for.

"Is everyone here? Are any of your roommates missing?" she asked.

The students began to shuffle about and look around, but no one seemed to respond.

"The two Hispanic girls were in their rooms the last time I saw them," a tall Indian girl said.

Her name might have been Prachi. Kimberly could barely remember the names of all these students that she had met only once. Some none at all.

"Could someone please knock on their door and tell them to join us?"

Prachi knocked, but there was no answer. She knocked again, and still no response.

With more than thirty faces staring at her, Kimberly began getting nervous.

"That's fine, Prachi," she told her. "We'll just start the meeting. I'll get anyone missing caught up some other time. Anyways, for the rest of you, my name is Kimberly Shaw. I will be your RA, or Resident Advisor, this coming year. Now does anyone know what an RA is or what an RA does?"

No one raised their hands. Nothing could be heard but the sound of chips crunching in mouths throughout the hall. Watching all those students sitting on the floor with their eyes on her made her self-conscious. She never realized how scary her first year as an RA would be.

"Well then, a Resident Advisor is just a student assigned to a particular hall in a residential building to aid freshmen in a variety of things. Having been at this university longer, as well as the intense training that we go through, we are full of knowledge on the resources this campus has to offer you regarding just about anything you need. If you have a problem, come see me. This could be for anything. Problems with a professor, problems with a roommate, emotional concerns, academic concerns, anything. Either I will help you, or I will find the appropriate person to help you.

"In addition to that, RAs also provide several programs for students. This year I have many programs planned for you, both educational programs and social, fun programs. The purpose of these programs are to have you all get to know each other better, as well as develop fundamental skills on how to survive being a college student. To keep the hall as safe and clean as possible, I am also the rule enforcer. You were all provided with a booklet containing housing and university guidelines. Read them and follow them. If you break any of those rules, it is my job to write you up, and there will be consequences for breaking rules. Are we clear?"

The room was still silent. Kimberly could tell that some of the students really didn't care what she was saying, like that British guy, Luca, and others weren't even paying attention, like Luca's trusty Asian sidekick, Sam. She was relieved to know that Ben and Amy, two students she had gotten to know a little better, were listening intently. Suddenly, she saw the hall entrance door open, and a girl wearing what appeared to be a tie-dye blouse made of some wool-like fabric came in.

"Hi, hello!" Kimberly called to her. "What's your name?"

"Hi! I'm Grace. It's a pleasure meeting all of you." She then curtsied while holding the sides of her skirt and took a seat near the back of the group.

"Oh, yeah, Grace! I was expecting you. Oh, and uh, that reminds me! I forgot to take attendance! Now please raise your hand when I call your name so I can mark you as having attended the hall meeting. Please also tell me something about you. It'll help me match the names with the faces, as I have yet to remember who all of you are. Got it?"

She fumbled around through her bag until she found a list of her students.

"Okay, Benjamin?"

Benjamin raised his hand.

"Hey everyone, I'm Ben, and um…. I don't know. I like turtles…"

"Great! Thanks!" Kimberly said. "Alright then, Jessica?"

A girl in an Air Force uniform raised her hand. "My name is Jessica. I'm in the ROTC program here at Sun Valley University," she said in her thick western accent.

"Thank you, Jessica. How about Prachi?"

Prachi raised her hand next. "I'm Prachi everyone and… umm… I'm from India and… my favorite color is indigo."

"Great! Luca?"

Luca raised his hand. "Hi everyone. My name is Luca, and one interesting thing about me is that I think this is boring as hell!"

Suddenly, laughter was heard from the whole group. Kimberly turned red with embarrassment. She fought her urge to cry and instead decided to change tactics.

"Okay, everyone. Due to time and it getting late, I'm just going to pass this sheet around. Please sign next to your name if you're here, okay? The next thing I'm going to do is go over the policy guide with all of you. Even though you all got a copy, it is a rule that I have to go over it with you at least once so I can make sure you know what the rules are."

Groans were heard from the students.

"Oh, it's not that bad. I'll try to make it as brief as possible. But first, I just want to remind you all that tomorrow morning is the official convocation ceremony for all freshmen at nine o'clock at the REC. Is everyone clear? Please don't miss out on this as it's one of the campus's biggest events. President Lambrick is a very busy man, yet he takes the time to attend and even speak to all of you at this event. There is also music from the band, guest speakers, prizes, and even some performances from our cheerleading squad! I loved it as a freshman and I know you will too! Now, onto rule number one. No alcohol in the residence halls!"

*****

Ben woke up in an instant as the sunlight from the window danced directly on his face. He looked at the time. Seven in the morning. He still had an hour to get ready. His alarm wasn't even set to go off for another forty five minutes. He slowly got up and went out to the semi-public bathroom he shared with the adjacent rooms. Zachary was already there in his towel. He had just gotten out of the shower and was shaving.

"You're up early," Ben remarked.

"It's a habit," Zachary told him. "I used to get up every day at five in the morning to help my dad with the farm. I also like to run in the mornings. I get too tired at night and it's way too hot the rest of the day. You're welcome to join me if you're ever interested."

"Thanks, I'll keep that in mind," Ben said in passing.

"Did you hear about the rich kid?"

Ben put the last of his toothpaste on his toothbrush. "No, what?"

"Apparently, his father is like, the CEO of some massive huge company or something and brought his son to school on his own private Learjet aircraft."

"Wow," Ben said in amazement.

"That's not all, either. Apparently, his father paid extra money to the school to put his son in the honors dorm, so that he's surrounded by all the smart kids. Talk about spoiled."

"Can schools even do that?"

"With the right price, they'll do anything."

Zachary rinsed himself off as he finished shaving.

"Well, I'm done here. Gotta go wake up my boneheaded roommate. He went out partying with Luca last night, no doubt drinking, and now it's gonna be hell getting him up for convocation. I'll see you at the REC?"

Ben smiled. "Yeah, sure. And what was your name again? I'm bad with names."

"Haha, Zachary. And that's alright. Aren't we all?"

Zachary left the bathroom as Ben finished brushing his teeth. He went back into the room, watched some TV, and then tried to wake his roommate up.

"Mattic! Hey Mattic! Get up! If we get there early, we can get better seats!"

Mattic's jet black long hair covered his thin face as he laid on his stomach on the top bunk. Ben tried to shake him, but he just groaned and turned his face away.

"Geez Mattic! Where did you go last night that got you so tired?" Ben asked. "Did you go partying with Dylan?"

Mattic groaned again and wrapped his covers over his head.

"Fine then, be that way."

Ben gave up trying to wake him up and decided to go to the convocation ceremony on his own. As he stepped out to lock his door, he saw a few students already on their way out of the hall. Amy walked with Kimberly and went to the elevator. Luca and his roommate Sam followed afterwards, with Luca checking out Amy and Kimberly from behind as they were walking.

Ben took the stairs down. As he passed the second floor, another student approached the staircase to go down as well. The student was a bit heavyset, with a chin strap beard going from ear to ear. It made him look much older.

"You on your way to the convocation ceremony?" Ben asked him. The student looked at him as if he just asked a very stupid question.

"Yeah, that's where I'm headed," he responded.

"Hi, I'm Ben. Just trying to get to know some of the people that live in this building."

"I'm Tobias. Are you a gamer?" he asked.

Ben was surprised to hear this question.

"Well, yes, gaming is a pastime for me. But what prompted the question?"

Tobias pointed at his shirt.

"You have a green one-up mushroom on your shirt. Either you're a Mario Brothers fan or a drugee. I took a stab and guessed gamer."

"Oh, yeah," Ben laughed. "Honestly, I forgot I had this shirt on. I haven't unpacked my clothes yet, so I pulled out the first T-shirt from my bag that was available. This is an old shirt."

"That's fine. Did you join the Gaming club?"

"What Gaming Club?"

"The one at the Activities Fair."

"There was an Activities Fair?"

Tobias slapped his hand on his forehead. "Seriously, dude. Did you not explore the campus yesterday? There was a whole section of booths on the east side of campus where student clubs and organizations were trying to recruit members. They'll be out there today and tomorrow too. You should check it out."

"Thanks," Ben said. This excited him a bit. Now that he was on his own, Ben was looking for a way to make new friends and involve himself in new activities. He figured that going to the Activities Fair would be a great way to do it.

Tobias and Ben finally reached the Renfield Entertainment Center. It was located on the east side of the campus. This part of the campus seemed like the Athletic Center for the university. A tennis field was there, as well as a track, a baseball field, and even the massive football stadium not too far from the REC. Inside the REC was even more amazing. The building looked much taller from the inside, with enough room to hold thousands of people. It looked like the entertainment hall was often used as a basketball court, since it looked like some hoops had been raised for the convocation ceremony.

Many of the students from Ben's hall were already there. He saw the ROTC girl Jessica and her roommate Prachi already at their seats waiting for the event to start. Neither of them had any family with them. In fact, it seemed that a lot of the students' families had already left by the second day of orientation, leaving the students to fend for themselves.

Dylan walked into the REC from the north doors holding hands with a girl.

"Rachel, you wanna go save us some seats? I'll get us some pop if you want," he told her.

"No, you're staying with me! I didn't get to see you at all yesterday since we arrived on campus. I had to spend the whole night without you! I'm not letting you go that easily," Rachel joked as she pulled Dylan towards the seats.

"Are you ever gonna quit giving me grief about that, Rei?" Dylan asked with a smile. "I told you, I was busy. I helped my roommate move in and then showed him around the town. It was the courteous thing to do. And see, now we have all day to spend together. No harm, no foul!"

"Oh, I know. I was just teasing. So when do I get to meet your brother Spencer? Is he as good looking as you?"

Dylan laughed. "He wishes! I don't know, really. Last I talked to him was on the phone on our drive here when he told me where to pick up our room keys. He said he'd be busy with some orientation stuff the next few days and that he'll let me know when he's free. Though he did tell me that he can't wait to meet you."

He glanced over to the entrance and saw Luca coming in.

"Oh Rachel, there's someone I'd like you to meet!"

He walked her over to Luca and Sam.

"Hey Luca, I'd like you to meet Rachel, my girlfriend. She came with me from North Carolina. Rachel, this here is Luca. He came all the way from England to come to school here."

"Oh, wow, an English boy!" Rachel said with a smile. "How sophisticated!"

"Heh, hardly," Sam added in.

"And this little Korean bugger is Sam," Luca said as he shoved Sam playfully. "Doesn't know when to keep his mouth shut."

"Ahh, shut it, you crazy foreigner," Sam retaliated. "You're just mad cuz you got turned down by that girl from our hall… TWICE!"

"Which girl?" Dylan asked. "Amy? You seriously went after Amy again? And you failed? Haha, oh boy."

"Hey, that bird's gotta be crazy. No one turns down ol' Luca here. I'm a hit at the club! You were there, Dylan. Didn't you see me chattin' up those babes in Downtown Sun Valley?"

"What?" Rachel asked. "You went to the club, Dylan? Didn't you say you were showing your roommate around?"

"Heh, calm down sugar," Dylan responded. "I did show him around. One of the stops was the club. What's wrong with that?"

"Oh, I don't know. Maybe because typically showing someone around consists of driving around seeing the locations of the restaurants, shops, maybe getting a drink. I didn't realize you went clubbing. And why didn't you take me?"

"Rachel, listen, it was a guy's night out, okay? It was just one night. You really need to relax."

"Oh, you owe me Dylan," Rachel said as she headed over to find a seat.

"Damn, mate," Luca said. "You told her you took Zachary out to show him around? Don't you think she'll find out that you didn't?"

"Shut up, Luca," Dylan exclaimed. "I know what I'm doing. Zachary's cool. He'll cover for me. Don't worry about that. It's just that Rachel drowns me every once in a while, you know? I need some space without having her breathing down my neck all the time. Anyways, I need to go before she gets even more upset. Later!"

Dylan ran off to meet Rachel on the stands. Sam chuckled.

"Poor, poor Dylan. Little does he know that weaving such a finely threaded web of lies will eventually tangle up and- oh my God! Look! Snow cones!"

Sam gave up his sentence mid-thought and ran to get a snow cone. Luca shook his head and walked on after him.

With everyone finally settled down, the band started to quiet down the music they have been playing the past 20 minutes. The stands were filling up pretty nicely, mostly with students, staff, and faculty, as well as some straggler parents who still hadn't left yet. In the middle of the court were some special VIP seats saved for some important people from the campus. RAs, orientation leaders, and other students who helped with the orientation process were seated in a portion of those seats. Kimberly and Robert were both sitting by each other near the back of the RA section. In another area, important university staff had a seat. Shandra Giles, Nancy Wei, and Travis Coleman were all sitting in this area. In the very front of the VIP section were the big bosses. University Provost Dr. Scott and President Lambrick were both sitting in the front, amongst some other university authorities.

As the music settled down, Dr. Scott got up from his seat and rose to the stage.

"Good morning everyone," he said. "How is everyone doing today?"

Standard cheers and applause came from different parts of the REC center.

"Aww, come on. That was weak! I know you can do better than that! I said how is everyone doing today?!"

The cheers were much louder this time, with applause roaring through the entire hall, surrounded by whistling and yelling.

"That's more like it! I am known around these parts as Dr. Scott. However, anyone who's cool calls me Scotty. No, I jest. Don't call me Scotty. Do so at your own peril. Anyways, welcome to Sun Valley University's forty-ninth annual convocation ceremony! Sun Valley University started out as a small, out-of-the-mill liberal arts college built by its founder and first president, Andrew B. Clifton. Around a time when the only college options were either state universities or expensive private colleges, Clifton's goal was to create a great new affordable college with just as much quality as the alternatives.

"We started out small, with only a few hundred students on our campus. It remained this way for several years, and then we began to grow. Our academic excellence as well as our athletics got us noticed around the state. Students began to enroll in higher and higher numbers each year. Now look at us! After being a small college for several years, we sprung up from three hundred students to almost fifteen thousand in less than twenty years! I would like to thank you students as well as your families for putting your faith in our institution. We will not let you down. To start off this convocation, I would like to call up Reverend Matthews on the stage to lead us in opening prayer."

The next hour went by pretty quickly. After Reverend Matthews' prayer, the band played one the university's battle songs as the cheerleaders ran up into the stage. They then performed one of their new routines to rally up the audience like an old-fashioned high school pep rally. A woman came up to announce the winners of the convocation raffle, followed by a guest speaker who talked a little about his profession and how college got him there. Finally, Dr. Scott got back onto the stage.

"Ladies and gentlemen, boys and girls, righties and lefties, I would now like to introduce to you a man with great power. His achievements both inside and outside the university are very widely known, even over international waters. His dedication to this university is topnotch, and he has made sure to keep this university #1 in all areas. He has also been known to leap tall buildings in a single bound. Give it up for President Jeremy Lambrick!!!"

The roar of the audience applause shook the stands as everyone got up to cheer. Although very few students even knew who he was prior to the introduction, they were already hyped up from the prior events from the ceremony, causing them to cheer for anything.

President Lambrick entered the stage and shook Dr. Scott's hand, then waited for the applause to settle down before he spoke.

"Thank you Dr. Scott. You know, if there's one thing I dislike about my job, is having to speak to a group of students after one of Dr. Scott's entertaining introductions. I think to myself, how do I top that? Anyhow, I would once again like to welcome you all to Sun Valley University. This institution is a big, if not the biggest, part of my life. Since I became president several years ago, I have worked hard to provide students everything they need for a great education. This means much more than just running the university like a business. It means getting involved in the finer details of college life, the things that people in the higher positions tend to miss. Now I know that Dr. Scott and several others contribute the success of this school to my hard work and dedication, but this isn't necessarily true.

"The real secret to this university's success is all of you. The incoming freshman class that brings a breath of fresh air to our campus. That's my secret. The truth is, you all run this university, not us. Sure, we have our titles, our experience, and our authority to run the school. But without students, all of that means nothing! This is why we place such high importance in students running the different areas of the universities. We have students work as RAs to make the residence halls a wonderful and safe place to live. We have our student government association so students like you can have a say on the big changes that take place on our campus. As I stand here speaking to you, I am looking at the next generation of leaders.

"Andrew Clifton was my college professor once. He is the one that inspired me to pursue a career in higher education. His inspiration is the reason that I am standing in front of all of you here today. On my first year here as president, before he passed away, I told Dr. Clifton how he inspired me to do such great things, and you know what he said? He said that I had it backwards. It is I that inspired him to do great things. Students like me who strived to achieve great things with their lives. Now that I am here, I say the same thing to all of you. Every single one of you serves as an inspiration for what I do. Don't just take this as a compliment. Take it as the driving force for your college career. I hope to one day see all of you up here giving a speech like this, speaking to a new generation of leaders waiting for their turn to rise to the top.

"So what I say to you now is don't give up. You've made it this far. You've paved your way through years and years of elementary school, middle school, and even high school. College is a whole different ballgame. The game has changed but the goal remains clear: you're here to win! Sun Valley University is currently ranked number one in many different areas: academics, athletics, customer service, and we're quickly rising up the ranks of the university giants even as a young university. We are well on our way to becoming one of the best, already being regarded by many as one of the "Ivy League schools of public education". And we could not have gotten this far without students like you!

"In closing, I want you all to stand up and give a round of applause for yourselves, for you deserve to be recognized for all that you have done, as well as all that you will do. So everyone rise, and give it up for the newest freshman class of Sun Valley University!"

Everyone stood up and once again cheered. Up until this point, college consisted of just a long drive or flight to the campus, hours spent hauling luggage and unpacking, and filling out forms after long lines for registration. It wasn't until now that students really felt the thrill of being in college.

Ben couldn't help but smile as he applauded. To see President Lambrick up there, having been a student just like him, having such power and motivating future generations to succeed, Ben had hope for himself. His mother always wanted him to do something big with his life. As he looked over at President Lambrick, he imagined himself up there, giving the same speech to his own group of college students. He knew it was a long shot, considering he was the first in his family to go to college. It was quite a big leap from where his family currently stood. But he knew he would at least try.

It was almost noon, and several of the students and their families were already getting up to go to lunch. As the audience applauded and the band played its favorite tunes, Ben noticed a woman walk up to Dr. Scott, who was sitting on stage behind President Lambrick, and whispered in his ear. As President Lambrick continued to smile and wave at the crowd, Dr. Scott got up from his seat and walked off the stage with the individual. His face suddenly turned into a frown as he talked to her offstage. Ben turned to see if Tobias noticed, but like everyone else around him, he was preoccupied with the music from the band. The woman pulled out her cell phone to make a call as they both hurried to the emergency doors in the back. Within seconds, they were gone.

CHAPTER 4: CHEYENNE WINTERS
JANUARY

Both alarms rang simultaneously, causing me to frantically get out of my bed and shut them off. I forgot to turn off my cell phone alarm I'd been using the past few days during my move. I turned off my desk alarm and shuffled through my purse to find my cell phone buried alongside my pocket dictionary, contact numbers, field notebook, and stationary. I remembered how annoying that alarm ringtone was, but, like always, forgot to change it when I had the chance. I finally found the cell phone and shut off that ear-splitting sound.

Still exhausted from my meetings the day before, I threw myself back onto my university-provided bed and stared at the chipped and slightly vandalized ceiling. Incomprehensible graffiti marks decorated one of the corners by the ceiling. The off-white paint coating was coming off the walls, and as I started to really inspect the room for the first time, I noticed just how badly kept it was. Although there were signs of mold blotches on the carpet, this was typical of any building located in the Floridian humid air.

I could tell that I wasn't a priority to this university. They threw me into whatever available room they could find, with no effort to at least clean it prior to my arrival, as evidenced by the gum wrappers lying on the floor around the trash can. Still, I was grateful they gave me a place to stay at all. My advisor at UF (University of Florida) was generous enough to make arrangements with SVU to house me in one of their residence halls free of charge for the duration of my study. They could have at least cleaned it.

In all honesty, I didn't want to get out of bed. I had been in Sun Valley for four days, and I had done nothing but jump through hoops to get the appropriate clearances for observing and interviewing twenty one students in a classroom. The big bosses wanted me to go through their lower level staff, the staff then sent me back up to the big bosses, and the big bosses would then send me to another department, where the whole process would start over again. Despite their initial resistance and apathy towards my study, the hardest part wasn't convincing them to give me the right approval, it was finding them. They were rarely in the office, never answered their phone calls, and forget about email! Administrators always seemed to be in a meeting.

As much as I wanted to just lie there all morning, I forced myself out of bed. Despite the hectic last few days, I got the necessary approvals. It would have all been for nothing if I didn't make use of them. I walked into my closet to find an outfit to wear. Though it really wasn't a closet; more like a small gap in the wall with a bar to hang clothing. I grabbed the first pencil skirt I could find and matching blouse. I walked over to the crawl space they called a bathroom and fixed up my hair in front of the mirror. Even the Florida sunshine wasn't enough to add color to my pale complexion. I fixed my black bangs that were all over the place and grabbed my small, rectangular-rimmed glasses by the side of the sink. I wiped them off with my blouse for good luck, put them on, and headed out the door to the College of Applied Sciences.

Dr. Garcia's office was located on the second floor of the Science College. It was smaller than the spacious offices with windows I saw down the hall. His office was cramped, windowless, barely had enough room for a second chair in addition to his things. The door was open, and he seemed preoccupied on his computer answering emails. I knocked on the door out of courtesy to grab his attention.

He was quite young for a professor. He couldn't have been older than thirty. As he got up to greet me, I noticed that he put effort in his visual appearance. He wore a neatly-ironed button-down shirt wrapped in a sport coat of a light fabric, with a pair of dark-washed jeans to round out his personal style. He had short, wavy black hair, a thin goatee around his slightly tanned face, and a pair of reading glasses he took off before he offered to shake my hand.

"Cheyenne Winters, I presume?"

"Yes, that's me."

"Hi, I'm Steven Garcia. I talked to Shandra who filled me in on what you were doing. Some kind of study, was it?"

"Yes, she told me it would be okay if I can introduce myself to your class this morning to explain the reason for my study."

Dr. Garcia walked back to his desk.

"And what is the reason for this study?"

"Oh, I thought Dr. Giles told you. It's for my dissertation as part of my PhD in Student Affairs Administration. I'm doing a four month ethnographical study on college students and their adjustment into college."

"Yeah, yeah, she told me all of that. But you didn't answer my question. What is the reason for this study?"

I adjusted my glasses.

"I… I don't understand your question."

"I'm asking why you chose to do this particular study. Now I'm certain that your dissertation advisor didn't just tell you to pack your bags and come to Sun Valley University to study our freshmen for a few months. What drove you to this school to study these students?"

I thought about his question for a moment, trying to find the right words to say.

"I don't know… I did a literature review, read past studies, and it seemed most universities in Florida were proliferated with studies except for this one. It was underrepresented in the literature world, so I thought I could add some data from here."

Dr. Garcia turned his computer off and got out of his seat.

"Walk with me to the Classroom Building. My classroom is in there and my students will start arriving in a bit."

He led me out of the office and locked his office door.

"Anyways, that's great that you're trying to add to the literature, but you still haven't answered my question. True research comes from passion in a particular subject. It comes from the desire to make a difference, wanting to not only learn as much as possible about what interests you, but to change the world in your own unique way. What's your passion, Cheyenne? Why does your topic interest you so much that you're willing to go through this school's insane approval system?"

"Umm, it's hard to say really. My advisor at UF was a firm believer of broadening your horizons and gaining new experiences. She's had an impact on me and I wanted to follow her advice. I found out about the first suicide here from a friend and I guess I thought I could make a difference. You know, maybe find out what makes these students tick so that I could prevent future suicides. I don't know, I'm still working it all out."

Dr. Garcia smiled.

"No, no, that's good. That's a much better response. Doing research is a tedious process. It will frustrate you and it will wear you down. Always remember what you're striving for to keep you motivated through the tough parts. That's the only way I managed to get through mine."

"If you don't mind me asking, how did you get a faculty position here? No offense, but you seem so young. Professors are usually in their thirties and above."

He laughed as he opened the door to the Classroom Building for me. The building wasn't as well kept as the Student Union Tower. It was made of brick, most likely to protect it from hurricanes. Patches of ivy decorated the entrance to the building, much like some of the other academic buildings around the campus.

"Yeah, I am pretty young. Went straight through my PhD after my undergrad. I studied science, and lucky for me, this school had a shortage of science professors. And voila! I got hired. It's tough, though. It's only my second year here, so not only am I the young guy, but also the new guy. And of course, administrators like Shandra look at me first when assigning rookie researchers to invade our classrooms."

I glanced away from him at the last part. I looked down towards the floor, feeling ashamed that I was disturbing his class. He noticed my embarrassment.

"I'm just kidding, Cheyenne. You're not a bother. Really."

I faked a smile. I knew he was just being polite. Past experience had shown me that people disguise their true feelings as jokes as a way to blow off steam.

We finally reached his classroom. Like the rest of the building, the walls of the classroom were painted green with gold trimmings at the bottom, most likely representing the school colors. The chairs and desks looked old, just like the furniture in my room. While the campus was beautiful from the outside, the inside could really use some work.

"If you'd like, you can read through some of these to give you some background information on my students. It's an assignment I gave them on the first day of class back in August."

He handed me a folder full of one page biographies the students wrote at the beginning of the year. I skimmed through them for a bit, but stopped when the first student walked in. She wore a light blue dress that almost reached her ankles. She had long, straight red hair held neatly by a blue headband.

"Good morning, Dr. Garcia," she said politely as she headed to her seat.

"Good morning Sarah." he said enthusiastically to her.

She pulled out a book and began reading.

"Her name is Sarah Holmes," Dr. Garcia told me in a quiet voice. "She's always here early. She tells me she helps out at a soup kitchen every morning, then heads to this class right after. Remarkable young lady. One of the most caring people you will ever meet."

More students started to arrive within minutes, all taking their seats. Dr. Garcia gave me little snippets of some of them as they entered. He told me about the two Hispanic girls that mostly stayed to themselves. He told me about the British student that became really good friends with the Korean student. He told me about Dylan, the student majoring in the same field Dr. Garcia graduated in, meteorology.

The students often gave occasional glances at me as they took their seats, wondering why I was there.

I saw an older woman, at least compared to the rest of the students, enter the room.

"Is she a teaching aid?" I asked him quietly.

"This university tends to have what we call nontraditional students. They're students of nontraditional age that come back to get their degrees many years later. That's Susan Price. She's a mother of two taking classes to further her career. I've had very fascinating conversations with her."

A student named Mattic was the last one to come in. Dr. Garcia told me that he was almost always late. Once everyone was settled in, he got the class's attention.

"Happy Monday everyone. I hope everyone had a wonderful winter break at home or wherever you decided to spend it. Hopefully, you've all come back refreshed and relaxed and ready for work!"

Some students laughed, others groaned.

"Now, as I'm sure you've all noticed, we have a visitor here with us today. Her name is Cheyenne Winters, and she comes to us from northern Florida. She will be working on a project here for the next few months, and we're all really excited to have her. So please let's give the floor to Ms. Cheyenne Winters."

Dr. Garcia gestured for me to speak. I felt the weight of all twenty one students' stares, examining me, trying to figure me out. I was never a public speaker. I was always the student doing the background work in group projects. I helped with the research, excelled in the editing and organization of the presentations, but I never presented. Just having my name acknowledged was enough, and I barely even cared about that. I loved to learn. I didn't do the work for the credit. I did it for the knowledge I gained by doing it, or by whatever discovery I could make through research. But standing here in front of all of these students reminded me how bad of a speaker I was. I began to revert to my nervous mannerisms. I fiddled with my glasses and unnecessarily fixed my bangs before I cleared my throat to speak.

"Hi... umm... Good morning everyone. Like Dr. Garcia said, my name is Cheyenne Winters. I'm a doctoral student at University of Florida working on my dissertation. I got my undergraduate degree at East Central Florida University majoring in Elementary Education. I then continued studying through ECFU's Master's program in Student Affairs Administration. I enjoyed it so much that I decided to pursue my PhD in Student Affairs at University of Florida, since I heard they had a great program there.

"What is Student Affairs, you ask? Well, to put it simply, it's a field that is dedicated to all of you. My field deals with learning all we can about college students to be able to make the college experience better for you. We work in many areas: university admissions, student advising, housing, student dining, counseling, Dean of Students, you name it!

"As I'm sure you're all learning, it's not easy being a college student. There is much more to it than just taking classes. It's almost like starting a new life. You all have the opportunities to reinvent yourselves, mold yourselves into the adult you want to be. Your decisions here will impact the rest of your lives.

"That's why I'm here. My goal is to meet with all of you a few times and get to know you better. You all bring unique experiences with you to college and your own ways of solving problems and persevering. I'd like to learn what college means to you, and how you plan to go about dealing with it. This can then help me assist future students who face similar problems but don't know what to do about them. And if there are any problems or questions that come up while I'm here, feel free to talk to me about them and I'll see what we can do.

"It's a great opportunity for all of you to contribute valuable information to society, and I'm excited to meet each and every one of you. I'll be leaving a signup sheet with your professor so you can sign up for an interview slot with me. I'll occasionally also be coming into the classroom to observe. Any questions?"

The class was silent enough one could hear a pin drop. Most of the students were still staring intently at me, still unsure as to the purpose of my presence despite my explanation. Other students just stopped caring halfway through and were playing with their pencil or just looking off into the distance. Dr. Garcia came to my rescue by breaking the unsettling silence.

"Thank you, Ms. Winters. And even though participation in this study is strictly voluntary, I'm going to provide extra credit points for anyone who decides to help out in the study. You each will receive 10 extra credit points for participating in class the days Ms. Winters is here observing, as well as 5 extra credit points for each interview you attend with her. This is a great way to boost up your grade after the lower scores some of you received from the midterm last semester."

I smiled, appreciating the support he gave me for my study. I thanked the class for their time, handed Dr. Garcia the signup sheet, and left the classroom.

Despite my awkward meeting with the class, I was starting to get excited. I had never headed my own research study before. In the past, my only research involvements were assisting professors and others with their own research. This time, I was in control. I picked the topic, wrote the proposal, and any results from this study would be my doing.

My smile faded as I exited the stairs back to the first floor of the classroom building. As I turned down the hall, I saw Detective Sawyer exit one of the offices. She saw me on her way out of the building, and looked at me like a wild dog protecting its territory. Her fierce stare relayed the message clear to me. She wanted me to back off.

I broke the visual confrontation by looking down into my clipboard, pretending to look for some documents that didn't exist. I waited until she went out the door before I continued walking. Due to my distraction, I failed to notice that Nancy Wei was standing by the office staring at me.

"Don't worry, hun. She gives everyone goose bumps around here," Nancy said.

I laughed nervously.

"You're Cheyenne, right? I heard about you. You're the one everyone's been complaining about. They say you've pretty much been stalking all the higher ups these last few days. My exaggeration, not theirs."

"Oh... I..."

"Don't worry about it. It's about time someone makes those lazy admins do some work for a change. Besides, with Detective Sawyer over there storming up the place, you're old news."

"What's she doing?"

"From what I hear, Detective Sawyer is sure that these suicides are linked. Possibly due to the same cause. Dr. Giles has told her that the cause is depression, but Sawyer doesn't want to hear it. She's sure that there's more to it than that. Three suicides in such a short amount of time is a big enough case to investigate anywhere else, but it's much harder here. Unless someone commits an obvious crime like murder or assault, it's difficult to get investigations on a college campus. The SVU administration doesn't want to subject students to constant interrogation and the inevitable media coverage that such a high profile investigation would bring in. You think you had barriers to entry in this study? You can't imagine what Detective Sawyer has to put up with."

Nancy and I walked out of the classroom building. It was still cold out like it was earlier in the morning, but that didn't say much. Florida winters rarely required more than a sweater to bear through, especially towards the central south where Sun Valley University was located. It was away from any major beaches so the area was free from the cold sea breezes that occasionally washed in.

"Have you been given a campus tour?" Nancy asked as she put on her sunglasses. The sun was out in full force, even in January.

"Not officially. Though I definitely got to know the campus as I ran from office to office."

"I thought so. Seriously, for the fame this school has in student customer service, they sure put all others out to dry, don't they? Walk with me. I'll show you around."

Nancy and I walked for the next half hour around the large campus. We walked around the four main colleges. I got to see the colleges of Science, Arts, Business, and Education. She also showed me the newly-built college of Medicine located further away. She showed me some of the residence halls, both freshman ones and upperclassmen halls. They ranged in size and in design. Some of them, like Miller Hall, had a more traditional dorm look.

Others like Terra Hall, the one I was staying in, had a cheap motel layout. Others looked more like fancier, indoor hotels, such as Scarlet Hall. She told us the honors students were put in those nicer ones. Then there were the apartment style halls. Those were reserved mostly for upper-class students, as well as some of the faculty and staff that chose to live on campus. They were also reserved for nontraditional students like Susan who had families and needed more room.

"Cheyenne, let me ask you something. What do you think you're going to find out from these students?"

"I'm not sure. I figured I'd ask them about their experiences getting here, their adjustments into college life, and maybe their reasoning for getting a degree."

Nancy looked off into the distance, engulfed in thought. We continued walking for a few more minutes saying nothing. I used the opportunity to look at the students as they traveled the campus. Compared to when I first arrived, the campus was full of life. Students were everywhere, coming out of every door in every building, overtaking the campus grounds like ants at a picnic. I was suddenly struck with a wave of nostalgia from my own undergraduate years, walking back and forth from class to class, seeing my classmates along the way, worrying about that test coming up.

The diversity of students was overwhelming. Nowhere else had I seen such a myriad of cultures from around the world coming together to this melting pot of a university. All of these cultures, races, and beliefs meshing together between students as they learned to cope and live with each other for the next four years.

"We need your help, Cheyenne," Nancy said, calling back my wandering mind.

I looked at her with confusion. "Excuse me?"

"Sawyer isn't going to get anywhere with this investigation. I was present for her last interrogation. She's questioning the students for facts. Facts alone aren't going to solve this case. If Dr. Giles is right, then we have to get to the root of the depression some of these students are facing. Up until now, no one's been doing anything about it, and it doesn't look like they will anytime soon. I really don't want to wait to see how many suicides it takes for the administration to take serious action. Right now, all we have is you and Sawyer. And I'm betting we have a better chance with you."

"Me? But what can I do? It's not like my students will know anything."

I noticed a look of concern in Nancy's face.

"Detective Sawyer may be a bit abrasive and impulsive with her conclusions, but I believe she's right. These suicides aren't isolated incidents. And it's not just depression, either, as everyone has conveniently concluded. Dr. Giles has put a few of us in charge of creating some depression prevention programs to take effect this semester, but I don't think it will do much good."

"Why?"

"I'm a student advisor. Advisors are at the bottom of the Student Affairs chain. Due to the nature of our work, we have the highest amount of interaction with students. Myself and a few of my coworkers have noticed patterns. Trends. Students talk. In my conversations with them, they keep on mentioning a student. Not any one student in particular, but a type of student. The type that acts as a sort of college bully. You know how student gossip runs about. Current rumors going around are that some student is forcing others to commit suicide."

"Forcing? But how can you force someone to kill themselves?"

"I don't know. The rumors are vague. But it's been mentioned by many students. Sure, some of them are just repeating what they've heard, but others seem to really believe it. I've actually seen fear in some of their eyes. Once I try to question them, though, they shut down. I can't get a word out of them. Unfortunately, due to my lower status position, I don't really have much say in implementing more extreme measures in the university. Upper management doesn't have nearly as much interaction with students, working mostly with budgeting, meetings, and paperwork. And they refuse to take any drastic action that is based on 'rumors'."

"But if student lives are at stake, why wouldn't they rather be safe than sorry? Students are dying!"

"They're aware of that, but it's not the whole picture. If university administrators begin to show visible concern over the suicides by forcing students to divulge information and treating it like an investigation as Sawyer is doing, a campus-wide panic can break out. You know how things like this play out. Once it's made known that students are becoming depressed and are killing themselves possibly due to another student, students will start to panic thinking they're suffering from depression, and others will begin accusing each other for being the 'student killer'.

"Then suddenly, others get involved. Do you know how many parent phone calls we deal with on a daily basis? Imagine if parents from around the world find out that students are dying left and right at their child's university. They would clutter up the lines! And once the media got a hold of the story, the campus would cease to function. Faculty and staff would spend more time dealing with all the interruptions than actually running the school.

"That's why they refuse to take any major action without actual evidence showing a prevalent danger for our students. You could be the one to find us that evidence, Cheyenne. Find out if there is any truth to these rumors. Maybe these really were three isolated cases of depression, or maybe there really is a student causing peers to kill themselves. But we need to do something! I can't sleep at night knowing that students are dying left and right and all I'm doing to stop it is construct a depression prevention workshop to force students to attend. Can I count on you, Cheyenne?"

The idea that some student out there was promoting suicidal tendencies seemed farfetched in my mind, but I could tell that Nancy was serious about this. She really cared about these students. Perhaps she was close to one of the individuals that died. Still, she was asking for a whole lot from me. I was already walking on thin ice at this school with my study. Getting involved in their institutional problems was just asking for trouble. But at the same time, I've always had a history of falling victim to my own curiosities.

"Where do you suggest I start?"

BIO: LISA PEREZ
MIAMI, FL

I came to the US when I was very young. The rest of my family was still in Cuba except for my immediate family and a couple of cousins here and there. It didn't matter, though. In our block in Miami we might as well have been in Cuba. Cubanos lived in every apartment down the street, they owned all the local shops, and you could even say Spanish was the official language here. It's like being in Cuba without its problems.

It's why I never had to worry too much about speaking English. Except for school, I always spoke Spanish. To my friends, to my family, even at work when I worked at Don Pepe's Supermarket. I didn't care much about the world outside of Miami. My mom always told me that I should stay close to home. She wanted me to go to Florida International University. She said it was the college of the Hispanics. She put that dream into me since I was a little kid. But she never told me how to achieve that dream. What did she know? She never went to college except for a couple of community college classes that she barely passed. She didn't know what these universities looked for.

I was shocked when I found out my senior year of high school just how hard it would be to apply for this school. I thought grades were the only thing colleges cared about. I was wrong. I mean, my grades weren't bad, mostly B's through my hard work, a few A's and a few C's. But this university wanted the best of the best. All A's in your report card, but not just that. They wanted community service. Volunteer hours working in as many places as you could. They wanted you to join all these clubs and organizations I didn't even know my high school had.

Recommendation letters from teachers were another big part. I never really took the time to get to know my teachers. Did they even remember me? Oh, and the cost. This school cost a fortune! One look at the tuition and I knew I couldn't go there. If it was that difficult to get accepted, how difficult would it be to get a scholarship?

Due to my lack of knowledge, I had to settle for something less. I was going to go to community college, until I found out about this school. In an effort to increase their diversity, they gave minorities special waivers to get into the school, even with my lack of credentials. Lucky for me. My mom wasn't too happy about it, though. She didn't want me to leave la familia.

CHAPTER 5: INTERVIEW #LP03
LISA PEREZ

[I meet Lisa at the local deli that makes her favorite meatball and melted provolone sub. Her shoulder-length black hair now has a dark red tint to it. She's wearing a pair of Capris and her signature hoop earrings. Our last few interviews didn't go as well as I'd hoped, as she seemed guarded and a bit uncomfortable. Changing the interview location to a place she was more familiar with seems to work much better. She appears more open and relaxed.]

Hey Lisa! It's good to see you again. I love what you did with your hair.

Oh, you like it? Thanks! I bought one of those hair-tinting packages that you can use at home. Yeah, there's this Asian girl in my class with some crazy green highlights and the other day I thought 'you know, I could probably rock highlights'. Of course, I wasn't gonna go green, but I felt I needed to do something with my hair. I looked at the different colors available, and dark red seemed like the perfect fit. I've always liked black and red.

[She starts to play with her hair as she's talking.]

Great! Wow, Lisa, you seem so chipper today. I'm guessing you had a good weekend?

Yeah, it was fun. Gaby and I went to the beach for the first time since we left Miami in August. It was too cold to go swimming during Christmas break, and temperatures finally got back up to the sixties on Saturday. That's

47

the best part about Florida. Whatever winter we get is usually gone within a few weeks. But anyways, the weather was nice, but the water was freezing. It was hysterical watching Gaby dipping her foot in the water, only to go running out as the cold waves hit her legs. Honestly, that girl can be such a pansy. You gotta love her.

From our talks, it seems that you and Gabriella are really close. Let's talk about her for a bit. What would you say your friendship is like?

Me and Gaby? Wow, I don't know where to start. We've been friends for a couple of years, since she came to the US. Even though we're about the same age, she looks up to me like an older sister. Probably cause I know more about everything, like she constantly tells me. I always laugh when she says that. Me, know everything? Ha! I know she's just joking, but it's still very flattering.

She came to SVU because of me. Did you know that? I wasn't complaining. She's the closest thing to family that I have in this school full of *gringos*. It's tough being one of the only Hispanics here, especially after living in Miami so many years. I can only imagine how hard it is for Gaby. Her English isn't as good as mine. She tends to be self-conscious about it, and doesn't want to speak it when she doesn't have to. She prefers to stay in her room and paint. We've only spoken Spanish with each other the first half of the year.

It's only recently that I've managed to convince her to practice her English more with me. I told her that she needs to speak English if she wants to succeed in college. She's getting better... slowly. I just wish... I just wish she was more willing to practice it with others more.

[Her smile fades away. She pauses for a bit to think as she takes a bite out of her sub.]

Does it bother you?

Well, no... sort of. See, adjusting to college has been difficult for us. I spent the first month here pretty much isolated from the rest of the campus. Gaby was just so scared to go out and meet people that she would just rather stay in the dorm and paint or watch TV *novelas* all night. I didn't want to leave her alone there while I went out and had a blast. She needed me. So I stayed with her. I tried to get her out of our room every now and then by taking her out to eat, just the two of us. We occasionally went for a walk in the park or shopping together. We also went to church every Sunday, but barely. It was an English-speaking church, so of course little miss Hispanic didn't feel comfortable there. At least she went. The last thing I needed was for her shyness to scare God away.

The students here didn't make it any easier. I recall this one time when I finally got her to join an organization with me. We tried joining the Student Government Association and tried to get involved. What better place to help her gain confidence than a place that teaches leadership? The contact person was another maverick like us that was elected as representative of students who lived in university housing. Considering the rest of the SGA reps were upperclassmen, it was more comforting talking to one of our own. He lived in Scarlet Hall, the dorm that was mostly reserved for honors students and VIPs. The SGA flyer said he held office hours in his dorm for students who lived nearby that wanted more info.

Well, he wasn't very friendly. His name was Renzo, a rich Italian student from New York. I didn't know him, but I did recognize him from somewhere. I think he's in our class with Dr. Garcia. Though that class only meets once a week, so I still don't know all the students there. He was the kid that came from the rich family. Apparently came to orientation in his own plane. Some say he's friends with the university president. Well, the guy was really rude, and I could tell he didn't think much of us. He opened his door and seemed a bit preoccupied. We tried to tell him that we wanted to get involved, but he was only half listening, continuously looking around and typing in his smart phone. I don't know what he was doing that was so important that he couldn't at least respect us enough to pay attention. I called him out on it, asking him to please listen to us when we were talking to him.

That jerk told us that if we wanted to get the rest of our illegal Mexican family into the US, a university SGA wasn't the answer. He told us to bring it up to Congress and then closed the door. I got super pissed, but I think Gaby lost whatever confidence she had that day. It's also why I stuck around with her for so long. I felt guilty that my constant pushing her to get involved got us both insulted by some jerk. Still, I felt I was missing out on that college experience everyone was talking about.

Eventually, I needed to go out and meet people. The rest of the students at the hall started referring to us as the Lone Latinas. Could you believe that? We were one entity. Kimberly, our RA, kept getting our names mixed up when she ran into us. It wasn't her fault, though. She always saw us together and we rarely spoke to her. Of course she didn't really get to know us well enough. Poor girl, she felt so bad whenever she called me Gabriella. She was afraid I'd think she was racist or something. I know she meant well.

Little by little, I finally started accepting invitations to go out. I would go to dinner with some of my hallmates, join study groups, and have movie nights. I figured that maybe Gaby would eventually join me if she saw how much fun I was having. I was wrong. She had much more fun in her room painting pictures of landscapes, wildlife, and candid shots of me sleeping. I told her to quit doing that. It creeped me out.

Eventually, the invitations for the both of us became invitations for just me. I was starting to get accepted with my own little group of friends. Ben, Tobias, Prachi, Ryan, Amy, and Lisa. We were like our own version of that show Friends. The more we hung out, though, the harder it became to hang out with Gaby. I usually had to cancel my dinner plans with Gaby since Ryan offered to drive us to a restaurant in town in his SUV. I asked her to come along, but she got all resentful and didn't want to go. We started to drift apart, and I started to fear for our friendship.

It looks like you two are close friends again now. What happened?

It happened right before Halloween in late October. Gaby and I were shopping for Halloween decorations to put in our rooms. Just because we weren't close anymore didn't mean we wouldn't take an opportunity to decorate our room. We both loved to decorate. It was the biggest thing we had in common. It was all business, of course. We talked, but we didn't really connect like we used to.

We were in the fake cobwebs aisle of the Halloween store when I got the call. It was Prachi. She sounded upset and panicky on the phone. She told us that Ryan was in an accident. I didn't fully understand. I thought he probably made a hole in the wall like Dylan did when he was roughhousing with Zachary. They made a big hole on the wall near their room and got fined by the housing department. However, Ryan's accident was much bigger than that. Like fatal.

I didn't really know the details, but he was involved in some kind of car accident and was rushed to the hospital. I had to rush back to the dorms to comfort Prachi who was getting hysterical. I've never seen her so upset.

It was hard for all of us. He was such a good guy. I mean sure, he didn't live on our hall, but like Tobias, they were both considered honorary members of Miller Third South. In a few weeks, things were starting to get back to normal. Well, not really normal. Prachi was more nervous than ever about school and tests. Ben got too scared to do anything, afraid that he would follow in Ryan's footsteps. Things got really awkward when Tobias asked Amy out. Things just never were the same with our group, and it slowly dissolved.

I started talking to Gaby again. Our conversations were short at first, but things got better. Later on I apologized to her for leaving her for my other friends so much. After seeing how easy it was for friends here to break up, I realized just how precious and durable my friendship with Gaby was. I told her that those college friends would come and go, but that my friendship and sistership with her would last forever.

Our friendship finally went back to the way it was. Even better, you can argue. Honestly, I didn't care if the other students thought we were weird. So what if we're the Lone Latinas? The truth is, I think the rest of those students were lonelier than us. While I knew I always had someone I could trust with my life and depend on when things got tough, they had to settle with fragile relationships that would eventually dissolve over time.

Were you aware that Ryan's death was a suicide?

I heard rumors about it, yeah. But then again, I heard lots of rumors thrown around here and there. Mavericks love their gossip, don't they? I heard it all. I heard that Ryan asked Prachi out, and that, when she rejected him, he had no choice but to kill himself. That one sounds a bit believable, I guess, considering how distraught Prachi was about it. But some of the other theories were just stupid. They say that Ryan got into a drunken fight with some guy and that he rammed him with his car on his way home. Others say that Ryan faked his own death for some inexplicable reason. Still others think there's a serial killer on our campus killing off the mavericks. And when the second death took place, wow did that theory gain some credibility!

I just tuned it all out. I didn't really care. I mourned the loss of Ryan my own way and then moved on. I mean, I have my own problems to deal with. Even though things are better with Gaby, school has gotten tough. My classes this semester are much tougher than last semester and I'm having a hard time finding available tutors. My nana is sick in the hospital and I'm worried for her. Family's very important to me, you know, and it pains me to know my nana is sick and I can't visit her. I'm getting homesick now.

Thank you very much, Lisa. This interview was very helpful. Enjoy the rest of your meal. Until next time!

[I get up to leave the deli.]

Hey, Cheyenne?

[I turn back to look at her. She has become a bit tense.]

Now, I don't know if it's true or not, but I've been hearing that you guys, you student affairs people, think that there is a student involved with these deaths. It's really none of my business but... After my encounter with Renzo, I went to vent with some hallmates, and I found out that we weren't the only ones that Renzo has verbally attacked. He apparently got into a huge dispute earlier on with another student in our group where he tore him up real bad. And from what it looked like, Ryan never recovered from it.

BIO: PRACHI DEVAL
FARIBADAD, INDIA

My father is the head of an engineering firm in Dehli. Our family lives in Faridabad, India. It's a very wonderful location, though a bit overcrowded. Growing up, we lived in a very communal environment. I had many friends who I spent a lot of time with. Though while the girls in my community tended to spend more time indoors, I loved to spend more time outdoors. I was an explorer, always searching for adventure.

Unfortunately, as the years went by, our district became very overcrowded and very dangerous. My mom wouldn't allow me to go out as much anymore. I was forced to spend my time inside. My adventurous spirit dwindled over the years. Rather than go outside and explore, I would stay inside and tinker with things my dad brought home from work. I became curious, inventive, and realized where my true passion lied: Engineering. My mother was shocked when I told her I wanted to come to the States to study aerospace engineering. I guess it was the adventurer in me, but I wanted to go out and explore. To travel those lands I imagined as a child.

My father wouldn't hear of it. He wanted our family to stay together. My brother had already left the family to become a doctor, much to my father's chagrin. He wanted my brother to take over the company. He didn't want him to leave, but he did. He went to a European college. Now that I was leaving, he didn't want to let me go and said he wouldn't finance it. It wasn't until I convinced my mother and she convinced my cousin to help fund my trip here. My father was devastated, and fought very hard with my mom. I feel really bad that I had to leave them that way, but I didn't feel like I had a future at home. I needed more from my life. More than what my family could give me.

CHAPTER 6: TRANSITIONS
SEPTEMBER

Today was the day. Rachel Davis was excited for the first day of classes, though she cared very little about the actual classes. No, today was the day she could try out one of the dozen new outfits she bought for the new school year. She had spent over an hour choosing the perfect sundress to wear around the school. As she finished touching up her makeup, she admired her work with much pride, seeing her healthy brown hair shine from the new conditioner she was using. She was glad she got ready early before the common bathroom was filled with other girls fighting for the shower or mirrors, which she anticipated would happen within the next ten minutes. After a few poses for her imaginary Vogue photo-shoot, she went back in her room to grab her purse.

Sarah Holmes was there, still in her pajamas, reading in bed.

"Rise and shine, roomy! We got class today!" Rachel said in an overly energetic tone for that morning.

"Our first class isn't for another thirty minutes. Where are you going so early? To see Dylan upstairs?"

"You say that like it's a bad thing. We're both gonna walk to class together. And knowing Dylan, he's probably still sleeping in bed, so if I want any chance for us to get there on time, I have to get there early to get him going. You should probably get ready soon. In a few minutes, that bathroom is going to get crowded with our neighbors, and trust me, you don't wanna use that shower after Cynthia washes her hair in it. That girl could probably make a wig with all that hair she leaves behind, yuck. But anyways, put that book down and get ready! What are you reading this early in the morning, anyways?"

"It's my devotional," Sarah said. "It's a book with a daily message for you to read throughout the year. Today's message is about change and how to accept it. Kinda fitting, don't you think? You should read it sometime. It's by Joel Osteen, one of my favorite inspirational writers."

"Maybe when it's not so early, haha! I'll see you in class, Sarah!"

Rachel reached into her purse and sprayed on some tropical ocean-scented perfume and left the room.

When she traversed up to the third floor to meet the man she went on about constantly in her online blog, she was surprised to find him already up and almost ready to go.

"Wow, Dylan. I don't think I've ever seen you up and ready this early in the morning. What gives?"

"Ask this guy," he told her as he nodded his head towards Zachary, who was fixing up his hair. "He convinced me to be his running partner to stay in shape now that football practice has started. I didn't realize he meant six in the freakin' morning."

"Hey, it's good for you and ya know it," Zachary said with a mischievous smile. "So, are we heading to class or what?"

Rachel raised an eyebrow. "Are you coming with us? I thought it was just me and Dylan today."

"Oh, I forgot to tell you, Rei. Did you know Zachary is in our University 101 class? Actually, a bunch of us from this hall are in the class together. Zachary, Luca, Sam, those girls that live by the RA. It's like having our own Miller Third South reunion right in class."

"Really? Wow. My roommate Sarah has that class with us too. I wonder if we'll know everybody in there..."

Once Zachary finished with his hair, the three of them left the hall towards the Classroom Building.

"So why didn't little preacher girl join us? Was she not done doing her Hail Maries?" Dylan joked as they walked.

"Don't be mean, Dylan," Rachel responded with a defensive tone in her voice. "She's a nice girl. And FYI, she's not Catholic, so she doesn't do Hail Maries. She said she'll meet us in class."

Once at the classroom building, they ran into Luca and Sam in the hallway.

"Dylan, the man of the hour! You still joining us for the party tonight?"

"What party?" Zachary and Rachel asked almost simultaneously.

Dylan gave Luca a look.

"Oh, it's just a party some trailblazers are holding to start the year. Mavericks are free to show up, but it sounds lame, honestly. I think I'll pass," Dylan told them. "Besides, we have football practice tonight. I'm probably gonna turn in early after that. Get myself some sleep for some early morning running with Zachary."

Rachel looked at him intently as if she was about to ask him something, but changed her mind at the last minute.

They finally reached the classroom, only to be met with some loud voices inside. Sam was the first to look inside and eavesdrop, followed by the others. A black male student was standing by Jessica Evans, the girl in the ROTC uniform, who was sitting in her seat trying to ignore him. He seemed agitated, and was confronting her in an elevated tone.

"You gotta problem with me?" Mitch Adams taunted. "What? Little country girl have a problem with blacks? There ain't none where you come from? If you got a problem, say it!"

Jessica did her best to ignore him, but they could tell she was getting furious. She wasn't big, but with her toned build, there was no doubt she could take him if she wanted to. Meanwhile, Ben was sitting in the back of the room, pretending to read his textbook, trying awkwardly to distance himself from the confrontation.

"Get... the hell... away from me," Jessica snarled at him.

Before things could escalate further, Dr. Garcia walked into the room carrying his folders and portfolios for his class. Mitch, upon seeing him, decided to let it go and took a seat on the other side of the room. With the crisis averted, Ben took a sigh of relief, and Zachary, Luca, Sam, Dylan, and Rachel took a seat in the classroom. Luca took a seat by Mitch.

Within ten minutes, most of the students had arrived in the classroom. Dr. Garcia took attendance, only to find that he was missing one student. After another ten minutes, a guy came in with long, straight black hair down to his shoulders, wearing clothes that you would normally see on a mechanic.

Dr. Garcia stopped his introduction of the course to pull out his attendance sheet once again.

"And you must be-"

"Mattic," he interrupted. "Just call me Mattic."

Without saying another word, he walked towards an empty seat in the side of the room.

"That's great, Mattic. But let me remind you that this isn't high school. That cool, mysterious, show-up-to-class-tardy attitude won't work here in college. Not the way you want to start your first day of classes."

Without saying much else, Dr. Garcia continued with the course introduction. He outlined the syllabus, the expectations for the course, and the purpose for the course. He made mention that the course would last the whole year, to which the students groaned, but that it was crucial to have an orientation class that taught students good study habits and other techniques to excel in their future college classes. He also stressed that they only met once a week for an hour, so it wasn't that bad.

He then went on to explain the first assignment for the class, which was a free-writing exercise. He asked the whole class to write a one page biography about themselves, consisting of whatever they wanted. He told them to write their name, where they were from, and then whatever they would like him to know about them. He told them not to worry, since it wouldn't be graded.

As the rest of the class worked and constantly interrupted Dr. Garcia with questions as to what they were and were not allowed to include in the biography, Luca leaned over to talk to Mitch.

"Hey, what was the deal with you and princess over there?"

Mitch looked over at him, then continued writing.

"That's cool mate. You don't have to tell me. It's none of my business. I'm just saying don't worry about her. Whatever she said or did isn't personal. She lives in our hall and yells at us all the time when we're just having harmless fun."

Mitch kept writing for a few more seconds then stopped.

"I was just thinkin, minding my own business, just looking in her direction. She thought I was lookin' at her, 'oggling' her as she called it. Yeah, she wishes. Anyways, she was all like 'quit oggling me you pervert! You're just like the rest of them.' I'm not gonna take that, you know? It's been a rough week, and I'm not in the mood to deal with this crap."

Luca smiled.

"I hear ya. Listen, there's a party tonight. A couple of us are going. You should come. It'll take your mind off things. Here's the address in case you decide to go."

Mitch took a look at the address Luca gave him.

"What's your name?" he asked him.

"Luca."

"Alright," Mitch said with a slight nod of approval. "I'll think about it."

Once a student turned in his or her biography, Dr. Garcia allowed them to leave. As Luca and Sam finished and left the classroom, Luca invited Sam for lunch.

"Man, I can't," Sam told him. "I got an email saying there are some problems with my financial aid. I gotta go to the financial aid office and find out what that's about. Later!"

Sam ran off just as Dylan exited the room and met up with Luca.

"Luca, did I hear you invite that guy in the classroom to go to the party with us? You don't even know him!"

"Yeah, I invited him. Listen, my car fits four people. The bigger the group that shows up to the party, the more respect you get. You know how it goes. If you got three of us and we meet four birds, one gets left out and we go nowhere. But with more of us coming in together, it's a better chance we'll come home with some babes. Besides, pretty soon we'll be losing you."

"What? Me? What are you talking about? Do you mean earlier? Nah, I lied. We're still meeting for the party. You just need to stop mentioning those things in front of Zachary and Rachel."

"Dylan, you can't just keep lying to them. You're going to get caught. I'm just future-proofing our group. When we lose you, I don't want it to just be me and Sam. I mean, Sam's a good guy, but come on! That guy won't be getting laid anytime soon."

Dylan looked into the classroom and saw Rachel turning in her biography to Dr. Garcia.

"Listen, you're not losing me. We're still gonna party. I'm just still trying to work out my social time, class, football, and Rachel. But I'm still game. Count on it."

Rachel exited the room, smiled at Dylan as she grabbed his hand, and they headed off to lunch.

*****

"It was probably just a practical joke," SGA Vice President Sandeep said to the rest of the executive board.

"Not when it happens twice in a row," Linda responded.

The SGA President looked to Shandra Giles for backup.

"Linda's right," Dr. Giles said. "George got one of these threats a week ago during orientation, and now Linda got this one this morning. Even if it is a practical joke, it is something that must be taken seriously at the risk that whoever wrote it is serious."

Renzo Moretti continued to look at the pictures taken of the message spray-painted all over Linda's dorm room door. "You will be punished." It all seemed a little too overdramatic to him.

"Hold up a second," Renzo interrupted. "Let's turn this back a notch. Now, I just joined SGA, so I'm sure I must be missing something here, because all I see is just some student being stupid with graffiti. This message just seems too silly to be taken seriously."

"Renzo, regardless of the intent of the message, it has to be taken seriously," Shandra told him. "Especially when it's a second occurrence. And this one is strangely enough a lot more tame. The one George had on his door was much worse, full of obscenities that had to be removed immediately before parents showed up to the hall with the new students. He felt so intimidated by it that he chose to step down from his housing and SGA representative position, which is why it was open for you."

"Vandalism is not tolerated at this university," Linda added. "If we don't do anything about it now, we're giving the students the message that we don't take such things seriously. It looks bad on me as President and on Dr. Giles as Dean of Students if we can't keep the university vandalism under control. But what motive would a student have for doing this?"

"Perhaps they had a bad orientation experience," Sandeep said. "I've heard tons of complaints from students about how bad orientation was this year, due to the blazing heat and sudden student rushes we couldn't handle. We were understaffed."

"Sandeep, you're VP. All complaints are directed to you by nature. That's why it seems like a lot."

"It's not just the number of complaints. It's the intensity of them. Luis didn't deal with such angry students as VP last year. I asked him. I'm just saying that it's a possibility."

"Sandeep's right," Dr. Giles said. "At this point we have to consider every possibility. I know it's hard for us as leaders to admit that we made a mistake. The truth of the matter is that this orientation was well below our usual standards. Everything that could go wrong did. The only thing that went right was convocation, and even then I had to bother Dr. Scott during President Lambrick's speech to see what we should do about George's vandalized hallway."

Shandra turned to Renzo.

"Renzo, now that you're the housing and residence life representative for SGA, we're going to need you to pay close attention to what's going on in the freshman halls. By the looks of it, it seems that one of our freshmen had a less-than-stellar orientation experience and decided to vent by using vandalism. The fact that the student has struck twice means that he or she may likely do it again. We need to stop it before that happens."

Renzo nodded.

"I think that's it for today's meeting," Linda said. "I'll be working with campus safety to see how their investigation is going. We'll set up another meeting later this week with an update, so please email me your availabilities. Meeting adjourned."

The SGA executive board quickly dispersed, except for Renzo, who stayed in his seat studying the photos. Linda walked up to him.

"Honestly, I think it's just some prankster having fun with the student leaders. These are freshmen we're talking about, after all, no offense," she told him.

"I just don't understand the kind of people that would do such a thing," Renzo said. He sounded annoyed. "Here we are, the hard working students trying to make something with our lives, and we have these stupid low-lives that have nothing better to do than to waste everyone's time with such nonsense. And then those people are the ones that complain about money problems and the rest of us have to come bail them out. Pathetic."

"Don't stress about it, Renzo. It's only your first day on the SGA board. Trust me, you'll have more to stress about in the coming months."

Linda patted him on the back and left the room.

After a long day full of classes and meetings, Renzo was looking forward to heading back to his room. He continued to ponder the stupidity that humanity constantly had to deal with. He wondered how bad a student's orientation could have been if it really did cause the vandalism. He thought back to his orientation experience which went pretty well. Though he did admit to himself that his orientation experience was privileged and one of a kind.

As he stepped out of the elevator to the fifth floor of Scarlet hall, he took out his keys while approaching his dorm room. He paused right in his tracks when he saw the message written across his door. It wasn't as big as the one he saw in the photo, but it was created using the same bright red spray paint. In bright letters he saw the message "Stay away from them rich boy, or you'll be joining them."

*****

Prachi Deval grabbed her hair in frustration as she tried to get her computer program to work. She had already spent three hours on that one program, not to mention the additional three hours she spent on her homework assignments for her other classes. She just couldn't believe how much work her professors were giving her on the first week of classes. While the other students spent their first week partying, socializing, relaxing, and getting to know the city of Sun Valley, she was stuck doing all this work. The work wasn't particularly difficult. It was just very time consuming. She had to work on overly-long problems and already had to derive complicated equations that took time and patience. And of course, her current Intro to Engineering class decided to give her a coding assignment without any instructions on how to go about it. No matter how many different ways she coded it, the program just wouldn't seem to work. It was almost two in the morning and she was no closer to figuring it out than she was two hours ago.

The whole building seemed empty from the study room she was sitting in. She occasionally saw students walking in and out of Miller hall from the study room's giant window. In a way, she cursed that giant window for providing too much of a distraction from her work. Watching the sun setting and all the people walking around kept her distracted for so long she had to turn her seat around away from it. Where the heck were the rest of the engineering majors? Were they all just that much smarter than her?

She saw one of her classmates, Ryan, open the door and enter the study room with a shopping bag.

"Prachi, what are you doing here?" he asked her.

"It's this program for Intro to Engineering. I just can't figure it out. Did you go grocery shopping?"

"Just some things I needed. Can I take a look at your program?"

"Sure, go ahead."

Ryan took her notes and looked at her computer, trying to see where she went wrong.

"Did you finish your homework already?" Prachi asked.

"Yeah. Okay, I see the problem. It's on line fifty three. You have your variables mixed up. Here, take a look."

Prachi watched as Ryan showed her how to fix her program. She couldn't believe how simple the solution was and how she could have missed it. She felt so stupid.

"How did you figure that out? I spent hours working on this!"

"Have you been here all evening, Prachi?"

"Yes."

"Prachi, didn't you know about the computer labs in the College of Science basement?"

Prachi remembered one of her professors mention them in passing, but didn't remember hearing anything significant about them.

"In order to survive the engineering programs here, the engineering majors usually meet in the computer labs at different times of the evening to work on their homework together. It's much faster that way. Trust me, I started to panic when I saw the amount of homework they were giving us on the first day of class. One of my classmates told me about the study groups, and they have made the work more manageable."

"But don't those labs close like at nine? My last class ends at seven, and I hardly think two hours is enough to get everything done."

"Don't worry about that. One of the aerospace engineering students works there and has keys to the lab. He usually shows up around ten to open it for us, one hour after it's closed to the general public. You should meet us there the next time you're stuck."

Prachi let a sigh of relief as she saved the program and turned off her laptop. She felt like a load had been lifted from her shoulders.

"Sounds like you had a rough night," Ryan said. "Ben and I are going to Tobias's room downstairs for a movie night. He was lucky enough to not get a roommate, so he has the whole room to himself. Would you care to join us?"

"Sure!" Prachi said with enthusiasm. After spending so many hours buried in books, notes, and computer screens, she was begging for any human interaction.

As she cleared out the table from all the papers and textbooks scattered around the table, she accidentally knocked over the grocery bag he had placed there.

"Oh, I'm so sorry!" she told him.

"It's no big deal. It's not like I had anything fragile in there."

Prachi quickly bent down to help him pick up the scattered groceries.

"You working on an art project?" she asked him as she handed him two cans of red spray paint.

"Something like that," he told her as he put them back in his bag.

CHAPTER 7: CHEYENNE WINTERS
JANUARY

I sat in my small temporary office located in the basement of Sun Valley University's 'Tower', their overly-emphasized student union. It was the only building I've seen so far that was perfectly maintained from every angle. It had a fresh coat of paint, probably done during winter break while all the students were gone. The furniture couldn't have been more than two years old. Even my tiny, cramped office looked like it was well-taken care of.

To be honest, I was actually surprised they gave me an office. I figured I would either have to bring the students back to my room to interview them, or run around the school meeting them in the office of their advisors like Detective Sawyer had to do. Even more to my surprise, they didn't put someone to watch over the interviews as I conducted them the way they did with Sawyer. Nancy Wei told me how either she or one of her colleagues had to be in the room at all times when Detective Sawyer interviewed the students. I could only imagine the kind of pressure that put the students in.

I figured they didn't see me as much of a threat to their school as Detective Sawyer was. In a way that made me feel better. Ever since I got here, I've felt like an intruder. A nuisance. In some dark way, knowing that there was someone they despised more than me made me feel better. Besides, I was nothing but kind and respectful to everyone since I arrived. Lynn Sawyer stormed into every area in the school like she owned the place and had every right to be there. Do they not teach manners in the police force?

It was getting late. Student response from Dr. Garcia's class was better than I expected. One week in and I had already conducted interviews with almost half of the class. It was amazing just how diverse their experiences were. Every student had such an interesting past. Their hobbies, their thoughts, and their goals were all deeply embedded to the environment around them as they grew up. Already I could start seeing the student development theories I studied in my Master's program applying to all of these students. Racial development, cognitive development, spiritual development, it was all there! It was all very exciting, as these weren't just case studies for class assignments anymore. These were real students with real struggles that I had the opportunity to help.

Unfortunately, I had yet to discover anything relating to the suicide cases. The first interviews were simply to get to know the students. I didn't want to start off the relationship with leading questions to get answers, as I was sure Detective Sawyer was doing. The key to getting answers from them was to build rapport with them. Get them to trust me and feel comfortable around me. Although I was the interviewer, they needed to be the ones to drive the conversation, not me.

As I concentrated on transcribing those interviews onto my computer, playing each sound clip at least four times since I was such a slow typist, Nancy came into my room through the open office door and knocked.

"Delivery!" she joked. "Did someone order a distraction?"

With the amount of work that I did at this school and general negative vibe I got from everyone around here, Nancy was really the only person I actually talked to about non-work-related business. In some strange way, you could say we were actually becoming friends.

"I certainly did not!" I responded in a playful tone. "But now that it's here, how can I refuse?"

Nancy laughed and came inside. I used to be a social person, at least in my undergraduate studies. But something about my Master's program got me secluded from the rest of the world. Everything in my life became about research and burying myself in books and studies. It wasn't for nothing, though. I graduated with a four point zero GPA and even honors in my class. My professors said I was the best they've ever seen, with more dedication in the field than any other student they taught. It's what got me into UF's competitive doctoral program. Despite the fact that I wasn't involved in too many extracurricular activities or had a good list of network contacts, the work I've done in the field had them impressed. It also helped that my ECFU advisor wrote a spectacular recommendation for me from what I heard.

Nancy walked over to me and started massaging my shoulders as I was typing.

"Wow, someone is very tense! How long have you been at this?"

"Well, I've been transcribing for the past four hours since my last interview. I still have three more interviews to transcribe after this, and since it has taken me an average of about five hours to transcribe each interview, then I have... oh, I don't know! A whole lot of transcribing to do!"

"Cheyenne, you need to relax. Come on, you need a break. Let's go get something to eat."

"I can't, Nancy. I have to drive up to Gainesville tomorrow for my weekly doctoral class, so I need to get as much transcribing done today, since I'll pretty much lose all of tomorrow evening. I start my next round of interviews on Thursday so I need to get these done before then!"

"All the more reason for you to join me for dinner. You have a lot of work to do. You need some motivation. Some work juice! Come on, we won't be out long! Besides, I gotta get you out of this stuffy office. You're starting to look like a troll."

"Gee thanks," I said sarcastically as I saved my document and locked my computer. "Fine, but no longer than an hour. I still have lots of work to do."

"Deal!"

Nancy took me to a local Italian restaurant on Town Square. Town Square was an area of shopping centers and a few franchises located on the northeast side of campus. Even though you were still on campus, it kind of gave you the off-campus experience. It was suited for students who didn't have a car and wanted something to do within walking distance. There was a small strip mall, a movie theatre, some restaurants, and even some recreation centers like an art museum and a martial arts dojo.

"So what have you discovered so far?" she asked.

I figured that question would come up sooner or later.

"Nothing relating to the suicides, if that's what you're asking. But a wealth of information about these students. It's amazing how this all ties in to what I've learned in my program. Like this girl Prachi, for instance. She was stressing out about her classes and the amount of work they give her. Three days into college and she was staying up until the morning hours stressing on assignments. That, Nancy, is a prime example of Sanford's theory of challenge and support. The theory suggests that a student needs a certain amount of challenge to learn, but the support needs to be comparable as well, otherwise the student will be overloaded and won't benefit from the challenge.

"That's exactly what happened with Prachi. She was given too much challenge but not enough support to deal with the challenge, so she wasn't really learning. The trick here is finding out what is the perfect balance of challenge and support she needs so that she can learn as much as she can without being overstressed. On our next interview, I plan to ask her some specific questions so I can find a way to help her with her issue."

Nancy took a bite out of her Italian bread, then began speaking before she finished chewing.

"That's great and all, but you're doing it again."

"Doing what again?"

"You're talking about your work again. I took you out to have a nice, distracting dinner with light conversation. Here you are getting all technical with me, quoting theories and such."

"Hey, you're the one that asked me what I've discovered!"

"Well, yeah, but I was expecting a short sentence or two. 'Oh, they're doing well' or 'I think I'm getting closer'. It looks to me like you're always thinking about your work. All the time. You should just shut off your brain for bit and enjoy an evening out."

The waiter showed up with refills for our drinks.

"Well geez, miss party pooper. There's nothing wrong with talking about something you're passionate about. Whereas other people's passions lie in sports, or sewing, or video games, mine are in this area. Can't fault me for that."

"Alright, I'm just saying. Your deal is your deal. But for all this challenge and support talk you have about Prachi, it doesn't look like you apply it on yourself."

"What do you mean?"

"Oh, nothing. Look, our food's coming. Just promise me you won't work too hard, okay?"

I smiled. It felt good that someone in this strange place so far away from home actually cared about me.

"Alright, Nancy. Let's eat!"

BIO: MIYU KANEKO
OSAKA, JAPAN

I've always been fascinated with the West. Since I was a little girl, I found myself watching Western animation much more than anime. I could never give a specific reason why I loved the West so much. It is a bunch of little things, you know? Ever since I learned to understand English, I learned as much as I can. I watched American shows, ordered American books online, and even made an American pen pal! She told me about all the latest bands, and I would listen to her recommendations. Pop, I love American pop. It's nothing like J-pop. There's just a type of… charm to it, I don't know.

I'm sure you're thinking that I don't like my own culture. That's not true at all. I love Japan, honestly. I love my culture, I love my family, and I love my friends. People just don't understand that I'm split between two worlds. I have a love for two cultures, but it's always just one or the other for other people. Sure, I applied to an American university and left my family for four years, but is that not the point of growing up? Experiencing what life has to offer out there before choosing to settle down in one particular place? I've heard so much about the Western culture, but I needed to experience it for myself. I wanted to know what all the fuss is about, see where some of my favorite books were made.

People here look at me funny. They see my green highlights and automatically assume that I'm out of place. But you know what? That's my way of keeping some of my own culture with me. My older sister highlighted her hair green. It was the thing to do with her classmates when she was in school. I do this to remember my sister, and my family in general. You know what they say, you can take the girl out of Japan, but you can't take the Japan out of the girl. I'm here to learn, understand this culture so much more, but I also want to retain mine.

That's why I want to get a counseling degree. I want to understand how people think, why they do what they do, and how it all works together. I want to use my counseling skills back in Japan to help those in need. Our city is very stressed and in need of counseling. People in my culture don't really put importance on feelings, so they live with stress every single day without learning how to deal with it. I want to help. I want to provide the relief and assistance that many people need back at home. Starting with my parents. They've done so much for me. I think it's time to return the favor, especially in the near future when they'll be needing me the most.

ROLAND NUÑEZ

68

CHAPTER 8: INTERVIEW #MK03
MIYU KANEKO

[This is my third interview with Miyu, a delightful girl from Japan with an interesting view to life. My previous conversations with her dove into her culture, her history with her family, and her move to America. She's always prettying herself up with dresses. Today she's wearing a pink, flowy miniskirt and an adorable white top. I have been trying to get an interview with Renzo due to some information obtained from another interviewee regarding the suicide cases, but he has refused to speak with me. Since Miyu lives in his hall, I figured she'd be the next best resource for info on Renzo.]

Hi Miyu! How are you doing today?

Well, school's going great, and things are going really well. Sigma Zeta Pi held a date auction last week that was a huge success! And I didn't do too shabby, either. The guy with the winning bid was pretty fine!

That's good to hear. How are things with your roommate Alia? Last time you told me there was some friction between you two.

Yeah, things have only gotten worse. It's a shame, really. Alia and I were so close in the beginning of the year. It was actually pretty smart of them to put two international students together in one room. Since we both faced a heck of a lot during our move to the States, we already had that in common, making our transition easier. She's a great girl, a bit quieter than me, but still willing to go out and try new things.

Like I told you last time, it started during rush week. Both of us pledged for SZP, but only one of us got in. Of course, she had to be a sore loser and insist that I quit the sorority because of it. I tried to reason with her, but she wouldn't hear it. It's like she became a whole different person. So we got into a fight, and we still kinda are.

Every time I get ready to go to a sorority meeting or event we're doing, Alia gets all upset. She doesn't say anything, as she tends to keep things to herself, but I could tell she's frustrated. I don't understand her. She's such a sweet girl. She's very respectful to everyone, as she says it's a big part of her culture. But then she gets upset over trivial things such as not making it into a sorority. But whatever, I'm having a good day. I don't want to upset myself.

Do you think there may be something you could have said to her that made her upset about this? Have you tried seeing it from her perspective? Maybe there's a deeper issue here.

I don't know, Cheyenne. I tried reasoning with her, telling her that she's acting childish. I guess I probably could have used some better choice of words, but in the end, it doesn't really matter. She's not going to stop being mad at me until I quit the sorority, and that's not something I plan to do anytime soon. My sisters are very nice to me. Say what you will about sororities out there. I know that Greek Life has a bad reputation in everyone's minds. They're all seen as conceited, power-hungry drinkers that care about partying more than anything else. But there's much more to it than that.

Since I've started pledging, I've seen the Zetas do all sorts of events for charity. Like this date auction, for example. All the proceeds went to the homeless shelter in southern Sun Valley. Not only are we raising funds, but we focus on both national organizations AND local ones. And we're always finding different ways to make people want to participate, other than your standard food drives and fundraisers.

But whatever. There's a lot more going on this semester for our sorority, especially this April. It's our biggest event of the year!

What kind of event?

[Miyu hesitates for a second before answering.]

Everything we say here is confidential, right?

Yes, of course, Miyu. This is an informal interview. Anything that you don't want disclosed won't be.

Okay, well... the Zetas throw a party every April to celebrate the end of the year. It's a very big party, but it's very exclusive. It's by invite only. Since it's a sorority event, the details of the party are kept secret. That's usually because every year they have a special event at the party for its members. Being part of the party committee, I've been given some information as to what this year's event is. Apparently Ashley, the sorority president, is working with another campus organization, I think it's a fraternity or something, to do something big. They've been raising money for a while now for it, as well as finding a venue for the party. The tagline for the party is going to say "It's a student revolution", celebrating the power of the student. It's based on Professor Lambrick's yearly speech that says that students have the real power in a university. It's supposed to be a lot of fun with some bands they're hiring to play, and don't even get me started on the after-party!

While the party is exclusive and strictly enforced, the after-party is unofficial and therefore not as exclusive. They still prefer it be only those who went to the party, but it's much harder to control for that.

That's great, Miyu. I wish you the best of luck with your party. It looks like you're getting along very well with your sorority sisters. You've mentioned that things are a bit rough with Alia, but what about the rest of the hall? How's your relationship with the others who live in Scarlet Fifth West? I recall you mentioning Brad, Lindsey, and Renzo in our last interview. How are they doing?

Oh, they're doing fine. Brad finally went ahead and asked Lindsey out. I am so happy for them! I always knew they would make a cute couple! Honestly, the last guy Lindsey dated was so beneath her. I don't understand it, either. She's a smart girl. She's in the freakin' honors hall! Where did she get the idea that dating an obvious womanizer such as this Dylan guy she talked about would be a good idea? But yeah, Brad and Lindsey are finally official. He surprised her with flowers one night, and actually sang her a song! It was the cheesiest, most romantic thing I've ever seen. Yeah, he did it in front of everyone outside her room.

He got in front of her door and started playing his guitar. People started popping their heads out of their rooms to see what was going on, and of course, good old Brad was on his one knee playing his guitar and singing to her. I don't know how I'd feel about that, you know, if a guy did that for me.

What about Renzo?

Oh, Renzo? Well, he's a complicated individual. If you work really, really hard at it, with much dedication and with an obvious goal in mind, you'll manage to catch a glimpse of his good side. I mean, he's not inherently a bad person, but everything he seems to do, including the good things, are usually for a selfish reason. But can you really blame him? Since he arrived at this university, they've labeled him as the snobby rich guy before they even met him. What's he gonna do? Give out fruitcakes and tell everyone he's just a nice guy? Frankly, he doesn't care. He's a politician. He only cares about the opinions of those who will directly benefit him. That's probably why he's nice to all of us in the hall. We're the 'gifted' freshmen. I'm not trying to boast or anything, but he figures he knows a good future when he sees one.

I met Renzo for the first time on the second day of orientation. He was the talk of the campus for having been the "Learjet guy", since his parents bought him his own plane as a going-away gift. Apparently, he was too special to attend the hall meeting our RA put on the night we all arrived. No one knows where he went or what he was doing, but it did make most of us mad at him. Call it jealousy, call it pride, but we joined the hate bandwagon everyone was touting.

But boy were we embarrassed when he showed up the next day. Apparently, the reason he missed the hall meeting was because he was shopping around for a good college laptop. Granted, he already had the best one anyone can afford, but he wanted a nice one customized with Sun Valley University engraved on it. Since none were available, he ordered his own and went to the local engraving shop to get it done. Not only that, but he got one for everyone in our hall! He said it was a gift for those of us who went the extra mile to achieve greatness.

He said he knew we wouldn't be too happy that he was in our hall even though he wasn't an honors student, but by having matching laptops, he wanted to show us that we all played for the same team. He wanted us to all get along. And it worked. He can be such a manipulative individual! Like I said, he's a politician. He came to my room and introduced himself to me and Alia. He was a lot more courteous than I imagined.

He told me all that mumbo jumbo about how he wants us to be friends and how the laptop was a token of peace between us. I knew he didn't really mean it, but hey, I got a free laptop out of it? How could I refuse?

Being the honors hall, the student government board came to visit with and speak to our group during our hall meeting. The SGA president, Linda, told us just how valuable we were to the university. She herself was admitted to the honors program as a freshman, and look at her now! She offered us all to join the SGA general board. She said that as freshmen, we couldn't run for the executive board just yet, but that by being in the general board we could learn the ropes in preparation for elections.

It didn't really matter to me, until I found out that Renzo was suddenly elected into the executive board. What was up with that? They tell us that freshmen can't run for office and then put a freshman in their office just a few days later? Talk about hypocrisy! It upset me a little, as I was thinking about running for office. Alia made me feel better, though. See, that's what I miss the most about being friends with Alia. She was such a great person to talk to. No matter how bad you were feeling, she knew how to make you feel better.

"Aren't you a counseling psychology major?" she asked me in her Kenyan accent. "Have you been applying what you've learned in your intro to counseling course?"

"...No," I hesitantly told her. I knew she was right, but it was hard to admit.

"Listen, don't worry about what Renzo is doing. If those on the SGA are being hypocrites, then let them. It is their loss for not having someone as wonderful as you on their team."

"Thanks, Alia. You're always flattering me. But you're right. I guess I shouldn't be worrying about them. It just upsets me, you know? That just because you have money you can get whatever you want. That's why rich people annoy me so much. Always superficial about everything. Since they can get whatever they want, it gives them some sense of superiority over others."

"Well then. Just pretend you are your own client at your counseling clinic. What would you tell your troubled self?"

I thought about it for a minute.

"I... uh... I guess I would ask myself to look at it from his perspective. See the situation from his shoes. Let's see... He grew up in a rich family, likely taught to succeed through whatever means necessary. He came to a public university here in Florida for whatever reason. I suppose he didn't have the grades to get into the Ivy Leagues. People seem to detest him because of his money. They define him because of his money. As a result, he defines himself by his money and prestige. It's all he has. I guess if I was in his shoes, I'd use my money to solve my problems too."

Alia smiled at me and gave me a hug.

"Miyu, you're going to be a wonderful counselor. Your family will be proud."

To be honest, her hug and her comment made me feel much better than my self-therapy did. But it did help me see things in a different way. I sorta made friends with him and began to understand Renzo more. I'd occasionally help him with his homework assignments and I could tell he was very grateful for the help. He seemed stressed a lot of the time. That SGA position he got was more trouble than it was worth. I'm glad I didn't have to deal with it.

Between you and me, he actually got a death threat spray painted on his door. I was the only person he told that to, since he trusted me. He didn't want anyone else to know. Pride, I suppose. He said he wanted to handle the situation himself. When he saw the message on his door, he quickly cleaned it up before anyone saw it and tried to find out who did it.

I don't know how he did it, but apparently he found the perpetrator. It was some guy named Ryan on Miller Hall. They got into some huge argument where Renzo berated him like it was nobody's business. I wasn't there, but I've seen the way Renzo treats people he doesn't like. He can be cruel. I was leaving my room when I saw him yelling at two Hispanic girls that went to visit him. Granted, one of them got a bit mouthy with him when he wasn't paying attention to her, so I can understand why he got irritated. He was already angry from his encounter with Ryan earlier and was dealing with some other issues that the SGA called him about when the girls came to bug him. That one girl's attitude towards him didn't do them any favors.

Well, anyways, once Ryan died, Renzo didn't seem the same. He secluded himself from the rest of us. He stopped asking for help in his homework assignments. No one understood why he changed so suddenly. He even stopped being rude to people. I think that's what concerned everyone the most. He seemed to thrive from berating others. I think it boosted his self-esteem or something.

Thanks, Miyu. That was some great information. Is there anything else you'd like to talk about before we conclude today?

No, don't think so. I just need to go home and get ready. Tonight is my date with the guy who won me at the date auction. His name's Zachary. He's in my University 101 class, but I don't really know him that well.

[My eyes slightly widen as I hear the name]

Did you say Zachary? Zachary Myers?

Yeah, I think that's his last name. Why? Is there something wrong?

Just curious. Thanks.

> *[As Miyu leaves my office, I search through my files for Zachary's interview transcript. My memory served me right. Zachary was out of town the night of the date auction. Based on his interview, he was never at that auction.]*

BIO: SAMUEL PARK
ORLANDO, FL

Well, first of call, call me Sam. I'm not Samuel, or Sammy, or Samsam, just Sam, got that? Now that we have that out of the way, let me tell you a little bit about myself. I am awesome. Yep, that about sums it up... But... apparently I'm supposed to write more. Okay then, what to write, what to write? Let's see... my family's from South Korea. Me, however, I'm from the magical land of Orlando. Yes, all fear the almighty power of Disney World, Universal, and Sea World! Hahahaha!

But seriously, I am awesome. I'm a supa fly guy with many skills. I ace at video games, I love to party, and I know things. Many things. I'm not saying I'm smart, no. In fact, school has whipped me several times over. What I mean is, I know many things on account of the fact that I'm part robot. Or alien, I haven't been able to decipher which. I know what you're probably thinking. It's what everyone thinks when I tell them. But I can assure you, this is real.

Back in Korea, my grandpa worked in the government for a while. My dad refuses to tell me what exactly my grandpa did. My mom says that that's just the way he is. Dad grew up in less-than-acceptable conditions in Korea, and just wants to leave the past behind. But I'm telling you, I know what my grandpa did. He was a spy! That's the only explanation! He worked on secret missions for the government! And they weren't too happy when my grandpa moved here to the US, so they started to track us while we were here! And when I was a child, they infused me with some type of machinery or alien DNA for some test project they're working on. I figured my dad agreed to it if they promised to leave our family alone afterwards.

Now it's just a waiting game. Just waiting to see when my amazing robot-alien powers will manifest. Now the question is, will I save the world or will I conquer it? Such alluring options, I don't know which to pick. I guess you'll just have to wait and see, ha!

CHAPTER 9: RECREATION
SEPTEMBER

The party was a blast. One of Sun Valley University's trailblazers owned a big house just outside of campus, which was perfect for gatherings throughout the year. The music was thumping loudly. The houses on the street were far enough apart that it didn't bother the neighbors. Besides, most neighbors were at the party.

The students were cheering wildly as two guys were chugging away at a drinking contest. Tyler still seemed conscious and alert, taking shot after shot with his own cheering squad behind him. Sam, on the other hand, was about to reach his breaking point, though it was hard to tell. Between his convoluted sentences, silly, empty stares, and laughing at nothing in particular, drunken Sam was hard to distinguish from sober Sam.

Sam's cheering squad was much smaller than Tyler's. It consisted of Luca, Mitch, the fashionably-late Dylan, and a few stragglers who just loved to watch Sam act like an idiot. It didn't help that he was a lightweight.

Tyler was a bit more heavyset than Sam, by at least thirty pounds. By the looks of it, this was far from his first drinking contest. The crowd continued to cheer as they downed yet another shot.

Sam turned around and leaned over to Luca, motioning for him to get closer.

"What is it?" Luca asked.

"Luca.. tell... tell the kids I love them!" he said overdramatically before he fell off his chair.

The crowd went wild as they celebrated the new victor. Tyler got up and soaked in the praise and applause, motioning for more. Dylan and Luca picked Sam's unconscious body up and carried him over to the couch.

"Why the hell did you let Sam enter a drinking contest with that guy?" Dylan asked. "He's so small and naïve. No way he would have stood a chance."

"I'm not his mother," Luca responded sarcastically. "But if you want to be, then maybe you shouldn't show up four hours late to the party. What happened? Did Rachel catch hold of your little lie?"

"Oh, shut up. Rachel went over to my room to ask Zachary where football practice would be so she could watch. Luckily for me, I was there to open the door so she asked me instead. What else was I supposed to do? I told her practice was cancelled, so she decided it would be a great idea to go see a movie. Luckily, she had homework to do, so shortly after the movie I was able to slip out."

"Dylan, Dylan, Dylan. What the hell mate? What kind of a man are you? Sneaking around, lying to your girlfriend so you can come party? Are you really that pathetic? I've met your brother and he's nothing like you. The guy has more class, style, and authority. But you... I think Rachel has softened you up, buddy."

Dylan raised his eyebrow, confused at what Luca was telling him but understanding at the same time.

"Please. Back in high school, I could have any girl I wanted. And I did! Now that I found Rachel, though, I decided to stay with her.." His sentence trailed off.

"Wow, Dylan. It sounds like even you didn't believe that."

"Piss off," Dylan snapped at him before walking off.

"What's his problem?" Mitch asked Luca as he left the next drinking contest that was starting up.

"The poor guy is just being a pansy and is now just realizing it. Who are the next drinkers?"

"Don't know 'em," he responded. "You know, that Tyler is an idiot. The guy's already on probation from drinkin' and what does he do? Gets himself piss drunk and then takes a girl back home with him. I hope the cops pull over his sorry ass."

"Ah well, campus is only like a block from here. He'll be fine. More power to him for scoring a win. Two wins, actually. Who was the lucky bird?"

"I don't know. Some tramp in a blue miniskirt. No question she was going home with somebody tonight."

He looked over at Luca for a response, but saw that Luca was distracted looking at a group of girls sitting in the couch across from them.

"Look after Sam, will ya?" Luca told him. "I got some girls looking for some Luca love."

He ran his hand over his hair and headed to the girls.

"Good evening, ladies."

Just as he expected, the girls practically swooned over his British accent. Mitch was almost impressed at how easy it was for Luca to sit right in the middle of the two girls in the couch, wrapping his arms around both of them as he complimented their features.

Mitch couldn't help but smile a bit. This party was the closest he's felt to being in Jersey for a long time. He was still deciding whether that was a good or bad thing.

*****

Sarah Holmes had just gotten out of a very welcoming church service. It was her first time at her new church. It was a bit different from her church back at home. For one thing, there were more students in this one. It wasn't just her and four other teens like at home. This church actually had a higher student percentage. It was most likely due to the close proximity to the campus. Even with the larger number of students, however, the church was pretty small, just like the one at home. Since it was welcome week at the church, she figured it was as full as it was ever going to get, and she saw barely thirty people in there.

She was used to this. The Seventh-day Adventist churches she'd been to in the past have always been small. She was sure there were bigger ones out in the bigger cities, but she had never attended one. Back in the small town of Grayson, Georgia, small churches were all she was accustomed to.

Regardless, she was very glad she had a good time at the church. The people were very inviting and did their best to make her feel welcome. She appreciated the effort, and couldn't wait to get involved. The group was very active in the community. She was already aware of places in Sun Valley where she could help out. She was excited to begin as soon as possible.

Her walk to campus was a long one. She didn't have a car, so she was limited to going wherever her feet could take her. The church was about a mile and a half away. Although really close by car, it took her almost an hour to walk all the way to church and then back. The heat wasn't helpful, either. By the time she made it back to campus, she was soaked in sweat and her long, red hair felt sticky.

She stopped by the student food court to get herself some lunch and something cold to drink. She grabbed the first empty table she could find and sat down to enjoy her meal.

About two tables away, she saw a large group of students huddled around a small table meant for a much smaller group. The way they had been laughing and enjoying themselves seemed like they have been there for a while. What else was there to do on a Saturday morning on campus? Most students were sleeping after a long first week of classes. Others were out and about on the town, or probably visiting the beaches on either coast. These students seemed just fine entertaining themselves at a food court, chatting and laughing for hours.

The ring leader was a darker-skinned fellow. She couldn't quite place his ethnicity. He could have been Indian, Middle-Eastern, or even Hispanic. Though he had a natural Jheri curl thing going. Maybe Black?

He was very well-dressed for a Saturday. He was wearing a light blue buttoned-down shirt. When he got up from the table to mimic some professor he had earlier in the week, she could see he was wearing some nice expensive jeans, and a pair of light brown dress shoes. He was about as well dressed as some of the guys she saw at church.

The guy was an entertainer. Everything he said seemed to instill laughter in the group. His impressions of that professor were apparently very spot-on. She tried to listen in but it was hard to understand him. With all the students talking at once, it was surprising that anyone could understand each other. He must have finished his drink, because he got up to get a refill. All of a sudden another student popped in to fill the ring leader void he had left behind. It was amazing how fluid group dynamics were in that aspect.

On his way back with his refill of lemonade, he saw Sarah sitting at the table eating her sandwich and walked over to her.

"Hey, aren't you in Dr. Garcia's class?" he asked.

"Yes, I am," she responded automatically. It was almost second nature to her and everyone else in the campus. One of the easiest ways to make friends, she discovered, was to ask someone if they were in so-and-so's class. Whether they were or not, it was a good icebreaker and conversation starter.

"I knew it! Me too! We're in his University 101 class together," he said enthusiastically.

Sarah thought back to the class and tried to remember him. She couldn't. Then again, she has had a lot of classes that week since Monday, and since Dr. Garcia's class only met once a week, it was hard to remember anyone she didn't already know.

"It's fine if you forgot. Too many new people can be overwhelming. The reason I remember you is because of your beautifully long red hair. I'm Mason, nice to meet you," Mason Cook said as he sat down in the seat across from her and reached out to shake her hand.

"Hi, I'm Sarah," she said, blushing at the compliment. Her cheeks matched the color of her hair.

"So what are you doing sitting here all alone, sweaty and well-dressed?"

"I just came from church."

"Church? But it's Saturday."

Sarah was used to that comment, as she heard it all the time.

"I'm a Seventh-day Adventist. We go to church on Saturdays."

Mason thought for a second.

"Seventh-day Adventist? Sounds interesting. I've never heard of that religion. What's it about?"

Sarah was surprised. Few people ever showed interest in her beliefs. Usually they just responded with how weird it was to go to church on Saturdays and moved on to something else.

For the next ten minutes, she and Mason had a nice chat. She told him about her religion, then talked to him more about herself. The conversation soon shifted to talking about the school, their goals, and their hobbies.

"Hey Mason, we're heading to the art festival. You coming?" one of his friends shouted.

He turned to them and motioned for them to go ahead.

"So Sarah, we're going to an art exhibit in Orlando. You want to join us?"

She smiled.

"Thanks, but I can't. I need to go back to my room and get out of these sweaty clothes and shower. Maybe next time?"

"Alright, but I'll hold you to that," Mason said as he left to catch up to his friends.

Sarah smiled to herself and headed back to her room.

*****

After ten minutes of looking, Ben finally found room 129. The dimensions of the building were still confusing for him to navigate, even after being in school for two weeks. He had missed the gamers club meeting last week due to some homework assignments he had to complete, but he did not want to miss it this time. To his surprise, the club wasn't filled with the type of people he was expecting. Rather than geeky-looking, glasses-wearing gamer-types his mind was led into believe populated these clubs, there was a variety of students that were playing games in the room. Granted, he did notice that most of them were males who seemed to be too insecure to hang out with people of the opposite gender, but there was still more variety. There were a few girls, most of them gamer types, but a few that were neutral at best. Some of the guys there would definitely surprise him if they were actually nerds.

He saw Tobias in the back of the room waiting for a turn on one of the games. He definitely looked more like the nerd type in comparison.

"So you decided to join us, huh Ben?" he asked as he saw him approaching.

"Yeah, I needed something to do."

Ben continued to look around, studying the interactions between the students. This was the first group activity he participated in other than anything that happened in class or back in the dorms.

Tobias noticed his curious observations.

"If you're looking for social outcasts, you won't find them here. Try the gamer guild club. They specialize in dungeons and dragons and other board games. We're a bit more progressive," he said in his World of Warcraft shirt.

"Oh, no, I wasn't-"

"Don't worry about it. I'm not insulted or anything. We're just gamers, people who have fun playing video games. After going through the clichés and judgments from high school, college is a piece of cake. No one really cares what you are or where your social status lies. People are just people here. It's not who you are coming in, it's who you plan to be when you get out."

Ben was amazed at how much Tobias knew about college in only two weeks.

"How do you know so much about college?" he asked.

"How else? My parents, my older brother, and a few cousins. They gave me tips and pointers. Didn't your family let you know what to expect?"

Ben hesitated for a moment before answering.

"I'm... the first to go to college. My mother's a cleaning lady at a hotel and my father passed away a number of years ago."

Tobias's face filled red with embarrassment, realizing how petty his comment must have sounded to him.

"Oh, I'm sorry. I didn't know..."

"It's okay. Like you said, it's college. It doesn't matter who you are coming in. It's who you expect to be when you get out."

Tobias smiled at the cheesiness of the reference and jokingly slapped Ben on the back, causing Ben to wince in pain.

"So you went to the activities fair like I told you to?" Tobias asked.

"Yeah, I did. There are so many clubs here! I didn't even know what booths to visit, much less what clubs to join. I had some guys try to recruit me to their fraternity, inviting me to rush week coming up, some girl wanting me to join their karate club, and some other guy wanting me to join this self-improvement club that is supposed to help you survive college. I thought about joining that last one, but this gaming club you mentioned seemed like the most fun."

"Great! I hope you enjoy! There's a bunch of different systems and games scattered across the room. Just find a game you like and get in line. When it's your turn, they'll hand you a controller and you have two rounds to play, depending on the game. Anyways, it's my turn to play. Good luck!"

Ben watched as Tobias started mutilating the other player in a fighting game he didn't recognize. In fact, he didn't recognize a lot of the games they were playing. Although he was an avid gamer, he could only afford to buy consoles that were two generations behind, and only then he bought a few games for them. Money was instead used on more appropriate expenses to help him and his mother.

He suddenly started to feel homesick, wondering if his mother was done with her double shift that she usually volunteered for around this time of the week. It saddened him to know that she would come home to an empty house, wondering what her son was up to. He made it a point to call her when he went back to his room.

*****

Dylan Wright woke up to Zachary's annoying alarm that was meant to wake up an elephant. When he realized that Zachary wasn't in his room to turn off the alarm, he angrily got up and slammed the alarm clock against the wall. Not even the sound of it smashing into pieces was enough for Dylan to fully wake up. He took a look at his cell phone and realized it was almost time for him and Zachary to go running, but Zachary was already gone.

Despite his strong desire to just blow off running and go back to sleep, he knew he had to do it. Their first football game was coming up and he wasn't as fit as he hoped to be. He spent his summer doing too much weightlifting and not enough cardio, so while he knew he would do great in his linebacker position, he wasn't sure if he had the endurance to last a whole game.

He got up complaining at no one in particular as he grabbed his running shorts out of the laundry basket. He wasn't sure if they were clean or not, but didn't really care either way. He was in a bad mood. Partly because of the huge hangover he had from the night before, but also because of his slight grudge against Zachary. Even though he played quarterback for his team in high school, winning them several games and even breaking a few records, he wasn't chosen to join the Sun Valley Sliders. However, Zachary, a mere runningback, was given a full scholarship as a runningback for the same team that rejected him.

Even though he didn't really need the money to go to Sun Valley University, he saw it more as a pride issue. For some reason, the football coach, Kevin Williams, found Zachary to be a better fit for the team than he was. He was finally able to make linebacker once he actually started here, but he was stuck playing defense, and with no scholarship. It was unfair and he knew it.

He went outside to their usual meeting spot and found Zachary stretching before running.

"You're here early," Dylan said as he attempted to change his mood. He knew that running with a bad attitude would do neither of them any favors.

"Yeah, I had to stop by Jessica's room to see if she was still joining us."

"Wait, what? Since when is Jessica joining us?"

"Don't you remember? I told you the other day. Jessica's ROTC group only runs on Mondays and Wednesdays. She was looking for someone to run with on Tuesdays and Thursdays in the morning, so I told her she could run with us."

Dylan thought back, but couldn't remember ever having that conversation. He did have a tendency to forget things easily, so he decided against arguing it.

"But dude, do you really want her running with us? I mean, you saw her in Garcia's class. Not a fun person to be around."

"Oh, relax Dylan. I talked to her. We didn't have the whole story. She's had a history of guys always hitting on her just because she's a short, blonde country girl trying to fit in with the guys. She mistook Mitch's glances at her and realized she unfairly lashed out at him. She tried to be reasonable about it, but he started shouting at her and yelling at her out of nowhere, even when she made no effort to retaliate."

"Fine, whatever. She'd better not slow us down, though."

Off in the distance, they saw Jessica approaching. Dylan's eyes widened when he saw her running towards them wearing just a pair of short light blue running shorts and a black sports bra. She waved at them.

"Holy S—"

Zachary covered Dylan's mouth mid-sentence. Since she had always worn her ROTC uniform every time they had seen her, they never realized just how fit and toned she was.

"Don't say anything you'll regret," Zachary told Dylan as he took his hand off his mouth.

Dylan gave Zachary an uncomplimentary glance.

"Oh, she's gonna slow us down, alright."

CHAPTER 10: CHEYENNE WINTERS
FEBRUARY

I had gone through my fourth magazine at the housing and residence life office as I waited for my meeting. Of all the places around campus I had visited in my few weeks here, this one was definitely the busiest. Student assistants running the front desks, RAs and RDs (Resident Directors) running back and forth through the office, ADs (Assistant Directors) and other administrators taking angry parent phone-calls and meeting with students and other campus representatives. It was like a madhouse in here. Had I known about this earlier, I would have made an appointment ahead of time.

The office seemed simple enough. It was nothing fancy, just enough space to get the work done that was needed. The furniture looked relatively new, much better than the interiors of other campus buildings that weren't the tower. It was most likely due to the fact that the housing and residence life department was an auxiliary unit on the campus. Whereas other departments received funds from tuition and other university income, this department received all its money internally, with no external help. Any income they made for housing-related renovations, salaries, and programming expenses came from dorm room leases and student fines.

I remembered how when I was a freshman I would complain about room prices and their increase when I became a sophomore. Little did I know that those price increases allowed my school to hire more RAs, of which I was one of them. The increase in room costs I paid my sophomore year essentially paid for the free room I got my junior and senior year. I smiled at the irony.

Ten more minutes had passed, and I was getting anxious. I knew they were busy, but I was sure I had seen walk-ins that came after me but were attended to first. Though it was probably because of who I wanted to see. I should have known better than to just ask for a meeting with the associate director of housing and residence life and not expect to wait. They asked if I wanted to meet with anyone else instead, since he was busy in a meeting, but I declined. Travis Coleman was the first person I officially met here at Sun Valley University, and besides Nancy, was the only person that was nice to me. I figured he'd be the best person to help me out with what I needed.

By this point, I had some information about the first suicide. The victim's name was Ryan Stallen, a freshman who lived in the second floor of Miller Hall. From what some of my interviewees told me, he had a really hard time at orientation. His parents in Germany sent him to Sun Valley University on his own. He wanted to go there because he grew up in Florida and wanted to go back, since his parents moved away against his will. Due to transportation issues, he did not make it to campus until two in the morning two days before orientation, well after the housing office was closed to get a room key. He didn't have any money with him, so he tried to go to the dorms to see if someone would let him in.

There were some RAs manning the front desk at one of the halls, and when he asked if he could stay in the halls, they declined. He pleaded for them to let him stay either in one of the rooms or in the lobby, but they refused. They even refused to call someone who had access to the keys so he could get into his own room. He didn't even bring a car with him. He took a taxi from the airport to the campus with the last of his money. As a result, he had to spend the night on a park bench.

Later on, I discovered through one of my interviews with Prachi that he had some red spray paint, and it was around the time that Renzo's room was vandalized. There were already two cases of vandalism prior to that one, and they were also caused by red spray paint. Renzo apparently found out it was him, an argument ensued between the two of them, and then he was found dead a few weeks later.

The thing that didn't make sense to me was his targets. If it was the housing department that made his first night deplorable, then why did he take it out on SGA? Sure, they had a hand in planning orientation with the orientation team, but, if anything, they were only indirectly involved. It didn't fit. I figured it would be at least the RAs' doors that would be vandalized, or any other housing staff member. I needed to find out more.

Travis's office in the back finally opened up. I cringed a little when I saw Detective Sawyer walk out of his office in her usual man-eating stare. For some reason, her looks always gave me the creeps. It's as if she made it a habit to scare the truth out of suspects and witnesses. It's probably why she was a detective. She turned around and looked back at Travis as he exited his office.

"Things are starting to come together, Travis. Believe me. If I find out that you're keeping any info from me, anything at all, I will make it my duty to make sure this whole department is shut down. You hear me?"

The student assistants looked back at Travis with their little freshman and sophomore eyes both frightened and exhilarated in anticipation of any action happening in the office.

Travis merely smiled in his usual, casual posture.

"I'm telling you Lynn, there's nothing more I can tell you. I answered all your questions as truthfully as I could. If you'd like, I'd always be happy to answer some more."

His entertainingly sarcastic attitude made Detective Sawyer even angrier as she stormed out of the room. As he looked around the room, the student assistants quickly went back to work in their filing and phone calls.

"Cheyenne, is that you?" he asked with a smile when he saw me.

I smiled back and waved. I wondered how stupid I looked.

"You wanted to meet with me, didn't you? I think I remember getting an instant message a while back while the detective was yelling at me. Come on back!"

I followed Travis back to his office. The look of his office matched his personality. Lots of souvenirs and knick knacks were on his desk and shelves, a lot of them being door tags that his RAs probably made for him. He seemed to have a few baseball trophies and posters of baseball stars, as well as pictures of his puppy on his desk. The room was full of color through the decorations. It was a pleasant change from the blandness I've seen everywhere else. In the university's efforts to appear classy and professional, they sure forgot how to make a place feel homely and fun, something Travis appreciated greatly.

"So what can I do for you?" he asked as he clasped his hands together on his desk.

I spent the next few minutes briefing him on the interviews I've had with the students in Dr. Garcia's class and the information I had gathered on Ryan.

"I'm sure you or one of your RAs worked with him at least somewhat during the semester. Do you have any idea what he had against SGA?"

Travis paused for a bit as he tried to take it all in.

"That's very interesting, Cheyenne. I had no idea about the stuff with Renzo. He didn't mention it to anyone as far as I can tell. No one knew that it was Ryan who vandalized the halls."

"No one knew? Considering his bad experience on his first night here, why wasn't he a suspect?"

"Cheyenne, this orientation wasn't one of our best. Every year we do such a great job of giving the students the best welcome imaginable, but this year just didn't work out like we had hoped. To start things off, a huge flu epidemic made half of our RAs sick during RA training. It was unbelievable! Training was relatively empty, and it really caused us problems. As we tried to reschedule events, it took time off of preparation for the students that were arriving.

"We had to ask for help from the students who worked at the orientation team. See, when it comes to orientation, the orientation team handles most of the work, but we as the housing department specialize in getting the halls ready for students. That involves inspecting rooms, doing key inventory, decorating the halls, and solving last-minute problems. We were stretched thin, and as a result we caused the orientation team to stretch thin trying to help us. Meanwhile, SGA was dealing with their own problems, so they couldn't step in to help us."

I took down notes as he spoke.

"What kinds of problems?"

"Budgeting problems, primarily. Due to economic problems in the education sector, massive budget cuts started affecting universities across the country. Unfortunately, since we didn't do as well on academics last year as we have in previous years, we got hit the hardest financially. It was sprung to us last minute, too. SGA members had to be called in early from their summer vacation to meet with their advisor, Shandra Giles, and Dr. Scott to make some adjustments. They had to make a plan to raise tuition, but due to the long process involved with that, it won't take effect until at least next year. They've been scrambling cutting funding for individual departments that don't output as much as they should be. We're at least lucky we don't have to deal with that."

"That makes sense. But that still doesn't explain the reason for Ryan to have a grudge with SGA. And it doesn't explain what happened to him. Students have told me that he died in a car accident. What kind of car accident was it? I've been getting different answers from everyone."

Travis's cheery complexion slowly faded.

"Cheyenne, with all due respect, this is confidential information. Aren't you here to do an ethnographic study? Detective Sawyer had to jump through hoops to have access to this kind of information."

"I understand, Travis. I didn't mean to pry. It's just that my interviews with these students have made me realize that they are a lot more involved in these suicides than we give them credit for. Even though it just looks like freshman gossip and curiosity, a lot of these students have been impacted by the suicides one way or another. One of my students, for example, told me how Ryan's death dissolved an entire group of friends and changed them. One of the students I'm meeting with is afraid to do anything due to his fear of ending up like Ryan. Another one just seems stressed all the time ever since it happened. I'm just trying to learn everything I know about it to be able to better help them. I'm not a counselor, but I'm a student affairs professional, and I can't just let them struggle like this if I have the capability to do something about it."

Travis didn't respond. He seemed to ponder for a little bit, then pulled out a sticky note and a pencil.

"You say you're interviewing Dr. Garcia's class?" he asked.

"Yes."

He wrote something down on the sticky note and handed it to me.

"Listen, I can't tell you anything about that suicide. It is confidential material and I can get in a lot of trouble for it, especially since you do not have the clearances for it. However, I do know of one student who might know more about the suicides. He's been going through a lot recently, so I didn't want Detective Sawyer bothering him with her investigation. She probably wouldn't get anything from him, anyway. I figured he'd feel more comfortable talking to another African American like me, but I was wrong. There's no way he'd talk to Sawyer. However, since he's in Dr. Garcia's class, I figured maybe he'll actually talk to you. You seem to be getting along very well with these students."

I looked at the sticky note. It was a room in Terra Hall, the motel-like hall that I was staying in. Up to this point, I had only had one interview with Mitch Adams. He didn't really say much. I knew it was time to take things up a notch.

BIO: MITCH ADAMS
NEWARK, NJ

I grew up in Brick City. It wasn't much, but it was home. I never cared about school. There was no point. The teachers didn't wanna be there, the students didn't want to be there. It was more like a waste of time. They told us to go to school to succeed, but we knew even they didn't believe what they were saying. Most guys just dropped off high school by their second year. Even if they were lucky enough to graduate, that was it. No college, no nothin. Yeah, I tried drugs for a while. Spent my time outdoors. No point in staying home. My parents were always going at it, always fighting. My dad eventually got arrested. I don't even know what he did. Didn't care enough to ask. I couldn't stand that guy.

My mom couldn't care less what happened to me. She was too busy with her own problems, her own addictions. Bringing in a different guy to the house almost every night. I did get arrested for getting into a fight in high school. This POS talkin' bad about my mom. This guy pissed me off. There were also suspicions he was kickin' it wit my girl. Got into a fight, cops got involved. But not before he pulled a knife on me. Stabbed me near the stomach. No vital organs were hit, but I did have to get stitches. The guy is still in jail, and will be for a long time. I got out with a year of probation. I got treated as a minor, he didn't. That year was both good and bad to me. My mother didn't want to have anything to do with me, so I was left to fend for myself. My girl left me when I got out of the hospital. I was spiraling out of control, sinking myself even deeper into the hellholes of my city.

My aunt here in Florida found out about what was happening to my family. She was upset that my dad went to jail and didn't want me to follow in her brother's footsteps. She tried to contact me, did everything she could to get me out of Jersey. She had some money. Offered to pay for my college if I came down to Florida. At first I didn't care and didn't wanna hear it, but it's the one time my mom showed that she gave a damn. She told me to go. I didn't know if she was just eager to get rid of me or if she really cared about my future. I wanted to believe she cared, but it didn't matter.

My aunt showed up a few weeks later and came to take me out of there. I spent a few months in Florida with her, finished my last year of high school, and graduated. Definitely one of the lowest in my class. It's a miracle I got accepted to this school, but here I am.

CHAPTER 11: INTERVIEW #MA02
MITCH ADAMS

[My first interview with Mitch was rather short and not much was said. This interview serves as a bonding activity so we can get closer. To achieve this, I asked him if there was anything he wanted to do in the next week or so that we could do together. He likes ice hockey, so I'm accompanying him to a home game today. We're sitting in the stands with some snacks and beverages. He's wearing a pair of baggy blue jeans and a white T-shirt.]

So ice hockey, huh? What got you interested in that? It's not a sport I hear about often.

It's a'ight. There was an ice rink I used to go to in Jersey. At first we all went there cuz of all the fights that broke out. It was the thing to do. Better than getting arrested for fightin fo' real, you know? But it grew on me. Being there so long, I started learnin' about the games, the rules, and the players. I caught it on TV when I was at my homeboy's house since Ma didn't have cable. Been hooked eva since.

Cool. I don't know much about the game. Is it like soccer, kind of, except with sticks? Are we winning?

Sorta. It's like soccer where you gotta get the puck to the other side, but the tactics are different. There are five players on each team, all really protected. You don't imagine how many injuries guys get from playin this game. See what that guy did there? It's called checking. Unlike in other sports, you're actually allowed to slam opponents against the wall to steal the puck.

As long as they're in possession of the puck, it's fair game. We're behind by a bit, but it's still too early to call a winner. There are three periods of twenty minutes in each game, and we're barely through the first one.

[He starts to cheer as our team scores. The fans around us go wild and start clanging their beers with each other, spilling some on my sweater.]

Yeah! Victory!!!! Hey, would ya be willin to get us some beers to celebrate?

You know I can't do that, Mitch.

A'ight, a'ight, it's cool. Just thought I'd give it a shot.

[He laughs.]

Yeah, hockey's pretty badass. Ya gotta be tough to play this game. I wanted to play hockey once. Watchin all the games got me all excited. It's just not something people around me did back at home. You'd have to travel two cities by bus to watch a live game. That's what's nice about here. The rink is only a few blocks away. I wish it was on campus, though, since I don't have a car. But thanks for bringing me. I appreciate it.

It's no problem, honestly. Speaking of your hockey interest, do you know if SVU has a hockey team you could join?

Well yeah, there's a team, but there's no way in hell I'd get in. The guys in that team are huge and experienced. Look at me. I'm skinny and I've never played a game in my life. I'd never make the cut. There is the intramural team, which I could join, I suppose. But I dunno. The teams I've seen are all white guys. I'm not sure what they would think if a black guy from New Jersey wearin' a typical white T-shirt and baggy jeans tried to play. I'm just not feelin' it. Eva since comin' to this campus I've felt like a minority for the first time. In Jersey we were all either black or 'rican. Even when I came down to Florida with my aunt I went to a diverse high school for my last year.

But SVU, it's mostly white people here. It's probably why I got into college so easily. They're trying to build up their minority numbers, so they let just about anyone in if they're not white. I'm livin' proof of that. I barely managed to pass high school. My grades were horrible. Only reason I applied for college was cuz my aunt said she'd kick me out if I didn't. Though thinkin back, she did kick me out anyways!

[He laughs again. He seems much more relaxed than he did when I first saw him today.]

She said that college was the first step to solve my problems. Yeah right. College, if anything, has been addin' to my problems. Classes are hard, it's hard to find help around here, and it just feels like no one cares whether you pass or not. I feel like all they do here is give you lots and lots of work to weed out the ones that struggle. Which kinda makes their minority admission worthless if they lose 'em all after the first year.

I'm already dealin' wit my own problems. Even though I left Jersey, Jersey just won't leave me alone. I found out my Ma's in some legal trouble up north. There's a court case that's been goin' on that is tryin' to get her locked up for a long time. Somehow she got my campus number and has been callin' to talk to me. Could you believe that? Eighteen years she spends ignoring me, and now that she's about to be locked up, she has the nerve to call me? What does she want me to do? Bail her out?

It just pisses me off. And of course, here I am tryin' to deal with my own junk, and I gotta have roommates to make things worse. For some reason, those housing peeps thought it would be a bright idea to put two black guys together in a dorm room. Why? Just because we're black means we'll get along? I'll tell you one thing. All my life I've heard of racism from white people to black people. You know what's worse than that? Racism from black people to black people. That's worse.

This guy, Tyler, looked down on me just cuz I speak differently, and that I "represent the stereotype that white people hate" as he told me. Well you know what? Screw him! Honestly, I have many worse words I'd like to use to describe him, but it would be disrespectful to your company. See, that's the difference between me and 'im. Yeah, I got my Jersey lifestyle wit me. But what am I supposed to do? I grew up in Jersey, and like it or not, it's my home. It's my culture.

I like my baggy jeans. I like my Fubu cap, even though they tell me that went outta style years ago. Who cares? See, this guy goes around parading his "white culture". The guy's a freakin' oreo. But you know what? He's an ass. He plays himself off as a nice guy, but he's really a douche to everyone around him. Including me. I apologize for speakin' ill of the dead, but the guy really knows how to get on your nerves.

Mitch, I have a question about Tyler. You say he was your roommate, but everyone tells me that he had a different roommate during the time of the accident. What happened?

I asked for a room change. I was with the guy for less than two weeks and I couldn't stand 'im. The RAs tried to have some sorta mediation thing to try and save our roommate relationship, but I knew it wasn't goin' to work. I think he was more happy to get rid of me than I was of him. It was before I really got to know anyone, so they didn't realize I used to be his roommate.

I guess I feel kinda bad, though. Apparently he had worse problems than I did if he had to kill 'imself. Or maybe I'm just the stronger man. I don't know. One thing is for sure. I'm glad I wasn't his roommate when they found him dead.

I was told that you knew a bit about the suicides that have taken place. Is this true?

Yeah, nothing too big. Just some info here and there. I know what you're thinkin'. Why would I go all detective on this case? It all comes down to student politics. Gossip. While it wasn't known that we were roommates, everyone knew we hated each other. Part of the reason was cuz Tyler badmouthed me every chance he got. So of course, the guy winds up dead one day and guess who everyone blames.

Sure, the bosses say it's a suicide. Though I wouldn't say that really "said" anything. More like "cover up". See, this school has a knack for keeping secrets. They're tightlipped about everything. No matter what they say their mission statement is, it's actually all about control. They let the public see what they want 'em to see. Are we the school with the highest minority enrollment in the country? Sure, let's let everyone know. But are we also the school with one of the smallest retention rates for minorities? Well, they forgot to leave that part out.

Makes me wonder if schools out there are really who they say they are. Buncha lyin' crooks is what they are. They wouldn't tell anyone what happened to Tyler. If someone asked, they merely said it was an "accident" and that they couldn't say any more out of respect to the victim's family. BS. They just didn't want their precious reputation ruined by having the headlines read "Suicidal Rush in Sun Valley University". So they didn't tell anyone. Well, almost. They did have to tell a select group of students, usually student leaders like SGA or RAs in charge of the residence halls. They were allowed to know the truth.

Well, here's the problem wit the truth. It changes with who's tellin' the story. Of course, stories of the suicide leaked out, and everyone and their mother was curious as to how it happened, why it happened, and, most importantly, if there was someone else involved. That was everyone's favorite part. After the first suicide, there were many questions but no answers. With this second one, now they were all too sure there was foul play. They knew someone was involved, and they wanted to find out.

And of course, everyone thought it was me. They say that I had the best motive to kill the guy and play it off as a suicide. Even though I tell 'em that it still doesn't explain that other guy's death, they don't listen. They figure I had some other motive for him as well. Rumors start spreading about Mitch the serial killer. Now me, I've been called lots of names growin' up. I'm used to that. But this was different.

I'm still in probation for a little while longer. They're watching me, considerin' I've already had some close calls in the past. I don't need no police pinnin' anything down on me just cuz I'm the black guy on probation. You know how it goes with rumors and gossip. When enough people say it, it becomes true. I couldn't have that.

I've already had a couple of close calls this year. These two guys I used to hang out with, Luca and Sam, they're always trippin'. Seriously, it's like they're always high. They've been meetin' up with some other guys during the weekend for a fix. They invited me and I joined them. Of course, the night I go is the same night that the cops are somehow tipped off, and a drug bust kicks in. People started to scatter. I managed to get out through a window, as well as Luca and Sam, but some of the others weren't so lucky. The kid who rented the house already got kicked outta here.

That was my wakeup call. My aunt gave me another chance. I'm not gonna blow it on something stupid like weed or even worse, getting falsely accused for murder. I mean, not that there was any evidence to charge me, but I needed to hush people up, so I began asking questions. I went to my old RA for information, who I assumed knew about the suicide since it took place in his hall. We got along well, so he gave me the info, as well as the names of others who knew more.

I started asking around, findin' out the specifics. I found out that the first guy, Ryan, crashed his car into a tree. Then Tyler apparently shot himself in the head. I cannot imagine what it must have been for his roommate to walk into his room and see that. At the very least the guy could have had the decency to do it somewhere else. Both were mavericks, but as far as connections, there weren't any. As far as everyone knows, they were two unrelated cases of suicide. They think that the added stress from schoolwork is causing the suicides. They're looking into providing more academic help for students, but it may take a while. In the meantime, they're creating some kinda depression-prevention program so students learn how to know the signs of depression in themselves or someone else so they can get the appropriate help. Also some stress-reduction workshops.

What about the third suicide? Do you know anything about that one?

Not really. Once I got the info I needed, I started giving people the facts, letting them know why their "theories" were so idiotic. There was no serial killer, I was not out to get anyone, nothin'. After it all died down, I just didn't care anymore. With this third suicide, I wasn't even around. I was still on break with my aunt in South Florida, so it couldn't have been me. I don't know who it was, since the few people that were here during the event were told to keep it confidential, and they actually did. Kinda surprising, but they did.

So you don't know anything about the third suicide?

Well, I do know that after Tyler's suicide, the housing department started to do room checks around the campus to locate and dispose of any weapons that students could use to kill themselves. They've also banned anything that could be used as a weapon, such as pocket knives and letter openers. We're lucky pens and pencils are still allowed.

Still, in Miller Hall, down the long passage of fourth floor south, people have been freakin' out about a ghost.

A ghost? Really?

Yeah. It's supposedly the same hall where the student was killed. Everyone knew who the dead kid was since he was obviously missing when everyone came back, but they didn't know the how or the why. But sometimes, as they wander the halls at night after coming back from a party, they claim to see his ghost hanging on a rope off the ceiling, still convulsing in front of their eyes.

BIO: SUSAN PRICE
ORLANDO, FL

Well, my name is Susan. I am a proud mother of two wonderful children, Lilly and Gavin. Lilly is five and Gavin is three. They are everything to me, and I would do anything for them. This is part of the reason I'm here. I used to work at a clinic as a receptionist. I've actually worked there for the past few years. It doesn't pay much, but it got the bills paid. Due to recent economic problems, the clinic was closed down and I was laid off. Fortunately, I was good friends with one of the doctors. He managed to get me another job at the clinic he was relocated to.

The job was temporary, however, and he only gave it to me under the condition that I go back to college and get a degree. That's the thing with society. You can't really get anywhere without a college degree. I figured that I'd study pediatrics. With the money from unemployment taking care of my bills and the money from this new job at the new clinic helping me with school expenses, I figured now was the best time more than ever. I barely managed to pay for this semester through my job, some financial aid, and a university loan. I guess that has me a little stressed. I can already see that paying for school will be an issue every semester.

It's not easy for a woman my age to start college. I barely managed to get the evening shift at work so that I can take daytime classes. But I don't have any time to spend with my kids. It's a struggle to find someone to watch them all the time. Lilly's in kindergarten at least, but it's almost impossible to find an affordable day care for Gavin. It's so much to deal with, and I'm not sure I can handle it. It also feels kind of uncomfortable being in a class with all these 18 and 19 year olds. I feel so out of place. I think I'm even older than the professor! But it's all for the best. If I can make it through these next few years, it'll be worth it. Once I get my degree in pediatrics, I'll be able to work in that department, and probably even be able to provide care for my own children. It's an uphill battle, but I have faith that it'll all work out. I've been blessed with these wonderful children, and they deserve nothing but the best from me.

CHAPTER 12: MIDTERMS
OCTOBER

"Mommy, look at my drawing!" Lilly Price pleaded with her mother.

"Lilly, go play in your room!" Susan Price answered in a commanding tone.

This had been the fifth time Lilly had bothered her mother with something that wasn't crucial. As much as Susan wanted to see her drawings of lollipops, camping trips, and some sort of unicorn and turtle hybrid, she needed to concentrate. Her first midterm exam was coming up on Monday, which left her just the weekend to study.

Between her work, her children, and her household duties, she was hard-pressed to find any time to study. The pressure was starting to get to her. She had been in school for two months, and already she was reaching her breaking point. She had constant bags under her eyes every day from her lack of sleep. She didn't even bother taking time for her appearance anymore, wearing her hair in a bun or ponytail, no makeup, and putting on whatever was closest to her and clean.

This, in turn, made her feel worse about herself. Not only was she the only student in her class that was in her thirties, but her messy, frizzy hair and exhausted look made her appear even older. Susan was a very petite woman. She was a runner in high school and her small frame was always an attractive feature on her. However, in her current state, it made her seem like a scrawny, elderly woman in need of medical assistance.

A few minutes later, Lilly came back.

"What is it now, Lilly?"

"Mommy, Gavin did a bad thing." She said in her overdramatic someone's-gonna-get-in-trouble voice.

"Oh great, now what?"

Susan got up and went to the bedroom of her apartment-style dorm. While all college freshmen were required to stay in freshman housing like

Miller Hall and Scarlet Hall, or mixed freshman and upper-class housing like Terra Hall, she was allowed to stay in exclusive upper-class and family housing at the Village due to her age and her children. Still, the apartment was too small for the amount of space her energetic children required.

Gavin wasn't in his room. She looked back and saw Lilly heading to the bathroom.

"Oh, God. Please no," she said to herself as she headed to the bathroom.

Already she could see water on the floor heading out into the hall. When she reached the bathroom, she saw the toilet overflowing with water, and Gavin trying to "clean" it up using three rolls of toilet paper.

"Gavin, what did you do?" she cried out as she picked him up. His clothes were soaking wet from sitting on the wet floor.

"He put some things in the toilet," Lilly tattled. "He put the remote, some toys, and your necklace."

"My what? He threw my necklace in there? And you watched him do this without saying anything?"

"You told me not to bother you."

"Lilly, I told you not to bother me for silly things," Susan said as she took Gavin's shirt off and threw it in the hamper. "This was an emergency. You can't just let Gavin play in the bathroom like that by himself. He could have hurt himself! Lilly, you need to be more responsible for your brother!"

Susan's agitated tone as she spoke to her made Lilly start crying.

"No, Lilly. Don't cry," she said as she dried Gavin up in a towel.

Lilly ran to her room and cried on her bed. Susan changed Gavin's pants and looked at the flooded toilet. She knew she would have to call a plumber in. She didn't know how much it would cost to fix it, but she was sure she didn't have enough. This was her life all semester up to this point. Dealing with problem after problem, falling behind on her studies in the process. She let Gavin go and told him to go cheer up his sister as she grabbed a mop to clean the water off the floor.

Once she finished and went back to her desk in the living room, she looked around at the rest of her dirty, messy apartment that was way past due for a cleaning. She just couldn't find any time for it. She looked at her two textbooks and her notes, realizing just how little she was prepared for the exam. She was already falling behind on homework, having to beg her professors for extensions. While Dr. Garcia was willing to work with her, some of her other professors in pediatrics were less flexible, since they did have a few other students her age and they managed to get their work done on time.

While looking at her study guides but not actually studying anything in particular, she put her elbows on her desk and sunk her forehead into her palms, closing her eyes and wishing for her problems to just go away. She stood like this for almost twenty minutes. She had reached her breaking point.

Even Lilly, having gotten over the incident from before as five-year-olds do, saw that her mother was in no state to be bothered and went back quietly to her room.

Susan's dazed state was interrupted by a knock on her door. She sat there, wondering if it was worth the effort to walk over and open the door, then did so by its fifth knock. It was Grace Collins, and she had brought over some dessert.

"Pie?" she asked with glee.

Susan didn't really associate with anyone on campus, as she was too involved in her responsibilities to pay any attention to her own personal life. Except for Grace. She was different. Whereas other students would either just stare at her and wonder why she was there or try to avoid looking at her, Grace actually walked over to her one morning before the start of Dr. Garcia's class and introduced herself.

The act caught her by surprise, and soon enough, the two of them became good friends. Though acquaintances was more like it, since she rarely had any time to see or even speak to Grace outside of class. Grace would still come over every now and then with baked goods she made in her portable oven she had hidden in her room since they weren't allowed on campus.

Grace immediately noticed that Susan didn't look very well.

"Susan, are you okay?" she asked with concern.

"Yeah, I'm fine," she lied. "I'm just studying for my midterm in my health sciences class."

Grace reached out with one hand and put it on her forehead.

"Susan, you're burning up! What do you mean you're okay? You have a fever!"

Grace walked into the apartment without being invited and put the pie down on one of Susan's cluttered tables.

"Susan, you need to take a break. I'll help you out."

"Look, Grace, really, I'm fine. It'll pass."

Grace looked at her as she wetted a rag with warm water in the kitchen and smiled.

"I hope I'm as strong as you when I'm a mother."

She came back to the living room and grabbed Susan by the hand.

"Trust me, you're not going to get any studying done when you're sick. It'll keep you from getting better and you'll have trouble concentrating. Now put this rag on your forehead and lie down. Let me take care of you for a bit. I'll tidy the place up and watch Lilly and Gavin for you. You take a nap for a few hours, and when you get up, you'll be nice and refreshed to continue studying!"

Susan watched in awe as Grace led her to her room and had her lie down on a bed. Who was this angel to come in and help her out like this when all was lost? Even though she repressed it, she suddenly felt the weight of the world on her shoulders being lifted, allowing her to gain a feeling of floating freely.

Without saying any words, she nodded at Grace and smiled before putting the warm, wet rag on her forehead and closed her eyes.

"Great! I'm going to make you a special tea remedy my mother taught me. It should have you feeling better in no time!"

Grace left the room to make her tea. But Susan was so tired, she fell asleep long before Grace managed to make it back.

*****

Dr. Steven Garcia looked at his impatient class as he started to put away his notes into his briefcase. He had made the mistake of telling them he would let them out a bit early, and now they were all anxious to leave every time he finished a sentence. He figured he'd chalk that one up to a rookie mistake.

"Alright everyone, there's still fifteen more minutes before class is over. I just have one more thing to tell you about, and then you're free to go. It's about your midterm."

The class started to groan and complain, some jokingly, some not.

"Hold on, let me finish. Since our class only meets once a week, we haven't really covered enough at this point to have an actual midterm. And since our class is a year long, our official midterm technically isn't until December. However, I do have an assignment for all of you that will be due next week. I would like you all to split yourselves into groups of two or three, preferably if any of you have similar majors, but that's optional. Your task for the next week is to find one professional in your field and interview him or her about the field. Ask them questions about their job, how they got it, what they majored in, how much they enjoyed it, and what advice they can give to you.

"This will not only help you practice your interviewing skills, but you can gain valuable information about the major you're studying or planning to study. Maybe you'll find out through the professional that the major isn't right for you, or maybe it'll further confirm your passions! Either way, you have one week to find the person, interview the person, and bring the list of questions and their answers, as well as a detailed biography of the person for the next class. Each group will give a brief presentation of the person they chose. So find a group partner or two. Once you're done with that and made meeting arrangements, you're free to go."

The class was still for a minute, some looking around waiting for some brave soul to make the first move, while others just looked down at their textbook trying to drown out the awkward silence. Mason Cook was the first to get up. He left his seat and walked over to Sarah.

"Hey Sarah, you want to be my partner?" he asked cheerfully.

She reciprocated the smile.

"Sure!"

That initial movement started a wave of students looking around for partners. Some partners were already chosen before they even starting looking. Roommates such as Lisa and Gabriella as well as Miyu and Alia already knew they would be partnering with each other. Since they were already roommates, Ben asked Mattic to be his partner, and he said yes.

Zachary, Dylan, and Rachel were in a group together, and so were Susan and Grace. Luca, Sam, and Mitch formed another group together.

Tobias walked towards Amy, cautious but determined, to ask her if she wanted to work with him. As soon as he asked the question, however, Prachi came in and interrupted.

"That's a great idea!" Prachi said excitedly. "Amy can work with the two of us! What do you say, Amy?"

"Sure," Amy said.

Tobias faked a smile. It was always the Ben, Ryan, Prachi, Lisa, Tobias, and Amy club at the dorms. He was really looking forward to getting some alone time with Amy for a change.

Jessica looked around and saw that just about all groups were made. Zachary saw her and felt bad, since he wanted to invite her in with him and Dylan, but Dylan volunteered Rachel before he got a word in.

Since Renzo didn't have a partner, Jessica partnered with him to round out the groups.

"Great!" Dr. Garcia said to all of them as they finished. "See you next week!"

As the class was leaving, Gabriella told Lisa to wait for her outside for a minute. She approached Dr. Garcia's desk.

"Hola profesór," she said to him in Spanish.

"Buen día, Gabriella. How's your day?" he asked her in Spanglish, hoping to transition her to speaking English. He was aware that she was deficient and didn't want to speak English out of embarrassment.

"It was good. I make you a present."

Gabriella pulled out one of her paintings from her backpack. It was a beautiful landscaping picture of a cliff blanketed with trees leading to a vast ocean.

"It's a picture of Honduras," she told him. "It is near my home."

"This is amazing, Gabriella! Having never been to Honduras, this really makes me feel like I am there, seeing the ocean crashing into the cliff. Your attention to detail is fantastic. Thank you, Gabriella. Promise me you'll never stop painting, okay?"

"Okay!" she said as she tried to hide her massive grin from happiness. She was very glad he liked it. She has had a huge crush on him since the first day of class, but had been too shy to say anything. It took all of her courage to hand him that painting, and she was delighted to know he loved it. Maybe there was hope, in some distant, magical future.

She closed her backpack and went back out to meet Lisa.

"So, did your lover like the painting?" Lisa taunted.

"Como tu sabias que-?"

"Oh, please, Gabriella. I'm your roommate. You can't hide things from me! I found your painting hidden in the closet when I was looking for my earrings. And I see the way you look at the profe in class. Lo amas, Gaby! Estas enamorada!"

"Is it that obvious?"

"Si, but don't worry. I won't tell anyone. Your secret's safe with me."

*****

Outside the classroom building, Sarah and Mason were struggling to find a time to meet for their assignment.

"Tomorrow won't work," Sarah told him. "I have a midterm for my world history class on Wednesday and there's a lot of material to cover. I really don't want to worry about anything else until that's over with."

"Well, I can't on Thursday afternoon. We have rehearsal Thursday and Friday afternoon all the way into the evening. Are you free any mornings before a late class?"

"I work at the soup kitchen in the mornings, so that's not gonna work."

"The soup kitchen? Couldn't you take off one day so we can get this done?"

"It's not that easy. Do you know how hard it is to find volunteers to wake up early in the morning to feed people? I need to give them at least one week's notice if I'm not going to be there. I'm the only one available. I get up early and set up, help with the cooking of the meals, and singlehandedly serve a bunch of people at the homeless shelter and other individuals that walk in. If I don't show up, they won't eat that morning. I'll try to ask to have off, but I won't make any promises."

"Alright, you let me know what they tell you as soon as possible. We need to get this interview done as soon as possible. Which brings up the next problem. Who are we going to interview?"

Sarah thought for a moment.

"Well, I was thinking of maybe interviewing the pastor at my church, since it's what I want to do when I graduate. Would that work?"

Mason hesitated for a minute.

"That's a thought, but we need to find one person for the both of us. Though I guess it would be a lot easier to find a pastor willing to do an interview than an actor. Do you think he'll be available to meet with us?"

"Sure! He seems like a really nice guy that would try to work around our schedule."

"Alright, fine. Give him a call and we'll see what happens. Hopefully we'll find some availability."

The two of them walked back to the dorm together in silence for a bit.

"Or, you know Mason, you could just come with me on Saturday and we can interview him there..."

Mason darted his eyes over to her and provided a sarcastic grin.

"Smooth, Sarah. Real smooth."

"What?"

"I know what you're trying to do. You Adventists are very evangelical. Trying every way possible to get us to go to your church. I'll go with you if it makes scheduling easier, but just that once. I'm not really a church-goer."

"I was just trying to find an easy way to meet the pastor. And what do you mean not a church-goer? Are you like... um..."

"An atheist, yeah. It's not an insult, Sarah. You shouldn't be afraid to say it."

Sarah's face was flushed with embarrassment.

"Oh, sorry, I didn't mean to- um... yeah. So you're telling me you don't believe in God? Like, not at all?"

"Nope."

"Never?"

"Don't think so. I went to church as a child when my family made me, but it was mostly routine and not really belief. What's the matter, never met an atheist before?"

Sarah was quiet for a second.

"Oh wow, really? You've never met an atheist?" he asked.

"I grew up in Grayson, a small town in Georgia. It has less than one thousand people and just about everyone there has traditional core values. While Seventh-day Adventists are in no way a majority there, everyone's a part of at least some religion. So you don't believe in God, huh? Why not?"

"It just doesn't make much sense to me. Everything about the concept is based on words that have been passed down for many, many years. It's like playing the game telephone through thousands and thousands of generations. How do we know that what we're being taught is true and hasn't been manipulated? Besides, if you look at ancient people, they believed that it was God who did things that science now explains through a more detailed, realistic method. Light used to be known as God's divine doing, now we know the properties of a star and a solar system. People used the idea of God as a way to explain what was not known. It was a great belief, as it kept them going and helped them make sense of the world. But as far as the present, we have science solving all of these mysteries at a rapid pace. The idea that a higher power controls everything we do just seems outdated to me."

"Well, that's the whole purpose of belief in God. It's based on having faith. It's about believing in Him without proof."

"True, but if you take such a stance and remove God from the picture, a lot of those concepts seem sort of silly. Take the story of Abraham, for example. He almost killed his own son because God told him to in order to test his faith. Religious people see this as an amazing act showing how much someone loves God. But if you see someone in the news today getting arrested for almost drowning their son or daughter in the name of God, are you going to admire them? No! People would chastise that individual to no end. It just seems to me that many people just use God to justify their actions, good or bad."

"I see. Well, I know I believe in Him. The wonders of this universe are far too amazing to not have had a higher power behind it all."

"Understandable. No reason we can't agree to disagree. And to shift gears a bit, I just thought of something. How about if I help you out at the soup kitchen this week so you can get done earlier? We can use the saved time to meet afterwards and come up with interview questions and other prep stuff. Would that work?"

Sarah's eyes lit up.

"You would do that? You do realize how early you'd have to get up, right? The kitchen opens at seven in the morning, meaning we'd have to be there at six to set up. Are you really willing to do that?"

"Yeah, sure. It's probably best to not sleep in so much anyways."

"Wow, thanks Mason!"

All of a sudden, out of nowhere, she gives him a hug. Mason could tell that working at that soup kitchen meant a lot to her.

"No problem. Considering I'm the first atheist you've ever met, it's probably best that I leave a good first impression, haha!"

CHAPTER 13: CHEYENNE WINTERS
FEBRUARY

My interview with Mitch gave me the idea to talk to other students who may have come across some information on the suicides. At this point, I knew a few things about the case. All three students were freshmen, male, and two of them had a problem with another student. Ryan was at odds with Renzo and Tyler was at odds with Mitch. I needed to find out more about this third student to see if there was a correlation in this third category as well. It wasn't a lot to go by, but it was better than nothing.

As I walked down the long, narrow hall of Miller Fourth south, I could understand the chill factor that other students experienced as they walked through here. The lights here were dimmer than in other parts of the building, giving the entire hallway a somber appearance as you walked. This must have been a party hall, as it was more damaged than the other parts of the building. Paint was peeled off in many places, some ceiling tiles were missing, and trash was spread throughout different parts of the floor, despite the trash cans nearby. The stench was unsettling. Unlike in other halls where tons of students were roaming around or sitting against their doors in the hallway, this hall was barren. There wasn't a single soul in sight.

The place gave me an uneasy feeling, probably due to the fact that someone had died here not too long ago. Even though I didn't believe in the supernatural, I did give a couple of quick glances around when something caught my eye. I could understand why students reported ghost sightings here. With the strange shadows given off by the lights, as well as the noises made by the old vents within the walls, it could make anyone's imagination run wild.

A few times on my walk, I could have sworn I saw someone hanging off the ceiling out of the corner of my eye, but when I turned to look, it was gone. It's one annoying feature about the mind. If enough doubt is put into your mind to make you question something, you are more susceptible to see what they tell you, rather than what's really there.

The RA's room was at the end of the hall, seemingly the only person in the entire hallway. I could see his lights on from under the door, so I knew he was there. I knocked on the door and waited. The door tag had the name "Robert" on it, so I knew I was at the right place.

A few seconds later, the door opened, and I was met by a short guy wearing a pair of shorts and a T-shirt. He had a remote in his hand. It seemed I had disturbed him from some leisure time.

"Do you need something?" he asked in a somewhat snarky tone, wondering why someone was bothering him at this hour in his room.

"Hi, I'm Cheyenne. I have a few questions for you. If it's too late, I could come back another time if you wish."

"No, no, come on in. I'd rather not have to get up again."

The room smelled like dirty socks and cheesy chips. It didn't look like the guy went out much or cleaned up very well. It looked like a typical college guy's room.

"I talked to Mitch earlier today. If you don't mind, I'd like to talk to you about the suicide that took place in this hall a few weeks ago."

"Oh, that Mitch. Gotta blab about everything to everyone. I probably shoulda just kept my mouth shut. Yeah, one of my students committed suicide across the hall. The guy hung himself in his room. From what I've been told, it wasn't pretty. The initial fall didn't kill him, so he just hung there, choking to death. It could have been a good few minutes before he actually died. I would've hated to be that guy."

"What was his name?"

"Caleb."

"Did you know him well?"

"I was his RA. Of course I knew him! He was a generally quiet kid. He stayed to himself most of the time. When he did go out, it was usually to church or to an art gallery out in the city. He never caused a blip on my radar until the suicide. That's probably what caught me the most by surprise. I had no idea the kid was suicidal. Though I guess I should've known."

"What do you mean?"

"I've been an RA for almost three years now. I'm graduating this year, so this was supposed to be my easy year where I coast through everything. I guess that made me lazy. I didn't catch the signs. Every year at RA training we are taught to look for signs of depression. Isolation from others is typically a sign of depression. Not always, but it can be. I probably should have checked up on him more, see how he was doing. I was so responsible at the beginning of the year, too. I got everything done for orientation, being one of the only RAs that didn't get sick with the flu. After that, though, senioritis kicked in and I just didn't care anymore.

"Now look at me. I got what I wanted. Ever since the suicide, most of the students have requested room changes to another hall due to the scare about a ghost flying around here. The few students that have stayed are rarely here. It's pretty much just me here."

"Do you believe there's a ghost?"

"Hell no. I don't believe in that crap! The whole ghost thing was just propagated by some drunk student somewhere seeing things and everything caught on from there. Students saw what they wanted to see, and others were just joking around to make the rumor spread. I've seen nothing, and I don't expect that to change anytime soon."

"Is there anything else you could tell me?"

"Like what? There really wasn't much more to the guy. He was a General Studies major, enjoyed listening to Simple Plan, and was a Seventh-day Adventist."

That last part caught my interest. Maybe Sarah knew more about him, assuming he went to her church.

"Well, thanks Robert. This was helpful. A word of advice, don't let this last semester slip away. Make sure you end your college years with a bang. It'll be worth it."

He got up to open the door. "I'll keep that in mind. Thanks for visiting."

I got up and headed out the door. The meeting wasn't as fruitful as I had hoped, but it did give me another lead.

"Detective Sawyer already questioned me, you know," he said as I was starting down the hall. I turned around.

"She's much better at this interrogation thing than you are," he told me.

"Well, I'm not a detective. And this isn't an interrogation. I'm just a person trying to understand how students think. Trying to keep this kind of thing from happening."

Robert scratched his head.

"Listen, I probably shouldn't be telling you this, but the night of the suicide, Detective Sawyer was one of the first people here to search for evidence. She was the first to actually go in the room after Caleb's roommate stormed out in fear. While campus safety was busy trying to keep all the curious onlookers away, I came out of my room to see what was going on since I just woke up from a nap. Detective Sawyer was coming out of the room with a piece of paper in her hand. It was a yellow sheet from Caleb's notepad, so I knew it was his. It had a message written in his handwriting. Evidence that apparently never got reported. When I asked her about it during my interrogation, she said she didn't know what I was talking about. But I saw the sheet in her hand, with a message in Caleb's handwriting."

"Did you manage to read what it said?"

He nodded yes.

"It said 'There are no second chances'."

BIO: SARAH HOLMES
GRAYSON, GA

My faith is very important to me. I grew up in a Christian family. It was my mom, my dad, and my little sister. I was raised a Seventh-day Adventist from birth, and I have been true to my faith ever since. I went to church a lot as a child, joined my church youth group, and even became a preacher by age 16. My life wasn't the easiest, but I wouldn't have it any other way. I miss my friends from my youth group. We were very close and supported each other through high school.

Unfortunately, Christian schools were expensive, and our parents couldn't afford to put me in a Christian high school, so I had to go to public school. The transition was rough. Students could be so mean, both to me and to each other. It made me sad to see so much hate thrown around. It's not a knock against public schools or anything, but that was just an observation about the school I went to.

Fortunately, I met this group of friends who made life so much better. In fact, I believe that this was God's plan for me all along. He helped me find these friends so I could help them find their way through Jesus. By doing that, they also helped me find my way through high school. They became members of my church and we spent a lot of time together. They were much happier for it. I miss them all, and I can't wait to see them again during the break. In my free time, I like to volunteer a lot and work to make the community a better place. I hope to make a difference here as well.

It's scary, though. It's my first time away from home. I really miss my family. My sister especially. She always looked up to me; I was her mentor. Now she has to fend for herself. I know that it'll do her some good, but I'm still scared for her, you know? Guess we each have our own paths to follow from here on out.

CHAPTER 14: INTERVIEW #SH05
SARAH HOLMES

[I've had a couple of interviews with Sarah by this point. After our last interview, she invited me to go to church with her. She was the guest speaker that day and did an amazing job. After church, we came back to campus to have lunch and conduct our next interview. Sarah and I are still in our church attire, with her wearing a long, flowy light blue dress. I had on a dress for the very first time in ages. I was used to wearing dress pants or pencil skirts. It felt a little strange.]

That was great, Sarah! I loved the message you gave today. You are a wonderful public speaker.

[She blushes]

Thanks. I've had lots of practice. Ever since I was little, I tried to get involved in the service either by leading a group activity with the kids, telling the children's story at the altar, collecting tithe, or even leading Sabbath School. Later on I was finally brave enough to actually preach a sermon. It was really scary at first. I nearly choked a few times and ended the sermon really quickly. The rest of the church was very supportive, though. Rather than laugh at me or judge me on my performance, they supported me and congratulated me for being one of the youth to step up.

Our church was having attendance problems with the younger members. While there were plenty of adults and children that adults brought with them, there was a distinct lack of teens and early college age people. It didn't help that we were a small town to begin with, but even those that went from childhood just stopped going when their parents didn't have control over them anymore. It's a bit sad, really.

I was good friends with many other children in our church. Little by little, they just stopped coming. They involved themselves in questionable things and just didn't care about God anymore. One of my close friends who left the church got pregnant at fifteen. Another guy got arrested. And a few more are just coasting through life without a care or any aspirations. They got a full time job right after high school at local fast food restaurants and just don't care about their future anymore.

Not that I'm saying that church would have fixed all of that. But at the very least being involved in the church family would have given them lots of support from the other church members. I had some tough times growing up. You read my biography, right? I mentioned there how tough high school was for me when I went to public school for the first time. It wasn't easy. The way I dressed, the way I behaved, the way I spoke was really strange to everyone, and of course, the default course of action for high schoolers when they see something they're not familiar with is to make fun of it.

They made fun of me because of the long skirts and dresses I wear that reach my ankles. I was raised to dress conservatively, not like the outfits other girls my age are wearing nowadays. Miniskirts and tube tops are just asking to be disrespected and taken advantage of by guys. They mocked me because I wouldn't drink underage or go to all the parties. They said that I spoke all proper like it was a bad thing. Is it really wrong to use proper grammar when you're having a conversation with your friends? Is it necessary that I speak in text-speak just to fit in? I don't judge them. I really shouldn't. If not, I'll be doing the same to them as they are to me. They didn't understand my reasoning for being the way I was, just as I didn't understand the reason that they were the way they were.

Sure, it's easy to assume that watching TV and being exposed to a world that promotes that type of behavior and lifestyle is what gets them to be that way, but I don't really know. For all I know, they could be hurting, longing for answers and that's the only way they could cope with it. They could be experimenting, trying to find their true identity but having to cycle through a bunch of other identities in the process. There are many different reasons for it.

That's why I focused my message today on identity. I talked about discovering your identity and learning to live through it. I think it was taken real well by the rest of the church, since they don't seem to look at it that way. The idea for identity was taken from those students in high school who may have acted that way because they didn't know of a better way to act that suited them. My idea for that sermon also came from my fellow church members.

See, while church is great, it does have its flaws. The people in my church tend to have such a close group-like mentality that they sometimes forget they are individuals. They are often seen as God's temple or as a church member that is a part of a collective group, but they often have a hard time seeing themselves as a unique individual. Everything they are comes as a result from God, and everything they do is what God wants them to do. In order to seem humble they don't give themselves enough credit.

That's why I talked about identity. It was about finding who you truly were, knowing your skills and talents, and making them work for you through life. Even though we are to worship God, we should not devalue ourselves in the process. God created us in His image, meaning that he must see us as at least somewhat important. Too many people don't acknowledge that at the risk of seeming too proud.

But yeah, thanks for all your help, Cheyenne. That talk we had the other day about Chickering's seven vectors of student development theory really helped me out.

Yeah, I noticed that you brought it up during your sermon.

Well, it made sense. Ever since you told me about it, I began thinking about how it affected me as well as the other high school students I went to school with. It can apply to just about anyone, really. All the steps were good, like managing emotions and handling relationships, but step number five was exactly what I needed. The name of the step was even called "Establishing Identity!"

Is that how you do it? Is that how you interpret these interviews and work with the students?

Yes. There are countless more development theories just like that one. When I interview all of you, and when other student affairs professionals work with students, it's all about finding the right theory to work with the right student. They are great guidelines to help the student out.

That's great! But what do you do if a student doesn't match a theory or if a student completely contradicts a theory?

What do you mean?

I mean, no matter how many theories exist, they can't possibly account for every student out there, can they? What do you do when you find a situation no theory has prepared you for?

117

[The question was unexpected to me, especially coming from a student. I felt like I was talking to one of my professors in class]

That's... an interesting question, Sarah. I'm not sure. Use your best judgment, I guess. To be honest, though, I don't think that kind of thing happens as often as you might believe. There are many theories and they tend to cover most general situations.

Okay.

So anyway, to switch gears a little, tell me about your semester so far. We've talked a lot about your past these last couple of interviews, as well as your first semester here, but what has been happening since you started your second semester in January?

Nothing much has changed, really. School has been school. Many people have been complaining that their courses have gotten much harder, but that isn't the case with me. Then again, I'm a sociology major. My courses deal with thought and writing papers based on different concepts. That's my area of specialty. It's something I have to do anyways whenever I prepare a sermon as a guest speaker for church.

Everything else has remained pretty stable. I have a few more friends now, some introduced to me by Mason, others that I've made in my classes. Boy, that Mason is an interesting guy. I told you how he's an atheist, right? It's so weird, though. He acts completely different than I thought an atheist would. Probably because of my high school experience once again. Many of those students I didn't get along with were Christian by identification, but didn't act like it at all. They believed in God, yet still got involved in drugs, alcohol, cheating, and other immoral things. I could only imagine what someone who didn't believe in God would be like.

But Mason is pretty cool. He accepts me for being a Christian while still being true to his beliefs, or lack thereof. We get along pretty well. Though every now and then we get into friendly quarrels and arguments over our faiths.

Like for example, in an interview project Dr. Garcia gave us, we struggled to find time to interview a pastor for the assignment. Our availability was working against us, and we had to do a rush job to get it in on time. It was bad work, like really bad work, but we didn't have much choice. I prayed with all of my heart for God to help me get a good grade. And wouldn't you know it, Dr. Garcia came back to us the next week telling us to redo the paper. He dropped the papers in the rain when he was going home and half of them were illegible. I told Mason that it was the work of God, but he said it was just coincidence. It was luck.

And that tends to happen all the time. I read a newspaper article about a miracle and he tells me the scientific explanation of how it could have happened. He brings up studies about how religious people tend to have lower IQs, and I bring up studies about how religious people tend to live happier lives. It's an ongoing rivalry.

Interesting. Sarah, I don't mean to switch topics again, but I want to ask before I forget. Did you know a guy named Caleb that went to your church?

Caleb? You mean the one that... had the accident? Yeah, sort of. He went to our church at first, but he didn't seem to like it too much. He preferred to go to the bigger SDA church in the city. He was a very quiet guy. He didn't really participate. He just sat there and listened. I approached him several times to talk to him. I figured he may have felt homesick and just longed for some company. But his responses to me were usually short and without substance. It's like he answered without ever really meaning anything he said.

After his accident, we had a memorial for him at the church. A couple of the members were actually surprised that SVU didn't hold a memorial service for him, or any of the victims for that matter. It's the honorable thing to do. I don't know what the deal was with that. But anyways, Mason and I got into a slightly more heated argument than usual shortly after the accident. When a couple of our friends brought up the event, I said that it was God's plan for him to go. I said that I didn't know why, but that maybe he wasn't as faithful to God and left His side.

Apparently, that made Mason a bit upset. He quickly replied that bad things can happen to good people, that they don't have to do anything bad. He said it wasn't God's plan, that if a god existed he wouldn't be that unjust to allow three students to commit suicide. I think those suicides hurt him deeply, and he didn't like it when judgment was placed on those who did it. I tried to tell him I wasn't judging, but he didn't want to hear it. It was quite the argument we had. We've made up since then, but it was still a bit uncomfortable for us. We found it best just to not mention religion around each other again.

What he said did get me thinking, though. My little sister got sick shortly after, and I really wanted to go home to take care of her, but my parents told me to stay here and go to school. They said they would make sure she was well taken care of. Well, she's been getting worse. My sister has asthma, and she can sometimes get some violent episodes where she has trouble breathing. It doesn't help that she's allergic to like half the things in Georgia. I've been praying to God to help her, but she's only been getting worse. It just reminded me of what Mason said about how bad things happen to good people.

Why would God allow these things? I mean, I know he has a greater purpose in mind, but I just wish he could give us a hint as to what that purpose is. All I can really do is have faith that he'll take care of my sister. I miss her so much and wish I could be there for her.

I'm so sorry to hear that. I really hope she gets better.

Thank you. You know, Cheyenne, you're seriously one of the only adults here in this campus that I feel really comfortable around, not counting my church family. Has anyone else ever told you that? It just feels like a lot of the administration here are a bit apathetic to their students. Maybe it's all in my head, but that's the feeling I get. Aside from a few others like Dr. Garcia and my writing professor, Dr. Richards, everyone else seems like they're just employees coming to their eight hour shift and that's it. If there's one thing I've learned growing up is that the company around you has a big impact on the person you become.

Like Caleb, for example. I forgot to mention it earlier, but Caleb, despite being quiet, would at least be a part of the church team in spirit. He sang the songs with us in church, showed up on time to the service, and every now and then stayed for the church potluck even though he didn't bring anything. But around October he started hanging out with some other people. People that I didn't know. I would see him walking out of Miller Hall with them, and it was around that time that he became even more secluded from us. He stopped going to church altogether by late November, not even the church in the city.

Did you recognize any of those people he was with?

No, not really. They were mostly guys, some older-looking. I wouldn't be surprised if they had anything to do with his death.

BIO: ALIA ATIENO
TAITA DISTRICT, KENYA

My name is Alia, and I am from Kenya. Back home, I live with my mother, my father, my sister, my grandmother, and my aunt. I also have a cousin my age who I love very much. We live in a small village off of Voi in the Taita district. We don't have much, but we do have a community. The people there are very nice. But I also see the poverty around my village. Even with what little we have, we are very well off compared to the others in my village. My father works for a man named Matu in Mombasa who runs a tourism business. Sometimes, my father may be gone for weeks to months at a time working in the cruise ships. It's our only income, but it manages to take care of all of us.

I almost didn't come here. I wanted to stay home and take care of my family. I couldn't imagine leaving them when I could offer so much for them. But my parents wouldn't hear of it. My mother, and especially my father, wanted me to continue studying, and to come to the US to study. My father has traveled the world in the cruise ships, and he's heard so much of the US but never actually been to it. He felt it was the best place of opportunity for me. He told me there was no future for me in Kenya. Education for women was not big around here, and he saw the education in the United States a much better option for women. He even offered to work extra hours and spend extra months working the ships to be able to pay for it. I couldn't believe he would do so much for me.

My father went to Matu to ask him for more hours so he could afford my education. Matu loved my father like his own brother. Hearing this, he offered to fund my education himself. That Matu is such a wonderful man. He has known my father for such a long time. Even with all his money, he remains a compassionate, caring person. In respect for both him and my father, I decided to come to the US to study. Also in respect for my father, I decided to major in International Studies so that I may be able to better help those in my village. This has been, so far, a wonderful experience.

ROLAND NUÑEZ

CHAPTER 15: FOUL PLAY
OCTOBER

Luca handed Mitch the recently-returned midterm paper for Dr. Garcia's class.

"Holy hell, I can't believe we pulled it off!" Mitch said with excitement. "We should get a medal for this or something."

He admired the giant A written on the top right of their paper on their way back to the dorms.

"What can I say? I'm a genius," Luca responded while jokingly popping his collar. "With the amount of detail I put into those interview transcripts, Garcia would have no idea that the person we interviewed didn't exist."

"How long that take you to write, anyway? I mean, with all the detail in this paper, wouldn't it have just been easier to find someone of our own to interview?"

"Who has time for that, Mitchy boy? You're studying architecture. Where were we gonna find an architect in a week? Sam and I are doing Film Studies. Who in the bloody hell were we gonna interview for film studies? And please, I wrote that whole thing in less than thirty minutes. Just made up a director, plugged in some great-sounding British movies, and voila! I doubt the prof was gonna waste time checking our sources."

"I guess. Where's Sam, anyways? He went storming outta class. Didn't even care to see what we got on the paper."

"Oh, poor Sam. The poor divvy got himself in a mess with financial aid. He filled out the wrong forms in the beginning of the year, and now they're threatening to remove him from the university if he doesn't get it straightened out. The financial aid office sent him to the scholarships office, they sent him to the records and registration office, and then they sent him to the enrollment office which was always closed or packed when he went there. He's trying to get there right now before the rush comes in."

They finally reached Terra Hall.

"Well, here's my stop," Mitch said. "You wanna hang out 'till your next class?"

"No, it's fine. I have a meeting with Renzo, the housing office and SGA representative. We're gonna discuss some ideas I have."

"Since when do you care about any of that?"

"Since I found out that Renzo is that rich guy with the Learjet! Do you know how ace it would be to be friends with him? To survive here, you gotta have connections. Just a few meetings here and there to get on his good side and we'll become best friends in no time."

"You're a clever bastard, you know that?" Mitch joked as he headed towards his room.

It was the first time Luca entered Scarlet Hall. He heard a lot about it, but didn't realize just how beautiful it was. The floors were carpeted like an expensive hotel, with Victorian designs and decorations in the lobby. It was no wonder only the smart and rich students were placed here. And the top athletes. Luca still couldn't believe that athletes were placed in the same caliber as the intelligent and the wealthy.

He wondered what it would have been like to live there. He knew he was smart, there was no question about it. He passed more than half the tests with Bs and Cs without ever cracking a book. He just didn't feel college was worth it. It was just a way to drive people into a sheep mentality where a degree equaled intelligence which resulted in a desk job where some guy yelled at you eight hours a day.

He came out of the elevator to the fifth floor really impressed. The elevator even had elevator music! The housing department seemed to play favorites, apparently. Disgusting. That was the trouble with college. It turned everyone into corrupt, capitalist politicians in everything they did.

He reached Renzo's room and knocked on the door. He waited. He knocked again, louder this time. Still no response.

"Where the hell is he?" he asked to himself in irritation.

An African girl came out of a room close by.

"Hey Luca," she said.

He looked surprised.

"I'm sorry. Do I know you?"

"Yes, we're in Dr. Garcia's class together on Mondays."

"Oh yes, that's right. You're... you're... umm..."

"I'm Alia."

"Oh, right right."

"It's okay, people tend to forget names easily around here. It's just a skill of mine to remember most people I see from only one occasion. If you're looking for Renzo, he had to step out for a minute."

"Step out? But we had a meeting!"

"He was in a hurry and told my roommate Miyu to tell you he had to reschedule. But Miyu had to leave too, so here I am."

Luca crossed his arms as he read the SGA announcement fliers hung on the bulletin board by his room door.

"Figures. He couldn't even take the time to leave me a note on the door."

"Don't let it bother you. People can be mean here. And the university culture makes it so that anyone who isn't mean turns out that way."

Luca walked over to her, having given up on the meeting with Luca.

"It's not about being mean, it's about being smart," Luca said. "Not book smart, but street smart. This country... hell... this world revolves around people constantly one-upping each other to reach the top. Being kind only allows people to step on you that much easier. You gotta compete to get to the top."

"I suppose," Alia said in a defeated tone.

Luca noticed she seemed upset.

"I didn't mean to offend you. Sorry if I did, I'm just one to speak my mind."

"No, it's not that. I've just had a lot on my mind. I pledged for a sorority recently, and the sorority leader was really mean to me."

"Really? Why?"

"The sorority president, Ashley, is like you. She speaks her mind, but she seems to have no regard to those she hurts. She blatantly told me that with my dress and my personality, I wouldn't be a good fit to their sorority."

Luca felt strange having a girl tell him about her problems. It's something he's never dealt with before, but didn't know what else to do but stay quiet and listen.

"You're right about the competition thing," she continued. "That's the basis of the sorority Ashley's running. She's turning all the pledges into one of them. That's what she's doing to my roommate Miyu and she doesn't realize it. I've tried to tell her that she shouldn't join that sorority, but she thinks I'm just jealous that I didn't get in. It's not about that. The things Ashley said to me and the way she said them showed me a side of people I never want to see in Miyu. Miyu can be a bit superficial sometimes, but she's got a good heart, and I like that about her. I don't want that sorority to ruin her. But apparently, my concerns seem to be slowly ruining our friendship."

Luca still had a hard time trying to find something to say.

"That's too bad" is all he managed to come up with.

"I get a bad vibe whenever I interact with Ashley. She seems like a bad person to me who disguises her true motives with fake smiles and pretty words. Someone you shouldn't be around. I don't know what it is, but I feel that Miyu could get hurt being around her."

"Well, good luck with that, Alia. Hopefully... things work out, I guess."

Luca waved at her and left the hall, feeling awkward. As he entered the elevator, he brushed it off and thought of the main issue at hand: getting close to Renzo.

"You can run, Renzo," he said to himself with a smirk. "But before you know it, that Learjet will be mine."

*****

It had been a long day full of classes, volunteer hours, and studying at the library. Sarah couldn't wait to get back to her room and rest her feet on her bed. Unfortunately, when she opened her bedroom door, she realized that wasn't going to happen.

Rachel was lying with her head buried in her pillow, crying and screaming into it. Sarah knew she was treading dangerous waters. If she approached her to comfort her, she might snap at her. But if she didn't do or say anything, she'll accuse her of being insensitive. She figured she'd do the most Christian thing and take a swim in the shark pool.

She walked over and sat on the bed beside her, resting a comforting hand on her back.

"What's wrong, Rachel?" she asked in her most sympathetic voice.

"He dumped me! That bastard dumped me!" she screamed into her pillow.

Sarah gasped, but in truth, she wasn't really surprised. She didn't expect their relationship to last. They just seemed like many of the other high school couples she'd witnessed at SVU so far. They were inseparable and destined to be married when they first arrived, then broken up and onto better things about a month later. She was actually surprised they had lasted all the way to October.

"There, there, let it all out," Sarah said to comfort her. "I'm here for you roommie. I'll be here as long as you need me."

Sarah sat in silence for the next few minutes as Rachel continued to cry. After a bit, Rachel finally calmed down and they were both silent.

"Guys can be such jerks, you know?" Rachel finally said. "And you know, it wasn't so much the breakup that really hurt me. It was his lack of emotion to it all. He dropped me like it was nothing! After all I put up with him!"

Sarah got up to get her a bottle of water from the minifridge.

"He didn't even have a good reason. He said that I suffocated him. What's that even supposed to mean?! He spent plenty of time this semester with his "pals", you know, Luca, Sam, and Mitch. And when he wasn't with them he was out running or working out with Zachary and Jessica! I know that guys need their space, so I gave it to him. Even when I knew he was lying to me about extra practice or homework he had to do. Guys will be guys. But I didn't realize he'd use it as an excuse to start banging other girls while still dating me!"

Sarah handed her the water bottle. She sat up and started gulping it down.

"He did? Really?"

"I'm sure he has. I've seen the way he looks at other girls. Looks like he's about to pounce at any moment. I've been hearing that there's this girl he's been flirting with at the parties he goes to. No doubt he's slept with her and has gotten tired of me."

Rachel began to tear up again and leaned onto Sarah's shoulder. Sarah wrapped her arms around her in a tight hug.

"Oh, Rachel. I'm so sorry. If you want, we can go for a walk and talk about it some more. Getting out of this stuffy room will probably make you feel better. Does that sound like a good idea?"

Rachel nodded yes. Her pout and large eyes made her look like a five year old girl looking for comfort.

It was late outside. The sun had already gone down and traffic on campus had dwindled. Rachel and Sarah talked and walked for a while, well over an hour. It was the first time the two of them really got to know each other. Rachel told Sarah about her cheerleading, the sorority she was rushing for, and some of the things she liked to do for fun. Sarah told her about her hobbies, her family, and her upbringing in Georgia. The weather outside was perfect for walking. The fall air made things chilly during the day, and even chillier during the evenings, giving anyone outdoors an adrenaline rush to keep moving. It was a strange, tingling feeling they could feel riding on their skin. It wasn't quite cold yet, but it was cool enough for them to feel goose bumps.

The campus also provided a beautiful sight at night. The lighting from the buildings was subtle but inviting, giving each building its own personality. As they walked around the campus, the same buildings they saw during the day looked different at night, with their lights pointing to features that weren't prominent in the daylight, almost like walking through a surreal version of the campus. The emptier campus was also a nice change. After all the traffic they were used to, walking through their typical paths felt like a ghost town.

In the middle of the campus was the all-encompassing tower, watching over everything within the campus's borders. To no surprise, it was the brightest building of them all, its lights shining all the way up its twenty floors. The top of the tower also seemed to have a sort of beacon, almost as if to help lost students find their way. There was no question that the student union was the center of the campus, not just by its position, but by its stance of authority.

By the time they were heading back, Rachel felt much better. Her face no longer looked flushed and she was laughing at jokes. Their laughter was interrupted by a loud noise coming from Miller Hall.

"What's that noise?" Rachel yelled out over the sound.

"I think it's the fire alarm," Sarah responded.

Both girls ran back to the building to see hundreds of students evacuating the building. Many were confused, others were drowsy having been woken up by the alarm, as evidenced by the pajamas they were wearing.

Sarah ran to one of the students standing outside looking up.

"What happened?" she asked.

"I don't know. We were just playing cards when the fire alarm started ringing. I have no idea why."

Laughter was heard as Sarah and Rachel saw Zachary exiting the building with just a towel draped around his waist. He must have been in the shower when the fire alarm was pulled.

"Hello Zachary!" Rachel cat called. "Looking good!"

Sarah looked over at her.

"What?" Rachel said to Sarah as she shrugged her shoulders. "I'm single now!"

Zachary hurried past them towards Kimberly, who was sitting in a bench chatting with Amy.

"Kimberly! Did you check your hall?" he asked his RA frantically.

"No," she responded. "I was already out here when the alarm sounded."

"Damn it, Kimberly! Our hall's on fire!" Zachary told her.

"What?" she yelled as she sprang up from the bench.

She started running back towards the building, but by that point, campus safety had blocked the entrances, only letting people out and not in.

"I need to get in there!" she yelled at Randy the safety officer.

"Sorry, ma'am. I'm placed here to direct traffic, and frankly, you're traffic," Randy said. "Now please get out of my way before I'm forced to escort you."

Kimberly gave him a dirty look, then ran back to Zachary and Amy.

"Any luck getting back in?" Amy asked.

"No, it looked like they've already sent some safety officers in there to scout the place and make sure there are no stragglers. Zachary, you were up there. Do you know what the source of the fire was?"

"No. I didn't actually see the fire, just some smoke coming out of one of the rooms."

"Who's room was it?"

"It was Ben and Mattie's room."

"Oh my God, do you think they're still in there?"

Kimberly started to panic. She knew the protocol for dealing with fire alarms and fire drills, having to knock on every door in her hall and check every room to make sure all the residents evacuated. She figured it was just a practice fire drill and that there was no real danger. She started to imagine the worst possibilities. She didn't know what she'd do if the housing department found out she didn't do her job, or worse, if any of her students were hurt or killed by a fire. She wouldn't be able to live with herself.

"Oh no!" she squealed to herself as she started to tear up in terror.

"It's alright," Amy reassured her. She grabbed both of her shoulders. "Listen, Kim, you'll be fine. They're fine. I'm sure they got out. Let's look around and see if we can find them."

Amy, Kimberly, and Zachary began to look around for Ben and Mattic, but it was hard to do in the wave of students crowding around outside. Not only were the Miller Hall residents out there, but residents of other halls had come out to see all the commotion.

"There!" Zachary yelled as he pointed towards Ben sitting on a bench with Tobias.

"There you are!" Kimberly yelled as she ran to them. "I've been worried sick! I didn't know if something had happened to you!"

Ben looked over at Tobias, who looked away.

"See what you did, Tobias? You made my RA panic!"

Kimberly looked over at Tobias.

"What did he do?"

Ben hesitated before he spoke.

"Well... he... we were hungry, and we were out of meal plans for the week. We figured we'd make some dinner. Tobias brought his own portable stove upstairs to help with the cooking. We left the rice cooking on it when we played video games. Things got very heated, both figuratively and literally, so we didn't notice that it was burning until it was too late. We tried opening the door to let out the smoke, but the alarms still sounded. And here we are."

"So you're telling me that all of this is the result of burning the rice? Really?"

Kimberly looked annoyed but also relieved.

"Was Mattic in there?"

"No, he's rarely in the room. Always out doing who-knows-what."

Kimberly sighed.

"Ugh, I'll deal with you two later. And Tobias, don't think that just because you're not in my hall you're getting away scot-free. I'm talking to your RA as soon as I find him. It looks like they're letting everyone back inside. Let's go, guys."

Everyone started migrating like herds back into the building. Ben and Tobias waited for everyone else to get inside before they started in. Amy stayed behind to talk to them.

"You guys are in trouble!" she joked.

"Oh quiet, Amy. Aren't things bad enough as they are without you rubbing it in?" Ben said.

"Relax. Me and Kim are tight. I'll try to convince her to let you guys off easy. That's what friends do, no?"

Ben and Tobias smiled at her.

"Speaking of friends, where are Prachi, Ryan, and Lisa?" Amy asked.

"Last I heard, Lisa went Halloween shopping, and Prachi was hanging out in Ryan's room."

"Really? Ryan's room? Is there something going on between them? That's kinda cute... or awkward... I don't know."

The three of them headed inside. As they walked up the stairs they bumped into Prachi, who despite her brown skin color, looked pale as a ghost.

"What's wrong, Prachi?" Tobias asked.

She held out a note in front of them.

"I found this in Ryan's room. It's a suicide note."

CHAPTER 16: CHEYENNE WINTERS
FEBRUARY

Things had hit a dead end for me. Days passed after my talk with Robert and his information about Caleb, but nothing more came of it. I talked to some more students to see if I could find out anything else, but the conversations tended to go in circles. It seemed there was nowhere else to go in my investigation. I was stuck.

After some stressful nights trying to figure things out, I started to think it was for the best that I didn't go further with the case. I noticed that I was starting to get too involved. After all, I was here to conduct an ethnographic study, nothing more. In fact, aside from a few people here and there, no one had any idea I was conducting these investigations on my own, and I could get in big trouble if they ever found out. Half of the information I gathered was confidential material that I wasn't supposed to know.

I talked to Nancy about my roadblock with the case and how I couldn't get any further. I told her that it would be best if I just quit while I was ahead. She didn't agree with my sentiment. Instead, she said that I should take my mind off of it for a little while and distract myself with something else. Maybe if I came back refreshed and relaxed, I might see the situation from a different angle and find something I didn't notice before. She suggested we go to the Sun Valley Historical Museum during the weekend for a girl's day out. When she asked me if I was free, I was shocked at how easy it was for me to say yes.

Due to the fact that I was always busy with schoolwork, research, and other projects, I never actually did anything fun. Ever since I entered graduate school, I became a full time scholar and put my social life in the back burner. The only times I found myself to ever do something was when Nancy encouraged me. It reached a point where I actually secretly begged for her to invite me to go out. It felt kind of pathetic, really. It was like I was some poor, secluded scholar who needed saving from my books and life of study. Like the lonely dog waiting all day inside the house, I'd instantly begin to roll over and beg when my owner came home and offered me a treat. What was wrong with me?

I found that thoughts like that were best put in the back of my mind, or else I wouldn't enjoy the few times we hung out together. Besides, the museum was gorgeous. It was a massive building surely built by some retired millionaire who had nothing else to do with his money. It was surprisingly packed for a historical museum. I figured that museums had stopped being popular once the internet came around and replaced them. I figured some people just appreciate the experience of seeing the exhibits and artifacts in person.

Nancy and I walked around the museum for a half hour on our own before we joined one of the tours that were starting up. We figured we'd gain a lot more to have one of them explain what we were seeing. I was never really much of a museum person. I preferred using books.

Much to my surprise, I recognized the tour guide as he approached us.

"Mason?" I unintentionally said out loud in an excited tone.

Nancy raised her eyebrow wondering why I got excited about seeing a student I knew. In a small town like Sun Valley, it was common to see people you knew around the town, working in the shops and restaurants, selling tickets for shows and movies, and even preaching at your local church.

I figured she wouldn't understand, but seeing someone I knew outside of my contained environment always excited me for some reason. I always had a strange philosophy in my mind regarding going to a new place. Whenever you move or relocate to a new area, you are never really a part of that group until you accidentally meet one of those people outside your element. In this case, Mason was the first student who I had met randomly wandering outside the university. Even though it was a very minor event, it meant a lot to me. It made me feel like I was finally part of SVU.

"Hey Cheyenne! Hey Nancy!" Mason said in his usual excited tone. It made me feel a little bit better I wasn't the only one sounding too chipper.

"Mason, I didn't know you worked as a tour guide!"

"Yeah, getting a job here isn't as hard as you may think. In a college town like this, students flock to get jobs at the fast food chains and department stores, but few students apply at places like museums. They figure you have to be a history buff to even be considered. It turns out that all you need is a great outgoing personality and they take care of the rest! They train you and everything. Though I did have to study up on my Sun Valley history before my first tour."

The next forty five minutes were very entertaining. There was something about Mason's personality that made all of Sun Valley's history seem much more interesting than it truly was. In reality, besides SVU, Sun Valley really wasn't anything special. It was a small town in south central Florida that used to be a giant orange grove before they started building houses on it. It was probably why about half of the museum's exhibits were SVU related. Regardless, Mason kept us engaged throughout the entire tour, cracking jokes every now and then and giving us interesting trivia. I really like Mason. I'd only had one interview with him due to his busy schedule, but it turned out to be great. Unlike other first interviews that relied on a question and answer format, my interviews with Mason were like regular conversations you'd have with your friends. He really was a people person.

He had his lunch break after the tour so he invited us all to eat at the museum cafeteria. The food wasn't all that great but he offered to pay for us using his employee discount.

"How are your classes going?" Nancy asked him as we ate our hot dogs. Nancy was Mason's academic advisor and had a hard time getting him in some closed classes for this semester. The problem with being a freshman was that they had to wait until all the other students registered for classes before they would be allowed to. This occasionally caused some required classes to be filled up, and the students needed that class that semester to stay on schedule with their plan of study.

"Pretty great! It was tough the first month with the fraternity events and the theatre rehearsals as well as this job, but I'm starting to get the hang of it. I used to multi-task a lot in high school, so it's prepared me for it."

"Great!"

He turned to me.

"So how are the rest of your interviews going, Cheyenne? Learn anything juicy for us to sink our teeth into?"

"Haha, no, not really. Just getting to know the students. You all have really interesting backgrounds."

I tried to avoid talking about my suicide investigations with the students unless necessary, fearing that it would turn my future interviews into interrogation sessions. That would ruin the essence of my dissertation study.

"Are there any people in my class you haven't talked to yet? Last I heard, just about everyone has jumped on the opportunity for extra credit."

"Pretty much most of the class has interviewed with me at least once. It's only a few that I haven't been able to sit down with, like Renzo and Gabriella. Renzo just outright refuses, and Gabriella is too shy. Otherwise, though, my interviews are going well. I just need about another two months of data and I should be finished."

He started to laugh.

"Good luck with those two! It's hard enough to get them to talk in class where there's a grade involved. Renzo thinks he's too good to participate, often just sitting back and watching the rest of the class go about their lessons, kinda like you do when you come observe our classes. He doesn't really feel like he's one of us. And Gabriella, she just doesn't like talking.

Lisa's the only one I ever see her talking to. I heard she has very limited English, but I'm not sure how well that excuse will hold. Her classes are only going to get harder from here, and mastering English is pivotal to passing her upper level courses. I wonder why she hasn't improved. Shouldn't the English Language Center be helping her with that?"

"Their hands are tied," Nancy responded. "Since this university has traditionally had a very small minority percentage, the ELC department was nearly non-existent here. I believe there has only been one person running the whole department. Seeing that the university was lacking in diversity, President Lambrick established a Diversity Initiatives program that would help the campus rise the ranks. The DI program was supposed to lower the barriers to entry for minority students, specifically Blacks and Hispanics, so that they would be encouraged to come to the university. The program was a success. So much of a success, however, that the ELC department wasn't prepared for the influx of students they received. And with the budget cuts we got last summer, they couldn't afford to hire any more ELC staff. As a result, poor Rita is stretched pretty thin working with all the new freshmen that have arrived this year."

"But why would they allow so many minority students who are deficient in English enroll in the university if they didn't have the resources to help them?" I asked in curiosity. "It just seemed like shortsighted thinking on their part."

"It was. When the decision was approved by the appropriate committees, all they were thinking was about the rankings. With their academic rank going down, they were desperate to increase their rankings in other areas: diversity, low felony rates, leadership, job placements after graduation. Plus, they didn't expect this many students would apply and get in."

Nancy's descriptions of SVU's resource management issues started to trigger all my studies from my Master's program. Cases like these were typical in my tests and class discussions. It was surprising that despite the in-depth preparation we received in graduate school to deal with these situations, they still managed to make themselves evident in universities. Did people not apply what they learned in school? I just didn't understand how college administrators could let things like this happen.

After lunch, Nancy and I said goodbye to Mason and headed back to campus. She was right. One day out really made me feel new and refreshed. My talk with Mason and Nancy at lunch invigorated my desire to help my students in any way I could. While I didn't have any power to fix the administrators' budget issues or staffing problems, I could at the very least help students deal with their day to day class issues and provide the proper support. On our drive back, Nancy got a phone call that made her lose her smile.

"What's wrong?" I asked when she hung up.

"It was Shandra Giles. She's calling for an emergency meeting with anyone in our staff who's available. There's an issue on campus."

"What kind of issue?"

"She didn't give me too many details, but she told me that they found a note in a classroom that may hint towards another suicide."

"Another one? Seriously?"

"Yes, and you'll never guess what classroom they found it in."

"Dr. Garcia's classroom," I finished her thought. I figured that's why she was upset, since that meant it involved me in some way.

The two of us got back to campus as fast as we could and walked over to Admin Hall and up to the third floor. We reached a room full of some staff members, and a few faculty members, which included Dr. Garcia.

As Nancy and I walked inside, Dr. Giles stopped us in our tracks.

"Sorry, Nancy, but she can't come in here," she said as she gestured towards me.

"But my input would be valuable," I told her. "I'm working with the class where the note was found. I have a lot of information that you may find useful."

"It's possible, but you cannot come in. This is for SVU employees only, and you are not one of us. Please leave, Cheyenne."

Nancy gave me a solemn look and walked inside the room. I stepped out of the way as Dr. Giles closed the door. At that moment, my feeling of inclusion left me as fast as it arrived. Dr. Giles was right. I was not a part of this school. I was involving myself in things that were way over my head and I needed to accept that. But I couldn't accept it. Not this time. The thought that another student's life might be in danger, no matter how minor the threat, was something I couldn't just ignore. At that moment I decided that my study had to wait. My primary goal was to find out what was happening in this campus and how I could stop it.

BIO: RACHEL DAVIS
RALEIGH, NC

I can say that I'm very spontaneous. I don't have a boring day. Whether it's at the mall, traveling to the beach, or just having a girls' night out with my girlfriends, I wrote the book on having a good time. I'm also up for new things. Just last week, I went scuba diving for the first time. That was amazing! Anyways, I'm from North Carolina. When I found out my boyfriend Dylan was coming to Florida, I was so excited! I mean, don't get me wrong, the beaches on the Carolina coast are okay, but the Florida beaches I heard are AMAZING! It was perfect! I mean, I was graduating soon, I didn't know where to go for college, why not go to Florida? It's been great here so far. I've been to the pool like every day, and the beach every weekend so far. Aren't the summers here wonderful?

Anywho, they had cheerleading tryouts during orientation. Guess my cheerleading experience accumulated since fifth grade has really paid off, cause I made the team! Practice has already started, and it's exciting. The girls are really nice. Well, most of them, anyways. We're practicing really hard for our competition in January. Thing is, when people think cheerleading, they just think about a group of hot girls cheering on a bunch of guys at the football games. While that is true, there's more to it than that. Cheerleading competitions are intense! Teams from all over the region will be meeting up with their flips, kicks, and turns. They haven't given me my placement yet in the squad, I guess they're still seeing where the best fit for me is.

Back in middle school I was a flyer since I was the smallest one on the team. Flyers are the ones that get thrown around in the air for those amazing flips you see in those kinds of competitions. However, once I began to... "develop"... I got too big to be a flyer. I got moved around to a bunch of different positions, but nothing really beats the thrill of being a flyer. So yeah, that's something to look forward to. College looks like a great experience. Dylan's in the football team, and I'll be cheering for him during his games. What more can I ask for? Some of the girls and I are already going clubbing next weekend in Orlando to see what's around. Can't wait!!!

CHAPTER 17: INTERVIEW #RD03
RACHEL DAVIS

[I went to meet Rachel at the REC after her cheerleading practice. She sees me approaching and runs towards me before I manage to get a word in. She's wearing her green and gold cheerleading outfit to represent the colors of the Sun Valley Sliders.]

Cheyenne! There you are! Guess what? We got third place!!!

[She had told me in a previous interview about the regional cheerleading finals in Jacksonville she was supposed to have in late February.]

That's wonderful, Rachel! How do you think you did?

Oh, I did amazing! We got third place! It was so crazy! Even though we practiced our routine like a million times, they almost dropped me during the competition. If they didn't catch me, I would have planted myself face-first into the ground. It wouldn't have been a pretty sight. They managed to recover very quickly, but that pretty much cost us second place. It was that close. Our teammate Lindsey did manage to win cheerleader of the year at the competition! We're all so proud of her! Her boyfriend Brad came to pick her up from practice early today to take her to Disney World in celebration. They are such a cute couple! Anyways, you wanna chat right here?

Sure, but don't you want to change first? Aren't you sweaty in that uniform?

Nah, we didn't really do much today. Now that competition is over, we're just doing some routine practices so we don't lose our touch. But the coach has decided to go easy on us for a bit. We've been working our butts off for the past few months. Between this competition, the basketball games, and homecoming, they've been working us down to our last sweat! To be honest, I'm glad I didn't have any other distractions this year. If I had still been with Dylan, I'm not sure I would have given it all my effort.

Ahh yes. The infamous Dylan. How's he doing, by the way? Do you still keep in touch with him?

Haha, that loser? No, I don't really keep up with his pathetic life. Ever since he dumped me, I swore to myself never to plan my life around some guy again. He's the reason I came to this school. He's the reason I continued cheerleading in high school even after I broke my foot and had to stop, and why I always wore high heels instead of flips flops because he said "it makes me look sassy". Well yeah, lesson learned. Look at me now, I'm stuck in this school as a General Studies major since I have no idea what I want to do with my life. I came here with him because I wanted us to begin our lives together. We were supposed to get married!

Stupid, silly freshman, huh? Don't worry, that won't happen again. Though I got nothing else in this school, I've got my cheerleading and my sorority sisters. The girls at Sigma Zeta Pi were very supportive when I was hurting in the fall. They told me about their own experiences with guys and how they were stronger because of it. Oh, and Sarah, my roommate. She has been a wonderful friend. She's a little bit on the simpler side. You've met her, right? She's the little red-headed church girl, always wearing those long dresses and reading those Joel Osteen books. She's kinda odd, but I have to admit, she has a lot of heart. She gave up her entire evening the night Dylan dumped me just to take care of me and make me feel better. Looking back at it, my reaction to our break up was pretty silly, but what can you do? I thought I was in love.

Dylan has long broken up with the girl he cheated on me with. He's back to the same old lady juggler he was back in high school. Guess he didn't change like he led me to believe after all. I haven't really kept up with him. Last I heard he was chasing after some bimbo in one of the other sororities. I hope one of these days he messes with the wrong girl who screws him over. It would serve him right.

But yeah, once I dropped him from my life, I managed to put my full focus on my sorority and my cheerleading. And let me tell you, nothing can cure a broken heart better than the monster that is Sun Valley University's homecoming. You should have been around for it, Cheyenne. Since it's a small town, just about everything focuses on homecoming. I heard so much about it coming in, but you never really understand its magnitude until you experience it yourself.

And being both a cheerleader and a sorority sister, I was involved in almost everything! They both had to fight to have me in their float in the homecoming day parade. My sorority won, if only because being on their float was a requirement. It was wonderful seeing all the students from the university gathered during the parade, then tailgating to the football game! Though frankly, the fact that Dylan was playing in the game kinda took away some of that excitement.

The campus was crowded everywhere. Students and faculty alike were wearing green and gold to represent SVU's spirit. Our mascot, Turt the red-eared slider, led the parade along with the marching band. I know it sounds weird having a turtle as a mascot, but he's actually pretty cool. He looks more like a snapping turtle than a slider, but no one really cares.

Spencer was there with a huge group of people throwing out candy to the onlookers along the way. They were all cheering him along, with some of them complaining that he didn't make it as a homecoming king finalist.

Spencer?

Spencer Wright. I never told you about him? He's Dylan's older brother. He's a great guy, definitely the classier of the two Wright brothers. He's been really nice to me ever since Dylan introduced me to him. In fact, even after we broke up, I do still talk to Spencer every now and then. He's a vanguard graduating next year hopefully. He's been very involved in campus since he started as a maverick and has worked his way to the top. Here in SVU, apparently the only way to get to the top is through SGA or through Greek Life. Spencer has shown us that it is possible to become well-known on campus without having to choose one of those two avenues. He was nominated for homecoming king, but was outvoted in favor of fraternity guys who had their brothers vote for them in droves.

I had a really great time. Unfortunately, we had some unforeseen showers interrupt most of our homecoming week, including the parade and the football game. It wasn't bad enough where we had to cancel or postpone, but some of the floats didn't participate and the football players and cheerleaders had to get wet out there. But despite that, we managed to make the most of it and had a kickass homecoming to be proud of! Granted, we lost, but it's okay. From what I hear, next year is going to be big. It's going to mark Sun Valley University's fiftieth anniversary. According to the rumors flying around, all gloves will be coming off and we're in for quite the treat!

So you're doing okay then as far as school and your personal life goes?

Yeah, I guess. Other than my aching feet from all the jumping and cheering, not really much to complain about.

And how about your friends in Dr. Garcia's class? Are they doing okay?

Dr. Garcia's class? Hmm, I'm not really friends with many people in that class. Let's see, Miyu's doing great. I see her in our chapter meetings every Monday. She apparently had a horrible date the other day, but nothing too major. She got over that quickly. I used to talk to Zachary back when I was dating Dylan, but we really don't chat much anymore. And Sarah... well... she's had better days. Her little sister is getting worse. Some sort of asthma attacks or something. She kneels down every night to pray out loud by her bed hoping for God to cure her sister. It's kinda sad, really. I don't have a sister, a real sister anyways. But I do have sorority sisters who I've grown to love like real sisters and I don't know how I'd feel if they were as sick as Sarah claims her littler sister is feeling.

Would you say that Sarah's distress is concerning? Do you think I should ask her to talk to me to see if I can help her?

Umm, I don't think so. I mean, she's not doing anything out of the ordinary. She has been praying more than normal, but that doesn't say much, since she prays a lot to begin with. And I wouldn't suggest you meet with her about it. She's very secretive about her problems, and she has just recently trusted me enough to pray around me and allow me to hear her. I'm pretty sure she'd lose that trust in me if she found out I was telling you this.

So why did you tell me?

I'm guessing you're trying to solve the suicide epidemic on our campus, right? Just thought maybe that would help you in your investigation.

What makes you think that? Detective Sawyer is the one investigating the cases.

Cheyenne, everyone's talking about it. The latest gossip going around is how you're trying to squeeze yourself into Detective Sawyer's investigation. They're saying you two are playing the whole good cop, bad cop angle. And to be honest, Cheyenne, I'm cheering for you. No one really likes that detective.

Rachel, I appreciate your comment, but you need to tell your peers that I'm not trying to infringe on Detective Sawyer's investigation. That is her investigation alone, not mine. I could get into a lot of trouble if some of the higher ups find out that I'm doing something I'm not authorized to do. Can I count on you?

Sure, I can do that. Anything for you! There's one thing you probably should be aware of, though. I heard some people talking at my last visit to the administration building, and it seems that Dr. Giles has been recently made aware of your involvement in this. And she's pretty upset about it. What's going to happen? Can you get arrested or sued?

No, I don't think so. Don't worry, Rachel, I'll figure things out. Thanks for the info.

[To be honest, I really didn't know what would happen.]

ROLAND NUÑEZ

BIO: TOBIAS GRAY
TITUSVILLE, FL

Hmm, I'm not really sure what to write about. There really isn't too much about me or my life. Let's see, I grew up in Titusville, Florida. It was a great place to watch the shuttle launches. I guess you can say I'm one of the few Floridians who actually grew up in Florida. Most people I know here have moved from the north. I've noticed that most Floridians come from New Jersey, New York, Pennsylvania, or Ohio. What's up with that?

But anyway, I didn't really do much as a child. My father was a pilot, so he often left for days, sometimes weeks at a time. My mother worked in a law firm, and also took evening classes at the community college. I spent most of my childhood with a babysitter. I found her pretty, but that's about all she was good for. She really didn't do anything. I pretty much fended for myself. Food, entertainment, school work, it was all up to me. I didn't really mind, though. I had the internet to take care of me.

Since I was a young child and learned how to use a computer in the first grade, the internet really helped me out. Whenever I had problems with homework assignments, I would look up how to do them online. I would try new dishes by searching for ingredients. Some of those meals were flops, but others turned out really good. My babysitter enjoyed my meals. The virtual world was really the only place I could feel safe and secure, so I invested most of my time on it. I love video games. I grew up playing everything, from your adventure games, to your platformers, to your FPS, RPG, puzzle, you name it! I also got into the MMO scene for a bit.

I wasted many years playing World of Warcraft. But that wasn't enough. I felt like I was just wasting my time. That's when I got into the hobby of programming. Do you know just how many possibilities there are in the world of programming? There's so much you can do! I learned Java, C++, HTML, Matlab, and then moved on to even more programming languages. It's an adventure, you know?

It's like the greatest puzzle of them all! Trying to find the right code to get your desired result. Spending hours searching for that bug that keeps my modded game of Super Mario Bros from working. While others find it tedious, I just find it a great way to fine tune my skills in preparation for my next project. It's probably why I'm doing Software Engineering. I feel I could put my skills to great use here.

CHAPTER 18: WINTER'S EVE
NOVEMBER

Sweat poured down Tobias's forehead as he walked over to Amy's room. It was the first time since school started that he finally managed to get some alone time with Amy. He had been crushing on her since Ben first introduced her to him. Now was finally the time. He decided that he would start admiring her from afar and that tonight would be the night he would tell her his true feelings for her. Just the thought of the awkwardness that would result from the conversation pained him, but he knew that if he waited too long, she would be taken by someone else.

With a trembling hand, he knocked on the door. Hundreds of different scenarios surfed through his mind about how their conversation would turn out. Perhaps it would be better if he just didn't say anything.

The door opened, but it wasn't Amy. It was Grace.

"Greetings!" she said with her usual cheery smile.

"Oh, hi Grace," Tobias said nervously. "Is Amy here?"

"She hasn't been for a while. She's been out with Kimberly last I heard. You're Tobias, right? From the hall downstairs?"

"Yeah, that's me."

"Nice to finally formally meet you! I've heard about you here and there but I'm not usually around when you visit. Hold on a second."

She quickly closed her door as she ran into her room. Tobias became confused and wondered if she was coming back. He heard some fumbling from behind the door, then heard it open again. She was holding a quilted patch in the shape of a rhinoceros. She handed it to him.

"Take this," she said enthusiastically.

"What's it for?"

"It's a gift, silly! I always cherish the moment that I get to meet new people, so I usually create these in my spare time for when I meet their appropriate owner. The second I saw you, I instantly paired you up with Rick the Rhino. You two are made for each other! You both look strong, fierce, and determined! Your size shows that you have character, something that rhinos are full of as well!"

"Umm, thanks?" Tobias said. It was an odd, though generous, gesture. His size was never seen as having character before. It was seen as having fat. He was surprised she even brought it up. One thing he loved about college was that students weren't as vocal about your imperfections as in high school.

All of a sudden, the room next door opened, making Tobias jump half a foot in the air. Amy and Kimberly were coming out of the room chatting about RA selection.

"So you promise me you'll apply?" Kimberly asked.

"I'll think about it. I'm not sure I can consider myself RA material."

"Alright, but remember that the deadline for application is the last day of school before winter break. You still have a bit of time to decide, but that deadline will approach faster than you may think."

Amy saw Tobias and Grace by the door of her room.

"Oh, Tobias! Is it seven already? Wow, time sure flies. Have you thought about where we're going to go?"

"No, I figured we could decide on the way there."

"Going to eat?" Kimberly asked.

"Well, yeah, but we're grabbing it to go. Tobias and I have a test to study for so we're going to go find a nice, quiet study lounge to study in. Wanna join us Kim?"

Tobias's heart almost stopped. After all of his waiting, he was about to lose his only opportunity to hang out with Amy alone. After Ryan's death, the group just wasn't the same anymore. Prachi was too stressed to do anything fun, Ben was too afraid to leave his room, and Lisa just disappeared altogether. He and Amy were the only ones left, and now it looked like Amy was trying to recruit more members.

"No, sorry Amy. I have to go to staff meeting. We have to go over winter break checkouts and other paperwork the RAs have to do before we all leave for home."

Tobias sighed a breath of relief as Kimberly finally left.

"How about you, Grace? Wanna join us for food before we have to study?"

At this point, Tobias wanted to kick her just as much as he wanted to hug her.

Grace gave a mischievous-looking smile.

"Sorry, Amy. I already ate. Besides, it looks like the goats need some herding over here. Have fun you two!"

She went back into her room.

"Goat herding?" Tobias asked in confusion.

"Tobias, if there's one word of advice I could give you, is to not try to make any sense of Grace. She follows the beat of her own drummer, and we'd best not get in the way of that. Come on, let's go."

The next half hour was like a trip to heaven for Tobias. He enjoyed every second of it, and had to mentally stop himself from reaching out to hold her hand as they were walking. They grabbed some sandwiches to eat from the university diner and found a nice study lounge in the library.

"Kimberly seems like a cool RA. Are you two good friends?" Tobias asked her in hopes to break the silence as they studied.

"Yeah, we've gotten to know each other really well. She wants me to apply to be an RA so we can work together next year. I'm not sure that's such a good idea, though. Seems like a lot of work and a lot of responsibility."

"Hey, at least you have an RA that cares about her residents. My RA is barely around. I'm not even sure she lives there anymore. Then again, she's a vanguard graduating this year. This close to finishing college and I guess she just stopped caring about her job. Kimberly's a pathfinder, right?"

"Yeah, it's her second year at SVU, first year as RA. Says she's learned a lot from the position. She's done a lot with our hall. She's taken us to the movies a few times, had a cookout the other night, and even helped them plan a surprise birthday party for me without me ever finding out. I still don't know how she pulled it off. You gotta love her."

She paused for a second and sighed deeply.

"What's wrong?" Tobias asked.

"Oh, it's nothing. It's just that... I'm still not over what happened to Ryan. I can't believe things could have been that bad for him that he had to kill himself. Kimberly took it really hard, too. She doesn't deal with death too easily. And look at what happened to us. There were six of us, and now it's just us. Everyone seems to still be upset over the whole ordeal. I just wish I knew what to do."

Tobias's heart began to pound. He knew this was it. Amy was vulnerable and seeking for his input. It was the perfect time for him to offer her words of comfort.

He opened his mouth to speak but nothing came out. He kept trying to force out a sentence, but the pit in his stomach seemed to swallow up all of his words. Fortunately for him, Amy was looking down at her textbook and didn't see how ridiculous he must have appeared.

"I know it's tough," he finally managed to say. "Ryan's death hit us all real hard. I know that I had to have some time to myself after it happened. I think that's what the others need. Some time to themselves to figure things out. Death tends to make people look at their lives in a different way. They start to question if they're making the most of it in case it ever came to them tomorrow."

Amy looked up from her book.

"Wow, Tobias. That was very insightful. That sounds like something I would say!"

Amy was a philosophy major, so he knew she would like that kind of response.

"I know Amy. Your inquisitive mind is one of the many things that I like about you. You're a pretty amazing person, more than I tend to admit."

"What do you mean?" she asked.

There was no turning back now. With the question, Tobias had reached the point of no return. The only way to get out of that question was to lie. While it did seem tempting, he took a big gulp and decided to go for it.

"Amy, umm, you are a wonderful person. You are funny, smart, and really helpful. I've always liked that since I first met you. More than liked, actually. I mean, you see... since the beginning of the year, I kinda hoped that maybe you and I... you know... became more than friends. Like... I'm just so shy and you're so outgoing so it's hard for me but... I have these great feelings whenever I'm around you, and I've never had the guts to do something about it until now."

"Tobias," she said in a low, enunciated tone. "Are you trying to ask me out?"

He froze as she said it. As silly as it seemed, he had hoped she didn't understand the barrage of cluttered words he threw at her.

"Yes, Amy. You know, if you'd like."

The resulting silence in the study room was only interrupted by the sound of the air conditioner humming throughout the room. The tension was thick, and Tobias was getting his hands, arms, and forehead sweaty as he tried to analyze Amy's blank expression. Why the pause? What was she thinking? He was about to have a panic attack.

After what felt like hours, she finally spoke.

"Tobias," she said in a very tired-sounding tone.

She paused again as she tried to find the right words.

"That was really sweet of you, and you are a wonderful guy. I've had a lot of fun around you, but I didn't know you felt this way. I've always seen you as just a friend, nothing more. I'm so sorry."

Tobias felt his heart drop to the floor. The rejection he saw coming from a mile away finally came true. He couldn't believe this was real and wished it all to be a dream.

"It's cause I'm fat, isn't it?" he said in reflex out of bitterness.

"No, Tobias, it's not that at all! I really like you but-"

"Of course you like me, just not as a boyfriend, huh? You said yourself I'm a wonderful guy. So what keeps me from being boyfriend material? Is it my appearance? Cause if it is, tell me! I can take it. Just please don't demean me and lie to me by saying I'm just a better friend. Please."

Amy sighed.

"Tobias, look. I'm not hiding anything from you. The reason I'm not attracted to you is because I'm a lesbian."

*****

Tony Brown downed his sixth can of beer at the pre-Thanksgiving bash. Like all the other "unofficial" parties at Sun Valley University, a trailblazer or vanguard who rented or owned a big enough house invited a large group of students to celebrate just about any event they could think of. This time it was hosted by one of the fraternity brothers of Kappa Chi whose parents owned some real estate property just south of Sun Valley.

It was the Tuesday before Thanksgiving and classes had already ended but not everyone had gone home yet. It was the perfect time to have fun before the inevitable flights or drives home.

Tony looked around for his fellow Kappa Chi brothers, but most seemed even more drunk than he was. He saw Mason in the living room, who was entertaining an entire group with his impressions.

"Yo Mason!" he shouted.

Mason looked over through the crowd.

"Hey Tony, what's going on?"

"Mason, I'm getting a bit buzzed. Won't take too long before I get wasted. You drinking tonight? Mind giving me a ride home when you leave?"

"Yeah, sure, no problem. I'm already DD for a couple of other guys."

Tony smiled and downed another can as he walked to the front of the house. He could hear loud cheers outside so he decided to check it out. Outside, there was a large group of students huddled together by the road.

They were staring out into the distance, as if looking for something.

"What's going on?" he asked.

No one cared to answer, but it didn't matter. Within minutes he saw two motorcycles approaching. With their positioning and speed, it was obvious they were racing. One motorcycle pulled in well before the other, winning the race. The guy pulled off his helmet and was engulfed in everyone's cheers.

"Any other takers?" Luca challenged.

The other racer finally pulled up, pounding his fist on the dashboard.

"Better luck next time, eh Tristen?" Luca taunted him.

"Get off your high horse, British boy. Next time I'm whoopin' your ass."

Luca, still seated on his motorcycle, revved up the engine as the crowd cheered for him. Another motorcycle pulled up into the front of the house.

"Mattic, is that you?" Luca asked with surprise. "Mate, I didn't even know you still went to this school! No one sees you anymore!"

Mattic's hair, despite the drastic hair-frizzing wind from his drive, was thin and flat enough to rest perfectly straight on his shoulders.

"Were you two the ones I saw racing down by Clark road?"

"Yeah, what of it?"

"You know that's illegal, right?"

Luca started to laugh.

"Are you serious? Are you really giving me a morality talk? The same guy who misses more class than he has friends?"

"I'm just asking if you knew. I never said anything about morality."

"Alright, pretty boy. Enough semantics. You wanna race? I could go for another win tonight before I turn in."

Mattic's face widened to a half grin as he pulled his bike up on the road. The crowd cheered again as Luca pulled up next to him and revved up his engine.

"Okay, we drive down all the way to Clark, make a right, get off on the road at the park, then maneuver back. You got that?"

"Crystal," Mattic said in his usual collected voice.

One of the girls walked over to Luca, gave him a kiss on the cheek, then went forward and waved them off.

On the signal, they both took off on their bikes, instantly leaving the group behind.

The race was even at first, with Luca slowly but steadily gaining a lead. The first test came when the road reached a curve. In this part of town, there were very few streetlights, so the roads weren't very well lit. All they could see was what their headlights would show them. The curve's edge ended abruptly around a lake, so they couldn't go too fast without risking falling in.

Both racers slowed down slightly as they prepared for the turn. Luca slowed down the motorcycle just enough to turn towards the inner curve of the road. Mattic instead chose to keep as much speed as possible and turned the curve much wider, skirting the edge of the lake by less than a foot. After the curve, while Luca attempted to gain back his speed, Mattic flew past him with very little effort.

Luca sped up as fast as he could. They were about to reach the most dangerous intersection where they had to turn onto Clark road. The intersection was monitored by streetlights, so they had to be careful for traffic when they arrived. As Mattic approached the intersection, Luca figured he would use the opportunity when Mattic slowed down to catch up to him. Much to his surprise, Mattic drove right through the red light and turned onto Clark with only minimal braking.

"What is this guy's deal?" Luca asked himself as he approached the intersection. Had there been a car crossing at that moment, Mattic would have been run over with ease.

Throughout the rest of the race, Mattic had a consistent lead as Luca struggled to keep up. Realizing that Mattic was taking high risks with his turns and maneuvers, Luca figured that emulating him was the only way to catch up to him. As they reached the park, Luca had to make a left onto the road that went right through the park. A car was approaching from the opposite way. If he waited for the car to pass before he turned, there was no way he would catch up to Mattic, so he went for it.

Luca turned the motorcycle as best as he could onto the left in advance of the car that was approaching him. He yelled out in fear as the vehicle honked its horn and he skidded right towards it. He missed the car by what appeared to be a few inches and drove into the park. His heart pounded against his chest as he tried to recover from his near-death experience. He was sure a cop would catch them doing this.

The road worked its way around as it directed itself back onto the road where they first started racing. Only one more turn and then it was a straight shot back to the house. Going top speed, he seemed to be catching up to Mattic. The turn was coming up, and the road they were in ended directly at the lake. They had to pull off that final left turn with perfect accuracy if they wanted to make it at high speeds without plunging into the water.

Much to Luca's surprise, Mattic actually slowed down for the final turn. It seemed he wasn't as crazy as he figured. Luca used the turn to gain some ground and was almost neck and neck with Mattic on the final stretch home. He sped up the bike to gain the extra distance necessary to catch up to him. Unfortunately, it seemed like he wouldn't have time to do it before they reached the finish line. In desperation he rode faster knowing full well it was over.

Suddenly, he started gaining speed. Out of nowhere he caught up to Mattic and even passed him. Only he knew he wasn't driving any faster than before. Mattic had actually slowed down! Luca gained just enough of a lead to cross the finish line first. He stopped the motorcycle in front of the house, but Mattic didn't stop. He continued going and drove off.

"Guess he's a sore loser!" one of the cheering students yelled out at him. "Right Luca?"

"Heh, yeah," Luca said as he caught his breath. He was still trembling from all the maneuvers he pulled off that last race. He couldn't understand it. Mattic gave him quite the run for his money but then let him win. He wasn't even sure if that's what happened.

"Alright guys, show's over. I'm done for the night," Luca said as he got off his bike and walked inside. "I need some water."

He was done racing for a while.

Tony followed the crowd back inside and found Mason.

"Tony, I was looking all over for you!" Mason said. "We gotta go. I'm parked out back."

The ride back was silent. The other two fraternity brothers were sleeping in the back. Mason looked over at Tony.

"I'm surprised you're still up. Figured you'd pass out like Beavis and Butthead back there."

"Nah, I didn't drink as much as I hoped cause *somebody* wanted to leave early."

"Hey man, I'm driving back to the Keys tomorrow bright and early. I need to get some sleep. I don't want to spend my whole Thanksgiving break sleeping at home. That's what school is for!"

They both laughed as Mason pulled up by Terra Hall.

"Alright man, here's your stop. Have a good break, alright?"

"Yeah, you too."

Tony waved as Mason drove off and then headed to the motel-like hallways of Terra Hall. The building seemed unusually empty. Most of the students had either already gone home, slept early for their upcoming ride home, or were still out partying. Tony walked down the outside hallway until he found his room near the end. He saw that the lights were still on in his room.

Weird, he thought to himself.

His roommate told him he'd be gone much earlier during the day. He figured he probably just forgot to turn off the light.

Tony fumbled through his keys while balancing himself on the railing. He was still drunk and tried to get back into his room before his RA found out he was drinking.

He finally found the right key and opened the door.

At first, he thought he was going delusional. He wasn't in any way a lightweight, but he had surprised himself in the past with how easily he would get drunk. It was probably why he hesitated at the sight he saw in his room. After he realized that what he was looking at was real, he began throwing up at the entrance to his room.

Lying on the floor was his roommate Tyler with a pool of blood spread out around his bloody, lifeless head and a nine millimeter handgun lying next to him.

CHAPTER 19: CHEYENNE WINTERS
MARCH

"What are you doing with your interviews?" Nancy asked as she wandered into my office.

My desk was filled with hundreds of index cards all over, each having sections and snippets of my previous interviews taped to them. I had been in my office at least thirty hours in the past two days. My eyes were weary and my body ached, but I continued to sift through the index cards for any hint or a sign.

"There must be a theme or a clue in one of these interviews. You said it. One of the students in Dr. Garcia's class, one of the students I'm interviewing, wrote a suicidal letter and is at risk. I need to figure out who it is. I've talked to them enough. I've gotten to know them. One of these interviews has to have the answer!"

I finished looking through a pile of cards and picked up another.

"Cheyenne, how long have you been in here? You're a mess! Come with me, let's go do something like we normally do. Take a break."

"No! I can't take a break. One of our students' lives are in danger and you want to go eat a burger? What's wrong with you?"

"Cheyenne, you need to calm down. You're not doing anyone any favors if you work yourself this hard. Look, whether we like it or not, Lynn Sawyer is looking into the case. Leave the detective work to her, okay? Let's just do what we're both here to do."

I stopped what I was doing and turned my chair around.

"Really, Nancy? You're bringing up Sawyer? That good-for-nothing that's found out squat about the case here? That nutjob that interrogates every student like they're suspects and tries to use her intimidation techniques on students that are already stressed from school, their home lives, and from neglectful college staff who care more about their pay checks than the students who keep them employed! You're just like all the rest of them

Nancy. You don't care about these students. You're just like Shandra and the rest of those cracks that worry more about the university's integrity than that of the students. At least they're upfront about it, though. You, on the other hand, try to conceal it with a fake smile and superficial words of support. Such as when you act like you actually care about Mason's classes or Gabriella's language deficiency. Give me a break!"

Nancy's smile faded.

"What's wrong with you, Cheyenne? You're not acting like yourself. You need to keep in mind that you're technically not supposed to be doing this."

"Well you know what, Nancy? This is your fault! If I recall correctly, you're the one that asked me to research this case, remember? Why did you do it? Was it another part of your facade? I bet you do this to ease your guilt of how useless you are, isn't it?"

"That's enough! You need to stop talking like that! First of all, I asked you to help with the case because I really do care about these students. But my hands are tied. What do you expect me to do? Follow the students around all day to make sure they're all happy and perfect? I'm not superhuman, Cheyenne. I help the students in the way that my position allows me to. I'm a student advisor. I advise them, that's it. And your job was just to interview them. It was a mistake to ask you to get involved. Especially since you'd use it as an excuse to obsess over your research."

"What are you talking about? I care about these students, unlike the rest of you."

"Save it. It's pretty obvious that these students are just another experiment to you. You don't care about them. You're just frustrated right now because you're dealing with a case study you can't solve. You're an obsessive overachiever. Your successes in grad school with your case studies and projects made you feel invincible. You thought you could conquer everything with your theories. Well let me give you a wakeup call, hun. This isn't a case study. These are real students with real problems. In real life, there are no right answers and sometimes, no answers at all! Your obsession with this case isn't going to do you or the students any favors, especially with that perfectionist attitude of yours. And frankly, I really don't feel like dealing with your attitude. Do whatever you want, but count me out."

Nancy stormed out of my office leaving me to my research. I looked back at all the index cards laying around the desk and even the floor and suddenly noticed the pulsing headache that's been plaguing me for hours. I covered my face in my hands and suddenly started crying.

I didn't know why, exactly. There was a mix of emotions running through me at any given time. I was angry at Nancy, probably because she brought up points that I was too proud to admit or notice. But I was also hurting. It hurt me that she could say that I didn't care about the students. My interviews with the students helped me connect to them in a way I had never connected with anyone. I cared about them like my own children, and to think that one of them could be in danger made me panic. I wanted to help them however I could. However, even only a handful of interviews apiece with them equated to over a thousand transcribed pages. It was unrealistic to think that I could go over all those pages of dialogue to find out which of my students were suicidal. But I didn't know what else to do. I felt so helpless.

I was so stressed and nervous that I started fiddling with my glasses and my bangs again. I took notice of my actions. It had actually been a long time since I had done those things. It felt unnatural to me. Looking back, I noticed that the last time I defaulted to my nervous gestures was the beginning of the semester back in January during my first few interviews. Ever since I got to know the students, my reactions of insecurity quickly faded away. I felt more comfortable around them and other people in general. As I continued to think back to my first interviews, I started to notice just how much my relationship had changed with the students since I first met them.

Nancy was partly right. At first these students were merely subjects for my own personal research experiment. I matched each of them with their appropriate student development theory, then proceeded to analyze them based on previous studies done on similar students. I didn't take into account everything that made them unique as individuals, or really care about their lives other than what was directly relevant.

But once I started hanging out with them, whether it was at a restaurant, ice skating rink, church, or cheerleading practice, I started to connect with them in a more personal way. I understood them and their feelings. And I felt much better about myself. They gave me the social interaction that I desperately needed. And part of my obsession now was to preserve that relationship. I didn't want my idealistic bubble to pop by finding out that one of my new friends was actually troubled and depressed. Somehow I made this a personal issue.

I had stopped crying and instead leaned back on my chair and closed my eyes. College is supposed to be a wonderful time to mature and explore the wonderful experiences of life. However, I already had my chance to go to college and it was time for me to move on. They were the college students now and not me. I needed to stop making this all about me and start thinking about what was best for them. One of them was in danger, and rather than obsess over whether or not I was capable of solving a real-life version of my graduate projects, I had to think more realistically and accept the fact that I might not succeed.

With everything in life there is a level of risk. Unlike in the perfect-scenario case studies we did in school, the issues that we deal with in life do not always have a resolution, and we will sometimes lose. I needed to do my best to solve this case to help these students out, but I had to accept the fact that I may be setting myself up for failure. But that shouldn't stop me from trying.

I quickly went back and looked at my index cards lying around the table. After my argument with Nancy and my own self-reflection, I had cleared my head enough to see the information from a new angle.

I glanced over the interviews and information I had on all twenty one students looking for any themes, details, or trends that could lead me to conclude they were depressed. A couple of the students showed symptoms, but it was hard to tell for sure. Mitch, for example, was dealing with family problems with his mother going to jail as well as pressure from other students who mocked him for being a "suspect" in the student deaths. Ben also seemed to be showing signs of depression. I didn't get this information from him, but from some of his friends who described him. In fact, Ben seemed to be following a similar trend to Caleb, the third suicide case. Both of them seemed to seclude themselves from the rest of the campus. Since Ryan's death, Ben had been keeping to himself in his room, not talking to anyone unless it was school related. I even recalled him telling me that his talks with me were the longest he's had in a while. He was someone I needed to watch out for.

I looked through some more notes just to make sure I wasn't missing anything. Rachel took her breakup hard, but she seemed to have recovered from it. And then there was Gabriella. I had very little to work with when dealing with her since I could never get an interview with her. Any info I had was given to me by Lisa. Gabriella had a very hard time starting school. She had a huge language barrier and couldn't get along with others due to her shyness. Her only friend abandoned her in favor of other friends. That could have kept her bitter. It wouldn't make sense, though, since she and Lisa made up. It would be hard to imagine that someone with so much support from her best friend could contemplate suicide. Then it hit me.

My eyes suddenly widened as I finally noticed a pattern that wasn't there before. I quickly sifted through some of the earlier piles of index cards that I looked over a few hours ago. I finally had found what I was looking for, and my suspicions were right. Nancy had given me a little bit of info on the suicide letter that they found. It was a student who was stressing over everything going on. It involved seclusion, too much responsibility, and having to watch over someone constantly. It was someone who tried to hide their own insecurities and problems by focusing on that of others. And by the looks of the handwriting, it was possible the writer was a girl.

After looking at the index cards, I pulled up the interviews I had with Lisa Perez.

BIO: GABRIELLA MONSÓN
MIAMI, FL

I've been in the United States for only three years. My English is very limited. My family came here from Honduras. After almost ten years of waiting, my father got approval from, how you say, immigration services, to come to this country. He came in a few years back and tried to make a life here. Then he asked for my mother and me and my three brothers and sisters to come. It was magical! I always wondered what it was like in America. My mother would tell me stories about it. All the clean roads, air conditioners, and a place full of the light skinned people we only saw near the capital in our country. I couldn't wait to go. I didn't even care that I was leaving my whole life behind me by doing this.

Once I arrived, though, all the happiness went away. My mother was a teacher in Honduras. Teaching was one of the most respected jobs there. She was paid well and got lots of vacation time and respect. Here, her Honduran degree didn't matter. It was the equivalent of a high school diploma and no one would hire her. She had to get a job as an underpaid cook at an asylum. My dad worked in construction. The money wasn't that bad, but I felt bad for them. Their jobs were so much better in Honduras. Here, they were treated like slaves.

My siblings and me didn't have a good time, either. My little brother and sister struggled in school and didn't understand American culture. The teachers discouraged speaking Spanish in the classroom, and that's all we knew how to speak. But it was worse for my older brother and me. My brother entered the country as a senior in high school. He couldn't pass his classes because he didn't understand the language. And the Spanish aid departments didn't help. They treated him like a remedial student unwilling to learn, but he tried. He really tried. I started as a sophomore. I knew very little, but my reading and writing was a little better than the rest of my family.

That was thanks to Lisa. I made friends with her when we moved here, and she helped me. She worked with me and with her help I managed to finish high school. I could read and write enough to help me graduate, but I couldn't really speak it. Lisa then convinced me to come with her here. Being her best friend, I decided to join her.

CHAPTER 20: INTERVIEW #LP06
LISA PEREZ

Hi Lisa, how did your test go?

It was okay. I got a C, but at least I passed. My professor really needs to do a better job explaining things in class. She just stands there and lectures all day without trying to see if we understand what she's saying or not. I can't wait until I finish that class.

How are things going everywhere else?

[She sighs.]

I'm not really sure, Cheyenne. Everyone just seems to be having problems everywhere. Gaby actually tried to go out and meet new people, actually be social for a change, but then she withdrew right back into her comfort zone. I'm not even sure why. She just chickened out. Meanwhile, I've been doing homework and studying with Prachi again. She lives in the room next to us, and I was kinda happy that I was starting to make some friends again, only to find out that she was in just as bad of a shape as Gaby.

It was great at first. Even though we didn't have any other similar classes other than University 101, studying together really motivated us. We chatted together, laughed together, and even had dinner together every now and then. We hadn't talked since the Ryan incident, so hanging out again felt like we were becoming friends for the very first time. I even started wondering what I would do about Gaby if the whole process from the fall started again where I would be making other friends and wouldn't have time for her.

It didn't matter. Soon, Prachi's true colors began to shine, and she started talking about all her problems. It was fine at first, but then I just started to feel overwhelmed. She kept telling me about how she felt that Ryan's suicide was her fault, how now she didn't have anyone to work with on homework assignments and didn't want to go to that crowded lab anymore. Her stress kept her from concentrating on her assignments. Apparently this semester her classes were twice as hard as the ones from last semester. She complained about how her roommate Jessica would wake up every single morning before six to go running either with her ROTC group or with Zachary and Dylan.

Prachi was usually up until two or three in the morning, well after I left the study lounge to go to bed. That's why getting woken up at five or six in the morning was causing her problems. She was really stressed out and didn't get any sleep. They fought constantly about it. Prachi wanted a room change but the only hall with any available rooms left was the one where Caleb died, and she didn't want to live anywhere associated with death after what she went through. Jessica just refused to move. She said she already had all her stuff there and she wasn't the one with the problem.

It felt to me like Prachi was going to crack. She vented to me almost every night we were studying. Honestly, I think that's the only thing that was keeping her sane. But once I left the study room and went back to my room, I had to hear all of Gaby's problems as well. She would tell me about her crush on one of her professors, and to help her decide where she should hold her fantasy wedding. At least that was amusing. But she complained about how she just couldn't get a grasp of certain English words, or how she felt constantly isolated from the rest of the campus.

"Well duh!" I would yell out. "Of course you feel isolated! You do this to yourself! You isolate yourself! Maybe if you went out and tried to make other friends like I've been trying to get you to do you wouldn't feel like this."

However, whenever I would say that, she would get all upset with me and then I had to deal with guilt for the rest of the night. It's really hard being everyone's stress reliever. I feel so bad for them. They have all of these problems and I just don't know how else to help them other than just sitting down and listening.

Lisa, there's a counseling center on campus that's designed to help students who are stressed and dealing with personal problems of any kind. Have you tried getting them to go?

No, it's not that extreme. They're not crazy or anything. They're just dealing with some personal issues and want someone to hear them out.

I understand that. But I think you might not fully understand the purpose of the counseling center. The counselors there specialize in all sorts of student issues. They don't have to be crazy to go see a counselor. They're here to do what you have been doing, which is hearing them out. They also have the added benefit of having a degree and many years of experience under their belt. I would really bring it up to them, maybe even offer to walk over with them if it helps. If you don't feel comfortable doing that, tell your RA and she can help you out. While I'm not familiar with the housing department here, I'm fairly certain all RAs go through training to deal with this kind of situation.

Really? I suppose I can try. I don't know about my RA, though. Kimberly seems scatterbrained most of the time. She was great at first, enthusiastic about getting to know everyone and even took the time to get to know me and Gaby. But as the year went on the only person she would really hang out with was Amy. She was always busy dealing with her meetings, paperwork, and classes. Apparently she wasn't one of the most popular RAs in her staff. She was kind of like the Gaby of the RAs. She tended to stay to herself often, rather than associating with the other RAs of the building whenever they got together.

I'm guessing maybe I can try bringing up counseling to Gaby and Prachi. Though that's kinda weird. How am I supposed to just go up to them and tell them they should see a counselor? Either they'll think I think they're crazy or they'll think I don't want to deal with them anymore.

That's the thing, though. I can't worry about their problems all the time. I have my own issues, too. My mom really wants me to go back home, and it hurts me to be away so long. I'm really starting to think it would have been better if I just went to community college. School's been tough and I'm not really having a good time. I'm out there helping everyone else with their problems, but who's worrying about helping me?

ROLAND NUÑEZ

BIO: JESSICA EVANS
ENID, OKLAHOMA

I'm an Oklahoma girl, always was, always will be. It's a wonderful state with wonderful people smiling at you at every turn. Me? I'm a nice person too, but people are sometimes caught off guard by my personality. I grew up with four brothers, so I spent my entire childhood playing catch-up in everything, even with my little brother Kyle. Sports, 4-wheeling, farming, you name it. Even though I'm a girl, they wouldn't take it easy on me. Except for Henry, he took it easy on me, and honest to God, that pissed me off even more. My other brothers at the very least saw me as an equal to them, constantly testing my boundaries to see how close I can come to beating them. Not Henry, though. God bless him, his heart was in the right place, but letting me win didn't make me feel better. It felt degrading more than anything.

Dan and Jacob taught me just about everything I know to this day. I was dedicated. Always have been. At one point I even managed to beat Jacob at football! That was quite the moment of shame for him when he got beaten by a girl. But it's all dandy. Our family is close, closer than other families. That says a lot, considering how close the families in our town tend to be. But we had to be that way, since we were limited in how often we spent together.

My older brothers were in the military. It was split, actually. Dan and Henry joined the army, while Jacob decided to do Air Force. I was always the pro-army side, planning to enlist when I got old enough. However, the loss of my brother Henry changed everyone's plans. My family no longer wanted me to join the army. They said it was too dangerous. Troops were being sent out in droves, with not many of them coming back. They were harsh times, and they didn't want me to be next. I protested and resisted, as I saw myself as an equal to Dan. But out of respect for my brother, I decided to heed their warnings. I joined the Air Force instead of the army.

They say it's much "safer." Safer, right. If going into the military you're too worried about safety, then you're looking in the wrong field. Even though I decided to join Air Force, I did it on my terms. Rather than enlisting like my brothers before me, I decided to join the ROTC program here. At the very least if I'll be joining the "Chair Force" as they call it, I want to be as involved in the leading process as possible.

CHAPTER 21: HUSHED HOLIDAY
DECEMBER

Florida winters weren't known for their freezing temperatures and blankets of snow. Instead, the season was introduced through the various holiday decorations around the campus and constant student excitement to go home for the break. Finals for most students were over, with only the sturdiest of professors holding out until the last day of finals week. The campus invited visitors and onlookers in with a festive design. Even the tower had Christmas lights from top to bottom that were turned on every evening. Its brightness consumed the whole campus in elegance and beauty.

The interior of the tower was just as beautiful, lined with wreaths, lights, and Christmas trees. Students were running back and forth getting their final affairs in order before heading home for the next few weeks. Shuttle arrangements were made to the international airports, as well as holiday parking arrangements for their vehicles.

Alia was at the records and registration department to register for spring classes, along with dozens of students who also waited for the last minute. After twenty minutes in line, she was finally called up to the counter at the end. Much to her surprise, Miyu was manning the counter. They still weren't on speaking terms, so the encounter felt awkward.

"May I help you?" Miyu said in her routine manner.

"Hi Miyu. I see you got a job."

"Yes, I did. How may I help you?"

Alia gave her the registration slip for her to input into the computer. Miyu took the slip and began typing away in silence.

"How have you been? Life treating you well?" Alia asked.

"It's been okay. Same as always," she responded without looking over.

"Miyu, why are you acting this way? This isn't like you. We got into an argument over a month ago. Are you still that upset over it?"

Miyu finished typing and printed out Alia's spring semester schedule.

"You had a web hold on your account which is why it didn't let you register online. It was a computer error. I fixed it and got you enrolled, so you're good to go. Have a nice day."

Alia took the schedule in silence and looked at Miyu one last time for a response. It seemed that Miyu was done with her. She picked up her backpack and walked away from the counter.

"It wasn't the argument," Miyu said as she walked away.

Alia stopped and turned around.

"What?"

"It wasn't the argument that upset me. I've gotten into arguments with people before. It's the way you treated me specifically. You stopped talking to me. Even after I got over the argument and wanted to forgive you, you just stopped all contact with me. I talked to you and you pretended I didn't exist. You and your childish grudges. That was very disrespectful and it hurt me. It hurt me more than if you had just yelled at me point blank."

"Forgive me? You're the one that was trying to forgive me? Don't you see what you're becoming, Miyu? You're turning into the rest of those shallow, superficial sorority girls that hurt others with your sarcastic remarks. When I merely suggested that you consider leaving that sorority, you attacked me and told me I was jealous. You made fun of me. No one in my family, not even my parents, treated me with such disrespect like you did. It shocked me and I didn't want it to happen again, so I just stopped talking to you. I was protecting myself from you. You started out as such a sweet person, but that sorority has turned you into someone else, and I don't want to have any part of it."

Alia walked off with a group of students awkwardly staring at the encounter. Miyu turned red with embarrassment when she realized how many people overheard the conversation.

"Next," she said sheepishly.

Sam walked up to the counter.

"May I help you?"

Sam slapped a registration form on the desk.

"Hey doll, I'd like to order a helping of spring classes and a side of fries, please."

His cheesy grin made Miyu feel uncomfortable. She took the registration form and began typing the courses into the computer.

"I'm sorry, but it appears you have a registration hold."

"Excuse me?"

"It looks like your funding didn't go through to the spring semester. You have nothing to pay for these classes."

Sam slammed his hands on the desk.

"What? You're telling me that I can't register? That I have no funds? Do you know what I had to go through to stay in this school?"

"I'm sorry, Sam, but-"

"Listen little green-haired missy, I have been given the SVU grand tour at least five times in the past few months to get my funding taken care of. Some unworthy pawn managed to screw up my financial aid and the forms ended up going to the wrong person. I had to go to the Financial Aid department, who then sent me to the Bursar's department, then the Registration department right here, then the student employment office for some reason, then the scholarship office, and then guess where they sent me? Right back to the financial aid office! It took me almost one full month of warnings and torture from this school before I got my affairs in order. And now you're telling me that I have to do it all again for next semester?"

Miyu looked at him, eyes widened, unsure of how to deal with an unruly customer. After spending the past few weeks looking for a job, she finally managed to get a job at the records and registration department after another girl quit. She was still new at her job considering she started last Monday.

"Yes," she responded in the quietest voice she could.

She felt Sam's glaring stare burning through her retinas. His expression suddenly transformed from a frown to a smile.

"Well then," he said in a suddenly more chipper tone. "Guess I'm on a race against time before I head off to Orlando land! SamMan away!"

He suddenly darted towards the door in a sprint, causing the papers on the counter to go flying in all directions. Miyu looked towards the door in confusion, as well as the rest of the students waiting in line.

"What in the world?" she asked before she took the next customer.

*****

Early in the morning, in her desolate room, Jessica shuffled through her things to find her only pair of closed-toed shoes. Her wardrobe mostly consisted of flip flops and her ROTC uniform boots, and she certainly wasn't going to use either of those for her checkride. The SVU regional airport only allowed closed-toed shoes on the ramp, something she didn't realize until she left Oklahoma. Back at home, whenever she wasn't barefoot, she wore her flip flops or her favorite pair of cowboy boots. She had to buy a pair of sneakers for flying purposes.

She often wondered why she decided to major in Aeronautical Science. The major itself was useless if you weren't flying a plane, and despite being in Air Force ROTC, the word on the street was that only about one percent of Air Force graduates actually got to fly aircraft. There was just something about soaring through the sky that excited her. She felt so limited on the ground and cherished the few moments she got to fly through commercial airliners. Still, her father told her that majoring in flying was ill-advised.

She went into the bathroom to brush her teeth before she left. The bathroom, much like the rest of Miller Hall, was empty for once. It was two days after New Year's Day and everyone was still at home enjoying their time with their family. Unfortunately for Jessica, due to the horrible weather they had during the fall semester, she fell very far behind in her flight lessons. Part of the reason for that was her badly-scheduled flight block. The school had her flying between one and five in the afternoon, which was the worst time to fly. Due to Florida's weather patterns, its afternoons were almost always filled with thunderstorms that grounded any planes which tried to fly. Even when the skies were clear, the air turbulence was so strong that small aircraft would have been torn apart if they attempted to fly through it.

The only way to catch up to her fellow officers by the time spring semester started was to stay on campus during the break to build more flying hours. The empty campus allowed her to schedule her flights in the most desired flight block hours, usually in the late morning or late evening. It was brutal and lonely, but she finally managed to build enough hours and experience to schedule her final checkride for her private pilot license.

She finished brushing her teeth and tied her hair up in a bun so the wind from the airport didn't make her hair go all over the place. She looked at herself one last time in the mirror before leaving. She was very tan for a White girl. All her time spent in the outdoors back at home made her appear much darker than the rest of the pasty-looking girls around her. She found it a bit ironic considering most of them were from the sunshine state. She didn't like it, however. Her tanned, toned appearance made her the target of many guys' attempts to hook up, especially those in her cadet group. Being one of the only girls there, the guys either belittled her out of jealousy or hit on her out of attraction. It annoyed her. Unlike the rest of the cadets, she often looked forward to wearing the insulated, uncomfortable ROTC uniforms as it hid her features.

She left Miller Hall and walked over to the SVU Regional Airport which was a few blocks away. It was very early in the morning, and the cool breeze made it feel more like summer morning than winter. The check-in counter at the airport was expectedly empty. Only the lone receptionist sat in the room. She quickly signed in and filled out her preflight information. The weather looked favorable so far, but that wasn't enough to make her feel comfortable. The weather around the airport changed constantly, often without warning. Microbursts were often an issue. They were little gusts of downward pushing air that could pop up even in a clear sunny day with less than a ten minute warning. If microbursts were detected, students weren't allowed to fly.

She rushed out to her plane after she finished her preflight log. She wanted to have the plane inspected and ready to fly as soon as she could. Once she was in the air, she was home-free. The plane was in great condition. Other than a few small dings along the wings and fuselage from hail, the

Cessna 172 was ready to go. Jessica sat in the pilot's seat waiting for her checkride instructor to show up.

Ten minutes later, an older gentleman walked towards the plane. He was probably in his sixties. She hadn't recognized him. She figured one of the younger pilots would be conducting the checkride. He did a quick walk-around to double check the aircraft and sat down inside next to her.

"Good morning, Jessica. My name is Harvey and I'll be your instructor today. How are you feeling?"

"I'm ready to fly," Jessica responded without hesitation.

Harvey seemed pleasantly surprised.

"Wow, you seem unusually calm for a checkride. Normally, students are fidgeting in their seats, unsure of their readiness for this exam."

"I've been waiting way too long to get this license, sir. I'm as ready now as I'll ever be."

Harvey smiled at her use of the word 'sir', then motioned for her to begin.

Jessica went through her operation procedures as she got the plane started and got clearance from the control tower to taxi towards the runway.

Everything went smoothly, from the enriching of the mixture to the checking of the flaps. She watched a Seminole take off before the control tower gave her clearance for takeoff. She watched as Harvey wrote down notes on his clipboard. The flight was very smooth and everything was going just as Jessica planned.

The winds started picking up during the second half of Jessica's checkride. She was completing her last required forty five degree steep turn when she started feeling the resistance to her flight controls. Not only were the winds picking up, but so were the gusts. Every maneuver she tried to perform instantly became twice as hard with the winds pushing the plane in different directions. At one point, she did so poorly on one of her maneuvers that Harvey told her to do it again. She did better the second time. Barely.

Jessica started to panic inside her head. She knew what she had to do. In the case of unforeseen weather, a student pilot had the option of stopping the checkride and landing the plane, rescheduling it to another day with better weather. However, Jessica did not want to do that. The students were coming back in the next day or two and it would be near impossible to schedule a checkride. She decided that she would finish this checkride one way or another.

Despite her best efforts, the rest of the exam went poorly. She did the bare minimum in some of her maneuvers, and she was sure she did below standards on others. On her approach to landing, Jessica felt defeated. She knew she wasn't going to pass the checkride. The closer they got to the ground, the stronger the winds were picking up. Her GPS was telling her that the winds on the airport were gusting at twenty to twenty five knots. She would be lucky if she even managed to land the plane.

On the back of her mind, she knew the test was already over. However, at the same time, she wasn't going to end it all on a bad note. Despite the mediocre flight, she gripped the flight controls as tight as she could as she kept the plane steady for the landing. The winds were pushing her left and right, with gusts springing the aircraft higher and lower. But she still kept the plane steady. She compensated just the right way and focused on the runway. The actual landing she pulled off was so perfect that she didn't even feel the aircraft hit the runway. It transitioned very smoothly the entire way. Even Harvey was impressed with the landing.

Jessica was pleased. Even though she failed her checkride, she at least felt comfort in knowing she made the best landing she's ever attempted.

"You passed," Harvey said as she taxied back to the parking area.

"Wait, what?" Jessica shouted in surprise.

"You passed the checkride."

"You've got to be kidding me!" she said in an impulse.

"Do you not want to pass?"

"No, of course I want to pass! I just didn't think I did very well. Was it the landing?"

Harvey chuckled to himself. The wrinkles on his face became more prominent with his gestures.

"No, Jessica. It wasn't the landing. I've flown for many years. So many, in fact, that I stopped counting ages ago. But in all my experiences I have learned to notice a good pilot when I see one. And you, Jessica, are a remarkable pilot. Your can-do attitude and determination from the beginning was already a great start. Your flight before the weather kicked in was nearly flawless. Sure, things started getting shaky when the winds picked up, but you didn't let that discourage you. Other students would have immediately quit, but you manage to push yourself as far as you could go while still keeping the aircraft safely flying. What I look for in a pilot is the ability to take a passenger from point A to point B, and that's what you did. Your perseverance and determination was an added bonus, something that they're really going to value in the Air Force."

"You knew I was in ROTC?"

"Oh come on. You call me sir and wear your hair in a bun. Call me an old geezer, but either I'm really behind in the fashion of the youngins or you're a ROTC student."

Jessica smiled as he laughed at his own joke. She passed. After years of dreaming of being a pilot, it finally became a reality.

"You do have some things to work on though," he added. "But fortunately, you have many more licenses to attain for you to work on them."

"No problem!"

The rest of the day went wonderfully. Jessica went out to treat herself at a nice restaurant. She then went to see a movie at the last possible hour they offered the cheaper matinee pricing. It was late as she headed back to Miller Hall. The sun had gone down and the streetlights were the only things lighting up the campus. The sidewalks were empty and the place was quiet. The only thing that seemed to be out of place was a set of campus safety vehicles parked outside of Miller Hall.

As she approached the building, she saw Detective Lynn Sawyer rush out of the building. Randy was outside trying to get her attention but she walked past him without stopping him. She seemed to be in a hurry.

Suddenly, Dr. Scott and Dr. Giles came out of the building doors right next to her.

"Shandra, you need to take care of this as quickly as possible," Dr. Scott told her. "She's poking her nose again. What if she finds something this time?"

"Don't worry, I'll take care of it. Meet me in Admin Hall. We'll talk to her there."

Dr. Scott walked back to the administration building as Dr. Giles rushed over to intercept Detective Sawyer before she left.

It seemed a bit strange, but Jessica was tired and just wanted to go to bed. She walked by Randy the safety officer who gave her an angry look as she walked by. She showed him her student ID to prove she was allowed to be there and he let her in just as Travis Coleman came out of the building.

"What's going on?" Jessica asked him.

"There's been an accident, Jessica. Just go directly to your room, okay? I'll check up on you in a bit and explain what's going on."

Jessica nodded and headed towards her room. She looked out one of the hallway windows and saw a lady in a light brown trench coat pull up into the nearby parking lot and approach Miller Hall. She stopped to talk to Randy and Travis. Jessica wondered if this woman had anything to do with the accident, but her thoughts were interrupted when the elevator door opened. Three guys exited the elevator wheeling out a body covered in a blanket. They left out the building doors and put him in the ambulance.

She didn't need an explanation of the accident anymore. It was becoming common occurrence at this point. What surprised her the most was that death on the campus was starting to seem normal to her.

CHAPTER 22: CHEYENNE WINTERS
MARCH

There was no time to lose. I hurried over to Admin Hall and went up to Dr. Giles' office. The reception area was empty for a Friday. Most people had probably gone home already. The only person there was a lone receptionist typing away on her computer. She had long, blonde hair ending slightly past her shoulders. Her dark outfit was contrasted by the white flower she had in her hair.

"May I help you?" Jasmine asked.

"May I please speak with Dr. Giles? It's very urgent."

"I'm sorry, but Dr. Giles is in a meeting at the moment. Would you like to leave a message?"

I started to grow irritated.

"No, I do not want to leave a message. I understand she's in a meeting but could you please at least tell her I'm here? I have something very important to tell her. Please, it's literally a matter of life and death."

Jasmine gave me guarded stare. After contemplating her options, she got up from her chair and walked to the back where the offices were. I sat down in the waiting area, nervous about what was going to happen. There was no doubt I would get in trouble for this. According to Rachel, Dr. Giles knew I was traversing waters that were off limits. I only wondered why she hadn't confronted me about it yet. If anything, interrupting her meeting to speak to her about it was the perfect means for her to kick me out of the university right on the spot.

But it was something I had to do. Someone's life was at stake here and I didn't care that my study would be ruined if it meant I could save them. Ideally, I would have taken care of it myself, but the residence halls were heavily guarded. It was better to get the right permissions to go in there before I got arrested for trespassing.

Jasmine came back after a few minutes.

"Dr. Giles said to go into her office."

"Thank you so much."

I hurried to the back offices. I had only been to Dr. Giles' office once to get her signature of approval so that I could interview the students. The office was very spacious, no doubt something that was earned for being a Dean of Students so many years. She had a large window with a beautiful sight of the campus and new, comfortable furniture around the room. Dr. Scott was already in there.

"Oh, hi Dr. Scott. I didn't mean to-"

"What do you want, Cheyenne?" Dr. Giles interrupted.

"Hi, Dr. Giles. I know this probably isn't something you want to hear from me, but I came here to tell you that I figured out which student wrote that letter."

Dr. Giles removed her glasses. Her stare without her glasses was even more intimidating.

Dr. Scott leaned forward on his chair.

"What letter? The suicide letter? How did you know anything about that? You weren't at the meeting."

My heart started to race faster. I was never good at interrogations.

"Dr. Scott, I know that I went out of line, but I found out about the letter through other means. The fact that it was found in the class that I was working with involved me in the case whether we like it or not. I've been working with these students for two months now. I've really gotten to know them, as well as their strengths, their weaknesses, their dreams, and their problems. You have to trust me when I tell you that I figured out the next student in danger of committing suicide."

"Cheyenne, you're wasting your time," Dr. Giles said. "We met with the whole classroom yesterday and discussed the letter we found. We gave them a lecture on suicides and the appropriate resources to get help. Despite whatever you may believe, Cheyenne, we are doing our jobs."

"I understand that, Dr. Giles, but do you think a discussion will deter a student who has already set their mind to commit the act? Students who are at this level of depression don't think rationally, and unless you confront them face to face, they're not going to listen to any warnings. It's just not worth it to them anymore."

"Cheyenne, I've worked in this field for over twenty years. Do not lecture me on suicides and suicide prevention." Dr. Giles started getting angry. Luckily, Dr. Scott intervened.

"Now Shandra, let's calm down, okay? I can see that Ms. Winters here cares deeply about her students. There's nothing wrong with that. We all tend to take some risks when someone we care about is in trouble. And besides, maybe a fresh new face is just what this situation needs. It may allow us to see things from a different angle. Now, Cheyenne, who is the student and what would you like us to do about it?"

I felt comforted in the fact that Dr. Scott backed me up. He was such a good mediator. It wasn't the first time he broke up fights before they started. He calmed things down between Dr. Giles and Detective Sawyer several times. I've seen how he's made students feel at ease with his natural humor and casual persona.

"Well, the student's name is Lisa Perez. I've had six interviews with her in the span of eight weeks. From my talks with her, I've concluded through racial development theory that she's struggling to find her identity as a Hispanic American. Growing up in Miami, she had no question of who she was, since everyone around her was Hispanic. She also had strong family ties. Once she came here, however, she finally felt what it was like to be a minority. Her family wasn't around to support her, and family is one of the most valued things in Hispanic culture. She tried to experiment by branching out and making White friends, but she was too scared.

"Since her roommate Gabriella was the only part of home she brought with her, she kept using her as an excuse for not expanding her horizons. She would constantly complain to me about how Gabriella is too shy to make friends, or how she had to spend so much time with her because Gabriella had no one else to turn to. In reality, it was Lisa that needed Gabriella more than Gabriella needed Lisa. It seemed like Gabriella was just fine in her room when she was painting. It was Lisa that struggled between staying friends with Gabriella and making new friends with the group she hung out with. It was merely the case of Lisa trying to decide between her Hispanic Identity and her newly-acquired 'White' identity. She struggled to manage both, and instead opted to stay isolated with her Hispanic culture."

"What's your point?" Dr. Giles asked impatiently.

"My point is, when I heard this, I started to notice that Lisa had a habit of hiding her problems and insecurities by projecting them on others. Everything she was feeling and struggling with she relayed onto Gabriella to make her seem like the stressed one. She did the same thing with her friend Prachi. Reading over the transcripts of the interviews I learned that she was in fact hurting a lot, especially since someone in her family was sick. I feel we need to talk to her and have her first accept that she's suffering from depression, then try to convince her to let us help her."

Dr. Giles looked at Dr. Scott in a concerned manner. They didn't say anything, but it looked like one knew exactly what the other one was thinking. Their eyes widened and both seemed to grow pale.

"What's going on?" I asked in confusion.

"We need to get to Miller Hall right now!" Dr. Giles exclaimed.

Dr. Giles and Dr. Scott got up from their seats and hurried towards the door. I was utterly confused, but I followed them.

"Jasmine, I'm heading out. I won't be back 'till tomorrow," Dr. Giles said as we rushed past the front of the office.

"Why are we in a hurry? What's happening?" I asked again.

"We got a call today," Dr. Scott responded. "It was Lisa's mother. She sounded a bit upset over the phone. Lisa's grandmother died this morning. They were very close and Lisa's mother was worried that Lisa didn't take it too well."

"Really? What did you do?" I asked.

"We asked her RA to check up on her. Family deaths happen all the time around here. We don't have the time to deal with every student grieving. It sounds harsh but it's true. That's why we have RAs. They take a look at the situation and if they gauge it's bad enough to warrant our intervention, they'll let us know and we'll act immediately. But her RA, Kimberly, didn't say anything, so we figured she was fine."

What he said made sense. As tragic as death can be, I knew that we didn't have the resources to sit down and work with every student who had problems. It was impractical and wouldn't allow any work to get done. But then problems like this would arise and we wouldn't be prepared for them.

We all hurried to Miller Hall and we didn't even know why. If Lisa was planning on committing suicide, there was no way we'd know exactly when she would do it. All I knew was that according to Nancy, the letter stated that the student who wrote it would be dead by the end of the week. That could have meant Friday, but it could have meant Saturday or even Sunday. There was no way to be sure.

We ran past Randy who was busy filling the entire Miller Hall parking lot with parking tickets from all the students who tried to get away with parking in the wrong zone.

"Randy, come with us. We may have a situation," Dr. Scott told him as we rushed by.

Randy nodded in his usual frowny expression as he placed a parking ticket on Sam's car's windshield.

As we entered Miller Hall, we started to attract students from all over the place. Three university staff members and a safety officer rushing through a freshman hall was out of the ordinary, and curious heads began popping up everywhere. We ran up the stairs to the third floor and headed to the south hall, with students following us. Dr. Giles tried to shoo them away, but to no avail.

It was probably our paranoia, but we were half expecting to find a dead body in Lisa's room when we entered. With all of the talk about depression and suicide, it was easy to jump to conclusions. Dr. Giles banged on the door and told the girls to open the door. She was not planning on waiting. If she did not hear movement in a few seconds, she would tell Randy to kick the door open. Students from the hall were now crowded around. The next few seconds felt like an eternity as we waited for a response.

Dr. Giles motioned for Randy to kick open the door, but it was finally opened right before he did. Lisa was at the door.

"Hi, are we having a party?" she asked with a smile.

I was honestly surprised to see Lisa smiling. I hadn't seen her smile for weeks now.

"Lisa, you seem very chipper today," I told her.

"Oh yeah, I feel great! I took your advice and went to counseling. I've seen a counselor twice this week. It really helped me out and I feel good as new!"

Even though I wasn't looking at them, I could feel Dr. Giles' and Dr. Scott's glares burning through my skin. I knew they weren't too happy with me.

"Cheyenne, you suggested she go to counseling and didn't bother to check up to see if she actually went?" Dr. Giles asked me.

"Well, I didn't exactly tell her to go. I told her to tell her friends to go for help with their problems. At the time, I didn't realize she was the one needing the help."

Dr. Scott began scattering the students.

"Alright everyone, nothing to see here. Move it along."

He began escorting students out of the hallway. Dr. Giles thanked Lisa for her time and she went back in her room.

"Cheyenne," Dr. Giles said in an almost muffled voice.

"I'm really, really sorry Dr. Giles," I pleaded. "I just thought it would be better to be safe than sorry. You know, it was my class and-"

"How can you be sure it was your class, Cheyenne? They're not the only ones that use that classroom! It's used by several classes a day. Dr. Garcia's class just happens to be the first one in there. It could have been placed there by someone in a later class, or a class from another day! See, Cheyenne, this is why we follow protocol. This is why we stick to the jobs we were assigned, so that we don't have to bring up all this commotion onto the campus. Don't you think this will spread like wildfire by tomorrow? Everyone will start to panic again, all because you quickly drew some poorly-organized conclusions!"

"I'm... I'm really sorry, Dr. Giles."

Things looked bad. I was glad that Lisa was okay, but I worried that my study was on the line. The amount of work it would take to start a new dissertation was too stressful to think about at the moment.

All of a sudden, a scream was heard from down the hall. Dr. Giles and I quickly turned around and ran towards the sound of the scream. We saw Amy running out of a room.

"What is it, Amy?" I asked.

Dr. Scott turned around from down the hall, and students who hadn't left yet once again decided to see what was going on.

Amy had tears in her eyes as she ran towards us and hugged me. I could feel her heart beating rapidly as she pressed against my chest.

"It's Kimberly! She's dead!"

BIO: JOHN MATTIC
SEATTLE, WA

I'm Mattic, and I'm a Leo. That's all you need to know.

CHAPTER 23: INTERVIEW #BB05
BENJAMIN BLAKE

[Today, Ben and I decided to meet at Clifton Memorial Park. Even though I drove by it every time I entered campus, I never actually took the time to go in it. Ben and I are sitting on a bench overlooking the pond. The weather is undergoing strong change. The brisk, cooler air of winter was starting to end, as today is the first warm day we had in months. The temperature is currently seventy five and rising. Spring is on its way.]

This park is very pretty. Considering it's surrounded by a circular road, I'm surprised it could be this serene.

Yeah, it's pretty nice. I come here every now and then when I just want a change of scenery. The road isn't really a problem. The trees around the edge of the park seem to cushion the car noises. The chirping birds also make a nice distraction. Whoever built this park was a genius. It's like adding their own piece of nature in the midst of all the madness that happens around here. I can't wait until the year is over. I wanna go home for a change.

Didn't you go home during winter break?

I wanted to, and I was really planning on it, but I got selected to join the Elite Freshman Task Force. It's a group that takes a certain number of mavericks from our University 101 classes who show signs of promise and capability and gives them some leadership opportunities for one semester. I was selected for some reason. Don't get me wrong. I'm a good student with some good grades, but the fact that I got selected over some of the other students in my class was really strange to me. If they look at intelligence for the organization, then my friend Prachi should have gotten in. She's one of the smartest people I know. As far as showing promise, I'm surprised that guy Renzo didn't get in. Despite his narcissistic attitude, he's definitely a good businessman who knows how to get what he wants.

Anyways, the EFTF offered us all a Christmas trip to New York for a conference where we would participate in workshops hosted by big business leaders and educational seminars. We even got a tour of Trump Tower! I didn't want to go at first, since I was anxious to go home and see my mom. But when I told her about that opportunity, she insisted that I go. She said it was the best kind of opportunity for me to get ahead. She said I could learn so much and network with important people. She eventually convinced me to go, and I'm glad I did. Spending Christmas in those fancy hotels around Times Square was amazing! I had never seen snow, and around that time it was full of it! Everything about the trip was amazing. The rooms, the atmosphere, and the food were all the greatest I had in my life. We even got to visit the Christmas tree at Times Square for New Years. Being around all those people counting down to New Years was exhilarating.

Still, I really miss being at home. I'm definitely going to go during spring break next week, so I'm excited for that. But the greatest thing I'm looking forward to is spending the summer in my own bed at home, and not in the bottom bunk of my stuffy, empty room.

Is your roommate still out a lot?

Yeah, Mattic is off doing his own thing as always. It's hard to figure that guy out. The first month that we live together he barely says a word to me. It wasn't until our midterm with Dr. Garcia that we teamed up in a group and we were forced to talk to each other.

I got to know him a bit better that week. I realized that he wasn't an uncaring jerk like I originally thought he was. He just seemed to have priorities in other areas. School wasn't a big deal to him. He did just enough to slip by, but spent the rest of his time in his hobbies. Up until then, I had no idea what those hobbies were. After the assignment, we began to talk a bit more and he told me. He was all about extreme sports. He loves the thrill of putting himself in danger. Every time he'd go out, he would take his motorcycle to different places to race other enthusiasts. I don't even know how they find each other.

In addition to motorcycles, he loves dirt bikes and goes riding out in the woods in the foresty parts of Florida. He skateboards, roller blades, bungee jumps, skydives, and just about any other physics-defying activity you could think of. This guy is crazy! I don't know how he can possibly go out there and put his life in danger by choice!

He asked me if I wanted to join him a few times. Now that was a crazy idea. Me, out there skating off ramps and such? No way! Now, call me a sheltered mama's boy if you want, but I fear for my safety. I'm a very careful person. I tried to get more involved in college, I really did. I even started hanging out with our Miller group, as I'm sure some of my friends have told you about. We would walk over to the movie theatre, go to the park, and the real park, not this SVU park imitation, and just have a great time. I didn't even care that we'd be walking down the side of a road at one in the morning back to campus, despite the obvious danger that put us in. Some drunk driver could have run over us for sure!

But after Ryan's accident, I just couldn't do it anymore. Rumors were flying everywhere left and right about how he died. While the general consensus was that he committed suicide, no one was fully sure. The fact that there was a possibility someone killed him frightened me to no end. I couldn't take it anymore. If I was scared to do things before, that incident scared me even more than that. I started to keep to myself. I stopped talking to Mattic again. I went to school and came right back home, avoided going anywhere and talking to anyone. I was afraid to trust anyone again. I feared that if I got close to them, they would either betray my trust and try to kill me, or do like Ryan did and get themselves killed which hurt me even more. I wouldn't say I was particularly close to Ryan, but his death traumatized me in a way. Not just me, but the rest of our core group. You see death in the movies all of the time, but until you experience unexpected death right there in front of your eyes, it fails to compare to the real thing.

It's amazing how quickly people get over death in the movies. Someone dies, people mourn, but usually someone else comes to comfort them and boom! They're better in a day or two. The only people you see suffer for a long time are usually depicted as crazy or mentally ill in at least some form. The truth is, unless you're exposed to death all the time, something like a friend's suicide can affect you greatly. Especially when you didn't see it coming. Ryan was a great guy. He would play with us, laugh with us, and offer a helping hand when we needed it. He seemed like a happy person. When he died, all we could ask was "why". Why did he do it? What went wrong in his life that he decided to kill himself?

And then guilt begins to wash over you. I know I felt really guilty about it. I felt stupid for not noticing any signs, or for not offering more words of encouragement. I felt at least partly responsible for his death. There is always more you can do to tell someone you appreciate them, and it's not until it's too late that you realize it. It was hard, but I know that Prachi took it the hardest. She and Ryan seemed to have a thing going on. I'm not much into gossip, so I didn't care to find out more, but whatever it was they had, his death really changed her. While I'm finally starting to feel better about it, I really don't think she has recovered. She's still stressed out at school more than ever, refusing to work with anyone until recently. I've seen her doing homework with Lisa again, but that's about it.

How did you cope with it?

Well, at first I really didn't. Like I said, I secluded myself from the rest of my world and just kept to myself. Most of my social interaction involved message boards. As a gamer, I often visited this website called Gamefaqs where people from all over the world discussed games and all sorts of other stuff from the comfort of their own home. I browsed its Current Events forum under the alias named AquaSphere. It's all I really needed. I kept up with current news and got to live vicariously through my online persona.

But after going to that trip during winter break, I realized just how much better I felt hanging out with others again. I felt so included and at home. I realized that college was the perfect place to get to know so many people, especially with opportunities such as that one where they'll pay for you to go out and have a good time.

As a result, I started getting involved on campus. I started going to the gaming club meetings with Tobias again. It was pretty funny, actually. I found out earlier on that Tobias visited the same online forum too, so even though I rarely saw him in person, I chatted with him all the time online without knowing it was him. But it was nice to be going out again.

I figured I'd join more organizations. I looked around at the Spring Semester Activities Fair to see what was available. There were clubs for just about every interest out there. Horseback riding, anime, choir, sports, cultural groups, and even rock collecting had representation. Unfortunately, there wasn't anything related to Marine Biology which was my interest. I found that kinda weird since we lived in Florida.

Did you find anything you liked?

Yeah, there were a few things here and there I tried out. I joined the business club for a day, but it bored me to death. I knew that wasn't for me. I also tried radio club to get some radio experience, but their meeting times conflicted with my schedule. Then there was this other club I joined which seemed very inviting. The guy at the booth was really nice to me. I wasn't sure about the premise of their club, but he said it was meant to invoke leadership and responsibility in all of its members. It sounded just like the Freshman Leadership Task Force I joined, but even better as you could join it for more than one semester. So I joined.

I got to meet some of the other members. It was a really big club from what I saw. But the mission statement of the organization was perfect for what I was trying to do. The club was called Second Chance, meant to help students who had lost their way find their way back towards their right path. It has really helped me out. I can't really share too many details as they have a fraternity-like secrecy thing going for members only, but our meetings often involved group activities and icebreakers meant to make us more confident and trusting of each other. They really know how to take care of you.

It has really given me a different view to my life compared to when I first arrived. Like my friend Tobias told me, it doesn't matter who you are coming in, it's who you plan to be when you get out. There's a lot of truth to that in college.

That's good to hear, Ben. It seems you really enjoy that organization. Who's the president?

Oh, like I said, I'm not allowed to say. We're sworn to secrecy. It's the family rule.

So there's nothing more you can tell me about it?

No, not really. To be honest, I probably wasn't supposed to tell you this much. But you're pretty trustworthy, so I figured there's no harm.

Thank you, Ben. Thanks for the interview. I'll call you if I need anything else, okay?

Anytime!

> *[Ben gets up and heads back towards his dorm. I sit there for a few minutes trying to process what he just told me. Second Chance. I had heard that phrase before. It was on the note Caleb supposedly wrote. The phrase repeatedly runs through my head as I try to determine if there's any correlation: "There are no second chances."]*

BIO: GRACE COLLINS
TITUSVILLE, FL

My name is Grace Collins. I am from Titusville, Florida. Some of my hobbies involve hiking, writing, and bead stringing. I especially enjoy bead stringing. In fact, I tend to make a lot of my clothes. The shirt I'm wearing as I write this is made from organic bamboo fabric that my mother gave me when she taught me how to sew. I believe that your appearance defines who you are, but in a much deeper level than some people make it out to be. If you exhibit a happier aura, people will react in happier ways. This aura can be expressed through more natural colors in your wardrobe, like the clothes I wear, and a much happier smile across your face.

I can say I'm a happy person. It's something I learned from my mom. Even with the suffering she went through in her earlier years, she never gave up hope. She would tell me stories of the abuse she suffered from her parents, and the consequences of running away from home. Yet she always looked to the positives in everything. She knows she made mistakes, she doesn't deny that. But one of the most valuable lessons she has taught me growing up was to always look towards a brighter world, as that's the only way we can get there. I've noticed the truth in her teachings as I grew up.

My smiles as a child always brought happiness to even the grumpiest of strangers. Even animals could sense my bright spirit, as they would give me a certain look every now and then, like they appreciated my presence. Speaking of animals, I have lots of pets that come and go as they please at home. I have a cat at home, a few birds, and two of the most adorable little ferrets you will ever meet! That's going to be the hardest thing about being in college. Leaving Max and Pax behind at home. I know my mommy will take care of them, but they are just too cute to be away from! Even though I'm only a few hours away, being without a car is going to be problematic when I want to go home. But things will work themselves out. They always do! :)

CHAPTER 24: SPIRITS
MARCH

The day was still young. The sun had just started to peak through the horizon, lighting up the Sun Valley campus slowly but steadily. The birds were coming back, their songs resonating throughout the buildings and beyond. The campus was quiet. Most students were still tucked away waiting for the last possible minute to get up and go to class. Only the ROTC cadets were up at this hour, running through the east side of the campus before the day got too hot.

Grace had almost made it to her secret spot. Over on the northwest side of campus was a patch of undeveloped land. In this land, there was an area covered by bushes and other greenery discovered and claimed by Grace as her own. She walked around with her small watering can to feed the hungry tulips, jasmines, and daisies she had planted there. A few of them had started to sprout, and she hoped to have some full grown ones by mid spring. A quick gust of air passed along the area, bringing her long, blonde hair to life as it danced in the wind. Her string of flowers was blown off her hair and onto the grass, but she didn't notice nor care. Grace closed her eyes and allowed the breeze to caress her skin as she enjoyed the day's welcome for her.

When she finished watering the flowers, she walked further back her floral sanctuary to another area she had cleared away from twigs, leaves, and weeds. She had it neatly trimmed, and picked the location so a gap in the trees above her would allow the sun's rays to shine through like a spotlight. She looked at the three memorials she had created, all resting side by side in the most peaceful area of the campus. Each memorial was created with a finely cut block of wood, sanded and polished to display the names of each of the poor victims that came to an unfortunate end. The memorials were surrounded by freshly-picked roses that Grace placed every few days.

The breeze had calmed down in this part of the area, as if to show respect and honor for those who had passed away. Grace occasionally sat down and spoke to them as if they were alive, telling them about her day and offering words of encouragement about the afterlife.

"It's not so bad," she would say. "Go on, make friends, then enlighten and comfort us when you become a part of nature again."

She would sometimes feel their spirits respond to her soft voice. Small rushes of air would sometimes pick up leaves around the site to almost form the shape of a human, or sometimes two. She didn't know the students very well, but she had met them at least once. She made every effort to meet and remember every soul she met at the university. It was her goal to spread the joy she felt inside with everyone around. She knew that even beyond their graves, these three students appreciated that and thanked her. Grace closed her eyes and took a deep breath, recollecting her last words with the students.

*****

"Hi, may I help you?" Grace asked as she opened the door.

"Hello, I'm Ryan. Is Amy available?"

"I'll be out in a minute!" Amy yelled from inside the room as she quickly got dressed.

"Amy just got out of the shower and is getting dressed. It might take a minute," Grace said.

"Oh, that's no problem. We're not in any hurry. Prachi and I were just going to go grab some dinner and wondered if the rest of the gang wanted to tag along. You must be Grace, right?"

"Yep, that's me," she said proudly. "Ryan, tell me, what's your favorite color?"

Ryan was surprised at the random question, but went ahead and thought about it.

"I guess I'd say it's orange."

"Great! Wait right here!"

Grace ran back in her room and closed the door. Ryan waited for a minute or two before she came out with an object in her hand.

"Here, Ryan. I would like for you to take one of my 'Glad to know you' ribbons I made. I made this in orange, in the off chance that someone's favorite color was orange."

Ryan looked at the ribbon. It was very simple, made of some party ribbon stuck to a piece of fabric with the words 'Glad to know you' imprinted on it. It was a very nice gesture.

"Thanks Grace. I'll hold on to this. When Amy is finished, could you tell her to meet me in my room?"

"Sure, no problem!" Grace said happily.

Ryan walked back over to his room and found Prachi watching TV on his bed.

192

"Amy will be down in a minute. Where's everyone else?"

"Well, Ben and Tobias are on their gamer club meeting, so they won't be joining us. Lisa said she had an errand to run and said that she'll meet us there."

"That's cool."

Ryan sat down on the bed and winced in pain as he put his hands on his temples.

"What's wrong, Ryan?" Prachi said as she turned down the TV volume.

"Oh, nothing. I've just had this splitting headache these last few days. I don't know why."

"I've got some Tylenol in my room. Let me run up and go get it."

Prachi got up to leave, but Ryan grabbed her arm.

"No Prachi, wait. Please sit down. I want to talk to you."

Prachi was confused, but sat down and listened intently.

"What's up?"

"Listen, we've known each other for almost two months now, right?"

"Yeah, I'd say it's about that long."

"Have you had a good time hanging out with me?"

"Yeah, of course Ryan! What kind of a silly question is that?"

Ryan's face became flushed, either from the headache or from what he was about to say next.

"Well, I was hoping that maybe you and I could go out sometime, on a date."

Prachi looked at him and smiled.

"Ryan, I would love that, honestly. But I really can't. This is my first semester in school in a very difficult program. I'm already here against my parents' wishes. I have a lot of stuff to deal with and I really don't have the time to date right now. Don't get me wrong, I really like you and under any other circumstance I would in a heartbeat. But you just need to give me some time. I need some time to adjust and get myself situated to college. Try again further down the line, okay?"

"Okay," Ryan said with a disappointed smile.

Amy suddenly came into the room.

"So, we ready to go?" she asked.

Prachi and Ryan smiled at each other and left the room.

A few days had gone by. Midterms were finally over and Prachi was finally relieved to have finished. She was sure that the past week she had spent more time studying that sleeping, even in the weekend. She had just gotten back her last midterm which she passed with a B. Excited, she ran back to Miller Hall to show Ryan the grade that he helped her earn with his hours spent tutoring her. She knocked on the door of his room but there was no answer. She tried the doorknob and noticed it was left unlocked. It was common for the Miller

Hall residents to leave the door unlocked. People rarely stole things and the students were too lazy to take their keys everywhere.

She figured she would wait around the room for him to come back and turned on the TV. She sat down on his bed, only to hear a crinkling sound. She got up and saw that she had sat on a piece of paper. She picked it up and read it, only for the fire alarm to sound at that moment. She was about to walk out of the room until she started reading the contents of the letter.

"To whoever finds this: I know this will come as a surprise to everyone I know and care about, but I just can't deal with it anymore. Behind all my smiles and laughs there has been hurting. My parents have disowned me. They've never really cared about me but when I left to college they said they wanted nothing to do with me. They weren't even there for most of my childhood, so that should not have come to much of a surprise to me. They moved me away to Germany against my wishes, and detested me for coming back. I can't say I blame them. I was never much of a good child, but at least I tried. Here at SVU, I tried to make amends for all my wrongdoings, and I thought it was working until everything blew up in my face. I quickly made enemies, people more powerful than me that I couldn't fight. And the incident last week was the final straw. I now know that I am not wanted, and the world would probably be better off if I wasn't in it. To all my friends at SVU and anyone else who cares, goodbye."

Despite the loud alarms and stampede of students heading out of the building, Prachi froze in the room rereading the letter. She could not get her eyes off of it. She hoped that she just misunderstood what it was saying, and that rereading it would correct her mistake. Unfortunately, it was crystal clear. And reading about the incident last week struck her the hardest.

"Oh God, it was me!" she yelled out loud. "I was the last straw!"

She lost all the color on her skin and became cold with fear as she thought over the implications of the letter. After what seemed like an eternity, she walked out of the room and headed down the stairs. She was looking pale and exhausted when she met up with Tobias, Ben, and Amy.

"What's wrong, Prachi?" Tobias asked.

She held out a note in front of them.

"I found this in Ryan's room. It's a suicide note."

Luca suddenly ran down the stairs.

"Guys, guys! Have you seen the news?"

The others just stared at him.

"There's been an accident on Rodney Way! A car was totaled when it slammed against a tree. They've identified the body as Ryan's!"

*****

194

Tyler's hands started to sweat as he paced back and forth throughout the room. He was feeling anxious and torn. He knew that whatever decision he made would end up hurting someone. The only question was which decision would hurt a smaller number of people.

He tried to think back to before everything went wrong. What could he have done different? His eyes started to water from both anger and resentment. He was starting to think Mitch was right, but that just made him even more upset.

"Tyler, man, you gotta stop tryin' to be White. You're Black, you were born Black, and unless you pull an MJ, you're always gonna be Black!" Mitch told him.

"Shut up! So you're saying that just cause I'm Black means I have to act gangsta and speak the way you do? Grow up, Mitch!"

"No. What I mean is that you gotta stop talkin' down to me because I am the way I am. And you gotta stop joining those white-ass clubs just to prove who you are."

"White-ass clubs? You mean like Second Chance? What the hell's wrong with you? It's a predominantly White campus. Of course the clubs here will be mostly White students unless you join the African Students Association or something. And even they have their first White president this year."

"You know damn well that's not what I mean, Tyler. I went to one of those Second Chance meetings. While the group is all lovey dovey wit each other, there sure felt like there was a lot of hate towards those that weren't a part of it. Don't you see it? They're manipulating you! They're getting you to think like them! Like who they like. If anything, they remind me of the KKK."

Tyler remembered rolling his eyes at Mitch's comments. What did he know? He was just an uneducated lowlife from the ghetto. Tyler was raised by a well-educated family who taught him the correct way to live and behave.

But now it didn't seem to matter. His actions got himself trapped in a hole that had no other options of escape. He was tasked to do some bad things, and he wanted no part of it anymore. Too many people had already gotten hurt through his actions, and he made the decision to end it.

He hesitantly picked up the gun from his desk drawer. Trembling, he walked over to his chair and sat down. He thought back to all the people that he hurt, and all the people that he was destined to hurt if he didn't go through with it. He thought of his parents, his uncle and aunt, and everyone back at home. Tears started running down his cheeks as the reality of the situation hit him when he pointed the gun to his head. Feelings of desperation and panic began to run throughout his body. Every emotion he had kept hidden and concealed suddenly blew up right then and there, forming a myriad of thoughts and feelings that were too overwhelming for him to bear. Perhaps it was that which caused him to pull the trigger. Perhaps it was his guilt of everyone he had hurt in the past. Or perhaps it was to relieve himself of the day to day pains that tormented him as he tried to lead on a normal life. Whatever the reason was, he finally let it all go. He was at peace.

*****

"I would like to call this meeting to order," Cody said as everyone started maneuvering their way to a seat.

"Our President had other things to take care of, so as Vice President, it is my responsibility to take over for today. I would like to welcome you all to our last official Second Chance meeting for the calendar year. Within a week's time, we will almost all be gone for winter break and will not return until the new year is upon us. We have made great strides this year, with many of our members increasing their test scores by at least a full letter grade and other members tackling their greatest fears. Manny, for example, touched his first tarantula today and didn't pass out. Let's all give a warm hand of applause for Manny!"

The dozens of students suddenly blasted into a roaring applause as Manny began to blush. He instantly began receiving hugs and handshakes from everyone around him. The cheers and hugs were very passionate, as if they came directly from the heart. Caleb sat in the back of the room watching with joy as Cody announced some of the members' highlights of the week.

Caleb had been waiting eagerly for this meeting all week. Through all the loneliness and seclusion he faced at SVU, he always looked forward to spending time with people that cared about him and loved him for who he was. He had been very loyal to them, attending every meeting, paying the required fee to get in, recruiting members, and following the Second Chance honor code, which was to involve oneself in positive thinking and actions that would result in the betterment of the individual and the organization as a whole.

He went through the entire meeting with much interest and vigor, listening to all the new announcements, the plans for the spring semester, and finishing it off with singing some lively music to lift spirits. Some of the older members, mostly pathfinders and trailblazers, brought their instruments to the front and began to play songs they wrote specifically for the organization.

At the end of the meeting, as everyone began to disperse, Caleb was stopped by Cody before he managed to leave.

"You're Caleb, right?" Cody asked.

"Yeah, that's me."

"Good! We have so many new members this year that it's getting hard for me to remember all of you on the first go around! Anyway, you're in luck! You're one of the next new members selected for initiation. Once it's complete, you'll become a full member!"

Cody gave Caleb a sealed envelope.

"In here are your instructions to become a full member. They are unique to you, so no one else has seen what's inside, not even me. Follow the instructions carefully and by the deadline listed. Is that clear?"

"Sure, no problem!" Caleb said excitedly.

This was the moment he was waiting for. After pledging for two months, he was finally going to become a full member of Second Chance! When he got home, he opened the letter and read it in its entirety. It started off very formally, thanking him for considering Second Chance as his family and home away from home, and that they looked forward to having him join the ranks as one of the Second Chance Elites. The letter then went on to say that he had to complete everything he was instructed to do to be considered for full membership into the organization.

The instructions were simple enough. He looked over at them and saw very simple tasks he had to achieve. Some of the tasks involved buying simple items like paint, tape, and office supplies. Other items involved talking to other Second Chance members and asking them specific questions. It seemed like a scavenger hunt! Once he completed the items on the list, he had to turn in the list with the required items and proof that the tasks were done (usually through pictures) and hand them over to the executive board.

Caleb spent the next few days trying to complete every item on the list, excited to get one step closer to being a full member. He talked to some other members and got to know them better, finding out their reason for joining and what they wanted to get out of the organization. Once he completed the list, he ran back to Cody the day before winter break to make sure everything was accounted for.

"Cody, I finished!" he said excitedly at Cody's place.

"Excellent! Let me take a look at this."

Cody reviewed everything on the list, as well as the proof that Caleb completed all the tasks.

"Great! It looks like you're done. I'll get you a meeting with the President so that he can direct you from here. You're just one step away from being a full member!"

Those were the last words Cody managed to say to Caleb. Cody lived in his own house in Sun Valley, so he rarely left during winter break. He didn't really have any family to visit, no one he cared about, really. His full dedication was to Second Chance and make sure that the other club officers did their job. As Vice President, he ran a lot more of the day to day operations of the club. The last he heard about Caleb was that he had to stay on campus during winter break to complete his final task. A few days into the new year, Caleb was dead.

Cody couldn't believe it. He started to get worried. That was the third member of Second Chance to die this year. He knew people would start to blame the organization for the deaths. Even with the organization's secrecy policies, he was afraid that something would spill out and endanger all of the other members. He had to take matters into his own hands.

*****

Grace opened her eyes.

It was starting to get late. Class was going to start in less than an hour, and Grace had spent enough time in her secret site. She heard some rustling in the bushes behind her and saw Amy approach.

"Good, you found the place," Grace said.

Amy nodded but stayed quiet. She hadn't said anything or spoken to anyone in the past few days. She looked malnourished and defeated. It was only due to Grace's soothing voice and positive spirit that she was convinced to join her.

"Now that you're here, I can finally place this."

Grace reached into her bag and pulled out a fourth wooden block memorial, this time with the words 'Kimberly Shaw' carved into it. She had already prepared a spot next to the other three while she waited for Amy to arrive. She placed the memorial until it fit snuggly into the ground, then scattered some roses around it.

"Would you like to say a few words on her behalf?"

Amy nodded no. She still seemed depressed, but Grace could tell that the memorial helped ease her a bit. The last item she took from her bag was a violet red ribbon, Kimberly's favorite color. She laid it down beside the memorial, just like the other three ribbons adorning the other memorials, each with the students' favorite colors.

Etched in the ribbons was the phrase "Glad to have known you."

CHAPTER 25: CHEYENNE WINTERS
MARCH

I tried to catch her before she left. The work day was almost over and I didn't know when I'd ever have another chance to speak with her. Universities function like a typical business. People clock in and out to help students in every way possible, but at the end of the day, it's all for a paycheck. Unfortunately, many administrators I'd met have taken this mentality to heart and value the paycheck over the student.

I reached Carrie Sullivan's office with only a few minutes to spare. As Student Activities director, Carrie spent many office hours working evenings and weekends to help out with student events and programs. From what I have heard, she seemed to take her role as director very seriously and always put the students first in everything she did. I was counting on that.

I found her locking up her office when I arrived.

"Hi, you're Carrie Sullivan, correct?"

"Yes, that's me. How may I help you?"

"Hi Carrie, I'm Cheyenne Winters. You may have heard of me and the study I'm conducting here at SVU."

"Ahh yes, Cheyenne. I've heard plenty about you, both from the students and the staff. You've been stirring up quite the movement here!"

I raised my eyebrow at her last comment.

"What do you mean?"

"Don't you know? The students are talking about the lady who's trying to solve the suicide mystery. But unlike Detective Sawyer who's doing the same thing, she's digging deep. Very deep. Getting not only the facts and figures, but also the thoughts and feelings of all the students, even the ones only remotely involved. The students are feeling heard and cared for, something the university hasn't been doing a good job of recently. The staff is starting to notice, too. You were actually mentioned in our crisis meeting a while back. People feel you are getting too involved. Congratulations, Cheyenne. You're causing waves!"

I almost lost my balance as my head became dizzy. I had no idea I was being noticed. I figured I was just a fly on the wall, as qualitative interviews usually recommend. This wasn't a good sign. If my presence affected the study, it would make my study invalid. I was trying to study the natural habits of university freshmen, but my involvement was possibly causing them to act differently. While Carrie saw this as a good thing, I didn't agree. Regardless, I had some more pressing urges to deal with, so I put the thought aside and proceeded with my original purpose.

"Carrie, I came here to ask you about an organization. Am I correct to assume that you have a list of all the campus student organizations?"

"Yes, of course. Students are encouraged to start any organization they wish for any interest. They just need to fill out the required paperwork through our office and get it approved. What organization did you have in mind? Is it for your study?"

"Do you know of a student organization called 'Second Chance'?"

Carrie's expression morphed from a peppy smile to an ominous glance.

"How did you hear of that organization?"

"It has been mentioned in passing by one of my students. I was wondering if you had any more information about it."

I could tell by her pause that she knew something.

"This isn't for your study, is it? You really are trying to solve this suicide case, aren't you? I figured it was just stories fueled by rumors. You're serious about this. Do you know how much trouble you can get into for dealing with private matters like this? Dr. Giles is already suspicious of your actions. All she needs is a semblance of evidence to get you kicked out of the school or even file a lawsuit. They're privacy laws you're violating!"

"Carrie, I really don't have the time to explain myself. I come to you not as an employee, or a researcher, or even a student affairs professional. I come to you as a rational human being with feelings. One of my students has joined this organization. He's in a very fragile state from homesickness and I fear he could be the next suicide victim. Please, if you know anything about the organization that can help me, I would appreciate it if you told me. I promise I will be out of your hair after that. I am prepared to deal with any repercussions, but only me. I will make sure that it doesn't get traced back to you in any way. You are the only person that can help me right now."

Carrie tried to keep a firm stare, but her sympathetic nature started to leak out. Her eyes showed a sincere caring for the student I mentioned, even though she didn't know who it was. If there was one thing that I learned in graduate school about student affairs professionals, it was that the field attracts a certain type of person. It attracts people who are in tune with their emotions, often allowing their emotions to drive their thinking. They are also individuals who cherished their college experience so much that they wanted to continue living it by helping other college students. College students are their weak spots. I realized that if I wanted to get anything done around here,

I needed to think outside the textbooks. I had to exploit those lessons that I didn't learn in my graduate classes.

"Second Chance isn't a registered student organization," she said. "They've been recruiting students for a long time now, but they've been doing it under the radar under unofficial terms. We've tried a couple of times to shut them down, but their pledge to secrecy has worked in their favor. I could never get anything other than vague rumors here and there, never anything specific. By the looks of it, we could be dealing with a cult."

"A cult? How could it be a cult?"

"Cheyenne, you need to understand that cults aren't like the high profile ones that you've seen in the past or the ones you see in the media. Cults are a lot more down-to-earth than you think, manipulate students into joining them through a friendly façade, and they are rampant throughout college campuses around the nation. It is a huge concern that universities everywhere do not want to acknowledge for reputation reasons. People think cult and they immediately think extremist religious groups with cloaks, rituals, and chants. In reality, the modern definition of a cult is a group with a devotion to a particular set of values that attempt to recruit students by approaching them through friendly means and then isolating them from the rest of the world."

Everything she said seemed to make sense with what was going on at this campus.

"Do you think that the suicide victims were a part of a cult?"

"It's possible. See, cults disguise themselves as student groups that give students a false hope that they can change the world. They particularly seek out students who are weak-minded or are facing serious emotional problems and thus are vulnerable. They reach out to them through events and community-building activities to make them feel like a family. Like fraternities and sororities, they make members vow to secrecy for the integrity of the organization, but unlike fraternities and sororities, their goals aren't as socially responsible. They tend to involve themselves in questionable acts through the use of its members. If they don't follow through, the consequences are usually drastic."

"But how could the students willingly participate in such things knowing they're wrong?"

"It's all just a big mind game. They build a sense of community with the students, getting them to trust their leaders and each other. They make the students become more dependent on the group by isolating them from their friends and other contacts. They reach the point where the cult is all they have left, and they're so broken down that they will do anything to keep them. They start them off with small things at first, small things that individually aren't too crazy, like petty theft. But once they get to the bigger things, they've done enough small wrongdoings that their leaders can blackmail them into doing whatever they want."

I started getting goose bumps on my arm. The fact that such groups could exist and actually recruit unsuspecting freshmen into joining them was a scary thought.

"I've tried to get an investigation going to look into it, especially after those suicides. But the higher ups don't want to turn it into a big scandal. Like other colleges around the country, they try to keep such things quiet. None of them want parents and students to know that such practices are happening right under their noses. The third suicide is what finally made them cave in and allow Detective Sawyer to investigate. Unfortunately, everyone is tightlipped about it and some don't even believe that Second Chance exists."

"So is there anything you know for sure about this organization?"

"I've heard the name Cody Nester pop up a few times in regards to Second Chance recently. It sounds like the suicides are getting to him. I told Detective Sawyer about it and she was supposed to go interrogate him. I'm not sure what happened with that. I'd warn you to stay away from him, but I could tell by the look on your face that nothing's going to stop you from pursuing this further. So instead, all I can say is to be careful, Cheyenne. This is a very sensitive issue and a lot of people can be hurt by this."

My phone rang as I thanked her and headed out on my way. It was Dr. Giles, and she wanted to meet with me immediately in her office. I didn't even need to hear the sound of her tone to tell I was in trouble. She knew that I was looking into a case that I wasn't authorized to get involved in. My involvement with it led me to the wrong person, so while Lisa was okay, we instead lost another student. Even though that couldn't have been my fault, I know that Dr. Giles believed it was. I figured it was only a matter of time before she called me in to talk to me. I was actually surprised it took her this long. At the very least I was glad I got to talk to Carrie beforehand.

I went to her office and sat down in the waiting area. I saw Jasmine again, typing away at her computer, acknowledging my presence with a careful glance. I'm sure she knew what this meeting was about. Her expression was that of a child when her parents were about to get into a fight. She instead chose to bury herself in her work and ignore what was happening around her.

My thoughts were interrupted by some yelling. It came from Dr. Giles office. Some sort of dispute was going on in there that I strangely enough wasn't a part of. Immediately, Detective Sawyer stormed out of her office yelling back at her. I had seen this happen so many times that by now it had become routine. This time, however, it was worse. She glanced over at me as she left the room, almost as if to warn me. From the looks of it, Detective Sawyer was being kicked out, relieved of her investigation. Could Dr. Giles even do that?

Dr. Giles came out and looked over at me. She didn't need to say anything. I quickly got up and walked down to her office like I was walking down death row. Dr. Giles told me to take a seat and closed the door behind me. To my surprise, she wasn't the only one in there. She was accompanied by Dr. Scott and two other administrators who I wasn't familiar with.

"Cheyenne, I've been telling these gentlemen about your visit to our university. You came here to study our freshmen, correct?"

I nodded nervously. Even if I tried to say anything I was afraid nothing would come out.

"And in this study, you were to interview them, talk to them, and get to know them. You wanted to see what adjustment to college was like for first year students. Am I still on track?"

I nodded again.

"So tell me then, Cheyenne, some of your findings."

I looked around as the men beat me down with their stares. My anxieties started to act up, and I started fiddling with my glasses and brushing aside my bangs.

"Well? We're waiting."

Her voice sounded tense and condescending, trying to crack me open and reveal everything I've been doing.

I knew I had to say something, but I was frightened. The pressure was getting to me. My lips wouldn't move, despite my efforts to do so. I felt as all the blood left my face, leaving a pale shadow of my former self standing in front of them. As fear, doubt, and frustration ran through me, I suddenly felt free. My mind suddenly went blank, and it took a few seconds before I realized I had momentarily passed out. I had lost my balance and was about to fall face first onto a chair. It was through Dr. Scott's quick reflexes and sharp judgment that he caught me just in time to keep me from injuring myself.

"Shandra, you need to cool it down," he told her as I slowly regained consciousness. "You're going to kill the girl."

Dr. Giles crossed her arms in annoyance.

"All I did was ask her a simple question. It's been almost three months. If she's been doing what she was supposed to be doing, then she should have no problem answering the question."

"Shandra, give it a rest, can't you see she just had a panic attack?"

Once I was fully aware, I realized he had sat me down on a chair. His support was a bit encouraging.

"It's okay, Dr. Scott. I'm better now. I can tell her."

I took a deep breath and looked over to Dr. Giles.

"Dr. Giles, I have been studying nineteen of Dr. Garcia's twenty one students so far and I can tell you I've learned a lot. Using the student development theories that I've learned in my Master's program, theories which I'm sure you're familiar with, I've been able to understand where these students come from and have outlined some ideas on how to assist them. For example, one of my students, Sarah Holmes, is dealing with spiritual development. Starting college, she came in with her strict values and beliefs. However, upon meeting other students and their respective viewpoints, she has started to place some doubts in her spiritual and religious beliefs as she's exposed to other trains of thought. She has been stressing about it recently and wondering if her faith is the correct faith. Other students, like Alia, are going through women's identity development. In her culture, women are expected to keep quiet and submissive with their thoughts. Alia is challenging the status quo by speaking up to her roommate about her concerns, but such a change in behavior as well as her roommate's antagonism towards her has frustrated her. These are just two examples of the kinds of things I'm dealing with."

The other two gentlemen in the back started to whisper to each other. Dr. Scott went to join them, and Dr. Giles merely waited. After a few minutes, one of the gentlemen cleared his throat.

"Dr. Giles, I understand your concern with Ms. Winter's actions. However, from what we see, she has been working on her study just as planned and there is no evidence to the contrary. We see no reason to dismiss her from the university at this time."

Their words brought a sigh of relief from me, only for me to tense up again when they addressed me.

"Ms. Winters, since you only have one month left for your study, we will allow you to complete it and report to us your findings. However, be aware that you will be watched, and if any more problems arise that have you involved with these suicide cases, the penalties will be harsh. You are dismissed."

I nervously got up from my seat and walked out of the room. I did my best to avoid eye contact with Dr. Giles. I was sure she was furious with the decision.

I went down the hall and downstairs to exit the building. As I stepped outside, I saw Lynn Sawyer sitting on the hood of her car in the parking lot smoking a cigarette. Despite the brutal meeting I had with Dr. Giles and the guys, I was sure that she had it worse. I walked over to her and stood there in silence.

"What do you want?" she asked me with a blank tone. I couldn't tell if she was angry, sad, or disappointed.

"Nothing."

We both stood there in silence.

"They kick you out too?" she finally asked me.

"No."

"Figures. They like you, that much I could tell from the beginning. Me? I never really stood a chance."

"If I may ask, why have you taken this case so personally? And why are you the only one working it?"

She threw out her cigarette onto the parking lot pavement.

"Funnily enough, this case isn't a priority down at the station. They would much rather deal with the thugs and criminals of Sun Valley than to deal with the bureaucracy of SVU. I'm the only one that was willing to take the case. Why am I so persistent with it? Because there's more than just suicides going on here."

I listened intently as she told me about her findings throughout the investigations. I was startled to find out that she had some information that the university had kept secret. She had found traces of evidence, both oral and physical, of incidents that had happened at SVU. They were mostly small misdemeanors, but among them were vandalized doors, dented cars, broken windows, and even break-ins. And most of the victims involved two major groups: university staff and student leaders.

However, these incidents were not publicized or even investigated. They were merely put on the backburner. Detective Sawyer had the impression that the administrators were hiding something and didn't want anyone coming in and snooping around. She knew that was the reason they didn't want her investigating the suicide cases. They were afraid of what else she was going to find. She went to talk to Cody, but when he wouldn't give her the answers she wanted, she started verbally harassing him. He reported her to the administration and they kicked her out of the university for it.

With that said, she got in her car and drove off. With the information she acquired, I realized that this situation was much bigger than I originally figured. I wasn't sure if everything she told me was the truth or just an exaggeration as a result of her frustration towards them. Regardless, I knew what my next move would be. I had gone too far at this point to stop now. I needed to talk to Cody Nester.

BIO: DYLAN WRIGHT
RALEIGH, NC

My name is Dylan… what the hell am I supposed to write on here? I was born in Ohio, moved to North Carolina when I was 7. Played a couple of sports as a kid. Some baseball in the third and fourth grade. Soccer in the sixth grade. Even tried my hand at basketball, but it wasn't really for me. Did some wrestling and football in high school. Played quarterback for my team by junior year, too. Fun stuff. I studied hard in school, thought of different colleges to go to, yadda yadda yadda, and now I'm here. Honestly, I didn't really care where I went. I only looked at this school since my brother goes here. Tried out for football. I made the team, but didn't get a scholarship. Bunch of pissants don't know real talent when they see it. Who cares that I'm the one that almost singlehandedly got my team through countless victories? They found me best suited for defense. Linebacker of all things. Even after the plays I was known for at Spartan High. Whatever. This school looks decent. Not the best my stepfather can afford, but at least I get my education fully paid for. What more do you want me to write? Want me to list my hopes and dreams? My aspirations and all that? Dreaming is for the ignorant. I'm a doer. I get in there and get dirty. That's how things get done. The only thing you can expect from me is results. If you want someone who has their head stuck in the clouds all day, go find a philosophy major.

CHAPTER 26: INTERVIEW #MK06
MIYU KANEKO

[With the arrival of Spring, I've been holding recent interviews outside. For this interview, Miyu and I meet for a picnic. The sun is out in full force and the breeze from the nearby lake is keeping us refreshed. Miyu made sandwiches for us.]

Hey Miyu, did you manage to find out more about the issue we discussed last time?

Yes, I sure did! It turns out that the guy who won me at the date auction wasn't named Zachary Myers after all. You were right, the real Zachary was out of town that weekend. This guy was Dylan Wright. Could you believe the nerve of that guy? He signed up for the date auction under another name just so that he could go on a date with no complications. See, he was seeing someone at the time and was starting to get bored of her. But rather than just ending things like a normal guy would do, he instead decides to see other girls using an alias. That just makes me so mad!

I can't believe I actually went on a date with this sleezeball. What's even worse, it's the same guy I criticized Lindsey for dating earlier in the year! I'm such a fool! Granted, I did have a good time, but that's probably why he gets away with these things. He's pretty smooth, no doubt about that. The fact that he's attractive is just icing on the cake. His older brother, Spencer, has a reputation for being the same way around here. He carries around so much charm and class around the ladies that he has no problem getting a date or a hook up whenever he wants. He goes through women like he goes through changes of clothes, and it looks like Dylan's following right in his footsteps.

At the very least Spencer is more responsible than his brother. Sure, he's a womanizer, but at least he's actively involved on campus and has done a lot of good around here. Dylan is just useless! He's in my University 101 class, which to be honest, I'm ashamed to admit that I couldn't recognize him even though I had class with him. It's tough, though. No offense, but to me, most of you White people look the same. I knew we had a Zachary and a Dylan in our class, and they were both football buffs. I had a hard time distinguishing them past that, especially since we never interacted together.

Luckily, he also forgot I was in his class when he bid for me at the date auction. I confronted him about the issue and he told me the truth with no reservations. It was almost as if he was proud of it! I think that's unfair to his roommate, too. Zachary seems like a nice enough guy, but Dylan's tarnishing his reputation by throwing his name around everywhere carelessly. I'm surprised Zachary hasn't punched him in the jaw yet. It's amazing what a friendship can do.

[She takes a bite of her sandwich.]

I had a suspicion that this wasn't Zachary's doing. Unfortunately, I couldn't get another meeting with him since then and the issue wasn't really prevalent enough for investigation. Thanks for finding out for me.

No Cheyenne, thank you! If you hadn't mentioned it, I would have never even noticed! We would have gone on our one date, moved on, and that jerk would have gotten away with it again. At least this time Zachary found out about it when I told him. Whether or not he does anything about it is his business, but at least he knows what's been happening. Seriously, guys can be so stupid! Why can't more people have a relationship like Brad and Lindsey? Did you know that for their one month anniversary he wrote her a song which he hired a band to play at the Student Union Tower restaurant? The place was packed with people and there he was singing lead with the entire band behind him. He is so romantic! More guys should be like him.

Great. Speaking of Dylan, I've been hearing rumors that he caused quite the debacle at Maverick Madness. What is that exactly?

Maverick Madness? Oh, that's that huge party I told you about a few interviews ago. It's Sigma Zeta Pi's keystone event at the end of every year meant to serve as a great sendoff to the mavericks before they go home for the summer and come back as pathfinders next year.

The festival this year was amazing! Some of the older members of the sorority said it was one of the best they've ever had! They pulled their funds to rent out the convention center in northern Sun Valley, which is arguably the only neat thing Sun Valley has that isn't SVU-related. They brought some bands, had amazing catering, and we almost reached full capacity! It was probably because of the weeks leading up to the event.

After the fourth suicide took place, students started going into panic mode. Since the first three suicides took place around the holidays, most students were gone so they mostly went unnoticed. However, Kimberly Shaw's suicide happened not only in the middle of March with everyone around, but Amy's cries about it were seen by a bunch of students from what I heard. It seems you and Dr. Giles went after the wrong girl? Poor Lisa. I'm sure all the sympathy stares she's been getting recently aren't helping her out. To be thought of as suicidal on a false accusation must be the humiliation of a lifetime.

But anyways, people started to go on a frenzy. Those conspiracy theories and rumors that were brought up after Ryan's death began to spread like wildfire around the campus again. The worst part is, everyone found out that the last person Kimberly wrote up for a housing violation was Mitch when he was caught bringing in alcohol with Sam into Miller Hall. Apparently, he was being accused for Tyler's death, and now that he had the potential motive for Kimberly's, the students won't leave him alone. I feel really bad for him.

As you can see, the school had gone into shambles, and it doesn't even look like the administration has done anything to fix it. All I've seen were some depression prevention workshops. What's that going to do? No one chooses to be depressed. It just happens. The students needed something to lift their spirits. I guess Ashley, my sorority president, used this to her advantage. She named the event Maverick Madness as a way to draw in the mavericks around the school. She even allowed her sorority members to bring in more guests, and even started to give out free tickets around campus to draw in more people. Never has our sorority opened up an event this much. She figured it would be a great way to get our sorority noticed, and it worked.

Soon enough, so many people wanted to go that we started selling the tickets instead of giving them away. You wouldn't believe just how much we made back from ticket sales. It pretty much covered the costs of the event!

But this wasn't an SVU authorized event, correct? Didn't you hit any obstacles trying to get this event approved by the administration?

You would think that, wouldn't you? We all thought that, honestly. But it was surprisingly easy. Carrie Sullivan, our Student Activities director, approved the event and told us that she didn't get the usual backlash from the higher ups the way they typically do. We figured that with all of the suicide talk going around, it was in the best interest of both the students and the staff to divert attention to something else for a change. I'm guessing they hoped that after Maverick Madness they'd be too busy talking about that than everything else that's been going on around here the rest of the year.

So we had the event and everything went great. There's no doubt that the Zetas will win Greek Life chapter of the year. It's about time Kappa Chi lost their reign at the throne! But the event was a huge success, and it really stayed true to its tagline: "It's a student revolution".

The whole event was planned by students without any planning or funding help from staff or faculty, and tons of students participated to make it possible. President Lambrick would have been proud.

Then came the after-party. That was a completely different story. With the event being unofficial, meaning that it did not get approved nor advertised through Student Activities, there was a lot less discretion in what went on. Of course there was the usual underage drinking and drag racing that SVU parties were known for, but things got out of hand very quickly.

I heard it was because of Dylan?

Not really. I mean, he sort of set things into motion, but things had gone awry long before he arrived.

BIO: LUCA PALMER
LONDON, ENGLAND

I've been here in the States for a few months now. It's alright. Don't really know what all the fuss is about, to be honest. I've seen New York, been down to the major cities in Florida. Even visited Cali a few years ago. London still has them beat. We've got the museums, the sights, Wimbledon, heck! You guys even base your zulu time on our GMT! It's nice here though. Can't really complain. I just had to get away from home. You know how it is. Parents pushing you this way, pushing you that way. In the end, what you have to say doesn't really matter. They want "what's best" for you. I needed a change of scenery. My parents wanted me to go to Cambridge, or Oxford. What in the bloody hell were they thinking? Did I look like Oxbridge material to them? Did they not notice that I just didn't care?

I needed a change of pace. I looked into New York. Some of my mates went to New York, but that place was too crowded. Wasn't my cup of tea. I like it down here much better. The weather's nice, and our location is perfect to visit the beaches on either side of the peninsula! You know what I'm talking about. Spring break can't come any sooner! All those fit birds in their bikinis gathered in one place waiting for the kill. See, here's my philosophy. I'm young. I have a whole life ahead of me. Why waste it worrying about the future when we don't know what will come of it? My mum studied all her life to do ballet. She trained and practiced all her life, doing what her mum thought "was best" for her, going to the right uni, but for what? Now she's nothing but a housewife taking care of my siblings. She wasted her whole life on something that never came. That's not a mistake I'll repeat.

I'm enjoying my time now. If things don't work out later, I'll at least know that I lived it up when I could get away with it. Besides, university is the best time to make mistakes anyways! Even if you have a horrible night from a piss up with your mates, you have the cushion to make it better. Once you get into the real world, you don't have that cushion. You'll lose your job, lose your family. I'm just doing what any student my age wants to get out of uni, and that's living it up.

CHAPTER 27: MAVERICK MADNESS
APRIL

"Come on, Sarah! You should really come with me. You'll have a great time, I promise!" Rachel said as she put on her earrings in preparation for the festival.

"I'm not really into that sort of thing. I prefer quieter, calmer events."

Rachel finished putting on her earrings and started brushing her hair.

"Sarah Holmes! I cannot willingly have fun at this party tonight knowing that every maverick that matters will be there except for my roommate sitting alone in her room. I mean, seriously, half the hall is going! Many already left!"

"I'm sorry, Rachel. I told you. It's not my thing. Please stop asking."

Rachel stopped brushing her hair and sat down next to her on her bed.

"Fine, you want to be that way? Then I'll tell you what I'm going to do. I am going to sit here right next to you and won't go to the party until you do. You can choose not to go, but I will sit right here next to you the whole night if I have to. Can you live with that guilt? Can you Sarah?"

Sarah raised her eyebrow as she tried to catch Rachel's bluff. Surely she couldn't be serious. Rachel, the girl who had been talking about this party for weeks, trying to pick out who she would take, what she would do there, and the inevitable Prince Charming she was planning to find there, could not possibly give that all up to sit with her roommate at home.

"Why do you want me to go so bad? You know I don't fit in with your sisters."

"Oh, don't be like that, Sarah. This isn't high school. Social status is irrelevant. What matters is whether or not you go out and socialize and meet new people. Do you really want to be like those Hispanic girls that stuck to themselves the whole year? That's no way to start college. You're a pretty cool girl and I care about you. You've been really nice to me when I've needed it the most. I just want to return the favor. And besides, I have no one else to take! I got you this extra ticket under the impression you would go. Pretty please!!!"

Sarah started laughing at Rachel's exaggerated pouty lips.

"Alright, alright. I'll go. What should I wear?"

"Excellent! We'll find something to make you look gorgeous!!!"

Rachel spent the next half hour trying to find the perfect outfit for Sarah. She quickly noticed, however, that none of Sarah's attire was appropriate for partying. Instead, she went into her closet space and looked through some of her own clothing.

"What size are you?"

"Rachel, you're not seriously implying that I wear your clothes, are you?"

"Come on, live a little! Step out of your comfort zone! Here, try this on. Let's see if it works."

Sarah tried on one of Rachel's skin tight dresses and looked in the mirror. She was shocked at just how defined her figure was in the outfit. She refused to wear it.

Rachel went through a few more outfits until she and Sarah could compromise on one. She ended up going with a pretty light blue blouse and a black miniskirt.

The ride to the convention center wasn't very long, but it did involve leaving campus, something that most first year students weren't used to doing. Upon arrival, Rachel immediately met up with Miyu and her other sorority sisters and introduced Sarah.

"So is it true that you went out on a date with Dylan thinking he was Zachary?" Rachel joked.

"Oh shut up! If you had introduced me to Dylan when he was still your boyfriend maybe that never would have happened!"

"Oh trust me, Dylan's not worth any introductions. You'd best stay as far away from him as you can."

The convention center was packed with students everywhere. Sarah and Rachel recognized many of their hallmates there. They saw Luca and Sam arrive together as usual, Zachary with a couple of his football friends, and Jessica arrived with Prachi. Even Renzo made a short appearance.

Once everyone was situated, Ashley, the sorority president, went up on stage to welcome everyone to the event, then introduced the bands for the evening. Roars of applause were heard from the crowd, almost trembling the entire building. Despite the limited standing space, every student was ecstatic to be there, cheering for just about anything and simply grateful they managed to get in.

Once the concert was over, Ashley gave away some door prizes and everyone was free to go. Even though no one said anything, they were all aware of the after-party that would take place in Ashley's mansion. Ashley was known for her wealth and her willingness to share it with others through parties, events, and giveaways.

As the students started to exit the building, Ashley ran up to Miyu.

"Miyu, hey! I was looking all over for you! Could you please make sure the cleanup committee sticks around and does their job? I have to get to the house before they trash it without me."

She laughed and then headed for the parking lot, but Miyu grabbed her arm to stop her.

"Sure, Ashley. But first, I want to know something. What's this?"

Miyu pulled out a flier advertising Second Chance.

"It's nothing. Just one of the tons of fliers that were passed around during the event."

"It's not nothing. I was put in charge of all the marketing for this event, and I've never seen this flier. Why were they being passed around during the event?"

"Geez Miyu, I don't know! People use these venues to promote their stuff all the time. How are we supposed to control that? There are tons of people here! I can't be the rule enforcer and event host at the same time!"

"I understand that. But haven't you heard what Second Chance is? They're saying it's a dangerous group to be around. For the integrity of our sorority, we should not allow people to be recruiting for that group around us."

"Listen, there have been lots of rumors going around lately about everything. You know what? I'm sick of it! I happen to know a couple of people who are a part of Second Chance, and the organization is a blessing. They have helped out many students who otherwise would have dropped out of college ages ago! Don't believe everything you hear. Believe what you experience firsthand. Now I really need to go!"

Rachel ran to her car while Miyu watched with a wary eye. She glanced down at the flier for a brief second then put it in her pocket to help with the cleanup.

*****

It was two in the morning and the party was wilder than ever. Students continued to come in every few minutes. Luca had just come back from winning another motorcycle race.

"Seriously, you Americans can't drive for beans! How about a real challenge for a change?"

Sam walked up to him with a mixed drink.

"Take it easy, Evel Knievel. Here, have some Rum and Coke."

The two of them sat on a couch and drank while Ashley walked up to the center of the living room and tried to get everyone's attention. It took a while, but the music was finally turned down and people were quiet enough to hear her through the microphone.

"I want to thank you all for coming to my party. I want to give an even bigger thanks for those who came to the party and the concert. Don't worry, I'm not going to take up too much more of your time. I just have one question for you. Did you have a great time?"

Cheers and applause were heard from the crowd, even those outside who didn't know what she was saying.

"That makes me glad. See, the theme of this entire event was student pride and power. I wanted us to make a difference, not just sit by the sidelines and watch the world turn. Through your participation and money we gathered from the ticket sales, we are going to go one step further and really show you how you have all made a difference. Thanks to your donations for the tickets, we now have enough money to open up the Sigma Zeta Pi scholarship foundation!"

She paused as the crowd cheered once again.

"These scholarships are meant for students who are struggling paying for college and cannot qualify for the limited scholarships they provide at SVU. You wanted to make a difference? Well how about keeping hundreds of students in school through your generous donations and promotion of these events? Here at Sigma Zeta Pi we strive to help all students, not just sorority members, succeed at everything they do. This is why we have partnered up with the organization whose sole purpose is to help students who need that extra boost. Please help me give a round of applause to the group that not only helped me come up with the idea, but who gave us the initial funding to make this event possible. Give it up for Second Chance!"

Cheers and chants were heard from the crowds throughout the massive house. Miyu, upon hearing the name, crushed her cup in anger and stormed out of the room.

"And now I would like to introduce you all to Second Chance's honorable president. Give it up for Spencer Wright!"

Spencer Wright ran into the room with air horns blasting to rile up the crowd even further. He ran up to Ashley, gave her a kiss in the cheek, then took the microphone.

"Thanks Ashley. I'm glad to be here everyone. I won't take up much of your time. I'm just here to tell you that these scholarships we're opening up next year do not have restrictions or qualifications to apply. You don't have to be a minority or low income or first generation. These scholarships are open to anyone who feels they need that extra help to succeed. The only requirement that you have to meet to apply is to join Second Chance. Our organization works hard to make college a wonderful experience. Originally started out as a group for students who were stuck in a hole with no way out, Second Chance is now broadening its horizons to help out every student out there! So put in your application! Spaces are limited! We hope to see you there!"

Spencer put down the microphone and the music was brought back up. Everyone once again started to party as if nothing had happened.

"How'd I do?" Spencer asked Ashley.

"You did amazing, hubbie bear."

Miyu walked up to them just in time to see them kiss. Spencer saw her and excused himself as he left.

"Well, I'm going to go mingle. I'll leave you two ladies to do the same."

Miyu waited until he walked away before she spoke.

"You lied to me," Miyu said in a powerful voice, very unlike her usual, passive tone. "What the hell do you think you're doing getting people to join that club? And then lying to me about it? Oh wait, I got it! You're screwing the president! No wonder he's got control over you."

"Oh shut up you whore! At least we're trying to help students out here. Like I said, Second Chance has helped hundreds of students over the years, and now with this scholarship program, we can help hundreds more. And what have you done? Dating around any guy that wins you at a date auction, then going around tarnishing his reputation just because you were too stupid to find out who he really was. Typical maverick. You know, Miyu, I have always had high hopes for you. You've been a very passionate member and have done a lot for this organization. There's potential for you, but we need to work as a team. One day, it's possible you can be running this sorority, but you have to become a visionary to do it. Can you do that, Miyu? Can you envision a greater future for our students?"

"Not a future with you," Miyu said in a sardonic tone.

"That's too bad, Miyu. I really thought you were better than this. Why don't you go back to your boyfriend? Looks like he's in the need for someone to hit the sheets with."

Ashley pointed towards a direction behind Miyu. Miyu turned around to see Dylan attempting to hit on Jessica but failing.

"Why not? You gotta admit we've had a good time this year. Let's go for a drive together and get to know each other better, this time without Zachary on our tail."

Jessica, who had been pretty quiet up to that point, started getting impatient.

"Dylan, I would, but there are a couple of things wrong with that. First of all, you're piss drunk, and I wouldn't get in a car with you if you were the last monkey on Earth. Second of all, Zachary's a good guy, and I'm not a fan of you and your buds mocking him all the time. And finally, I have already said no. You ask me again and you'll be going home with one less testicle tonight."

Students around them started laughing and cheering, trying to instigate the situation further. Dylan simply smirked.

"Is that how it is? You think you're a hot shot or something? You think that you're too good for anyone here? Well I'll tell you one thing, Jessica. It's not that I find you attractive or even really care about you. I'm just really in the mood for some action and you seemed like the most vulnerable piece of ass around here. You think you're so tough? Just know that I'm not afraid to hit a girl."

As his voice got louder, more students started huddling around. Miyu walked over to get a closer look. Luca and Sam had also gotten up from the couch to eavesdrop.

"You want to hit me? Then hit me!" Jessica taunted. "Let's see how much of a man you really are behind your muscles and cheesy grins."

Before Dylan could react, Zachary walked up to him and grabbed his shoulder.

"Dylan, don't turn this into something ugly, okay dude? Seriously, let it go and move on."

"Sorry Zachary, but this bitch needs to be put in her place. All year long she walks around like she's untouchable, like she owns this campus. She needs to get a reality check."

Zachary started to get annoyed.

"Don't do this. I'm warning you. You're drunk and you're not thinking rationally. Remember that I'm your friend, Dylan. Even though you've screwed me over a couple of times, I've stuck by you. I need you to trust me on this. Let me take you home."

Dylan looked down as he absorbed Zachary's words. He was right. Dylan had lied countless times and had Zachary cover for him so he wouldn't get caught. He even stole his identity for a night and ruined his reputation among some people, yet Zachary stood by him since. Dylan looked at Zachary and smiled.

"Alright, let's go. I'll deal with this bimbo when I'm more sober."

Groans were heard from the audience of college students when they realized the conflict didn't go anywhere. Luca wasn't pleased.

"That's right. Go home, Dylan, just like your mum Zachary tells you," Luca shouted.

"What are you on about now, Luca?" Dylan asked.

"Just what I told you would happen. You're weak! Instead of just living it out, you've been lying your way around just so that you don't make others angry. Stand up for yourself, mate! First Rachel, and now Zachary? What's the deal?"

"You'd better shut up if you know what's good for you," Zachary responded. "You have been a pain in my ass since I've first met you. Dylan is a jerk and lying womanizer, but he does have his merits. Unfortunately, hanging out with you digs those merits even deeper. You better stay away from him if you know what's good for you."

Luca started to laugh and was joined by the group around him. Many of those students were so drunk they would laugh at anything.

"Oh look! He speaks! You know Zachary, you've spoken so little to me, I was beginning to think you became mute! And for good reason. Being a bit of a poofter, eh mate? Look at you, standing up for your little girlfriend Jessica. But she's not your girlfriend, is she? In fact, have you ever been with one? I don't imagine too many birds chattin' up a Nancy-boy like you.

Probably why you're so close to Dylan, eh? Don't want any other girl around him? Want him all to yourself, pretty boy?"

Zachary's glance suddenly turned into a fiery glare.

"Oh look, he's getting upset cause I'm insulting him and his lover! Would you like a hug to make it better?"

The students laughed as Luca cracked jokes at Zachary's expense. Dylan's headache started to get to him so he left the room, leaving Zachary to take care of himself. Zachary couldn't control himself anymore. An entire year of hatred and annoyance towards Luca was unleashed as Zachary launched directly at him.

Upon seeing the six foot tall angry runningback charging at him, Luca panicked and backed up, stumbling over the people behind him.

Zachary caught up to him and grabbed him by the collar of his polo shirt and pulled him towards him. He reached out to punch him, but Luca kicked him as hard as he could in the shin, causing Zachary to wince in pain. As a result, Zachary punched him with a right hook to the face, knocking Luca onto the floor. Some of Luca's friends suddenly pounced on Zachary in retaliation, with three guys knocking him down and kicking him.

By that point, massive fights started to break out. Some of Zachary's football friends went in to defend him, which led to more people getting involved. The living room was filled with punches flying and crowds cheering them on. Ashley started to get worried that her things were in danger of being broken. Her parents left her the house for the weekend and she didn't want to know what would happen if everything was destroyed from a fight.

Ashley ran to the living room and started yelling at them to stop, but her cries were drowned out by the cheering of the growing crowd that was approaching from the other rooms in the house and outside. Soon there was little wiggle room as everyone crowded around each other and students began to be pressed against the walls. Others fell on the floor and were trampled.

"Stop it, everyone! Stop it!" Ashley pleaded. No one listened.

*****

It had been one week since Maverick Madness. The term was more popularly used to describe the incidents of the after-party than the festival itself. Sigma Zeta Pi was on probation as university officials began to investigate what had happened that night. Someone had called the police and they arrived to break up the fight. Zachary was arrested for assaulting Luca, but Luca did not press any charges. He did not feel it was worth his time. Zachary was instead let out with a warning and was placed in academic probation for the rest of the semester.

Things began to quiet down at Sun Valley University. Finals were coming up in two weeks and everyone was busy getting their term papers and other assignments finished. Others had already started making travel arrangements to go home for the summer. The Miller Hall study lounge was packed with students studying a variety of subjects, some in groups and others individually. Mason, Rachel, and Grace were working on a project for their Humanities course.

"So the party was that bad, huh?" Mason asked.

"You wouldn't believe it. People were fighting everywhere, half of Ashley's furniture was destroyed, and people are still walking around showing their bruises from it."

"Too bad I missed it, then. Probably for the best, though. Fighting isn't really my style. Grace, what are you working on there?"

Mason noticed that in addition to the documents they were using for their research paper, Grace also had some books for Pediatric Cardiology.

"I'm helping out Susan create a study guide using index cards so she can study for her final while she's at work. She is so busy that there's hardly any time for studying."

"Susan? You mean that older lady in Dr. Garcia's class with us? Doesn't she have kids too? Gosh, I can't imagine how hard it must be to deal with everything she does."

"Yeah, it's tough. Even worse, she's having a hard time finding financial assistance for school next year. Even with all the budget cuts we've had this year, they're going to cut more financial assistance next year, making it hard for many students to come back."

Mason turned to Rachel.

"Maybe she could apply for your sorority's new program. Didn't Ashley announce that they started a scholarship fund for people with those types of problems?"

"Yeah, but I'm not so sure if that's gonna go through anymore. After the events of Maverick Madness, they're keeping a close eye on our sorority and we can't really do anything until we get out of probation. Since then, there's been nothing for me to do. I've been stuck in my room with a moody Sarah for the last two weeks."

"Moody Sarah? What do you mean?"

"Oh, the girl has become insufferable! She gets mad at me all of a sudden and yells at me for no reason. Other times she's just quiet and to herself. She hasn't been acting like herself. I don't know what's happened to her. I think she might still be mad that I took her to the party. Though I don't know why. Other than the fight, it was a great party!"

Mason began to get concerned.

"This isn't good, Rachel. If there's one thing that Sarah's always been, it's happy, just like Grace here. No one suddenly changes that quickly. I need to check up on her. We could have another case of depression on our hands. The last thing we need is another suicide!"

Mason got up and went to Sarah's room. He knocked on the door, but realized it was unlocked, so he walked inside. He saw Sarah lying on her bed. Her eyes were open but she wasn't looking at anything in particular. Rachel told him she's had that look for days.

"Sarah, it's me, Mason. Are you okay?" he said as he approached her. She didn't say anything.

"Remember? I'm good ol' atheist Mason who you got a kick out of lecturing."

She continued to lie there silently. Mason attempted a few more times to get her to talk, but she wouldn't respond or even acknowledge his presence. Not knowing what else to do, he just sat there. For twenty minutes he sat by her side in silence, attempting to offer her support through his presence.

After a while, she finally started moving and darted her eyes towards him.

"You were right," she said in her quiet, tired voice. Mason had to lean in to hear her.

"Right about what?" he asked in his most sympathetic voice.

There was another pause. Mason wasn't sure if she didn't hear him or was trying to formulate the words.

"God isn't real, Mason. You were right."

"What? What happened, Sarah? This is nothing like you. Sure, I've been stating my case to you all year long, but why do you now all of a sudden choose to believe it?"

Sarah stood quiet for a few more minutes after that. The next thing she told him gave him the biggest shock of his life. It wasn't so much what she said, but how she said it. Her blank stare coupled by her monotone, uncaring voice made his heart race with anxiety as she spoke.

"Mason, I was raped."

CHAPTER 28: CHEYENNE WINTERS
APRIL

Cody Nester was a simple guy. He donned a pair of jeans and a plain T-shirt. His interests consisted of watching TV and listening to music. There didn't seem to be anything genuinely unique about him except for whatever information regarding Second Chance he had. He had spent most of our meeting so far scratching his head and talking about nothing in particular.

"Is there anything else you need or can I go?" Cody said in a passive aggressive tone.

"Cody, you've been skirting around the issue our entire talk. I know you're vice president for Second Chance. How is it possible that you aren't aware with what happens in your own organization?"

"I'm telling you the truth. I know very little of what goes on. Spencer only uses the other officers for routine club management stuff. He's the only one that gets involved in the meat and potatoes of the organization. He's the visionary. I don't know what more to tell you."

I sighed. "I want you to understand that I am not Detective Sawyer and I will not act like her. Harassing you the way she did was wrong and I know it. I would really appreciate it if you worked with me. I can tell you're a reasonable guy. I'm sure you aren't happy with the suicides that may have occurred as a result of membership in Second Chance. Any information you may have can help me prevent suicides from happening in the future."

Cody began to contemplate what I told him. We sat there in silence for almost a minute.

"All I know is that the students who died were applying to be full members of Second Chance. It happened during their final initiation test. I don't know what those tests were. Spencer is very secretive about that stuff. To be honest, I didn't originally think that the suicides had anything to do with the organization. I figured it was just coincidence. It wasn't until Caleb's suicide that I figured something was wrong. But that's the thing, though.

Kimberly wasn't even a part of Second Chance, so that kind of blows that theory out of the water."

"Not necessarily. I have talked to Amy, one of Kimberly's close friends. She told me that Kimberly was very stressed. Her RA job took a lot of effort, and other than Amy, she didn't have any friends. She often felt like an outcast in the groups she was involved with. This leads me to believe that suicide seemed like the best option. After seeing so many students solve their problems that way, she figured it might work for her as well. Don't you see the bigger issue here? The suicides are starting to spread outside of Second Chance! Students suffering from depression are starting to consider it as an option after seeing other students doing it! Students with emotional issues can be very impressionable. The last thing we need is to give them this kind of outlet to escape."

"Well what do you want me to do about it?"

"Where can I find Spencer? Ever since I found out he was president, I've been looking for him but have failed. He seems to have gone into hiding."

Cody brushed his hair with the palm of his hand.

"I couldn't tell you. After his plan at Maverick Madness failed, he decided to retreat from the group. He found it too dangerous for us to meet since now that word has spread out, everyone's keeping an eye on him. I have no idea where he went. He hasn't been at home or in class for days. Some leader he turned out to be. Leaving us all behind when things started going awry."

His puzzled look as he spoke seemed to suggest truth to his statement. I needed to find a different way to gather information.

"Let me ask you this, Cody. Why did you join Second Chance?"

"I don't know. It seemed like a good idea at the time. Josh, the old president before Spencer, was recruiting students and I decided to check the meeting out. I was bored and had nothing better to do. I guess I liked what I saw and I stayed. You have to understand that Second Chance isn't all bad. Its leaders are truly there to help students in need. The founder of Second Chance meant to provide exactly what it was named after. It was meant for students who had followed the wrong path or had nowhere else to turn in college."

He took a deep breath.

"The organization offered tutoring services, counseling services, and all sort of support groups for students with alcohol problems or anger management issues. What made it so popular was that it was fully student-run. No administrators to take control over everything. It was a service provided by students for students. I was a nobody when I came to SVU. Just like high school, I was invisible. But once I joined Second Chance, I was amazed at how friendly everyone was. There were other students who had the same problem as me and could understand me. I felt heard and appreciated. That's why I became VP. I want to be able to continue helping students have a second chance at college. It just makes me mad that someone like Spencer had to take the organization and turn it into something ugly."

I could tell the organization meant a lot to Cody, which made me question Carrie Sullivan's description of Second Chance as a cult. Was that really what this was?

I thanked Cody for his time and left his room. Although he couldn't help me find Spencer, I figured I could talk to someone who would. Hopefully Dylan, being his younger brother, would have some idea what he was up to. Unfortunately, since the Maverick Madness incident, Dylan had also been keeping low profile. The humiliation he must have felt from being told off by Jessica as well as singlehandedly starting all the commotion that brought in the police must have gotten to him. It also didn't help that he as well as several others were underage drinking at the party.

However, that had to be saved for a later time. My next appointment was an interview with Lisa. I had hoped to conduct a follow-up to the mess that I got her in by rushing to her room the other day. I felt bad that students looked at her as "the suicidal girl" because of me. That was the problem with suicides. If you fail at it, you are branded as suicidal forever. Even though she never actually attempted it, through all the gossip and rumors about the evening she might as well have. Students would watch her or talk about her behind their back wondering if this would be the day that she would do it. Students have almost come to expect suicides at the university. It had gotten that bad.

I showed up to her room when I saw she wasn't waiting at my office. After waiting fifteen minutes I figured she might have forgotten. I knocked on her door and waited as footsteps were heard on the other side.

Lisa opened the door, her eyes red and puffy as if she had been crying.

"What's wrong Lisa?" I asked sympathetically.

"I'm leaving," she responded in a defeated tone.

"What? Why? What's going on?"

"I can't take it, Cheyenne. It's just too much. Counseling helped for a little while, but I can't hide from the truth. I don't belong here. I never did! I really miss my family and they miss me. They need me! They don't want to tell me, but I can feel that my nana died because I wasn't there for her. We were very close and I just left them all! I can't handle all of this. I'm failing my classes, students are looking at me expecting me to kill myself any day now. I need to be with my family. I'm needed there much more than I'm needed here. They're all suffering, both from the loss of my nana and from the loss of my income there. My old boss at Don Pepe's told me that my mom would ask for handouts from him since they didn't have enough money for food. Could you believe it? She was begging!"

Lisa was getting upset again as she began to hyperventilate. I acted out of impulse and hugged her, something I was advised against in my counseling classes. But I knew she needed it. We stood there for a while. Lisa cried as I wrapped my arms around her, holding her as if she was my own daughter in pain. These past few months had been the most emotional in my life. Seeing the pain in these students really struck a nerve with me. I never expected this. Through all my books, research, and case studies, I was never prepared for the amount of emotion I had to deal with as a student affairs professional.

"When are you leaving?" I asked her once she calmed down.

"Tomorrow. I've already withdrawn from my classes and have started packing my things. I haven't told Gaby yet. I know she'll be crushed when she finds out. I'm also scared she will hate me knowing that I abandoned her this way."

"Don't worry about that, okay? Gabriella is your friend. I'm sure she will understand. You just do what you need to do and tell her when the time is right. I'm so sorry that you couldn't stay, but I wish you the best in whatever you decide to do. I'll miss you, Lisa."

It was very hard for me to keep myself from tearing up as I spoke to her. I never realized just how attached to her I had become until now. Seeing her leave made me realize that I failed at my job. I came here to help students succeed in college, and I couldn't do it. If anything, I helped Lisa leave much faster through my meddling into her personal affairs and marking her as suicidal.

Unfortunately, this was only the beginning of a downward spiral. I had only two more weeks left at Sun Valley University. Two weeks I still look back at with dread and affliction.

BIO: MASON COOK
KEY WEST, FL

Why did I come to college? Interesting question, really. Most will tell you it's to get a job, or because it's "the thing to do." I'm here for the theatre! Yeah, I know, it's a bit stereotypical. I know what you're thinking, "of course the gay guy does theatre!" But I've always loved theatre! Even before I "knew" I was gay. I went to a private school, you see. Catholic school to be specific. Oh, the irony, right? Well, in the school's typical money-hungry nature, they put on two shows a year that every class had to participate in. The teachers had to take time off of class to practice with students these musical numbers and dance steps that they had to choreograph with their non-existent experience, then charge our parents $10 a piece to come see us perform in that musical fest.

My parents, just like the others, hoped that our class would perform first so they can watch it then get the hell out of there with me. Then the school had the audacity to charge the families money yet again to sell us the recorded tapings of that show! The students hated it, the teachers hated it, and aside from seeing their student on stage for a few minutes, the parents hated it. But I loved it! You know why I loved it? Because I enjoyed the limelight! Ever since fourth grade, I started getting the lead male roles in the musical. No, not because I was a great actor, or a great singer, or even the most willing (though that became apparent later on), but because I was the loudest. Yes, the loudest. All our principal cared about was that we sang loud and sang proud so the parents can see our fake enthusiasm. But I didn't care, I loved it! And after that year, every one of my teachers up until eighth grade chose me as the lead again, partly due to my late puberty.

The thing is, by that year, I was the only male in my class to have a high tenor voice to sing all those lead parts. It was great. The parents knew to expect me on center stage, and the principal knew to expect a ravishing performance from me. I enjoyed myself and had a great time, and kept it up through high school. But I wanted more! Then, I came to Sun Valley University with my high school class to see their showing of "The Wizard of Oz". After that day, college theatre became my passion! I set my sights to this school and the rest is history. I can't wait until my first production!

CHAPTER 29: INTERVIEW #SH08
SARAH HOLMES

[I am sitting by Sarah's bed on one of her chairs. Sarah is in her pajamas drinking a cup of hot cocoa. She had gotten sick and missed school for a few days. I made sure to treat this interview with as much caution and sensitivity as I could.]

Sarah, before we begin, are you sure you're comfortable talking about this? I don't want to pressure you into anything you're not ready for. I can turn this recorder off right now if you want me to.

No, it's okay. I think I'm ready to talk about it. It's about time I talk about it. I've been keeping it secret for weeks and it's been killing me inside. It wasn't until I finally told Mason that I started to feel a bit better.

Okay then, go ahead. But please, if at any point you want to stop, just let me know and we'll stop.

Well, it happened at the Maverick Madness after-party. Like I told you before, Rachel convinced me to go with her. I was hesitant the whole time, but I had fun at the festival, so I figured the after-party would be just more of the same. I'm not a party girl. I don't feel comfortable at large, crowded events like that. I only did it because Rachel was my friend and she really wanted me to go. Rachel handed me a couple of drinks. I couldn't even tell you what they are. I don't know much about alcohol other than beer and wine. All I know is that some of what she gave me tasted fruity.

That was my first mistake. I really shouldn't have accepted any drinks that night. Unfortunately, I was still pumped from the festival and I guess I let my guard down more than I should have. Underage drinking was immoral and I should have held my ground. It also didn't help that apparently I was a light weight. I was drunk within a half hour of getting to that party. Rachel told me afterwards that I was a flirtatious drunk, hitting on every guy around me. I still get chills when I think about it.

But that's what happened. I flirted with guy after guy, and each of them would offer me another drink and I'd take it. A lot of what happened that night is a blur to me, as I got so drunk I'm surprised I didn't die of alcohol poisoning. From what little I can remember, I did make out with a few of those guys. I still scream at myself inside for it. What was I thinking?! This was nothing like me! I can't believe those pigs had the nerve to take advantage of me like that.

I don't even know at what point it happened, but one of the guys invited me upstairs. By that point I was laughing like an idiot and willing to take chances. I knew what things like these led to but it just didn't fully register in my head. All that mattered was that I was having fun. And of course Rachel wasn't around to watch me. Once she saw me flirting with a guy she left me alone to 'work my charm' and went to hang out with her other sorority sisters. That might have been the last time I even saw her that night. What kind of a friend just leaves you there all drunk and inexperienced at these events?

Well, the one guy took me upstairs. We fooled around for a bit in one of the bedrooms. I sat with him on the bed and he started kissing me. He then started unbuttoning my blouse. My mind was rushing with emotions and excitement from being such a bad girl. But somewhere inside, my conscience was trying to get through to me. Not just my conscience, but my common sense. Even in my drunken state, I started to realize what was happening and I wanted to end it.

But my body wouldn't respond. Even though my mind lifted red flags everywhere, I just couldn't get myself to stop him. As he kissed me, I told him to stop as sternly as I could, but it came out as weak and even playful. I laughed as he laid me on the bed, telling him that we shouldn't do this. He toyed with me and told me that playing hard-to-get made him want me even more.

Once he started pulling my skirt down, I started to panic inside. My smile faded and I tried harder to tell him to stop. I tried to push him away, but he overpowered me. I barely remember what happened in that room, but the feelings I felt were still crystal clear to me. I was horrified inside. I knew that I was in danger, but I had no control over the situation. The guy was drunk, and all my pleas went unnoticed to him.

I started to pray in my head, begging God to get me out of that situation. I wanted Him to intervene somehow, make it all go away. But nothing happened. The guy continued to force himself on me and I started to cry. At least I think I started to cry. I'm not sure. I continued to plead to God for some help. I started to silently cry out to him in despair, and asked him why he wouldn't help me.

It wasn't fair! All my life I had been devoted to Him and my church and now that I needed Him the most, he abandoned me. And it wasn't the first time. As I lied there on the bed, my feelings of despair started to turn into feelings of grief and frustration. Despite all my prayers, God allowed my sister to get sicker and sicker. He allowed her to be admitted in the hospital in critical condition. Her asthma attacks almost killed her. She had stopped breathing and her fingers turned purple. My family started to panic. That was all I could think about at that moment. I thought of how God had abandoned my sister, and how God had abandoned me.

Then he did it. He raped me. I had never felt so alone, so betrayed in my life as I had right there. At that point I was sure I was crying. My God left me lying there, as if he was punishing me for some reason. I didn't deserve this... My sister didn't deserve this...

[Sarah starts crying and cannot talk anymore. I stop the interview for a while as I try to comfort her. I tell her that we should stop here, but she insists that we continue. I hesitate, but I let her continue.]

It was a horrible night. I don't remember how I got home. I think one of my hallmates saw me lying there after the cops came in to bust up some fight that went on downstairs and offered me a ride home. I can't remember for the life of me who it was. It could have been Prachi. I don't even remember if I was dressed when she found me. I think I passed out after the incident, because everything after that feels like a big hole in my head.

The next few days felt like a dream to me. More like a nightmare, really. I was awake, but I still felt I was asleep. It all felt unreal, like everything that happened that night and afterwards was part of a long dream that I just wouldn't wake up from. I still wanted to believe it was the night of the party, and I was safely tucked away in my bed waiting for the next day to ask Rachel how it went. I didn't want to accept the truth.

Afterwards, I started to get angry. Like really violent. I would snap at Rachel for no reason. I had finally started to realize that I had indeed been raped and I felt like it was all my fault. I felt I deserved it. God had punished me for being such a whore and leading those guys on. I hated myself. I hated everyone. I even hated God. I stopped going out or to my classes. I stayed locked in my room every day and didn't bother to get out of bed. I guess I got sick from my malnourishment. I wasn't hungry and I wasn't in any mood to talk to people.

By the third week, I had finally come to a realization. There was no God. No God would willingly put one of His servants through such horrible torture. He wouldn't allow that kind of suffering on a person. I remember in a health class in high school how our teacher warned us about rape. He told us that rape wasn't what most people expected, which was some random stranger pulling you into a dark alley. He told us that the most common rape was date rape, which was caused by someone you knew who you were comfortable around, and could be aided by intoxication. Obviously, I didn't think I would ever be a victim of something like that.

Not only was I a good girl, but I knew I had God on my side. What a joke. I realized that in this world, you had to take care of yourself. There was no omnipotent being watching your every move and solving your problems for you. You had to be the one to take action and take responsibility for those actions. I'm the one that went to that party, I'm the one that got drunk, and I'm the one that went up to the room with that guy. I deserved it.

When Mason came into my room, I couldn't help but tell him what happened to me. He seemed to be the only person who cared enough about me to really ask. And in some weird way, I trusted him. He was always honest and sympathetic with me. He always had a smile on his face and that smile usually spread to me. So I told him. I told him that I was raped at the party.

Mason tried to hide it, but I could tell the shock he experienced when he heard that. He might be an actor, but there are some feelings you just cannot hide.

I told him how he was right and that there was no God. I knew he would give me the 'I told you so' speech. I had just hoped that he would be a little more sensitive with my situation that he wouldn't rub it in so thick. What he did tell me, however, was completely unexpected.

"What the hell are you saying?" he asked me bluntly.

His question shocked me. Only once had I heard him talk to me in such a strong tone and we didn't speak for days after that. I couldn't believe he chose this moment to use that tone again.

"You don't believe that one bit, Sarah, and you know it," he said.

"What are you talking about? You spent the whole year telling me how God doesn't exist! Are you seriously arguing otherwise?"

"No, of course not. But you have to understand something. Beliefs are beliefs for a reason, Sarah. They are what drive us and motivate us. They are what keep us going. There is no way to know whose belief is right and whose is wrong. I argue with you just for fun. I never actually expect to prove that your belief is wrong. I've seen your faith. You are one of the most devoted Christians I know. And you are much better for it. Through your faith, you bring happiness to others. You do everything you can to help those who are down. Look at what your lack of faith has done to you!"

I started to tear up in anger, but mostly because I knew that what he said was true and didn't want to admit it.

"My belief is that there is no such thing as God," he said. "But that is my belief, not yours. You're only saying this because you are upset, and it is how you are choosing to cope. You need to accept this just as you accepted what happened to your sister. God does everything for a reason, and you need to trust that everything will work out in the end."

Tears ran down my cheeks again as I tried to make sense of his words.

"But it hurts so bad!"

I cried onto his shoulder and we just sat there in silence for the rest of the night. Mason had a test the next day that he didn't study for so he could take care of me. I am very grateful for what he did. I still hurt and ache from the event. I still wake up screaming at night as my nightmares replay that ingrained memory. What really haunts me about all of this is the uncertainty of it all. I don't remember much of it, only what was going on in my mind. I don't remember who it was that raped me, or even if he went to this school.

Is there anything you can remember regarding his identity?

All I remember is that he was wearing a red windbreaker. It was cool that night and there was a chance of rain. He put it on me when we were outside before he led me upstairs. That's it.

[I thank Sarah for her time and wish for her to feel better. She is going to need a lot of therapy to get over this incident. Once outside, I pull out my cell phone and call Detective Lynn Sawyer.]

CHAPTER 30: RETRIBUTION
APRIL

"Hey Zachary, wake up! It's almost eight. A couple of us are going to dinner. You wanna join?"

Zachary woke up with a headache. It was dark outside. He felt dizzy as he sat up on his bed.

"Whoa, I must have fallen asleep while studying. I really haven't gotten much sleep lately."

Dylan laughed and patted him on the back.

"Yeah dude. You really need to relax. What are you doing with all your time? Now that you're suspended from football for the semester, I can imagine you have lots more free time."

"I do, it's just that I have a lot on my mind. Now that I'm under academic review, they might revoke my scholarship. I can't stay at SVU without that scholarship money. And I don't know what my dad would do if he found out I got into a fight and got suspended from football."

"That sucks. So you coming with us or what?"

"Yeah, just give me a minute to find another shirt."

Dylan nodded and headed to the door. He opened it and stepped outside, but not before momentarily turning back around and looking at Zachary.

"Oh, and Zachary. I, uhh, never thanked you for standing up for me back at the party. Not that I needed any help. Seriously, you made me look like a freaking pansy in front of everyone! But thanks."

He left the room immediately after.

Zachary laughed to himself as he changed his shirt. After everything he went through, at least he got through to Dylan's thick head. Back in the beginning of the year, Rachel had talked to him about Dylan and his horrible living conditions. His parents divorced when he was very young and his mother married a few times before settling with the rich stepfather he had now. His stepfather didn't care for either Dylan or Spencer, and sought to pay for their college if they promised to go out of state. According to Rachel, his mom didn't really seem to care either way. Zachary felt bad for him and wanted to help him out. He knew that Spencer wasn't exactly the best role model for him. Having relatively uncaring parents himself, Zachary couldn't help but sympathize with what Dylan was feeling.

As he left the room to meet up with Dylan at their usual meeting place in the Miller Hall lobby, he wondered what the future would bring for him. Being his first offense, he figured they couldn't be too hard on him. At the same time, he was a great runningback and they needed him. Hopefully they would let him play next year.

His eyes darted over to the voices coming from Luca's room as he walked past. Luca was sitting with three girls by his side, laughing and joking.

"Yeah, I held my ground," he told them. "You don't get black eyes like this one from just sitting around and taking it. I'm not a fighter, but when the situation calls for it, you have to be ready, you know?"

Zachary clenched his fist in anger. How Luca always managed to end up on top was beyond him. He had half the mind to walk in the room and confront him, but figured it wasn't worth it. That was all behind him now. He ran down the stairs to the lobby to meet with Dylan and some of his pals from the bar. Dylan, however, wasn't present among them.

"Where's Dylan?" Zachary asked.

"Outside. He had to take a phone call. It sounded bad," one of the guys said.

Zachary ran outside. He saw Dylan on the phone, his face pale as a ghost. He could almost hear his heart pounding from where he was standing.

"What's wrong?" Zachary asked when Dylan hung up the phone.

"I gotta go," Dylan said frantically as he ran to his car.

*****

"Yeah, Second Chance is being disbanded," Cheyenne said on the phone. "After Cody started talking, other members started talking as well. They started telling university officials everything they knew. They mentioned the hazing techniques they used which forced them to vandalize property as a rite of passage to become full members. It's a complex system, actually. When first joining the organization, students talked about their problems and who caused those problems or at the very least didn't help them with their problems. Spencer took down all that information and compiled lists. As their final test to become a full member of Second Chance, he would randomly assign the student with one of those people who has screwed over his or her fellow member in the past and do something bad to them.

"That's why they targeted all those people. They scared the SGA members because they had done something to piss off a Second Chance member. Like

Ryan, for example. His problem was with the housing office for making him sleep on a bench the night of orientation. Another Second Chance member was assigned to take care of the RAs who wouldn't help him by breaking into their rooms and stealing their things. In return, he had to help the other students by getting back at Renzo for treating them like crap. It was like some sort of demonic Secret Santa. Unfortunately, some requests were harsher and more violent than others. After the warning spray painted on Renzo's door, Ryan was asked to hurt Renzo if he didn't quit SGA like he was asked.

"I don't know how exactly. Maybe stab him with a knife or something. Point is, Ryan didn't want to do it. However, by that point, he was so deeply involved and invested in Second Chance, he had no other choice. If he didn't comply, Spencer would turn him in for the vandalism and other illegal things he did for the club. Ryan was already depressed, hence joining the club to begin with, so he had no other place to turn. He had one more fight with Renzo and one more fight with Spencer, and he was overwhelmed. He saw suicide as the only way out."

Cheyenne heard a car pull up in front of her apartment.

"Listen, Lynn, I gotta go. I have my final interview with Ben tonight and it looks like he's here. The point I was trying to make was that it's over. That's why those cars were vandalized, homes were broken into, and death threats were sent. They were a part of Second Chance's initiation process. And fortunately, Miyu decided to speak up and mention how Spencer was dating Ashley. They were working together to get Sigma Zeta Pi involved with Second Chance recruitment as well. Sigma Zeta Pi is now in probation."

She heard her door knock.

"Come in!" she shouted. "The door's open."

She turned back to her phone.

"Yeah Lynn, I'll call you back later so we can talk about your findings on the rape case."

As much as she didn't want to do it, Cheyenne gave in and asked Detective Sawyer for help on the rape case. Sarah didn't want to report it, so no official investigation was called. She knew how passionate Lynn was about helping students, despite her abrasive personality in dealing with the case. She figured that made her perfect for dealing with a rapist. No one who rapes a girl deserves to have it easy. She could think of fewer worse punishments than to deal with an angry Detective Sawyer. She had made a deal with her that she would keep her updated on the Second Chance case if she could help her with the rape case.

Cheyenne turned around as the door opened and froze as she saw Spencer Wright enter through the door. He was holding a gun in his hand pointed right at her.

"Spencer!" she yelled all of a sudden.

"Shut up!" he yelled back. "Drop the phone and kick it over to me. You're not going to need it."

Cheyenne's heart started to race. She did as he asked and kicked the phone over to him. She wanted to talk to him, to reason with him, but her mouth could not come out with any words. All she could focus on was the gun pointed straight at her.

"This is all your fault!" Spencer yelled. "You did this to me!"

"What?"

"You just couldn't butt out, couldn't you? You had to get involved. I bet you even think of me as a murderer. Do you think I wanted all of this to happen? I was doing just fine fixing this mess until you decided to stick your head in and trick my members into turning against me!"

Cheyenne took a big gulp and forced herself to speak. Her voice was squeaky and trembling.

"Spencer, I didn't mean any harm to anyone. I just wanted to stop people from dying. How can you fault me for that? Your actions, regardless of their intent, were hurting people!"

Spencer laughed sadistically.

"You just don't get it, do you? You think I'm the only one at fault for this? Don't you realize that the people you work for are just as guilty? They're the reason for all of this!"

Cheyenne raised her hands to show they were empty and stood up.

"I don't know what you're talking about. Please, Spencer, talk to me. I'm not Detective Sawyer. I'm not Dr. Giles. I'm just a doctoral student trying to help students like you. Tell me what you mean."

Spencer reacted at her sudden movement. She feared he was going to shoot. She had only seen Spencer twice before from afar. Everything she knew about him was from her interviews with Rachel and Dylan. The guy they described was not the guy that was standing in front of her. This guy wasn't friendly and outgoing or bold and assertive. Spencer wasn't well. His current state seemed to be a result of months of built up anger and depression being triggered by the pressures he was dealing with right now. She feared that neither of them would leave the room alive. His suicidal stare looked like he was planning on taking them both down.

"It's this school," he said after a pause, still pointing the gun at her. "They did this to me. I wasn't always like this. I was a great student. I rose the ranks easily through the years. I ran for SGA President and lost, but that was okay. I was so well known around the school that just about everything I wanted to get done would get done regardless of how much official authority I had. I worked hard to make Sun Valley University a better place for the students. Unfortunately, the staff and faculty here didn't have the same goal. With them, it's all about money and prestige. That's all they care about. You know that speech President Lambrick gives at Convocation every year? It's all a bunch of lies! They don't care about the students. All they want is the power of being the number one campus in the country."

His hand started trembling as he spoke. He could pull the trigger at any second the way he was shaking the gun around. Cheyenne closed her eyes.

"I was supposed to graduate in four years and get a well-paying job to pay off my student loans. But you know what I found out my last semester? My advisor didn't bother to check or review my plan of study before he signed it. As I applied for graduation, I found out that I took some of the wrong courses and that I was still missing some critical ones. What the hell was I supposed to do? My scholarships only paid for up to four years of schooling, that's it. I needed to stay an entire other year with no way to pay for it. I tried to apply for other financial assistance, or at least have someone work with me to solve the problem. No one bothered. All they did was send me to another office so I could be someone else's problem. I got upset and talked to my friends about it. Guess what I found out? It wasn't just me they were screwing over. Students all around SVU were being ignored or tossed aside.

"And you know for what? For only a select few. The administrators at this school were handpicking the students they thought would bring back the biggest return investment to improve their credibility. All of their aid, assistance, and privileges went to their SGA officers, honors students, and wealthy VIPs. I found out that all their schooling was paid for, but that's not all. They received exclusive tutors who pretty much did their work for them and provided special workshops that prepared them to be leaders. What did the rest of us get? Nothing! Once they got their first pick of courses during registration, we had to fight over whatever was left. And the worst part is that everyone is in on it. Dr. Giles, Dr. Scott, and all of those people you've been working with know this is going on and no one cares to do anything about it."

Cheyenne could tell that he was hurting. He was trying to hold back tears of anger as he spoke. The only sense of relief she felt was that he had put the gun down.

"I didn't know any of this, Spencer. Please, sit down and talk to me. I'd like to know more."

Spencer didn't listen, but he continued talking.

"Everything I had worked for in the school was the result of a bunch of lies. I believed Dr. Lambrick's speech at my Convocation. I believed I had the power to make a difference. That's why it hurt me more than ever to know that it was all a pile of shit. We had no power in this school. The university chose from the beginning who would be the winners and who would be the losers. If you didn't come into the university meeting their requirements for success, you were pretty much destined to fail. That's when I came across Second Chance. I heard about the organization, but never really looked into it. They helped me so much! They found a way to help me fund my fifth year here. They managed to do within one month what an entire team of university administrators failed to do. I felt indebted to them and ran for president as a result. Due to my popularity, they were honored that I joined their club to begin with so they all voted for me. The organization was effective, but it was small. They needed a leader who could help them grow and provide a force that would turn this university around."

"And you did that by taking revenge on everyone that made you angry?"

Spencer glared at her but let the comment go.

"It wasn't that simple. I wanted everyone in the group to trust each other. I wanted us to work as a team. The best way I could think of doing it was to have each member feel like they helped someone solve a big problem. It's why I had them get back at the enemies of others. Your enemy is my enemy and all that jazz. I'll admit, I did go overboard. I let my emotions get the best of me and some of my tasks became self-serving. I got a little rough and pressured them into doing something they didn't want to do. I didn't want to accept that the first suicide was my fault. Not even the second or the third. I figured that they were depressed and they would have done it anyways regardless of my actions. You have to understand that the students who joined Second Chance were emotionally disturbed. They didn't think straight. It wasn't too much of a stretch to think they were capable of suicide for whatever reason."

Spencer finally sat down. He looked a bit calmer than when he came in through the door. Cheyenne breathed a sigh of relief.

"It wasn't until Kimberly's death that I started to panic. She wasn't a part of Second Chance. Not only was her suicide more public, but that meant the deaths were reaching outside Second Chance. People were saying that the suicides from the students in my organization were setting a trend for others to follow suit. Eyes were starting to be turned towards me and my organization, so I needed to change tactics. That's why I partnered with Ashley. I wanted to work with a respected official organization to gain credibility and trust from the student body. Part of the problem was that we were working in the shadows. We were relatively unknown to the outside world, only existing through rumors and vague references. I wanted to change that. I tried, Cheyenne, honest. I hated these suicides as much as anyone else did. I hoped to make Maverick Madness the first venue to turn the organization around into a reputable force for dealing with SVU's corrupt administration. I wanted to make a difference, but that all turned to shambles when the after-party was ruined. Then you came along and started a chain of testimonies from my members before I managed to turn the club around. Do you see what trouble you put me in? I'm wanted for harassment, abuse, and hazing."

Spencer started to get agitated again, but this time in a more reasonable context. Cheyenne felt that she would have a better time reasoning with him.

"I'm sorry, Spencer. I didn't know any of this. But you have to understand that your plans to improve the organization and admitting to your mistakes are admirable actions, but you still did something wrong. One way or another you have caused many deaths at this university. If you want to truly be a leader and an example to the students, you can't keep hiding. You need to get out there and take responsibility for your actions. Trust me, students will appreciate that. You may even teach the administration a lesson or two about honesty and integrity. One of my students said to me that it's not who you are coming in, it's who you plan to be when you get out. Tell me this, Spencer. Who do you plan to be? How can you improve yourself to become that person?"

Spencer absorbed all the words Cheyenne told him as he sat in her chair. Cheyenne felt she was getting through to him and started moving towards him to comfort him. At that moment, the door was kicked open, making Cheyenne and Spencer jump in shock. Detective Sawyer ran in with a gun pointed at Spencer.

"Drop your gun!" she yelled at him as she moved in.

Spencer instantly pointed his gun at Cheyenne.

"You set me up!" he shouted.

Cheyenne froze in her spot.

"No, I didn't, really!"

Spencer looked at her with fear and hatred in his eyes.

"I said drop your gun, Spencer!" Detective Sawyer yelled again.

Spencer put his gun down. Detective Sawyer moved in and reached for her handcuffs.

He took the opportunity to whip his gun back up and then shot her in the arm. Detective Sawyer winced in pain as he sprinted out of the room. She shot at him but missed.

Cheyenne ran to Detective Sawyer and watched through the open door as Spencer got in his car and drove off.

*****

Lynn Sawyer put down her cup of coffee as she finished up her interview with Prachi.

"Prachi, I really want to thank you for everything you told me. And thank you for agreeing to keep this meeting a secret. I'm not allowed on the campus, much less talking to students, so I appreciate you coming over to the coffee house to meet me."

"No problem, Detective Sawyer. No offense, but I was nervous when you asked me to come talk to you. You have a reputation of being rough and mean with your interrogations."

Lynn laughed.

"Yeah, I tend to get caught up in my work. I'm off duty right now, so no worries about that. Besides, anyone who treats Ryan as great as you did is okay in my book."

"If you don't mind me asking, why were you so interested in having me tell you about Ryan?"

Lynn took another sip of her coffee and looked down for a second to collect her thoughts.

"I knew Ryan when he was a boy. Aunt Lynn is what he used to call me. He would get into all sorts of trouble growing up, and I was usually the cop to catch him. He was a troublemaker, but there was a certain charm about him. They were mostly mild misdemeanors, but we would always butt heads about it. I usually just drove him home. Unfortunately, his parents could care less what he did. They didn't even care that he was escorted home by a cop. I realized he wasn't being educated at home so I spent time with him myself. Every now and then after school I would take him riding in my cop car and show him around. I took him to workshops and taught him valuable life lessons. He learned to care for me. One day, his parents decided to move to Germany and he didn't want to go. He wanted to stay with me. Shows how much he cared for them.

"His parents were upset and forced me to get him to leave. If I didn't, they would report me for breaking a lot of rules with him by not taking him in like I was supposed to for some of his crimes. Could you believe that? They blackmailed me for helping their son! My only option to get him to leave was to tell him I didn't want him around. Despite his wishes, I told him he had to leave and we got into a fight. I really hurt him that day, but I convinced him to leave. It was one of the hardest days of my life. Guess that's what you get for breaking the rules by being a softy. When I found out he came back this year, I was surprised to find out how bad his first few days were. He had no place to stay and he didn't even bother to find me. I would have helped him. I guess he still hated me, so I didn't attempt to contact him. But I'm glad that he made friends. I was so worried about him. I'm glad that he managed to change his ways and had a good time in college, relatively speaking. Thank your friends for me, okay Prachi?"

Prachi smiled.

"No problem. And just so you know, I really did want to date him. He was a great guy and we all miss him terribly."

"Alright Prachi. You're free to go. And I'm warning you. Tell any of this to anyone and I'll find you. Deal?"

"Deal," she said as she left.

Lynn sat at the coffee house thinking to herself for a little while before her phone rang. It was Cheyenne giving her an update on the Second Chance case. Lynn had agreed to help Cheyenne with the rape case if she told her what was happening regarding Spencer and the organization. Even though she was no longer involved in the case, she wanted justice to be served for what happened to Ryan and the others.

Right before she hung up, she paused when she heard Cheyenne shout out Spencer's name. Apparently Cheyenne hadn't hung up the phone.

"Hello?" she said onto the phone. There was no response.

She heard a loud crash through the phone and then it went dead.

"What the hell's going on?" she asked no one in particular.

She got up from her seat and left the coffeehouse.

She reached for her phone to make a call but realized it was already ringing.

"Hello?"

"Hi, Detective Sawyer? This is Miyu. You left one of my sorority sisters a voicemail earlier. You were asking something about a red windbreaker someone was wearing at the Maverick Madness party. Well, I remember someone wearing one of those so I got your number."

"Well, who was it?"

"It was Spencer Wright. He's the Second Chance President. He was wearing a red windbreaker that night."

"Are you positive?"

"Yes."

"Thank you."

Lynn quickly hung up the phone and got in her car. Spencer was in Cheyenne's apartment, meaning she could be in danger. She grabbed the gun from her glove compartment before she called for some backup.

CHAPTER 31: CHEYENNE WINTERS
APRIL

I called the ambulance as fast as I could. Lynn was bleeding profusely from the wound on her shoulder.

"I had it under control, Lynn," I told her as I applied pressure to the wound.

"Well sorry for thinking your life was in danger and coming to the rescue," she said as she struggled with the pain on her shoulder.

We had to wait a while for an ambulance to arrive. Randy the campus safety officer came into my room escorting the emergency personnel.

"What took you so long?" Lynn asked in anger.

"Sorry, we have our hands full. There's a collision right near the entrance to the campus. Two cars were totaled. Last I heard, they were SVU students."

Lynn and I exchanged glasses, both asking in our minds the same question.

Suddenly, my room phone rang.

"Hello?" I answered.

"Cheyenne, it's Nancy! Why won't you answer your cell phone? I've called you like five times!"

"Sorry, my phone, umm, died."

"You need to get over to the hospital right away! There was an accident! The victims were identified! The students in the vehicles were Spencer and Ben!"

I felt a sharp pain in the pit of my stomach. Ben was in the accident. Even before she told me, I felt like I knew. And the only reason he was in Spencer's way as he drove off was because he was on his way to see me.

I hurried to the hospital as fast as I could. I met up with Nancy in the waiting room.

"What's the status?" I asked.

"They haven't told me yet," she responded. "It was a bad accident. I've called their parents already. I left messages for them and am waiting for them to call back. I told them it's urgent, but want to give them the details live, not through a recording."

A doctor came out and asked for the parents of Ben and Spencer. Nancy raised her hand and hurried over to him.

"Hi, their parents aren't in town right now. I'm responsible for getting in touch with them. What's going on?"

The doctor looked into his clipboard and cleared his throat.

"Spencer was hurt badly, but he seems to be stable. It looks like he was intoxicated during the crash, which may have actually saved his life. The fact that he was disoriented kept him from stiffening his body up during the accident which in some way lessened the brute impact. Ben, on the other hand, wasn't so lucky. Are you aware of his condition?"

Nancy and I exchanged confused looks.

The doctor continued. "We tested Ben when we realized that his wounds kept getting worse, and we found out he has hemophilia. It's a rare condition that not only causes the individual to bruise easily, but it prevents the blood from clotting and thus prevents healing. Nothing we've done has been able to seal up the wounds sufficiently to stop the bleeding. I'm sorry to say that it doesn't look like he'll make it."

Just then, Nancy's phone rang.

"It's Ben's mother," she said. "I'm gonna go take this then call Dylan to tell him about his brother. I'll be back, okay?"

Nancy walked away to take the call. I could see the pain in her expression as she had to break the news to his mother who lived hours away and had no way of getting here. The thought of her pain and the guilt of knowing it was my fault was too much to bear. I started to feel faint and had to lean against the wall to hold my balance.

"Are you okay, ma'am?" the doctor asked.

"I'll be fine," I barely managed to say.

I saw Shandra Giles walk into the hospital doors and approach me.

"Who told you to come here?" she asked in an irritated manner.

Before I could respond, she changed the subject.

"So I heard that Spencer got caught. Not exactly the way I imagined it, but at least it got the job done. He won't be hurting students anymore. Guess karma caught up with him."

I didn't say anything, but the feelings inside of me almost burst with anger. The boy was in a hospital bed and she was validating it?

Nancy came back after her phone call with Ben's mother. She looked crushed.

"Dr. Giles, you're here," Nancy said.

"I got here as soon as I got your message. What did the doctor tell you? We need to immediately make some calls and find out how we're going to handle this. A cult leader crashing into one of our freshmen doesn't bode well for us. We need to set up a town hall meeting instantly and address the issue before it goes public. We'll talk to the students and tell them that we are doing everything in our power to keep something like this from happening again. Spencer is very popular among the student population. If we don't keep this under control, someone else will take his place. And let's keep the media away from this case. We also have Detective Sawyer shot on our campus. If any of this gets out, we're screwed."

Dr. Giles walked off with Nancy giving her instructions on how to contain the incident. I looked in horror how everything that Spencer said was suddenly proven true. Dr. Giles didn't care about the students. She cared about the university's integrity.

I stood there in the waiting room for the next few hours, wondering and worrying about Ben. He didn't deserve this. I should have never gotten involved. Ben's accident was my fault, and it was something I had to deal with for the rest of my life. I couldn't imagine how his mother must have been feeling. I had no children, but my time with these students made me care for them like they were my own. They were lost and confused, trying to find their way in this world through the crutch that was college. Their parents worried night and day hoping that their children will come home safe. This was not the case for Ben's mom. I ached at the thought of the news that she may never see her son again.

This was too much for me to handle. I had two more days at Sun Valley University. I planned to quickly conduct my final interviews and leave the campus for good.

BIO: AMELIA "AMY" CALDWELL
LANCASTER, CA

There are only two things you can control in your life: the present and the future. And sometimes I even have doubts about the former. Regardless, the past is the past. You can't change it, you can't manipulate it, so there's no point in dwelling on it. See, I'm a forward thinker. If I'm not one step ahead of myself in everything I do, then it's a slow day. That's how I see my life. I look to the future, and only refer to the present to decide how I'll get to that future. People have told me I'm wrong. Learn to live in the present, they say. You can't forget your past, they say.

They simply don't understand. I am a girl of many interests and many talents. My greatest talent is multi-tasking, you might say. Since as young as I can remember, I'm always tackling a bunch of things at once. In kindergarten, when I wasn't busy drawing my works of art in the classroom, I was creating stories at home in my journal. Granted, I could barely write, but I believed I could. That's the key. I didn't care that everything I wrote in the book was just nonsense that I made out to be a story. That's living in the present. No, I looked at that story and wondered how amazing it'll be 20 years from now when I became a famous writer! That was always me. The forward-thinker. Busy in the present and always dreaming about the future.

I took several instrument classes. I can play the piano, the guitar, saxophone, flute, and I even tried my hands at drums. I've taken 2 different martial arts classes. Tae Kwon Do and Judo are two very different martial arts, don't let anyone tell you otherwise. I was always juggling extra-curriculars back and forth between school, home, and my part time job. I worked in a library during high school. Worked a few hours every day after school. I had a plethora of books around me, so I always took the time to read them and learn more about everything. I guess you can say I'm a jack-of-all trades kinda girl. Dating? No, no time for that. No interest. I was busy enough as it was. I hope to gain a lot from my college life. There are just so many possibilities here I don't know where to start! Clubs, service organizations, honors societies, programs, any free time I used to have will be long gone when I'm through with this school. People worry that I take on too much, but again, that's only a problem if you live in the present. Those who fret about being too stressed or having too much responsibility can easily get overwhelmed seeing how much I do. They key is to look forward. Look at the result of your labors, that's how you get through it all. I'm an inquirer. I love to learn and I love to do.

CHAPTER 32: INTERVIEW #RD05
RACHEL DAVIS

[For my last meeting with Rachel, we decided to meet in my office at the tower. It's the evening before checkout.]

So Rachel, did you say you were leaving tomorrow?

Yeah, I finished my last final this morning. I'm almost done packing everything up. It's insane how much stuff you can accumulate in the course of a year. I'm leaving with tons more stuff than I came in with. I don't know what to do with it all!

Everyone in my hall is getting ready to go home. They're throwing out or giving away tons of their stuff. Others are trying to find storage areas to keep their things until they come back in the fall. That's one thing that's really annoying about living in the dorms. No matter what, by the end of the year you have to pack everything up and leave.

My friends in the third floor aren't having it as easy as we are since they no longer have an RA. At least the housing department is working with them. Since Kimberly's incident with the pills, Travis Coleman decided to personally go to their hall and help them out with check-out procedures. He's going to be doing their room inspections before they leave. He also got Amy to help him out with returning keys and other tasks. I never got to know her well, but I did know she was close to Kimberly. Like, very close. As a result, she knew just about everything she needed to deal with the checkout procedures that were coming up. I can only imagine how hard it must have been for her to deal with it. I talked to her a little bit the other day to see how she was doing. Sarah wasn't talking to me so I figured I'd visit Grace upstairs and ended up talking to Amy. She seemed to deal with it really well. She said something about living in the future and leaving the present in the past. She said that Kimberly's wish was for her to become an RA so they could work together.

Amy said she didn't really want to do it, but after Kimberly's death, she decided to honor that wish. She went through the interviews and is waiting for a response. I hope she gets it. To be honest, I think Amy would make a better RA than Kimberly. I don't mean to speak ill of the dead, but Kimberly wasn't very good at her job. She was very nervous, insecure, and while she was friendly, she didn't really exert the proper authority necessary to be in charge. From what I heard, people got away with a lot of things in that hall.

I heard there was a university town hall meeting today. How did that go?

It went pretty well. Dr. Scott stood up and cleared everything up for us. Everyone cheered when he went up. After Dr. Giles' boring intro, he was definitely a nice change of space. He admitted that this year had its troubles and that they have not gone unnoticed. He had us all hold a moment of silence for all of the students who died this year. He also told us about the car accident between Spencer and Ben. He wanted us to hear it from him first before we heard it as a rumor. He said it was better to present the information in a way that was more respectable to them.

He also told us the university's plans to improve. Many programs were going to be implemented starting the following year to support students. He mentioned the minority scholarships that were started this year and how they were a step in the right direction to helping out the students. There would be more opportunities in the coming years, but what we could expect starting in August was a strong college retention program to keep students not only in college, but to provide a safe environment where they could be heard. He really pumped everyone up with his speech.

He finally mentioned how Spencer was recovering, but that we should not fear Second Chance infiltrating our campus anymore. The organization was permanently disbanded and Spencer would be arrested as soon as he healed in the hospital. He had many charges filed against him, but he didn't really go into any details on that. He just wanted us to know that the campus was once again safe and still on its way to the top.

[She sighs.]

Do you not believe him?

It's not that. I'm glad that they're making all of these improvements, but I won't really be around to benefit from them.

What do you mean?

It was a difficult decision, but I'm leaving Sun Valley University. I just can't handle all of this. The only reason that I came here was to be with Dylan. Once I broke up with him, there was really nothing else for me here. I'm a General Studies major, which is pretty much worthless right now since I don't know what I want. I did have my cheerleading, but that's really the only bright side in all of this.

When I found out about Sarah being raped, I almost threw up. The guilt that spread through me was insane. It was my fault that she was raped. I'm the one that pretty much forced her to go to that party. I'm the one that left her alone with all of those guys. And to top it all off, I'm the one that gave her a hard time for the next few weeks for being so moody. No wonder she was mad at me! I deserved it!

Even now she still won't talk to me. I guess she's still bitter about the whole thing. That was really the last straw. My presence here has been nothing but problems. I just talked to my advisor today and filled out the paperwork to withdraw and cancel my classes for the fall. I'm going to go back to North Carolina and see what lies for me there. I might go to community college or maybe skip college altogether. I don't know for sure yet.

Are you sure this is what you want, Rachel? Is there anything I could do to convince you to stay? I really think you should give college another chance. This was a bad year for everyone, not just you. You shouldn't let it deter you from succeeding.

I appreciate your support, Cheyenne, but my mind is made up. You say that I should try to succeed, but who's to say that my definition of success is a college education? Maybe that's not what I'm meant for. This school was Dylan's plan, not mine. And I'm tired of living in his shadow months after we broke up. I am done with him and I am equally done with this school. I do wish the rest of my friends here the best of luck though. My goodbyes tonight and tomorrow will be the hardest part of leaving. I did make some great meaningful relationships here.

At the very least I hope Sarah can forgive me long enough for me to say goodbye to her. I really want her to know that I am truly sorry for what I caused and that I wish it was me that had happened to instead of her. And I hope that Spencer gets what he rightfully deserves. From what I've heard, he finally admitted to the rape and that charge will be added to all the others. Figures that one of the Wright brothers would be the ones responsible for this. Like brother, like brother, I suppose.

Who knows? If I had stayed with Dylan, that very well could have been me. But like Amy said, no use dwelling in the past.

Thank you very much for all your interviews this semester. I really appreciate all the time that you took to speak with me. I've had a great time getting to know you and wish you the best in whatever you do.

Thanks, Cheyenne. I've gotta say, you have been an amazing person and you're the closest thing I've had to a mother at this university. I'll miss you.

> *[Rachel gets up from her chair and comes over to give me a hug. Like with Lisa, letting her go was very difficult for me, and I wished that I could have done more to help her.]*

Goodbye, Rachel.

BIO: RENZO MORETTI
ALBANY, NY

I'm from upstate New York. When people think of New York, they immediately think of NYC or the Bronx, or sometimes even Manhattan. Overcrowded, polluted, filled with the country's filth, both through trash and people. Upstate New York isn't like this at all. It has a much nicer feel to it, a much nicer view. The place that I live in particular has a wonderful panoramic view. We've actually had tourists come to take pictures around my father's property every now and then. As far as myself goes, I'm a visionary. New York is great, but Florida is where the future is at. Originally a place for older folk to retire, the migration movement to Florida has spread to all ages and ethnicities. Families from all over the north are moving to Florida due to its tropical climate, attractions, and wonderful beaches. As a businessman, this brings some great opportunities for business down here. It's why I'm here. I'm scouting the area, learning what the market looks like. I've already dipped my feet into the business sector, running a couple of small businesses in New York with moderate success. However, I have some ideas that if panned out just right, I'll be the next CEO up there with Steve Jobs and the like.

What I will tell you is that the market is changing. Trends are showing which sectors will survive, and which will fall into obscurity. My job is to keep up with those trends, studying them, watching them mature like a good wine. My father built his entire empire from scratch, and now he's one of the most respected figures in the aerospace industry. He hopes to entrust the company to me when the time comes, but it's not enough for me to just take it. I want to earn it, prove to him that I can make it on my own as well. It's true what they say. The rich get richer and the poor get poorer. It makes sense. Having been raised in a family of wealth I've received a very in-depth financial education.

That's the problem with this country. The education system is subpar. Schools spend an awful amount of time teaching you about Christopher Columbus's journey to America year after year. In fact, schools are wrapped up on history. What they need to do is stop worrying so much about the past and care about the future. Why aren't courses teaching budgeting, parenting, or entrepreneurship required courses? Why do they seem less important than reading and analyzing Shakespeare? Well, if anything, they're just making it easier for me to get richer. Less competition

CHAPTER 33: FAREWELLS
MAY

After a few minutes of organizing and mingling, Linda called the final Student Government Association meeting of the year to begin.

"Thank you for agreeing to meet everyone. I know that finals are over and everyone is anxious to go home. However, we have a couple of things to get done before we leave for summer break. First of all, I would like to congratulate the new executive board of SGA. Congratulations to Sandeep as next year's new SGA President, Renzo as SGA Vice President, and Clara as SGA Treasurer. I'm sure you will serve Sun Valley University in the best way possible."

Applause was heard by the several SGA members around the room.

"As you heard in the Town Hall meeting earlier today, Dr. Giles and Dr. Scott have managed to bring our university back to normal by removing the rotten apples that were polluting our campus. Spencer Wright, as you know, is being charged with the harassment and abuse of several students on campus and will be locked away for a long time. Ashley Stout, President of Sigma Zeta Pi, has not been charged with anything, but has been kicked out of SVU for working with him.

"Unfortunately, their actions and words have started to shake the students' faith in SVU's administration. They feel that our faculty and staff, as well as SGA, are corrupt. To alleviate this, Dr. Giles has asked us to create a student retention task force led by non-SGA members that will work hard to meet the students' needs. They will be seen as the voice of the campus and will work to improve our image by making all of their efforts public."

One of their members raised their hand to speak.

"Yes, Dominic?"

"But Linda, this concerns me. As SGA, we are the student representatives of the campus. We make the important decisions. Wouldn't having a task force like this undermine our authority? We tend to work behind the scenes while they're being set to work in the spotlight. What if their influence on the students gives them more power than us?"

"That's not going to be a problem," Dr. Giles said as she walked into the room. "Sorry I'm late everyone. I had to take care of some angry parent phone calls and reassure them that everything is okay. As far as your concern, Dominic, you do not have to worry about the task force. Their entire purpose is simply for show. They won't really have any power. Everything they do has to go through and be approved by us. The goal here is to let the students feel that they have someone to believe in. It's supposed to be a morale booster. We will still be doing what we have always done, except this time we'll be presenting these ideas and plans through their own representatives. That way we're not the bad guys. Realistically, it's not possible to give so many students much control over what happens at this university. People need to understand that students who come to college directly from a family setting characterized by dependency and parenting are not yet fully prepared for the freedoms of an adult life without the continued active intervention of university officials. The system is too complex and we're struggling with it as it is right now."

Linda nodded, then looked over at the new executive board.

"Okay then. Sandeep, Renzo, and Clara, I will assign you to each choose a representative to lead the student retention task force. They need to be students that the rest of the student body trusts. And they need to be rising sophomores. Having young blood leading the committees will make it easier for us to keep control over them. We need three people to lead the committees of the program. Do you have any recommendations?"

Clara looked at the handout with the different committee descriptions of the task force.

"I've got someone in mind. He's a very outgoing fellow. He's very actively involved in Kappa Chi and well-known by most of the population. His name is Mason Cook. I think he'll do well in the Allied Arts College building renovation project since he's a part of that college."

"Great," Linda said. "We'll put him in the College Renovation committee. What about you two?"

She looked at Renzo and Sandeep.

"I nominate Miyu Kaneko," Renzo said. "I've worked with her in Scarlet Hall and she seems to be the only one with any common sense over there. For a bunch of smart people, they sure lack simple logic. She'd be a perfect fit for the Human Relations committee. She's a counseling major, after-all."

"Great. The Human Relations committee will have the most direct contact with students and we need to make sure it's someone charming and approachable. Alright Sandeep, we need someone for the Strategic Planning committee. This committee will be in charge of relaying any major changes in policies and procedures to the student body so they know what's happening on the campus. We need someone with vision, determination, and obvious leadership skills. But it needs to be someone who can also follow our orders and not try anything without our approval."

"Oh, I have the perfect person," Sandeep said. "She's in Air Force ROTC with me. Her name's Jessica Evans. She's one hell of a cadet but exhibits loyalty like you won't believe. She won't let us down."

Linda smiled and clasped her hands together.

"Alright everyone. Let's contact those three students and offer them these lucrative positions. I'm sure they'll be ecstatic. As for the rest of you, I'm glad to have served as your SGA President for the year. Even with all the craziness we've faced this year with the deaths, budget cuts, and even threats against us, we managed to pull through. Thank you everyone for your support. Meeting is dismissed. Have a great summer!"

The SGA board darted to the exits, anxious to pack up and go home. Renzo stayed behind to talk to Linda.

"So did you ever find out who vandalized your room door in the beginning of the year?" he asked her.

"Not exactly. No details were given. From what Dr. Giles gathered, Second Chance members did each other 'favors' where they got back at each other's enemies as some sort of bond-forming ritual. More than likely it was some pissed-off student we punished last year for some academic violation who asked another member to get back at us. Be glad you didn't have to put up with this crap. Now that it's all over, we can finally get back to dealing with all the regular crap we deal with on a daily basis. Again, congratulations on winning Vice President. Now go home already!"

Linda shook Renzo's hand, then he watched as she headed out the door. Renzo never told the SGA committee about the vandalism on his own door. He never told them how he found out it was Ryan that spray painted his door as one of his Second Chance membership requirements. He never told them that it was due to his own constant harassment and berating of the boy that eventually drove Ryan to the breaking point. He held the guilt of Ryan's suicide silently, hoping it would die down eventually through his efforts as SVU's new student Vice President.

*****

Miller Hall was filled with movement down the entire hall as students walked back and forth moving their belongings out of their rooms. Down in Miller Third South, Amy gave Grace a tearful hug as they both parted ways.

"You've been a wonderful roommate, Grace. I don't know how I would have survived without you."

"Same to you, Amy. Good luck on your RA hiring process. I hope you get the job!"

"Thanks! You too, Grace! I hope you get it as well! Thanks for applying with me for support! It meant a lot!"

They finally released their hold and Amy grabbed the only bag she hadn't already put in the car. Grace watched as Amy walked down the hall and towards the elevator to prepare for her flight back to California.

Grace looked around and saw a bunch of the residents walk around with the farewell pins she made for all of them. It made her glad to know they cared enough to wear them. She saw roommates saying their goodbyes, ranging from simple handshakes to complete waterworks as they parted ways. She saw Gabriella leaving her room and turning off the lights. It had been a few weeks since Lisa left and she had stuck to herself since then.

Grace ran over to her room to give her the last pin.

"Here you go, Gabriella. Something to remember your first dorm with."

Gabriella took the pin with caution. "Thank you."

"Are you coming back to us next year?"

"I don't know. I don't know what I am going to do."

Grace smiled. "Well, just know that I will be here when you come back if you need a friend. Best wishes!"

Gabriella sheepishly smiled back, nodded, and went on her way. She walked past Tobias, who had come up to the third floor to say goodbye to Prachi. He knocked on her door.

"Hey Tobias," Prachi said when she came to the door. "Are you leaving now?"

"Yep. Just came to say goodbye. I just missed Amy who already left and I wanted to see at least someone from our initial group before I left. It seems you and I are the only ones left. Lisa's gone, as are Ryan and Ben."

Prachi's expression seemed to dim.

"Do you know how Ben is doing?"

"No idea. No one would tell me. He was in critical condition last I heard. Has some sort of disorder or something. They say he won't make it. It's such a tragic ending for a year. He was such a good guy."

Prachi looked into Tobias's eyes.

"Tobias, promise you won't leave my side. I've lost too many people I've cared about this year. Please promise me you won't be next."

Tobias's solemn expression turned into a grin as his face lit up.

"You won't get rid of me that easily, Prachi. I'll be seeing you again, don't worry. First thing in August. Deal?"

"Deal!" she said happily as they hugged.

Tobias finally picked up the bag he laid down and headed down the hall, only to run into Grace, who had watched the entire exchange.

"Do you still have your rhinoceros?" she asked him.

He reached into his bag and pulled it out.

"Hasn't left my side since."

Grace smiled, gave him a kiss on the cheek, and ran off. Tobias touched his cheek and suddenly had a rush of joy run through him. By the looks of it, college would turn out to be a much better experience than the terrible one he had in high school.

*****

It was near closing time, and Miyu was excited to finally finish her last work day until next year. Unlike the rest of the students, she planned to be in town for an extra week after finals, so she was the only one available to work the registration desk at the Records and Registration office. Even after finals, students kept coming in with scheduling issues and registration for the summer and fall semester. It was only a minute until closing time and Miyu breathed a sigh of relief as she got up to go back to her dorm. Just as she was about to leave, she saw Sam approach the desk.

"Aww, come on!" she said to herself.

"Hi, are you still open?" Sam asked eagerly.

"Sure, why not? What do you need?"

"I came to turn in my change-of-course form. I'm joining band next year and their practice was conflicting with one of my courses. Can you do that?"

"Sure!" Miyu said as she took the paper.

She started plugging the data into the computer.

"Uh oh," she said.

Sam's eyes widened. "What do you mean 'uh oh'?"

Miyu looked up nervously at him.

"It looks like you have a... registration hold. One of the documents you turned in to the financial aid office wasn't signed, and they can't approve your funding until you do."

"WHAT?" he shouted out loud. "Are you gosh darn serious? Why me? Why?"

"I'm really, really sorry Sam. I'm just the messenger."

Sam suddenly leaned in very close to her, close enough where she could smell the cologne he drenched himself in.

"Oh, they'll get what's coming to them, yes they will. A time will come when you will be asked to choose. Us or them. The power is yours."

He suddenly went darting out of the office.

Miyu rolled her eyes and closed down the office.

Sam angrily reached the financial aid office, glad that it was still open. The last thing he needed was to stay an extra day on campus just to get a hold released on his account. There was one person ahead of him, and he started getting impatient when she wouldn't leave. He recognized the lady. She was an older woman that attended his class with Dr. Garcia.

"So there's no way to cancel my loans?" Susan asked the teller.

"I'm sorry, ma'am. If you leave the university without graduating, you are forced to pay back any loans you've accumulated immediately. There's really nothing else I can do. Are you sure you want to withdraw from the university?"

"Yes, I can't afford to stay here anymore. My financial assistance was taken away and I have no way to pay for next year."

"Very well then. Let me see your ID card and I'll start the paperwork."

Susan handed the teller her SVU ID card and waited for him to come back. She looked at her watch and was worried. Lilly needed to be picked up from school and this was taking longer than expected. She tried to figure out what she was going to do about her job now that she couldn't get her degree. The teller came back, but did not have any forms with him.

"Ma'am, I have some information you may want to hear."

"What is it?"

"One of our students, Rachel Davis, just withdrew with us yesterday. She was under a scholarship that you qualify for. Since she left, the funds were transferred over to you. It should cover most of your costs. All you need to do is apply for a small loan to cover the rest. Congratulations!"

Susan's eyes lit up upon hearing his words. "Really? Oh thank you! Thank you so much! You do not know what this means to me!"

Susan walked out of the office with a wide grin on her face. This news was even better than when she found out she passed her Pediatric Cardiology final. She managed to dodge another financial bullet, if at least for another year.

*****

On her way back to Scarlet Hall, Miyu saw Alia in the parking lot getting into a taxi.

"Alia, wait!" she shouted as she ran towards her.

Alia stopped and turned around.

"Alia, listen. I know we had a rough year. I know you have a plane to catch, but I just wanted to say goodbye to you. Despite our ups and downs, we were roommates and nothing's gonna change that. I'm so sorry for being a jerk to you. Can you please forgive me?"

Alia stared at her calmly in a thoughtful manner. She slowly smiled and got out of the taxi.

"Where would we be if we didn't know how to forgive?" she said as she reached out to hug Miyu. "And for the record, I'm sorry too. I guess I misjudged the actions of one individual like Ashley and generalized them to an entire sorority. Your sorority is indeed very nice."

"Thanks Alia. And just so you know, I'm still looking for a roommate for next year. The offer's open if you want it."

"Thank you very much, Miyu, but I'm not sure if I'm ready to think about that yet. This year was very difficult for me and I need a break. We've been at odds with each other for several months and I feel it is best if we take it slow from here."

"Fair enough," Miyu responded.

Alia got back into the taxi and watched the university shrink in size as they drove away. The residence halls and other campus buildings became smaller in size until they fully disappeared into the horizon. The only thing left standing was the massive Student Union Tower peering off into the distance, standing strong and watching over the students as they went their separate ways.

The weather was steadily increasing as spring progressed and made its way into summer. Though not as hot, Alia thought back to her first day of college, inexperienced and confused as to where everything was. Now, as she left to go back home to Kenya, she realized how much more she knew in the course of a year which seemed to fly by. She knew the campus like the back of her hand, having traversed its sidewalks hundreds of times and being able to navigate them like a pro.

Matu and my father will be so proud, she thought to herself.

She managed to achieve something no one in her family could have imagined. She could feel that Matu's investment on her was already starting to pay off.

As they hit the highway towards Orlando International Airport, Alia finally saw the tower vanish into the horizon, which marked her departure from Sun Valley University. She smiled, knowing she would see it again in a matter of months. She learned a lot this year, and her entire trip back home was filled with thoughts and speculation about what the future at the university would bring her.

ROLAND NUÑEZ

CHAPTER 34: INTERVIEW #MA04
MITCH ADAMS

[This is my final interview at Sun Valley University. My office is empty except for a few boxes I have yet to move out. Mitch is sitting in a chair I borrowed from another office. His aunt will be picking him up shortly to take him home.]

Hey Mitch! I promise I'll keep this brief. I know you're anxious to go home.

It's a'ight. Don't rush.

Now that you've completed your first year at Sun Valley University, do you have any final thoughts you'd like to share?

Final thoughts? Not a lot to share. I was pissed when I found out people were blaming me for all those deaths again. What are the odds that the RA who wrote me up would die the day after? And why would people think I'd be stupid enough to kill her knowing very well I'd be the first suspect? People don't think around here.

Anyways, I'm glad things got cleared up. Dr. Scott announced who the real culprit was and announced he was getting what was due to him. I'm in the clear for now. I figure as long as I keep my head low, I should manage to get by these next few years without a problem.

SVU as a whole is okay. Definitely much better than any other school I went to. The people here are nice and generally don't get in your face if you don't get in theirs. Hopefully with this new student retention program things can get better around here so people would stop complaining.

Are you going to miss it here when you go home?

I guess so. I got to know a few people. Better than not knowing anyone back at home. Luca left a few days ago. Lucky son-of-a... excuse my language. He didn't have any finals and managed to go home early. He was pretty cool, if a bit obnoxious at times. But you gotta admit, he knew how to have fun. Things have been pretty quiet since he left, though. Dylan doesn't really hang out with him anymore since that whole incident at the party. Besides, he's all bummed out about his brother, so he's not much fun to hang around anyways. And Sam's being his crazy self as usual. That's one thing I'll miss about SVU. There's always something going on worth talking about. Back at home with my aunt all there is to talk about is whatever's on TV at the time. That's pretty much what I'll be doing all summer.

Based on your experiences as a maverick at Sun Valley University, what would you tell a new student who's about to start college?

I'd tell him if he plans to get high, don't get caught!

[He laughs.]

Naw, I'm just playin'. I'd tell 'em that college is nothing like high school. Classes aren't a load of BS to keep you busy for a while. In college, you have to wanna be here to make it. I'm not the best in my classes, but I'm at least makin' the effort. My aunt worked too hard and spent a lot of money to get me outta Jersey and gimme an opportunity, and I don't plan to waste it. I realize that I wasted a lot of years of my life and I'm hoping to make it better. Especially this year. I made a few mistakes and I paid for them. What I would tell a new student is this: Try hard in school and avoid getting into fights or people will think you're a murderer.

[He laughs again.]

Thank you very much Mitch. This has been really helpful.

So is this really your last interview ever here?

I'm afraid so. My time at Sun Valley University has come to an end.

That's a shame, really. This school could use someone like you.

I don't think so. Since I got here, I've caused a lot of unnecessary commotion and even managed to get some students hurt and others to drop out of college.

Cheyenne, take it from someone who grew up in the hood. Bad things happen to good people all the time, regardless of who's at fault. Life isn't fair. I used to take that to mean I could do anything I wanted without concern. Now I see I was wrong. Even if I make mistakes, hurting others in the process, I keep those mistakes in mind so that I don't make 'em again. Don't bust your chops about the mistakes you made here. The important thing is the good you've done for all of us. For me at least.

Anyways, thanks for that. I really enjoyed goin' to those hockey games wit you. You're the only staff member to take the time to get to know students like that. Like I said, it's too bad they have to lose you. You could probably teach 'em a lesson or two about how to do their job.

[He looks at his phone.]

My aunt texted me that she's here. I gotta go. Thanks Cheyenne!

You're welcome Mitch. Have a great summer.

[Mitch leaves my office with his bag. I turn around and grab the final stack of papers that are left on my desk. They are from my final round of interviews with the students of SVU. On top of the stack lies a card. I pick it up and look at it once again. It is a thank you card that Dr. Garcia gave me. He got all of the students in the class to sign it and write me a little thank-you message each. Each time I look at it, I begin feeling sentimental. Out of the hundreds of hours I spent interviewing and transcribing the thousands of pages of interviews, none of them, even collectively, were worth more to me than this simple card.]

EPILOGUE

Dr. Eric Johnson got up from his chair and removed his glasses after reviewing all of the documents.

"That was an endearing story, Ms. Winters," he said with a slight hint of both amusement and sarcasm. "However, I'm trying to understand what all of this has to do with the crisis of Sun Valley University. According to this information, even though you were contracted to be there for only four months, you stayed there much longer. Why is that?"

Hundreds of eyes focused on me as they waited for my response, ready to judge and evaluate whatever I said next to fit their agenda. This time, however, it didn't faze me.

"The crisis of Sun Valley University originated through this group of twenty one students I interacted with. My involvement at the university was a big factor that led to the event. I failed as a researcher, for an experienced researcher does not let her presence affect the actions of the participants. However, my failure as a researcher also brought my success as a mentor and a leader. I stayed at Sun Valley University because these students needed me. The university administration ran through a corrupt system through which the students suffered, and they attempted to cover it up through motivational speeches and shallow programs meant to deceive. My goal was to protect these students from the same fate experienced by Spencer. I take full responsibility for what happened."

Dr. Johnson sat back down in his chair and looked to the rest of the committee who all shared a similar disapproving look.

"Ms. Winters, do you expect us to believe that you singlehandedly managed to stop a university which is apparently full of corrupt, self-serving administrators who lie to their students?"

The murmurs of the crowd didn't bother me anymore. No more panicking. No more fear. I knew what I was doing.

271

"Of course not, sir. I never claimed to have achieved my goal by myself, nor that the administrators were corrupt. I said that the system was corrupt. The university political system is very complex and often leads to self-serving actions. My intervention of that system merely started ripples that were felt throughout the campus. My students, those that I interviewed, turned those ripples into waves, and those waves are what led to the crisis. As you can see in those documents you reviewed, it was my students that helped solve the case of the Sun Valley University suicides. They are all leaders, and they will continue to be leaders regardless of what you do to me."

The committee members huddled to talk amongst themselves. I couldn't hear what they were saying, but I knew that it wasn't boding well for me. My students and I worked together to shake a corrupt system. We all deserved whatever consequences came from that. By releasing them from all the blame and putting it all on myself, I could give them a chance. A chance to graduate and make something of their lives. They deserved it. Even as my career came to an end in this hearing, I knew my students would be safe. That's what we do in my field of work. We keep our students safe.

STAY TUNED FOR THE NEXT BOOK IN THE SERIES:

HALLS OF IVY: PATHFINDER

Things start off bright at Sun Valley University as Dr. Steven Garcia's former freshmen begin their second year. Attempting to move past the previous year's suicide scandal, the students quickly come to realize that Sun Valley's secrets don't end there.

Meanwhile, after recently being hired as a student advisor, Cheyenne Winters notices suspicious activities taking place at the Sun Valley campus. Inaccessible university records. Questionable practices in the athletics department. A cunning university attorney who knows more than he leads to believe.

With the aid of Steven, Cheyenne sets out to uncover and expose a large-scale system of corruption employed by the university for many years. She discovers the administration is planning something big, and the only way to stop it is to take down a firmly-rooted hierarchical empire.

Follow the intertwining stories of Cheyenne and her students and how their roles lead up to the crisis of Sun Valley University.

Follow the Halls of Ivy series at
HallsOfIvySeries.com

ABOUT THE AUTHOR

Roland Núñez has been writing since the third grade, with most of his works being written on napkins or extra pieces of lined paper. It has always been a passion of his to write poems, screenplays, and music, having published or produced at least one of each. He later began writing novels. As he began his college career, he became so involved in many extra-curricular areas that writing took a back seat to theatre, games, research, and flying planes. Since entering the field of student affairs, however, Roland has once again found his passion for writing by writing about his vibrant college experiences through works of fiction. Roland hopes for *Halls of Ivy* to be the first of many college-related novels that engross the reader into the unique world of higher education and the complexities, struggles, and joys of being a modern-day college student.

Roland and his wife Jasmine live in Oklahoma with their dog and two cats.

19054976R00167

Made in the USA
Charleston, SC
04 May 2013